CRY 'GOD FOR GLENDOWER'

Also by Martha Rofheart
CRY 'GOD FOR HARRY'

CRY 'GOD FOR GLENDOWER'

MARTHA ROFHEART

BOOK CLUB ASSOCIATES · LONDON

This edition published 1975 by
Book Club Associates
by arrangement with Talmy Franklin Limited

*Printed in Great Britain by
Richard Clay (The Chaucer Press), Ltd,
Bungay, Suffolk*

To my husband

AUTHOR'S NOTE

The facts about Owen Glendower before the years of the rebellion (1400–10) are meagre; even his birthplace is not certain, and the sites of his grave are numerous. Welsh records were lost during the almost total devastation of the country; one must depend upon the biased documents of the enemy English and the scant information from the French allies. I have invented Owen's character from these scraps, rejecting most of the conflicting legend. It is almost certain, however, that he was sophisticated, traveled, and unusually knowledgeable; it is equally certain that he was tall and 'beau.' All contemporary references to him mention his prepossessing appearance, his wealth, and his princely lineage. Out of documented history, legend, and myth emerges a man ahead of his times, a man who might better have fitted into Renaissance life, and it is thus that I have portrayed him.

Of the narrators, Nathan ben Arran and Sibli are invented, as well as a few of the minor characters; most of the people in this novel are mentioned in history.

I have chosen wherever possible to Anglicize the Welsh spellings of names for purposes of readability. To one not familiar with the Welsh language, the many consonants are formidable; in fact, however, some of these consonants are used as vowels in Welsh. (The *w*, for instance, has the sound of, literally, a double *u*, and the *y* sounds like a short *e*. Owen's name, in Welsh, Glyn Dwr, would be, phonetically, Glen Doo-er.) Among the many English renderings I have used Griffith for the Welsh Gruyfydd, and Meredith for Maredydd. (The 'dd' is pronounced 'th.') Iolo and Iestyn are spoken as Yolo and Yesten.

7

CONTENTS

BOOK I

MOEL OFFRWYM

(THE HILL OF OFFERING)

Told by Owen ap Griffith of Wales,

known to the English

as Owen Glendower

ONE

My earliest clear memory, strange to relate, is of my dog, Cabal. I say strange because, though I have had many passions, hunting is not one of them. Nor is war, though the world would not believe it. I am come, in latter years, in my countrymen's eyes, to be Owen, the Man of Wrath, Avenger of Wales, like Brân the Blessèd, or Arthur. A thought that makes my insides shake with silent mirth.

This dog, Cabal, was named after Arthur's white boarhound; in my country the bards still sing of Arthur's dog, and the folk point to his paw print, huge as an elephant's, in the stone of a hill. Cabal, too, was the name of Llewellyn's dog, or so they say. In our manor in Dolgelly, Rhug Hall, there is, in the great hall, a foot-long iron spike fixed to the high table, where Llewellyn tied this beast when he sat at meat.

My own beast was given me by my uncle Vaughan when I was four, or thereabouts. He was of the same pure strain as Arthur's hound, and his pedigree was older than my own. A foolish thing, but men are bound by such sad fantasies; in these ways they cry out against their own inevitable extinction.

This Cabal was nearly as tall as I, though a puppy still, and I was afraid of him. I did not say so, for I was more afraid still of my uncle Vaughan. Cabal was white, with a bald, shaven look, and liver-colored spots on his underbelly. His mouth too was liver-colored and his jaws slobbered. He was never still, running in circles and leaping up above my head.

One day, when none was about, I took him into the great hall, myself thinking to play lord of the manor and sit in the high seat like my ancestor, Llewellyn the Great. I had tied a bit of hempen rope about the dog's neck and thought to tie the other end to the spike (I had just learned to make a knot). Cabal, in his twistings and leapings, caught his teeth in my flesh, just under my heart. It only stung, but the red blood oozed out, trickling down my side under my boy's tunic. I stood still, watching the thin trickle, while the dog, pulled free, and with the rope trailing, ran in circles on the stone floor. I saw my own mortality then, in that blood. Always I had thought, as animals and small children do, without thinking at all, that I would live forever. Coldly and in stillness I stood, while waves of thought washed over me: You, too, will die, you, too—you must die.... I do not know how long I stood there—it cannot have been more than a moment—but time stood still. I mark it as my coming of age, as other men will remember their first kill or the first girl they lay with. For this, I think, is where the human animal differs from all others; he alone knows his end. And he must carry it with him always, this knowledge, this frailty.

After, Cabal licked the blood. Another man would say, in devotion; I have always loved people more, with all their faults. It is in a dog's nature to like the taste of blood; we must not give him human qualities. Though he was a good and gentle beast, Cabal, and I kept him by me many years, until he grew old and died. I lost my fear of him early; he was, in fact, a traitor to his hunting strain. I never saw him kill a flea, even.

This manor, Rhug Hall, was not my birthplace; that was in Sycharth, a little to the north, in the shadow of the great mountain of Snowdon. Mother always brought us children here, when summer was over, I thought it was to escape the hard winters of Snowdon Valley. It was not so, I know now, though the winds blew gently around Dolgelly, and the snow fell lightly, if at all.

No, I see now that Mother removed herself from choice, out of her melancholy. They did not get along, she and Father; summers at Sycharth the halls rang with their quarrels and she went about red-eyed. I think she would have gone farther south, to her home in the Deheubarth, but that she feared to shame herself before her kin. I never knew why they did not agree; he had other women, but that is a common thing among nobles.

We are descended, my brother, Tudor, my sister, Laura, and I, Owen, from the three great princely lines of the Cymry. My father, Griffith, is of the strain of Powys and Gwynned, and Helen, my mother, can trace her forebears right back to Rome and Arthur. Men set great store by such things; myself, I know it matters little, if at all. Trace far enough, if you can, and we will have, all, a common ancestor; one who went on all fours, like as not, and ate slugs out of the earth. But we are fortuned anyway, our princely family; we have great wealth, the greatest in our country, and it can buy much, land and power and riches for the mind.

My mother, Helen, grew sadder every year; she suffered from what our old scholars call 'accidie,' a kind of sickness of the soul. Once she was merry, by fits and starts, when I was a small child; she used then to call me her 'little cherub,' for I was fat and dimpled, I am told, with a round head covered in silver-gilt curls. This is hard to believe; I remember myself only as a big little boy, taller and more timorous than any other, so that even my brother, Tudor, two years younger, could vanquish me with a raised fist. I was squeamish, too, and would run, retching, from the sight of a rabbit mangled by the housecats. I was too big to laugh at, and my mother's darling besides; but for that I would have been wretched, for there were none others about me who shared my tender sensibilities. Except perhaps for Griffith Lloyd, who was studying with the great bard, Iolo. But Griffith was older, and a lofty personage who never noticed me. Bards and their students are greater than princes here in the Cymry-land.

As I have said, I was big for my age and always growing; my hands and feet were huge and clumsy, and made me slow. I was slow to anger, also, and would take all manner of boys' insults with a shrug and a smile; my thoughts were always other places, far away, for the mind inside my awkward hulk darted like a weasel.

There was another manor-house near, at Nannau, belonging to my uncle Vaughan, my father's brother. He had eight daughters, all beautiful as images, right down to the three-year-old; their beauty made me shy as a bear. There was a son, also, the only one, and much spoiled by all the household. This was Howell, my first cousin, and just my age. We were much forced upon each other, for these reasons, by our families, but it did no good; fire and water do not mix.

He was a handsome lad, Howell, with a ruddy color and

quick bright eyes, good at all manner of sports; hunting and hawking, too, though he would not study his Latin. He had a cruel streak, though he was likable and it passed for mischief in those days. I never saw him pull the wings off butterflies, but I saw the sad little corpses, like worms, and the thin bright membranes scattered over the ground when he leaped up to the sound of the hunting horn. He teased his little sisters till they wept, and lamed Cabal with a stone, though he swore, after, it was an accident; I could not like him. There was jealousy there, too, for he was like a boy Apollo, compact and muscular, with neat, lithe limbs; when we were ten, he looked like a small and perfect man, and I towered above him, head and shoulders, with my great hands hanging and my feet getting in my way at every move.

When we were ten, also, our friendship, if such it could be called, ended, for I broke his nose; it was so easily done that my jaw dropped in amazement, my anger gone. I had been reading, Giraldus Cambrensis, I remember, for the book still bears the scar. I lay beneath a big oak tree, on my stomach, among the fallen leaves, for it was autumn; he would not let me alone, Howell, for he hated books and had nothing to do. He baited me with words, but I would not hear; then he took out his meat knife and began throwing it close to me where I lay, just missing whatever part he aimed for. I refused to be angered and went on reading as though he were not even there. He had a kind of choler even then; I could almost feel his fury. Suddenly the knife whizzed past my ear, pinning the parchment of Giraldus to the earth. Something broke in me, seeing the little knife quivering above the book. The months and years of suppressed hatred brought me to my feet, quickly, for me, and I smashed my fist into his grinning face. It was as if a mace had hit him; blood poured out, and his face looked like red jelly. He fell to the ground, unconscious; I thought I had killed him and ran, terrified, for help.

The thrashing that I got from my uncle Vaughan made bad blood between our families after, and Howell had a nose like a sheep's, flattened across his face and spoiling his pretty looks. I was sorry, though no one would believe it; I had not meant to hit so hard.

It made an end of my foolish frights, though, all of them. I was never again afraid of a bully like my uncle, with his knotty muscles and hairy chest; the beating he gave me was the worst he could do, and I had weathered that. Besides, I would soon be too big for it. The other boys, too, stopped their teasing and went about with awed looks; Howell's face had warned them off. Indeed, in afteryears my fame spread in all these parts; I have heard myself called a lion of wrath! As for my squeamishness, well—I have learned to keep a stony face in the sight of blood, so none knows my weakness. To this day, though, I cannot watch torture, and have never ordered it.

As I have said, I was let alone, from that day, and was free to pursue my own interests, that were shared by only a few. I pored over my precious books, learning of the great world, antique and modern, that pulsed beyond our hills. And from the bards I heard hour-long songs and tales of our land of the Cymry, that the English folk name Wales.

Wales is beautiful as all mountainous places are, with its sudden sharp contrasts that catch at the heart; purple hills wreathed in mist falling sheer and wild down, down to a gentle green valley carpeted with yellow daffodils; torrents breaking across the jagged rock, flinging spume out onto a sky as blue as the Virgin's robe, and, lower on the mountain, turning into a little laughing stream. Snowdon country is wild, it is giants' country; Dolgelly is kinder, with gentler slopes; the Romans lived hereabouts, leaving a patina of old grandeur. Everywhere there are Roman ruins, smoothed by time and lichen-grown. There is Ffynon Well, on Nannau property, that dates from the days when that manor was a Roman villa; this would have been late in the Roman occupation, for a wealthy commander lived here, perhaps, with his family, in summer, to escape the heat of Rome. Or it may have been the home of a Roman Briton, newly civilized. I studied this ruin, seeing it more complicated than any of the wells that our people use nowadays; though it is eroded and fallen away in spots, still one can see it did not work in a simple hand-over-hand way, but used some lever or pulley system, for the traces remain to this day. I am still given to prodigious imaginings; when I was a boy, I used to sit alone on the rim of this ancient well, seeing in my mind a slave-boy, Greek, perhaps, or an Ethiopian with tight-curled hair, winding the pulley to lower the buckets, his short tunic splashed with water and his sandals muddy. Or I would picture the daughter of the house, thin and proud, the blue veins showing at her temples, sitting where I now sat, sick for her sunny Tuscan home.

And then there is Caer Gai, farther down the valley, which scholars say was the home of Cei, or the English spell it Kay, one of Arthur's men. It is a noble ruin, truly; it must have been a great mansion once, though only one wall remains above the foundations. My tutor, Iorweth Sulien, said that under these foundations lies a very early Roman camp; he pointed out to me the stones, of a different size and shape. This man, my first teacher, is dear to my memory still. He was a small and wiry Breton, with a young-old face, the vicar of St. Sulien's, though he was almost not Christian even. He much loved the ancient ways out of books and modeled himself on the Greek pedagogue, that noble boys had about them in the old days of Rome or Greece. Our studies were spent much in the open, walking, examining old ruins, or digging for blackened treasure among antique graves. I loved him well.

There are two Roman–British forts a horseback ride away. There is, first, Pen-y-Ddinas, known as Arthur's camp, but to my mind it looks too early. And there is the famous circular fort, almost intact; in my boyhood travelers came to see it, not so much for its Arthurian connection, but for the fact that it had been rebuilt in the time of Owen Gwynned in his long stand against Henry II. My people of Wales are fierce patriots, as all losers are.

The most glorious spot, though, in these parts, to my mind, is the footpath that goes high, high, up the side of Moel Offrwym, the Hill of Offering. It was a name that whispered to me of dark blood and ancient mysteries, older than the Druids, but the hill itself is lovelier than a mountain in Paradise; indeed, the valley below it has been named Eden for as long as any can remember, time out of mind, as we say. One can climb to the hill's summit and stand, quite literally, with one's head in the clouds. When they are low-lying, as at sunrise or setting,

they are purple from below; as one climbs, they turn rosy, but
at the top they are thick and white, and to breathe the air is
like choking on water, until the lungs grow accustomed. The
path is strongly marked still, though it is almost never used
anymore. But the feet of old worshipers wore it deep, even into
the rock; it was a place of sacrifice, that is clear, though what
manner of men came there and what gods they placated, none
can tell. Iorweth thought they might have been of the old race
that came to these shores from Troy, eons ago, and, for sure,
there are remains of altar-stones, and fallen columns, carved
roughly with the double ax. But it may be older still; my
father in his youth found there a huge thighbone of some unknown animal, long gone from the earth. It served as a hitching post for our horses, where he had set it up in front of the
stables. As hard as stone it was, but a bone, clearly, all knotted
at the joint.

The path is too steep for horses; we used to dismount and go
by foot. It winds clear round the hill, but at the foot it passes a
beautiful abbey, Cymmer Abbey, a house of Cistercian monks.
These men were very industrious; one saw them, with their
gray habits hitched up round their waists, walking behind the
plow, brown as any peasant. They were kind, too, and would
give us milk, still warm from the cow, or sometimes a bowl of
their own dark-red wine, made from the wild hill berries that
grew upon the slopes. They had honey, too, in the comb, but it
was nasty, tasting of garlic and onion; we ate it out of courtesy,
rinsing the wine round our mouths after.

I say we—for years, when I was still very young, I walked
there with my tutor, Iorweth, and he pointing out something
new each time. Later, I took my sweet Joan, pointing out these
same wonders, while her beautiful eyes gazed gravely upon
them.

Joan, lovely and lost, whom no bard sang.

TWO

Joan was the daughter of our seneschal, there at Rhug Hall, a good man called Hugh of Clyde. This man was of fine yeoman stock, decent and proud, that the bards trace back to the Saxon invasion. That family must have been watered, long ago, with that same Saxon blood, for they were fairer than any of us Britons; skins of milk, and hair like tow, silver-pale. This Hugh had served under my father in the Scottish wars, where he had lost an arm. He grieved much that he could not be at Crécy with the Black Prince; in those days the Welsh were loyal Englishmen, for all the Edwards were kind and gentle masters, just kings and impartial, treating us Welsh as well as native English. (Scotland and Ireland were another story—but I did not know that then. No king is just to all—nor no man, neither. A harsh statement, but true.)

Joan was not her given name—she had been christened for some Welsh saint, Winifred, I think—but in those days many maidens were called Joan, in honor of the Black Prince's bride, she they called the Fair Maid of Kent. This Black Prince was beloved, the hero of Crécy, that was leading our British peoples to glory. The year his son was born, 1367, the village was peppered with Richards; every other infant bore his name. Indeed, there were so many baby Richards and nubile Joans that they were nicknamed to tell them apart; such as Richard of the Squint, Fat Joan, Joan the Swart, and so on. My Joan was called Joan the Angel, for her beauty that seemed not to belong to this earth.

She was tall for a girl, Joan, and delicately made. Her body was as long and slender as a flower-stalk and seemed to sway as she walked, like a blossom bent by the wind; her hands were thin, almost transparent, with long fingers that were pretty but chapped, for she worked hard. The seneschal had a large family and his wife had been taken by the plague, along with her last-born; the older girls kept house, cooking and washing-up, and spinning and weaving too. I never tired of looking at Joan's face, though I cannot describe it; it was perfect, but changing always with her thoughts. Her eyes were not blue, but a pure light gray, when she laughed, they looked like little silver fishes in a stream.

I cannot remember when I first saw Joan; the seneschal lived in our gatehouse, and his children were always about, running errands for a penny, or tumbling in the grass of the courtyard. We of the great house played with them as though we were all one family, for my father was a plain man, without airs, and fond of Hugh besides.

My father joined us at Rhug Hall perhaps once each year; I remember those brief times as idyllic, for he and Mother were reconciled for a little then, and she went about with a light step and humming at her tasks. As I have said, it did not last long; inevitably the great quarrel would come, and Father would take horse and spur north to one of his concubines, fury in his face. But they were short golden days, in the fall usually, and all of us were happy then.

Father and Hugh liked to sit of an afternoon and talk of old battles; Hugh had been his body-squire in Scotland in their youth. In spite of his one arm, Hugh made the best ale in those parts; I remember it still, rich and brown, with a full body to it and a subtle taste of nuts from the shell. Father always gave me a sip from his tankard; he said it was good to grow on. Sometimes they would finish a whole jug between them, and Mother would scold, but smiling all the while. I think Hugh brewed it for my father only; I never saw him drink alone. When my father was away north, Hugh drank the same thin watery beer as all the rest of us, mild, tasteless stuff that the women made in the spring.

Joan, even when she was little, had a long plait of hair tied with a coloured thong; it was pale as a moonbeam and hung between her shoulder blades, bouncing as she walked. I remember it in front of me where we sat in prayer-school at St. Sulien's, like a gilt snake it was, thick and curving and catching the light from the little high church window. Mother used to send all the children of our household, even the kitchen-sluts' by-blows, to the chapel there to learn the Latin responses. She did not know them herself, Mother; in her day girls were not taught to read. She did not even go to mass regularly, for my father would not go except on a feast-day, and when he was away from us she never went outside the manor. She sent us all, though, to pay lip service to things holy; we were her offerings, her acts of contrition, I guess.

Our cousins of Nannau went, too, to the prayer-school, before I broke Howell's nose and estranged our families. Howell sat directly behind Joan, his fertile mind, as ever, wandering, and his fingers working what mischief they could. He had a sling-shot, and would aim at birds through the window, when Ior-weth, the master, was not looking. And once he smeared the end of Joan's braid with the sticky gum from a peach tree; it was almost black at that time of year, and evil-smelling, and would not wash out. They had to cut off the hair, six inches of it, and Joan wept bitterly. Iorweth thrashed him for it and made him sit till sundown copying his letters, but Howell only laughed.

Later, as she grew, Joan became most devout, spending all her snatched moments in the chapel on her knees. Her brothers and sisters teased her for it, and Mother's old nurse shook her head and said, sadly, that 'the poor girl is too good to live.' Iorweth Sulien said the mystery of holy church had caught her, as it did long ago with the early saints. Once, at Christ's Mass —I must have been about twelve then—I saw her eyes, raised to the altar; the look in them stabbed me through with a sudden hot agony, so beautiful they were and so alien. As beautiful and as void as the stars.

I used to talk to Joan sometimes about the lives of the saints, for I read everything I could get my hands on, even those childish stories, cruder than any myth. It was a flagrant deception, for they could not interest me, those deluded holy men and women with their blind devotion and their strange sick martyrdoms. But it made her notice me, and listen, and turn her wonderful great gray eyes upon my face. I would grow red, then white, and my hands would sweat. For I loved her so that I thought I would burst with it.

Except for my giant growth and my learning out of books, I came to most things slowly. I was fifteen, and had not slain a deer or unhorsed another boy at tourney, for always, at the last moment, I turned aside spear or lance. Tudor, at thirteen, had got a girl with child already, or at least she said so. I turned away from the ripe glances of the village wenches, too, though there were a few who looked, as girls always will, at big male creatures. I thought them delightful to watch, pretty as fox cubs; their soft arms and swaying hips moved me no more than the play of puppies. I looked but did not touch. Perhaps I knew then, under, that once I started, I could never get enough of them, women. For so it has been with me, always.

I had not known that my feelings for Joan had anything of the flesh in them, though I burned with love, as I have said. Until the Dawns Epona, the Dance of the Horse-Goddess.

This is an old, old dance that the maidens do here, every year in the early days of spring; the bards all say it came over the sea with the Cymry-folk centuries ago, when they came from Greece or Troy or wherever the place was—who can tell? Sure, it has an ancient feel about it, like priestesses before an altar.

It is said that, long ago, in more barbarous times, there were horses, and that the maidens courted them, like fillies, and even, at the end, played a ritual coupling. For sure, Epona, the Horse-Goddess, is one of the very oldest, and my people were a horse-people, and worshiped those beasts for their service and the advantages that they gained from them.

But down the years the dance has changed, and no one can remember such a thing. The maidens play the horses now, the prancing, dancing, provocative fillies; all the maidens take part, the youngest ones, from thirteen perhaps, every year until they are wed. The young men stand around the circle of dancers and clap their hands in a curious compelling rhythm.

Father said that when he was a boy, the maidens, at the end, took each a boy, drawing him into the dance; so it was, long ago, a courtship dance.

Joan did not know this, of course, for she would never have taken part; she would not even sit astride the old Derfel-horse in the town square, like all the other girls, and wish for a lover to quicken her; indeed she would hurry past that time-blackened horse-image, head averted. One could see that she thought it nasty, with its huge phallus.

But she was there, with the others, for the Dawns Epona.

Her sister, Olwen, too, was among the dancers, though she was almost too old for it, and promised already to a page of our house. My big sister Laura was lined up with the girls, all flushed and laughing, her red dress sewn with little beads of glass. All the dancers wore red, the color of maidenhead blood, perhaps, or of love; it is lost, the meaning, in the mists of time.

The clapping began, slow and monotonous; as it increased in tempo, one could hear in it the stamping of stallions. The girls began slowly too, a toss of the head, a lifted knee, an arched back, proud. The movements were clear-cut, doll-like. At measured intervals they came together in pairs, and lightly rubbed their bodies together, their round arms lifted above their heads. As I watched, clapping still, a curious feeling came over me, a kind of pity—for those sweetly made creatures forced into those strange ritual postures by that clapping—by that simulated stallion rut-stamp. It was a sensual feeling, I know now, compounded of pathos and cruelty, and over all an empty, crawling, sick desire.

Olwen was ripe and round as a fruit; her heavy breasts bounced under the thin red stuff of her gown. My sister Laura was big-breasted too, and tall, like all our family, with long, long legs; she looked like some antique goddess on a vase, her face stern and Attic-pure. The maidens, all, made in different sizes and shapes, wore a look of Artemis this day. It had rained earlier; their feet, bare, were beaded with moisture from the still-wet grass. There was that strange light, too, that comes sometimes after a rain, washed-looking, with something of emerald in it and something of gold.

The girls' hair was unbound from its knots or braidings and fell loose to their hips; Joan's was like a sheet of pale hammered gold. She wore her sister Olwen's old dress from the year before; it was short to show her ankles, for she was taller, and a little rip was beginning at her armpit, in the back, where the fit was too snug. Once, in a sharp turn, her hair caught in Laura's sleeve, held by one of the sharp glass beads; I saw Joan's face ripple in a sudden little spasm of pain, unholy-sweet to watch, and the two girls bend together gravely, still dancing, to free it.

The dancing, though still ritualized, grew faster, the long hair tossing like manes, and the knees lifted, prancing, the legs showing in all their length. The hips swayed, the stomachs rolled, and the waving arms made provocative beckoning patterns in the bright air. The clapping-stomping grew faster too, and wild, a kind of frenzy under. Toward the end of the dance, the maidens' faces, drenched with the sweat of their exertions, lost the look of purity, and glowed with a mad ecstasy, innocent of shame. At the last, they faced, those prancing fillies, inward, in a circle, their bare feet planted wide apart, spreading their maiden hips. The backs arched sharply upward, in a bend that did not look human, jutting the breasts sharply outward. The long throats stretched, the heads thrust upward above the blowing manes, eyes to the sky. The pose held for a long moment; the clapping reached its crescendo, and, all at once, the girls' arms stretched high to the sky. The little tear widened at Joan's arm, showing dazzling flesh, whiter than her face, between the torn red edges of her sleeve.

Something broke in me, like an underground explosion; a sudden hot sweet emptiness, draining my loins, and leaving me, after, sick and weak. The clapping stopped then too; the dance was over. I felt all eyes were upon me, though of course they were not.

I had been wearing my loose scholar's gown over my hose, so I was not shamed before them all. My father must have seen something, though, because he sent a girl to my bed that night. She was one he had lain with several times, so he meant it well.

I could not take her there, though, in the wall-bed beside my brother Tudor, though he was snoring already. Instead I took her by the hand and we crept outside, lying on my fur cloak in the grass of the courtyard. Her flesh was warm, and glowed in the moonlight; her eyes were deep dark pools, though by day I had seen them narrow and sly.

She was my first girl, a rosy-dark hill-girl come down to work in the manor. I lay with her all that spring, and Tudor after, so we never knew whose child she bore. It might have been our father's even, or the hill man she went back to. She called her son Rhys Gethin, after that man, at any rate.

My life—and Tudor's, too—was all entwined, later, with this same boy-child, this Rhys, called the Savage. But his mother ... it is so long ago that I have forgot her name.

THREE

I should have been cured of Joan, but I was not. As she loved God, so I loved. I was a man by moonlight, but in the day I still stood before her with my mouth dropped open and a witless look. I would see her blond plait swinging ahead of me, on the path to the well, and race to catch up, only to slow beside her, wordless and without even the sense to take the heavy buckets from her hands. Or I would find my voice and talk and talk and never stop, keeping her from her work.

I took to waylaying her at chapel, too, lurking outside the door to meet as if by accident, and making her walk with me up the mountain. She could not refuse, for I was her baron's son, though she was missed at home and scolded roundly after.

Hugh must have spoken something of it to Father, for one day as we rode about the holding he took my horse's bridle, turning it so that I faced him and looking at me straight. 'Does she not please you then—your bedmate?' It was the first word of that girl from his lips. I flushed and swallowed, not answering. He smiled a little, wryly. 'It may be I will take her back ...'

I spoke then. 'Oh, Father, she pleases me well, but——'

'Why, then, do you moon after Hugh's Joan? She is promised to God, I have dowered her.'

'It is not the same,' I said, shaking my head. 'I would not touch her—Joan ...'

'How not?' he said, still smiling. 'She is pretty enough—and we are none so pious, our house, either ...'

'I think she would not have me ...'

'Try her,' he said, shortly. 'It may be she plays a waiting game.'

'You said it yourself, Father ... she wants to go to Aberystwyth—to be a nun there.'

'Girls of that age do not always know what they want,' he said. 'Usually it is a man. Try her.'

Next day, upon the mountain, the Hill of Offering, I reached out my hand to her; I meant to touch her neck, white under her hair, but my fingers closed upon her plait. It was warm from the afternoon sun, and felt like a thing alive. I put it to my lips and kissed it wildly, as though it were her flesh; when I put out blind hands to take her, I felt her shoulders stiffen, and drew back. Her eyes were turned to me; there was a look in them like a horse's eyes when it is ready to bolt. I let go then, and said, miserable, 'Can you not—like me, Joan?'

'Oh, yes,' she said quickly, her breath nearly going from her, 'oh, yes, Baron—I like you ... I like you well ...' She had not called me baron before that, in all our years. I would not have her that way, in her fear and all unequal.

I stood up, pretending to brush the grass-dust from my tunic, and then straightened, pointing. 'Look,' I said, 'there is the altar where they sacrificed—the Old People ...' In the clear light I could see plain the rough-carved double ax on the altar's face. 'Human sacrifice, they say ...' I had not heard this said by anyone and do not know why I lied; perhaps to be cruel, for she had hurt me. I looked at her, seeing her all red and shamed, and now frightened again.

She crossed herself; I saw her lips move.

'What is that?' I said, brutally. 'It is no worse than any other sacrifice ... it is no worse an offering than to give Christ a bride!'

She stared at me in a kind of horror, her mouth in a little 'o.' Then she turned and ran down the mountain, leaving me to beat my fists into the stone until the blood came, and I cried weak angry tears. I never spoke with Joan again, and only twice did I see her.

We removed to Sycharth again that summer, with all our household, bards and minstrels, too. Mother and Laura, with the house-women, were packing for weeks, though it was not far, just over a mountain or two; still, we had a train of forty-odd pack-mules. The seneschal stayed on, of course, with his brood, to look after Rhug Hall, and my hill-girl disappeared, back where she came from. She was not even mine anymore;

my heavy humors had wearied her, and Tudor's love was lighter and sweeter. Still, she had not stayed with him long either; these hill-women are very independent and give where they please; they are princesses, all, or bear themselves so.

Sycharth is a fine, fair manor, timbered in stout, carven oak, with mountain slate for roof. My father had built it on an old site; it was all new-appointed, and stood on a little knoll, with a view of all the valleys. It boasted a deep moat, too, with a drawbridge, borrowed from the Normans; we swam there on hot days, for my father would allow no offal to be thrown there, and the water was clear and clean, fed by a fast-running hill-stream. It had no turrets or keeps, and no fortress-look, but a pleasant picture-look of peace and plenty, with, over all, in the distance, the wild peaks of Snowdon hunched and brooding.

Our bards went with us there, and I was much in their company that summer. I say 'our,' but of course they belonged to all Wales and to the ages. My father drew these men to him, though, and mummers and minstrels, too, for he was prodigal with gifts and hospitality to all such folk. We children had studied with them all our years, and Tudor and Laura, too, were fair harpists even when their fingers could not reach to all the strings; Father had little harps made for them, pretty things inlaid with ivory and gold. I was not really musical, though I learned the notes, for I was clever enough. I could make words flow, though, and translated songs from the Latin, besides making some of my own. The older bards would not play them, shaking their heads and clucking; they said they were too modern and that the rhythms clashed. Only Griffith Lloyd the Younger would try them out for me. This Griffith Lloyd was a young man, twenty, perhaps, but balding already; he was becoming my good friend, for we two had much love of learning, ancient and modern, and would talk and argue by the hour. He was the son of another bard so named, long dead, and had been reared by his uncle, that all Wales called Iolo Goch, or Julius the Red, for his hair and long mustache that gleamed like copper fires. There are many Roman names among our Welsh people, from intermarriage centuries ago. My mother, Helen, was proud of her Roman beginnings, and spoke Latin on feast-days, though we children smiled behind her back, for she got the words all wrong. But names like Madoc and Caradoc were once Madocus and Caractacus, and there are many more. So is named Red Julius, whom I will call by its Welshing, Iolo Goch, for he is famous as Homer ever was in Greece.

Iolo was old already when I knew him then, as a boy, though his hair was bright still and his step all vigor; he was born before this century began, so he must have been over sixty when I first knew him. He was Lord of Lechryd, in the Valley of Clyde, and claimed descent from Merlin. I take all this with a grain of salt now, for I have read much, all contradictions; Merlin has many names, and maybe did not live at all. But, for sure, Iolo comes of ancient lineage, and the Lloyds are petty lords but proud.

All of our Welsh bards are pagan in thought; they date, after all, from Druid times. Iolo, in particular, writes odes to the old gods, as if there had been no Christ, no church, and no priests ever. He writes of Hu Gadarn, the Husbandman, inventor of the plow, Hu the Mighty; he writes of Morrighan, the fierce war-goddess, and of Lleu, the Celtic Hermes, and of Myrrddhin Willt, that the English call Merlin. He has written many odes also to the Virgin, but they are almost love-poems, such as one might address to Aphrodite, and would make any churchman blush. Iolo is an old libertine, still; one cannot trust him near a young serving maid, though the pages are safer than they are with visiting monks. He is a poet for women, war, and Wales, a fierce patriot is Iolo. All his work is in the grand manner and old-fashioned to make the younger bards smile behind their hands; true it is that his words are empty, without the music. But his harping would bring tears from Snowdon peak; he is the finest harpist in the world, Iolo, and it is his harp that speaks closest to the common folk. They crowd the courtyard whenever he plays; no one knows how they hear of it; it is as though a fairy called them, or old Merlin, perhaps.

There was at Sycharth too, that summer, another bard, David ap William; Father had had him carried in a horse litter all the way from the south, in Glamorganshire. He was older than Iolo even, and very weak, afflicted with a kind of palsy in his hands, so that he could no longer play. His voice, though, was beautiful beyond any other, with a range of notes like a young man's, and much vigor, too. He would not let Iolo play for him; he said his harping stole away thought. So the other bards would play softly, while David sang. He was a poets' poet, David, too fine for the common ear; they called him, all, the Welsh Ovid. His poems, like that old Latin, were all of love and beauty and the little secret speaking of nature; beautiful they were to hear, and I wrote them down when I could, to have them by me always.

My grandfather, Griffith of Rhuddallt, was alive still then, and his father, Madoc the Cripple, too. These two old men were like brothers, instead of father and son; I guess Madoc had married young, as the old folk often did. They would sit in the upstairs chamber all day and gossip in thin old voices. More like ancient dames they were, those two, with their long gowns and hair, and their faces clean-shaven as babes. Thinking on it now—they cannot have been so very old, for my father was still not near his prime, but neither of them could walk. Old Madoc had a twisted spine from birth, which got worse with the years; the doctors said it calcified. And Grandfather had had two cruel strokes, leaving him like stone all down one side. They sipped possets of honey and wine all day and ate little; I think they were always a little drunk from it, or perhaps there was a drug mixed in. We children always used to creep in and listen; they seldom noticed us, and their talk was often very lewd, too good to miss. Once, that last summer, though, old spidery Madoc looked up and fixed his rheumy eyes on Laura, all ripe by them, like a golden peach, and called out to her, a name we could not catch, some doxy of his dim youth. 'Come sit on my lap, little dearie!' Lap he had none, his legs were shriveled to nothing by then, but she drew near, not wanting to offend, and leaned over to catch his words. He thrust out one tiny claw-hand, quickly, for all his infirmity, and grabbed a breast, holding on tight so that she cried out, and he cackled in glee, squeezing harder. Mother forbade us to go there again, calling it a scandal. She hated those old men anyway; she disliked all my father's people.

But, before, we had heard much; the memories of those old sires were prodigious, going back to Llewellyn's time, though maybe it was all lies, who can tell?

That was where we heard the tales of the wild youth of the bard David ap William, though; tales to curl the hair on your head, if you could credit them. How he, a beautiful lad of twenty, with yellow love locks and a fine-turned leg, seduced his patron's daughter, following her to the nunnery, where she had been locked up for safety, and abducting her, sending her back to languish when he had tired. How he composed a poem to a rival bard so vile that the man, hearing it, fell down dead (we laughed ourselves sick at this, though some sober folk believed it, our Welsh will swallow anything where it touches on the magic of genius). According to his poems, David had been faithful and loving throughout to one Morfydd, to whom he had been joined in a Druidic ceremony. Church law forbade such marriages, and her parents wed her to an ancient hunchback. She promptly fled to David's arms again, and they lived awhile together in some sylvan glade, until they were discovered and separated and he flung into prison. The men of Glamorgan, though, not wanting to lose their finest bard, rescued him, risking their souls, for they all were excommunicated for it.

But the most comic tale is the one they told most often. It seems that David had, in a certain county, a great many mistresses. Once upon a time, in the month of June, he made secret rendezvous with each of them, all at a certain hour and under a certain oak in the forest. Before the appointed time, he climbed into the oak and watched through the leaves as these willing nymphs arrived, all twenty-four of them. For some moments they stayed, all beneath the oak, staring at one another. Finally one spoke, and the whole swindle came out. 'O, that monster,' they cried, in one voice. 'O, that traitor ... only let him show himself and we will tear him to pieces!'

'Will you?' cried David, from the branches of the oak. 'Here I am. Let her who has been most wanton with me strike the first blow!'

All were speechless; then suddenly, enraged, they flew at one another, tearing hair and scratching cheeks. While the fray was at its greatest height, David slipped down from his perch and ran away. A likely tale. Griffith Lloyd composed a song about it, after the manner of some of the Italian tales, but it is too licentious for any ears but mine.

Indeed, much of what is told of all these bards must be winked at. Iolo, for instance, is reported to be somewhere in the neighborhood of a hundred and ten years, and to have sired half Wales. But then many of the older songs attributed to him are not his at all, but have been handed down, with a word changed here and there and using a different key. As for all the redheads that abound in these parts—well, we are Celts, after all, either red or black, or that tawny in-between like my own family. Iolo never married, though there is a woman in these parts who claims to be his wife in the old faith, or some such thing; it is a strange story. Iolo never spoke of her to me or my brother, but Griffith Lloyd has heard the tale and met the lady, too, when he was a young boy. And one day that summer, having nothing else to do and adventure-bound, we set out, Tudor, Griffith, and I, to consult this lady and learn our fortunes.

For she is a prophetess, and has the Sight, or so it is said. She is the priestess of some old cult; they hang on still, here in Wales, dating from some time before the Christians came. They are harmless little religions, for the most part, and tucked away out of sight, though the ignorant folk still bring offerings at certain times, when the moon is high or low, or whatever; the churchmen mostly pretend blindness.

It was a fairish ride away and took the whole morning; the sun was high overhead when we came to the place at the foot of Dinas Brân. This is an old, old castle or fortress, said to date from the time of Brân the Blessèd; of course this is impossible, he is pure myth. But it is old enough to look as if a race of giants built it, before the coming of man; if you look close, though, and without awe, you will see Roman traces, and Norman even, in its structure. Perhaps it is built on an ancient hill-city site, all sunk into the earth by now; I will come here one day and dig, when I have time.

Indeed, I was so busy examining the ruin and musing upon what lay beneath that I did not see the thing in front of me till I had almost ridden into it; I was checked by my horse, which reared high, nearly throwing me. In front of me was a tall column, painted wood, and winding round it a large snake, its head pointed at mine; the little forked tongue was an inch from my eye. It took a moment before I saw it was painted too, a cunningly made thing. I heard my companions sniggering and got down from my horse, feeling foolish.

There was another column, too, its twin, holding up the roof. Seen close to, the whole job was crude and did not look built to last. A long low building, wooden, with a flat roofline and no walls, a kind of rude temple. One could see at the other end a cave-opening, hung with some spotted fur. Griffith had told us about this place as we rode; it was called the House of the Snake. There is a snake-goddess, of course, in our old religions, but she is old, so old, I should have thought forgotten. There is one in every faith, back far enough; it is a very ancient symbol of earth and the Mother, before the man-gods. The newer one, but old still, is our Welsh Horse-Goddess, called Epona; one can find her little stone images, fallen in the forest, beside rough shrines, fallen too; they are as common as dirt, or were then, when I was a boy. They have disappeared now, hidden away, or smashed by the churchmen.

But she had her image there, too, Epona, in that temple; there was a little pitted stone figure, the size of a doll, seated sideways on the back of a horse. Derfel was there, too, on *his* horse, with his captive maiden flung across his knees, and the horned helmet on his head; this image was wood, and the paint worn away, so that the god had no face. He has been made a saint, Derfel; his worship could never be put down, so the Christians took him for one of their own. It is a wry thought; Derfel-worship is an ugly thing, with the ritual deflowering of virgins. But the holy monks wink at it and, some say, make profit, too.

I have thought often that St. Derfel may be our Welsh devil; he is cruel and sly, and commits outrages in the night. Perhaps he is a kind of Pluto; he is said to take a virgin for his own each year, in the fall, and keep her all the winter, somewhere in a cave underground, while the land lies snow-locked, much like the old Greek myth. His horned helmet, though, may

come, not from the devil's image, but later, from the Saxon
enemy, who wore such helmets into battle. It is a thing I would
like to study; it will be difficult, though, for even to countenance the Derfel-tales would be to lay oneself open to a charge
of witchcraft.

As we entered that rude temple, looking about us curiously,
I saw the leopard-pelt twitch aside for a moment, and smelled
smoke, acrid and heavy with some herb, though beyond all was
dark. Near the door place was an altar, very small and low; as
we drew near I saw little corpse-skeletons, bats or mice, upon
its blackened surface. Tudor held his nose, looking sick, but
Griffith laughed. 'It is all child's play now,' he said, gesturing
at the black stone slab. 'There you may see the sacrifices ... I
think they keep a grass snake or two, just for show.'

Two maidens came out then through the opening, pushing
aside the skin hanging and bowing before us. One of them
giggled and held her hand before her mouth; she could not
have been more than seven years of age. The other was a ripe
maiden, one could see; they wore the oddest clothes, full skirts,
dyed red, the color of dried blood, and little sleeveless jackets
that did not meet in front. I stared; we all did, for they wore
nothing beneath. The little one, of course, had nothing to
show, but the other—I did not know where to look and be
polite still. Their long hair fell behind, loose, and there were
flowers stuck in it here and there; their feet were bare and
stained red too, as though they walked in blood. At wrists and
ankles they wore slim circling snakes, wrought of some bright
metal, redder than gold. Gold braid, too, trimmed their scanty
jackets; when she came close, I saw the older one's braid was
tarnished, and frayed in places. A flower fell out of the little
one's hair; she stooped to pick it up, giggling again. I saw her
hair's color, like old bronze; she would be beautiful later.
Griffith whispered that she was Iolo's daugher, or granddaughter; the older girl put a finger to her lips, frowning. I
counted in my head; granddaughter, surely!

'The Lady will see you now,' said the riper maiden, low.
From somewhere she had got a rushlight; as we followed her, I
saw it was needed. Behind the leopard hanging was a great
cave, going far back into the hill, its walls lost in the darkness.

Beside the rushlight, there was only one other light, a bowl of some stuff that burned steadily, with a little bluish flame; it was this that smelled, catching in the nostrils. It stood on another altar, and behind it sat a woman of surpassing loveliness. She was not young, far from it, but a thrill went down my spine, fugitive, at the sight of her. I do not remember what she wore; some loose robe, rusty-red like the others', and her hair, knotted high, that same red, or nearly. 'It is the Lady Morgan,' hissed the big girl, in my ear. 'Kneel!' It seemed natural for me to do so, she was so beautiful, like a very goddess, but I heard Tudor give a little clucking sound and put out a hand to make him kneel with me. I am tall; even kneeling, I could look into her eyes, though she sat on some sort of dais. Her eyes were a very clear light blue, like colored glass; close to, I saw little lines around them, and threads of gray, too, were in her hair. Even so, I think she was the most startling beauty I have ever seen. The face was without flaw, the jaw's clench ageless, but there was more. If those lips had leaned out to kiss mine, I would have followed her to the world's end, old as she was. A kind of sorcery she had, a woman-thing, and beckoning. I thought to myself: She is true-named, this Morgan. The French tales were coming into fashion then, Arthur, and his queen, and the fairy Morgan in her enchanted wood.

The rigmarole we watched was meaningless and silly, and I cannot remember it today; in any case I watched the Lady Morgan and not what she did. I remember she threw a pinch of some powder on the flame before her, making it flare suddenly, almost to the cave-roof, and making us jump, too. I heard the little maiden choke then, laughing loud. The Lady looked at her, her brows drawn down, but I saw a tiny indentation at her mouth's corners; she was an indulgent mother—or was it grandmother? She looked a little look at the other girl, barely gesturing with her head, and the giggler was taken out.

The flame had died down again, and I saw the Lady take something from the dish, a kind of wax, between her fingers, rolling it into a little pellet. She put it in her mouth, and I saw her jaws move; perhaps she swallowed it. She made an incantation in Old Welsh, hard to follow, for the words are different and the meanings obscure, but I heard the name of the goddess she called; Diis, it was, or Di, an old, old name for the Mother. As she stretched her arms above her, her sleeves fell back, and I saw, with some shock, that the snake-bracelets on her arms were real; one was black and one tawny-spotted, and they were tiny, but their little tongues went in and out and their heads moved from side to side, the gem-eyes glittering. And then she told our fortunes, Morgan.

I do not remember what she said to Tudor, or to Griffith, either. Something of war and bloody death, cruel to hear. But after, she turned to me, speaking of glory; foolish words to hear, even from her sweet swooning lips. I suppose she had heard I was the eldest son of our princely house and wished to do me honor. But at the end she took my two hands in hers, cradling them; one of the little snakes slithered onto my arm, leaving hers and making me shudder, though I knew them harmless and managed not to flinch. 'We are all entwined now, Lord Owen,' she said. 'Our houses and our fates ... Our blood, too, will mingle ...' She smiled at me; I nearly kissed her then and there—I am very susceptible to fair women. She shook her head a little, still smiling. 'Not us two,' she said. 'I am too old ... older than you think. Though I much regret it ...' And she leaned forward, placing her lips against my eyelids; it was a touch like a bird's wing, but I felt it deep, in my loins. 'No,' she said. 'I will give you Lowri—my own Lowri, Daughter of Earth ...' I wondered who she meant—it is my sister's name in Welsh.

She held me so, while the snake wriggled back, winding, onto her arms. The flame in the saucer guttered out then, and she loosed my hands. We stumbled out of there somehow, in the darkness, blinking when we came into the light of the temple and looking at each other, sheepish.

Before the temple was a flat patch of earthy ground where no grass grew. The small maiden sat there, no longer giggling. Her hands were busy as a housewife's, digging into the earth and kneading it with water from a bowl. 'Mud pies,' I thought, 'she is very young ...'

She lifted her eyes to me then, for I stood over her. They were the eyes of the Lady Morgan, sea-blue and beckoning, and her face, too, was the Lady's face, in little. All round her were the little objects she had fashioned. Not pies, then, I thought, and bent to pick one up. I blushed then, dark red, clear down into the neck of my tunic. It was a perfect phallus, erect, and with all the rest, too, clustered tight. I heard Tudor snicker behind me and put it down quickly, as if it burned my fingers.

The little maid looked up at me, solemn as Minerva. 'It is an offering,' she said. 'An offering for the Mother ...' I watched her little fingers shaping another. She had skill, for sure. She held it at arm's length, squinting critically, then indented it sharply with her fingernail at the tip. I winced.

She stared up at me again, her eyes unwinking, her hands in her lap now; butter would not melt in that full-lipped, child's mouth.

I could find nothing to say to her; the toys she played with were too potent. Finally, uncomfortable under her look, I asked her name.

'I am Lowri,' she said.

FOUR

In the fall, back again to our winter quarters—like those old Roman-Britons moving camp, like birds. In truth, the habit was wearing thin by now; it seemed a weary trek, the forty sumpter-mules, the packing and unpacking, the settling in with all our house-folk. And then, Father came too, he and Mother were reconciled now, in a sort; there had been no angry voices raised all summer, for a wonder. Rhug Hall seemed cramped, though, for all its size; Father had a whole new set of minstrels, and some apprentice-bards as well, besides the old ones. The two old sick men, our grandsires, father and son, came too, and the palsied David ap William, by litter all the way and slowing us to a snail's pace. And Father brought his women, too, along with their children. Mother did not seem to mind, and even nursed one of the little bastard boys when he caught a fever; perhaps she was past jealousy now. Indeed, when I came upon her in the sunny courtyard, our first day back, I saw with a little shock that her look of youth had all gone from her. She had been airing the bedclothes with some of the servingwomen, and counting linens, too, frowning over the task. When it was all settled, she looked up, feeling my stare, and smiled; the deep crease between her brows was there still, and some new lines, too, around her mouth.

Sycharth had been a pleasant place; I think we young people all felt discontent, one way or another, to leave it. My sister Laura was betrothed, or nearly, though no papers had been signed. But I think she liked him well, the young man, a son of a Sycharth neighbor. He was just her age, but half-English and very worldly, dressed in the latest fashions from court. She met him once only, a formality; toasts were drunk and hands clasped, but I saw her eyes bright and fevered and her cheeks red with excitement. He was a goodly fellow with some wit, old for his years; his English was as good as the king's, and he wore a little pointed beard, the latest style; he had just come back from Oxford. So we all gawked, feeling like mountaineers, and out of it. I think she daydreamed about him, Laura, all her idle moments. Or perhaps it was of the fine clothes she would wear as his wife. His name was Robert Pulestan, and he would have knight's tenure when he came of age, and a baronetcy, too, after his father died. It was a good match and would probably come to pass, so it was just as well she fancied him. It is not always so with our heiress-maidens; they are bartered in marriage, even here in Wales, though not as cruelly or odd-matched as in other places. I think my father would not have forced her to wed against her will, anyway, whatever the cost; he is a feeling man, for all his faults, and she his only true-born daughter and very dear.

Tudor and I, also, were much put out to leave our summer place; we had had to part from our girls there, a vexing thing. I had two laughing damsels that summer; they shared me willingly, light as thistledown they were, and making all my nights day-bright. One was as Saxon-fair as my sweet Joan, but of a different make, and no saint.

As for Joan, I avoided her; an easy task, for she made it so. I would see her sometimes in the distance and walk the other

way; once, as I rode about the holding, I saw her ahead of me
on the path and turned my horse aside into the woods. The
look of surprise on its face, swiveled round at me, was almost
human, but it bent its head gratefully to the little grasses that
grew beneath the trees. I was not cured of Joan, far from it;
but though I clasped her slender length in many an imagined
feast of love, the dream face she turned to me always wore that
look of fright. To this day I cannot put out my hand to a
woman, and she not willing.

I spent, still, long hours with my tutor, Iorweth, though it
was clear there was not much more he could teach me. We
talked the sundial round, though, in pleasurable discourse and
dialogue; I think we both fancied ourselves as copies of Plato
and the great Socrates, his master. Philosophy was Iorweth's
god, too, though he was learned in all the churchly abstrac-
tions and could quote all the good fathers clear back to the
first Paul. I can see him still, small and intense, his monk's robe
tucked under him where he sat cross-legged upon the yellowing
grass, the late sun dappling him with its gold. He had never
taken a wife, Iorweth, as so many of our clergy did, though it
was against canon law; I think, too, that he did not love boys
either, he was a solitary, and a thinker. He lived on pure
thought, as other men feed. I know he neglected himself; his
tonsure was always growing out, and under his habit he was as
thin as a weed. Mother used to worry over him, and scold;
sometimes she would burden me with all manner of delicate
victuals to tempt him, but I think he gave them, all, to his
pupils. 'Boys are always hungry,' he would say, with a smile.

We dug for treasure, too, as I have said, though none else
would name it so. Bits of pottery, and splintered bones, rusty
weapons and old coins covered with mold; I kept them all to
study, though the serving folk clucked their tongues when they
had to dust it all. There are old grave-places dotted all round
the countryside, mounds of earth built by the Old People that
were here before our Cymry-folk came. There was a huge bar-
row nearby, rich in old hidden things; you could dig with a
trowel only, not a foot down, and find something each time.
And once we rode all the way to Mathrafal; the mound-grave
there had been struck by lightning, exposing all one side. It

was a sight of much fascination; inside were several small chambers, each with its separate poor bones, and little clay pots, and blackened bronze, unrecognizable by now. Those folk must have been tiny; their bones were no bigger than the bones of children, and they lay upon their sides, curled as if in the womb, with their knives and their drinking bowls buried beside them, for use in the other world. So we knew that even then, so long, long ago, men put their faith upon another life, after death. I wept within to look upon these sad traces of mortality, though Iorweth signed himself and said a prayer; he was a Christian, after all, and bred to his own blind faith.

In one of those chambers, deeper in the mound, where the soil was all chalk, we came upon a girl's body, still clothed with flesh, though her grave-wrappings had rotted away; she looked as though she might have died just yesterday, and I caught my breath, looking. She was about the size of a ten-year-old maid, but formed as a woman, small and perfect. Her skin was the color of some rich wood, and her hair was black, spreading about her like a cloak. We could see her little hands, with almond-shaped, curving nails, and the sooty lashes that lay against her cheek as if she slept. She must have been preserved by the chalk. I thought to take this treasure home, and put out my hand, carefully, to lift her. At the first touch, though, she crumbled into a fine dust, like a dream that dissolves. I have told this later, and seen the sneaking look of laughter flicker behind eyes, for none believed me, but it was so. For just that one moment of time, I saw, clear, one of the Old People as she had been; beautiful as a princess she was, so small and strange.

We wandered far afield, Iorweth and I, in our searchings for old knowledge. Once we spent a whole week away, and came upon, unwitting, a horrid sight.

As I have said, Wales has been at peace for many years, under the last English kings; I have not spoke about the borderlands, though, which are held by the Marcher barons. These are English–Norman lords, granted these lands long ago by the Norman conquerors. The land itself is part in England, part in Wales, and always there is strife of some sort there. For the Welsh peasantry will not bend to the Norman feudal yoke; they will not be serfs and un-free. From time to time there are raids by these would-be English masters, upon the sleepy peaceful villages of the Welsh. Maidens are dragged off to be used and thrown away, or kept for low work when their looks are gone. Young strong men are taken too, by force, and branded, and an iron collar soldered about their necks, in the Norman way. It is illegal, of course, but these are isolated instances, and have not grown large enough to come to the ears of the king.

In one place, I have forgot the castle's name, but right at the border, we saw revenge taken. The lord of that place had been away, at war somewhere on the Continent; they are always fighting somewhere, these Normans, to them it is as natural as breathing. There were none left in the castle but women and boys, and a few old men, too old to go to war. From the villages roundabout, as we surmised it, the folk had banded together and fired the castle. It was of stone, of course, and would not burn, but the walls were blackened and everything inside destroyed or carried away. Somewhat was left, though, a grisly sight, and a reminder that tyranny breeds savagery and devastation.

For there were upwards of thirty corpses there, flung anyhow upon the flags of the great hall, stripped naked and mutilated. Women with their breasts cut off, old grandsires with eyes gouged out, and tender pages, barely come to puberty, castrated and rotting in their own blood. It had happened some while before, for the smell was dreadful, and crows and mice had been at the bodies, too. But upon the foreheads were carved rude crosses, and upon some the old Derfel-sign, horns, or at least it looked to be. The worst sight was the little babes, skulls smashed and bellies gutted. In blood, darkening now, were filthy names written in Welsh upon the walls, and 'vengeance' and 'death,' too, scrawled there. So we knew it had been done by our own people, and it saddened us. Men are beasts under, and have always been. Perhaps in time we will change; our time on this earth is a drop in the bucket of eons, after all, a snap of the finger, no more. For the world is many, many millions of years old, and man has been upon it a mere million, if that. A thought to numb the heart and awe the soul. But what thought does not? The part that is not beast thinks, and finds no meaning. But think we will, no matter. It is our destiny.

I never saw such a scene repeated, in all my early days. But I knew there was violence hidden, even in our pastoral life. And in the remoter hill regions, it was whispered that men lived as in the old days, tribal fighting, and heads, and worse, taken as trophies. For our Wales is wild and rocky, and there are places hard to get to, where no native eye has looked upon a stranger. One day will we be welded, all, into a nation, that protects its borders, and knows its neighbor within, and thinks as one. It is my dream, and I have thought much upon it.

But mostly were our days pleasant, and fine discourse upon old deeds of beauty and glory, of Rome and of Greece that was greater still, of philosophy and art and ancient lovely song.

Sometimes, as I sat at talk with my master, Iorweth, another scholar would steal up and take his place beside us to listen, eager as a child. He was the miller, Iestyn by name, but his mill ground at night only, for he spent all his daylight hours over his books. He was an odd scholar indeed, this man, for he was upwards of fifty, and a cripple, too. None knew his beginnings; it was said that he had been exposed at birth, for he had a deformed foot, hideous and clumsy as a hoof. He used to boast that he had been suckled by wolves, like the twins of Rome, but his eyes danced as he spoke. The miller that was before him, a widower and childless, had heard the babe crying on the mountain, and brought him home. He was a likely lad and clever, for all his limp, and so he prospered, inheriting the mill and grinding now for all the village. The lust for learning came to him late, or perhaps he could not spare the time in his youth; a strange sight it must have been, for sure, to see this big maimed man, white-haired already, sitting on the low benches at St. Sulien's, mouthing Latin with the restless little boys.

He never married, either, Iestyn, most like he feared a wife's scorn; the village women are a crude lot, and do not love unfortunates. But he had contentment of a sort, and wealth enough, with his mill, to buy his precious books. Like that other scholar, Iorweth, he much suffered from self-neglect, forgetting to eat, or to brush his clothes. They were always cov-

ered with a fine white dust, mark of his trade. The mill itself
was fine and large, situated in goodly beauty upon a fair
stream; the great wheel, idle by day, brooded above, while the
water flowed by gently, a pastoral scene. Once, by night, I came
upon it, though; I liked sometimes, when I could not sleep and
the moon was full, to walk abroad, walking away my thoughts.
The noise of the wheel was loud on the still night air, and the
water black and churning, vicious. With the windows all blazing with lights and the unholy noise, it was like a mill in hell,
worked by demons. The folk all thought him touched by
fairies, Iestyn, with his books and his hoof and his night-flying
wheel, but he got the work done on time, and finely, so none
did more than shrug, and perhaps make the sign, behind his
back, against the evil eye. He was a good man, the miller; he
lived to a great age and served me well, later.

Tudor had no such love of learning as I, and did only those
lessons he could not get out of, though he would play his harp,
a full-sized one now, by the hour, and willingly. But his days
were dull, and autumn setting in; sometimes he, too, would
walk abroad with us, silent, but listening, for want of something better to do. We climbed Cader Idris that fall; we had
been too young before. It is the highest peak in those parts,
named for the giant Idris that the bards sing. The name
means 'Idris' Chair'; in the legend, one who falls asleep in his
chair—that is to say, one who loses his way on the mountain—
runs mad forever after. It is none so hard a climb as that; we
made it in an hour, we two, while Iorweth rested below on the
lower slope, reading a new manuscript. True, the climb was
simple; one could see, though, that it would be easy, in a fog,
to stumble, or come down the wrong way. I had thought there
must be something on the summit, some natural formation of
rock, roughly shaped like a seat, but it was flat and bare as a
loaf, worn smooth by the snows of winter. A disappointment,
truly; I liked always to think on these old names, and how they
came about. But when I spoke of it to Iorweth, he said that in
his youth there had been a kind of rocking stone up there; it
had become dislodged in a storm and hurtled down the mountain, killing two sheep. So there was something in it, after all.

Our cousin of Nannau did not study now with Iorweth but

went to Egryn Abbey, a mile or so away, for his Latin. I saw him once in the village square, tickling a girl as she sat astride the Derfel-horse; she was a sluttish wench with dirty ankles and rough hair, and I would not touch her, myself, with the point of a lance. But he had a name for tumbling them all, a new one every day. He looked up as I passed, laughing. I saw his face had grown up to his broken nose and was handsome again; he wore a purple cloak, like royalty, clasped at the shoulder. I thought it went ill with his reddish hair and hot brown eyes. His smile faded as he saw me, and he turned away; I shrugged within and rode on.

We had been used, in years past, Iorweth and I, to walk upon the gentle slopes of the Hill of Offering, but he said, this year, the climbing was too much for him and tired him. I much loved this place, the most beautiful in the countryside, and then, too, I had read somewhat in Roman writings of that double ax symbol and wanted to check the altar-stone and its scratchings. So one day we set out, Tudor coming too. We went the long way round, stopping at Cymmer Abbey to sample the good monks' new wine. I had not seen these men since the year before; I fancied I caught an odd look in the eyes of one of them, a man I had much liked and spoken with often. It was a look of sadness and knowledge, but fleeting; perhaps I imagined it, for he poured the wine after and looked at me straight, with pleasant small chat. We spent a good while there, eating and drinking and discoursing upon growing things and the seasons. It was late afternoon already when we climbed to the top, the shadows long before us.

There was someone there, at the altar; two figures. A girl lay upon it, on a purple cloth; I knew it for Howell's cloak, and stopped in my tracks. Her legs showed long and white, her dress rucked up; a long gold plait hung almost to the ground. I thought he was raping her and started forward, but Iorweth gripped my arm. 'Gently,' he said. 'Let it go ... all summer they have come here, up the mountain. Let it go ...'

As we watched, I saw her arms go up to clasp him, and her head fall back. Tudor, before me, turned; I saw the look he gave me before he went past, something of pity and something of scorn; he had known, then, my feelings for Joan, perhaps everyone had. We turned, all three, and went silently down the mountain. My heart, or something there in my chest, was like a lump of ice, and I could scarcely swallow in my dry throat. I was very young, and sick and shamed.

FIVE

All the Nannau people moved away shortly after, Howell with them; my uncle Vaughan's father-in-law had died, somewhere in the south, and he went to take up his inheritance and order things upon his holdings there. They left none in the manor at Nannau, not even a caretaker, leaving it to the crows and mice, till they should come again. This was never our way; my father taught us care, and responsibility, too, to those who worked our fields. They were tenants only, for the feudal way had never caught on much in Wales; still, in a bad season, these poor folk could starve, without some charity to tide them over. But those two brothers were different in many ways; Vaughan was greedy, as well as a bully. In the winter that followed, my father had to feed them all, the Nannau land-pensioners, though Mother grudged it, saying that bad Vaughan would make beggars of us all.

Autumn blew cold that year; by early November the trees were bare-stripped as skeletons, gnarled and black against a dirty-gray sky. It snowed too, that month, in gusty flurries; the top of Cader Idris was white with it, and even the gentle mound of the Hill of Offering wore a thin crust. Most years at Dolgelly we had the first snow round about Christmastime, a tender blanket of pure fluffy white under a blue sky, and good to roll into balls and pelt one another with, laughing. But that year the old crones spoke of demons and Derfel, crossing themselves and muttering by the fires, and when we rode out, our horses' hooves crunched loud in the crusty frost; like frozen spittle it was, covering field and road.

I did not see Joan; Olwen, her sister, did all her work; they said she had caught a cold. This girl, Olwen, came often to the big house, for she had her sweetheart there; she was of an age with my sister, too, and they two would spend much time together, after Olwen's work was done, giggling and talking girl-talk; they had been friends since childhood. Once I caught Joan's name, as I passed through the solar where they sat, and glanced sharp at them; they fell silent, and picked up a cloth, looking close at the stitches worked small upon it.

Once my mother bundled up and went to visit Joan, carrying her own good broth in a covered pot. But Joan would not see her, sending one of the littler children to say she was too sick. It hurt Mother and vexed her too; she went out of her way to scold Olwen and Laura after, calling all the young girls ill-bred and a bad generation. As for me, I thought Joan grieved for her lover, Howell, and had a bitter taste from it in my mouth, hating them both.

December came, biting. We did not leave our hearths, the breath froze on the air, even two feet from the fire. The three poor old sick men stayed under fur robes all day, within their beds; we thought they would not last the winter. Father chafed, restless, and paced the floor, and I played knucklebones with Tudor, or read by the weak light of a candle, the windows all shuttered against the cold.

It was too cold to snow, they said; the ground was frozen hard as rock, and ice formed on all the ponds and streams. The miller could not work the wheel, and my father sent serving-folk to all the cotter-people, taking gifts of flour and dried corn, though the servants grumbled loud to go abroad in the icy air. The grip of this young winter held us near a month; it was almost Christmas before the air softened and the ice began to melt.

Three nights before the eve of Jesus' birth, the bitter winds stopped howling outside the shuttered windows, and a gentle snow began to fall, big white flakes that drifted slowly down. We opened the shutters to see; the air was milder, fresh-smelling and a little wet, and the fallen snow sparkled under the moon. In the dawn hours we were wakened, all, by a loud thumping at the door.

The miller, Iestyn, stood there when we opened, covered with white like a snowman and breathing hard. He had run all the way on his thick clubfoot; his face was terrible to see, his eyes sick with shock. 'It is the seneschal's Joan,' he gasped out. 'I knew her by her golden hair ... All broken she is—in the millrace ... all broken by the wheel—and drowned. And her dead babe floating beside her ...'

I scarce heard his words, though they beat in my ears as we ran before him, Father, Tudor, and I, to the millstream. We waded out into the water; like the grip of death it was, squeezing us to take our breath. The wheel was stopped now, but we saw her, wedged beneath it against the rocks, her hair spread like straw on the blackish water.

There was ice, too, broken up; we had to fight our way against it, swimming; the water was dammed here for the mill and very deep. We got her out, tugging hard; I hoped that she had drowned first. She was all mangled and crushed; one side of her face dark blue where the wheel had caught it, and both hands gone. A baby-thing floated beside, the long cord trailing, miscarried in the torrent; it was no bigger than a frog, but with all its fingers and toes. As we took it up, I saw it would have been a man.

We gave her decent burial in the churchyard of St. Sulien's, my sweet, battered Joan, and the poor babe, too. Mother wept that it had not been shriven, but Father said never mind, it had not lived anyway.

Hugh died not long after, Mother said from a broken heart; he had loved this daughter well. I did not die, though I grieved much, and hated, too, that cousin Howell. I did not doubt that he had forced her, at the first, and made her love him, leaving her after as if she were a light doxy. Tudor, though, whispered that maybe he had not known of the babe. I brooded upon this, and in the first spring thaw sent a page over the mountain, to inquire of those girls I had lain with, in such lightness, in the summer past. All was well with them, though, and that page even boasted, after, of a wild night with one of them. So I breathed easier. But always, after, I had much care for my women, even the lightest of them. Men have said, in later years, that I peopled our hills with my bastards; it is not so. I have them all by me, in my keeping, even some that mayhap are not mine at all. For I would have no fair woman suffer, for my doing.

SIX

It was the coldest winter but one, in my remembrance, and the grimmest, too. The three aged men died, within days of one another, Madoc the Cripple, my great-grandfather; Griffith of Rhuddallt, my grandfather; and the Welsh Ovid, David ap William. They lie, all, in St. Sulien's, along with Joan and good Hugh.

Many of the poor folk died, too, our own tenants and those of Nannau as well, for there was not enough fuel to keep them warm, and their stores of food froze in the bins. We lost cattle, too, and horses; even with hides piled over them, they froze in their stalls. We all of us caught colds, also, from the drafty halls that ran with damp under the hangings; Rhug Hall was ancient and not built for comfort. Mother, in particular, was very sick; she recovered, but the cough stayed with her. I never remember her without it after, even in the heat of summer. It became a part of her, that cough, a little, hesitant, apologetic sound that punctuated all her sentences. I think now that it was a habit, truly, that she could not shake, like the wringing of her hands that came later; Mother was always nerve-ridden, from a girl.

Even the spring thaw was a miserable thing that year; the swollen mountain streams overflowed their banks and water lay in the valley, inches deep; some of the cottages were flooded and uninhabitable. Our minstrel-house was converted into a sort of refuge for the homeless, until they could rebuild, and the manor itself crowded with the displaced minstrel-folk. They are my favorite breed, these, merry and kind, for the most part, and taking things as they come. They lightened my heavy heart with their easy humors and prodigal talents; I

spent much time among them, aping their ways and listening
to their lewd songs. Mother scolded and fretted, for the house
was always noisy with the sound of strings attuning, or musical
phrases tried over in key after key; also they kept the maids
from their work, teasing and snatching gay careless kisses. The
bards, too, held themselves aloof with drawn-down brows and
clucking tongues and would not play unless the hall was
cleared. These bards are the aristocrats of the mummer-folk,
and scorn the tumblers and mountebanks for that they do not
observe the strict rules of poetry and cadence. It was comical
indeed to see them draw their robes aside as they passed a low
minstrel-fellow; they were like old dames twitching their skirts
out of the midden-heap. I speak of the lesser bards, of course;
old Iolo would strum a lute a-times with the lowest and sing
the bawdiest air.

In spite of all our tragedies, and even in the grave discom-
forts of that spring, we had a wedding in the manor, and a fine
betrothal, too, later. Olwen married her page, a lad called
Rawlff, and my sister Laura stood up and was handfasted to
her squire, Robert Pulestan.

The wedding was a merry event, though the bride did not
wear red, but went all in white, still mourning for Joan. She
was fairer than I had ever seen her, though, Olwen, with her
flaxen hair all curled beneath her bride-veil, and her round
cheeks pink as blossoms. They were married twice, and, in a
sort, three times, for the Latin was said over them by Iorweth,
and Iolo bound their hands, after, in the old Druid rite. There
was a huge feast, too, and Father gave her the dowry that was
meant to be Joan's nun-portion, and presented Rawlff with the
seneschal's post and a good annuity. They would live in the
gate-cottage there, with a built-in family already, for there
were eight of Olwen's brothers and sisters to be cared for.
There were some few ribald songs about this, you can imagine,
minstrel-folk being what they are, but the young couple took it
in good part, though Olwen's cheeks flamed and she drew her
veil across her face to hide her smiles.

I made a great fool of myself, on purpose, for the first time,
though it was by no means the last. I had got a taste for mummery these last weeks, being so much among these minstrel-

men, or maybe it was there within me all along. True it is, I could always mimic folk to the life, even when I was small, making my sister and brother weep with laughter and Mother, even, smile behind her hand. At any rate, being flown with wine, though we had planned it earlier, we staged a great silly mock-wedding after the supper, myself and some of the minstrels. I had wanted to play the priest's part and show him all drunk and hiccuping over his Latin, but the others thought it would be a waste; they coaxed me to mum the bride! There are no women mountebanks in Wales, so some male creature would have to do it. I was the funniest, with my great height towering head and shoulders over the groom (we had picked the smallest man for that part and the daintiest). I wore an old dress of Laura's, with a piece let in so it would meet behind, and two pig bladders, filled with milk, stuffed up front. The sleeves were too short, and my great hands hung out like hams, I twisting them nervously among the folds of my gown, and simpering. At the last moment we had had to change the hair; I had thought to wear wood shavings curling beneath my veil, but Olwen's tortured curls made them too like and a little cruel. We found some black-dyed wool and braided it; I was ugly enough to frighten crows. I stumbled and shambled in shoes like longboats, and once pulled the groom down with me. The laughter that greeted my every move made me bold, and the whole thing got bawdier and bawdier; at the end, to a special song, very lewd, I pricked the bladders in my chest, making the milk spurt out and running about spraying all, even the clergy. It sounds disgraceful, as such things will when told soberly, but at the time it seemed as brilliant as a court masque.

Spring came, though late, and pale new green covered the scarred land. The cottages were rebuilt, finally, and the fields sown. The hard winter and its tragedies were not forgotten easily, though; the little church was crowded to bursting every Sunday with folk praying for a good harvest and a gentler fate. We resolved, the manor folk, to close the house there and take up permanent quarters at Sycharth. I sighed to think of the bustle this would create, when forty mules had been too little for our summer moves.

It would be hard to part with Iorweth, but there was little more to be learned from him; he was a small parish priest, after all, for all his love of learning. It was thought that Tudor and I would both go to Oxford, to study there, though he groaned at the prospect.

My sister's betrothal-ale was a fine, fair feast; her squire, that Robert Pulestan, I came to like well, for all his worldliness. He came, with his father and a great train of servants, when the floods had subsided and the roads were passable again; they stayed near a fortnight. My sister bloomed in her new import-ance, going about with a bold step, her head held high; they agreed well, those two, one could see it plain. Often and often I came upon them cuddling in corners or saw them ahead of me on the forest paths, holding hands.

At night, though, after supper, the women being shut away in seemly wise in their chambers, we young men would sit over a flagon of wine, talking long hours away. Robert's worldly looks were all show, I found; beneath he was as eager as a kestrel, on fire to fly the world. He named Oxford slow and clerkly, though; I had thought it a marvelous, fine learning-place. 'No,' he said, 'you can learn nothing there but Latin and a little theology. You yourself are already beyond it ...' For we had read some Latin together, and I had lent him some books. 'And then, too, there is much brawling there, the townsfolk, bumpkins all, hating the scholars. Not a night goes by but some head is broken ... it is the only sport. There are no wo-men either, but serving-maids and bawds ... and constant dis-putes over religion. A wearisome place...'

He said he would go in the fall to Westminster at London, to learn the law there. 'There are fine Inns of learning there, all having goodly courtyards and with parks and walks about. All the humanities can be learned there, too, philosophy and logic ... astrology, too, and the sciences. There is no place like it in all the world...'

He fired me too, Robert, for this Westminster-place and its wonders, and I spoke to Father, begging to change my plans. 'It costs a leg and both arms,' he said, tugging at his beard and frowning. 'And there are years of study ... would you be a lawyer-sort then?'

'We have need of law-knowledge here in Wales,' I said, with some cunning, for in his youth Father had lost some of Mother's dower-portion through ignorance and bad advice.

'Well—we will see,' he said, as all parents have spoken since time began.

He gave his consent, though, as I had thought he would, Mother clucking at the expense, though we are the richest house of Wales. One must have knight's tenure, too, for Westminster; they do not suffer upstarts there. And so all was settled, and I would go to London in the fall, and Robert, too. We made our plans, thinking to lodge together there, for company and ease. I was much elated, for Robert was my elder by some two or three years, and already I looked up to him in all things, resolving to trim my beard to a point, like his, when it should grow; there was nothing but a fine down on my chin as yet, I was almost as smooth as a girl.

Much excitement reigned at all our new futures; Laura, after Robert had gone, stitched and embroidered for hours at a time, a-making of her dower-clothes, washing her hair in camomile, too, and putting cucumber-pastes on her face, though she would not be wed for a full year; Tudor, too, looked forward to Oxford-town now, after Robert's tales; Tudor loved nothing more than a lusty brawl. As for me, I could not believe my good fortune. London, for the taking!

I said my long good-byes to my tutor, Iorweth, and the miller-scholar, Iestyn, too. Many a good talk we had walking the woody trails or lying upon the new mosses, smelling of violets under. Iorweth talked of Paris, where he had studied with the Gray Friars long ago; that city, too, I resolved to see and know. The world lay all ahead, and I ready to walk its wild wonders.

Once I went hunting with Father and Tudor, stalking the young timid deer where they came to drink in the fast-running stream. I made my first kill then, coming late to it, as I have said. It was not so bad, a clean death, an arrow in the throat, and the venison was good, a change from the winter's salt meat. I had practiced long on the crossbow, and the longbow, too, for I had almost a man's strength for it, but I had not known my aim was so good. Tudor's buck was wounded in the hindquarters and had to be finished off with the knife, its great eyes begging. Cabal went with us, old now for a dog, but he ran away, whimpering, when the wounded buck crashed toward him through the bushes. He is a worse coward than I, even, poor great fool.

We climbed Cader Idris again, Tudor and I; it might be for the last time. It was no more than a steep hill to us now; we were scarcely short of breath when we reached the top.

I walked the slopes of the Hill of Offering alone, though, to say my private farewell. The monks were busy in their fields, their gowns tucked up and bound around their thighs; I saw them from far off only and waved. At the summit I stopped for a little, seeing in my mind those two there at the altar as I had seen them last, the purple cloak beneath them on the gray stone.

As I walked forward, slow, a white bird flew up, startled. It had been nesting in the hollow of the sacrifice; I saw the little bits of straw and chaff, all neat and flattened where it had lain. And, looking closer, I saw among the straw some broken bits of pale shell; the nestlings had all flown away. I stirred them gently with my finger; one was almost whole, and small, so very small. I saw a spot of blue; the thong, thinner than a snake, of some dyed skin. Joan had used to tie it round her braid to keep it neat. The blue was gone from it in spots, faded by the long-lying snow. I picked it up and put it inside my tunic, under my shirt. It was all I ever had of her, my Joan.

BOOK II

THE HUMANITIES

Told by Geoffrey Chaucer, squire,

customs clerk,

justice-of-the-peace, and sometime poet

ONE

Londoners are bred to noise from their first breath, and I among them, for I was born here, in the city, upwards of thirty years ago. The house where I was born, in Thames Street, beside the river, shook with the clash and rumble of the great wool barges, and every hour shivered to the bells of St. Martin's, next door. I never remember noticing these sounds, except once when the tenor bell of St. Martin's cracked and was silent for a whole day, till it was repaired. And then, too, when a great noble dies, the river traffic is halted and the barges are black-draped; it is the hush only that one hears.

I say one grows used to these sounds, and the cries of vendors, the brawling, and the games of boys in the streets; for these two years last, though, there is one din that plagues me, and most like ever will. Two years ago I was given, with some ceremony, a job of work, among my many others, carrying a long title with it, and a house as well. The title is Comptroller of the Customs and Subsidies of Wools, Skins, and Hides in the port of London. The house, municipal property and leased to me by the city, was most desirable in many ways. It is built over one of the city gates—Aldgate, nearest to Wool Wharf, not half a mile away. These houses once had held the families of sergeants-at-arms who guarded the gates, but it is long years now since London has been in danger of attack, and so various city officials occupy them now.

Philippa, my wife, is happier in our new home than I have ever seen her; she loves bustle and gossip and rises earlier than the hens she insists on keeping in our little garden. But I, who fall asleep only at first light, after reading or scribbling the dark hours through, rise in anguish at the clatter of the carts beneath us as they bump over the stones, stopping to pay their tax-tolls, the gates grinding and squeaking like the portals of hell. Perhaps, in time, I will sleep through it all, and not yawn in my poor wool-merchants' faces as I stamp their goods in the raw mornings. Philippa says, in her warm and homely scorn, that if I blew out my candle at night, like other good Christian folk, I might rise bird-bright and seemly at cock-crow, and be gone about my business before the carts pause under us. She is right, of course, according to her lights, but all us human kind are different; I must have my books, and pen and ink, too, or die. If there are not enough hours in the day, then I must make do as I can and go groggy at my work. I get it done, at any rate, and none complains. And I only curse the noisy carters now and then.

For, in fact, I cannot think of a finer place to live than this, our house over Aldgate. There are no neighbors crowded next us, as happens in most of London, and God's good light floods in our windows from all sides. To the west we overlook the tile roofs and church spires of all the city, with the gilt cross of great St. Paul's pointing its finger to heaven beyond; eastward are the green, green fields of Essex, and roads ribboning to far woods, faery-dense. Upon the little roads are bright ant-figures hurrying to what end, on foot or horse; my mind runs lively on these, what time I have to watch them at their comings and goings. I saw once a party of pilgrims, bound for some holy shrine; I was late for work that day, for I saw them, all unlike, each with his own look stamped plain, even in the distance, and set myself to imagine each life as it was lived, in those far-off hearts. Almost I made up a thread of story, but I lost it, for Philippa came to scold me on my way. But, another time. It will wait.

Most luck of all, there is ample space over Aldgate, as there is not anywhere else we have lived these married years. Lewis and little Tom are not underfoot and have a garden to play in, with no danger from horses' hooves or wagon wheels; Philippa has a great kitchen, with pots hanging from the rafters, and a fine, fair hearth and bake-oven; a good solar she has, too, with wheel and loom set up and still not crowding it. She has two little kitchen-maids, also, to push about and cluck at when they are tardy or dull; she is competent enough to do it all, however much housework, alone, except that these small scold-ings give her much pleasure, and do not hurt the girls either; all must live, as I have said. As for myself, I have shelves built in for my books, and I have a flat-topped table for writing, and money for candles, so I am happy as a cuckoo nesting in the spring.

We are not rich, we Chaucers, far from it, but we are main comfortable, as London folk go. I have the revenues of our old Thames Street house, for it was left me in my father's will; the neighborhood has gone down lately, and the street is full of Lombards and even some Jews, so the rents are not high. Still, it is something. And I have several jobs besides my official one; it is not straw that comes to my coffers from them, though I must bustle a bit to keep them all going at top profit. And then Philippa has many bequests from high places; she was a favored waiting-woman of the old queen, for whom she was named. Ten marks a year for life she got from her, poor old dropsical creature, when she died. For they were countrywoman, Flemings both, and Queen Philippa was sentimental and lonely, too, I fancy, here in England. She kept to her bed in her last years, all swollen and sick as she was, while the old king fumbled in Alice Perrers' bosom, drooling like a babe. A sad story, and only funny around the edges, like all of life.

Philippa has monies, too, all hoarded, from the king's son, the Duke of Lancaster, the great John of Gaunt. They are presents all, and gossip runs, for London is all gossip. But you have only to look at her to know it is not so. My Phil is sweetfaced, and sweetly plump as a partridge, and suits me well— but Lancaster ...? It is main ridiculous. He is wild for love of Phil's sister, Katharine, and spills his largesse for her sake. Some of it falls on us, that is all, and God be praised. Though I must say, with some pride, that the great duke rewarded me handsomely for my *Book of the Duchess*, that was writ after the lady's death. It was a labor of love, my book, too, for never did lovelier lady live than the most douce Duchess Blanche; I mourned her greatly and with my little heart. And so the poem shows, in its little way. God grant I could have been great Dante for her!

Strange to say, court gossip has not caught up to those two yet, Duke John and my beautiful sister-in-law; sometimes folk cannot see what is under their noses. But she is governess to the royal children that were the lady Blanche's issue, another Phil-

ippa, Elizabeth, and the heir, young Henry. Her own romp
among them, the little Swynfords, Blanchette and Tom (for
she was married to a knight, Sir Hugh Swynford, now dead in
the Spanish wars), and several bastard babes got on her by the
duke. The court ladies mislike her for her beauty, which
blazes, but still I have heard none call her whore. She is not
that either, but main faithful to Duke John, and loves him
true. It is an antique saga, that; one does not often see its like
in our day.

As I think on it, I have writ so that some would say I slighted
my Phil, making her out to be scold and shrew, and plain to
boot. This is not so, and I have not meant this; it is the fashion
to make little of one's spouse, among us rhymers, a legacy from
the Courts of Love, where only pure love, unsullied by the
marriage bed, is granted room to live in beauty. It is an old
joke, which should have run thin by now, this wife-belaboring,
but it has not. Like the mother-in-law jibes, and the absent-
mindedness of all learned folk, it will go on forever. But let it
go.

I speak plain now, and from my heart. My Phil is good and
kind, a lively humored lady, and with a fine, sharp wit. She
cannot help that she can do all things better than the rest of
us, and does not even show impatience often. She is a good
mother, too, to our sons, not smothering them with sticky kisses
or stuffing them with food, or neglecting them either. Strict she
is in some small matters, such as clean hands and face to
church, and no filth spoken before her lady-friends; but in the
main she lets them be, giving them the rough side of her
tongue only when they are rude as street-boys, or give back
answers. Her scoldings of me are naught of matter either; it is
habit only by now, we have been wed a full ten years. There is
much loving kindness in her, under.

She is fair, too, in her way, my little Phil, bonny brown hair
shining from the brush where it shows under her wife's coif,
smooth brown skin (for she is often out of doors at her garden
tasks), and bright dark-brown eyes, round as a rook's. Small of
stature she is, and rounded where she should be, with little
dimpled hands that move as she talks. The brown-bird look of
her is all changed to bright-feathered peacock in her sister,

Katharine. There is the hair touched with carnelian, and the eyes great blue sapphires, and the skin roses and cream, the body long, long, and filled with a languid grace. Still, under, one can see they are sisters, all unlike as they are.

I have writ my Criseyde after the pattern of my fair sister-in-law; it is main true and lifelike, though I say it myself, this character; often they will not come out real for our pens, these creatures that we invent, but I am pleased with my Criseyde. One thing, though, bothers me. The tale of Troilus and his Criseyde is got from an old Italian; I have but translated it. In the story she proves faithless in the end; I cannot change it, for it is not my own. I fear the duke will withhold his patronage because of this, for surely he will see his lady-mistress mirrored there. I ponder on it as I go about my day-business, how to reconcile this odds, in story and character within it. But I have not solved it yet. I have writ it in the London tongue, too, which may please no one. But it is my stubborn wish to conquer this language, which does not rhyme well; I have always loved a challenge. I have Englished many another romance, but they are small things all, not worth contention; most people find them amusing, though some say French is the only language for poets. Ah, well, I have writ in both, and Latin, too; to make our English speech sing is reward enough in itself!

My versings buzz in my head as I go about my small affairs, side by side with my account-figures; Jesus knows how my mind sorts them out! But the brain is a most marvelous thing, a mystery in its workings, and makes its own fine order. Many a time have I tallied up hides, and no mistakes neither, while Criseyde's voice cooed loving in my ear!

One fine September morn I had business in the Inner Temple near the City, for I am a member there, though I am not nobly born; they have let up lately on those class restrictions, and several of us poets and clerks have been admitted, so be it we can pay the fees, and have some law-knowledge. My friend John Gower is a member, too, and good Tom Pynchbeck. There is much favor to be had in the Inner Temple, scribe work and clerking, and some of lawyering-work may come later; we writers must turn our hands to many things, for not much monies can be made from scribbling, and we, like all folk, must live. I remember the day well, for it was impossible to go on donkey; the streets were crowded with the new students just come to register at the Inns and to find lodgings in the area. Footpads were out, too, for it was fine pickings; the raw new boys stood gawk-faced in the lanes, staring at the sights, while their purses were lifted under their noses and they none the wiser. I counted nine within the half hour with purse strings dangling empty from their girdles and London stars in their eyes.

My business did not take long; I was on my way back across town, thinking to collect my Thames Street rents while I was in the neighborhood. It was near noon and hot; sweat streamed beneath my new wool robe. I had told Philippa it was too heavy to wear this day, but she was insistent, for she likes me to go seemly and fine at my work. There were beadings of moisture on my forehead, too, and I threw back my cowl, for all that my hair is thinning on top. My mouth was dry, and I remembered me a drink-shop in Fetter's Lane, nearby, and turned in there to wet my lips and sit a minute in the cool.

It was a wine-shop, run by a Lombard; my father had done business with his father, years back, for in those days the Chaucers were vintners. This Lombard, a Messer Vitelli, was a man I much liked for his love of learning and his merry humors, and I thought to have a small chat with him as well. The shop was called Grotto of the Purple Grape, and a sign hung over the door, depicting a Bacchus with a great bunch of grapes in his hand and a wreath set awry upon his head.

I saw no sign of the Lombard, but the place was as cool as a cave and nearly as dark. Wine-casks stood along one wall, brought up from the cellar below, and straw-bound bottles, still cobwebbed. Behind a long counter sat the wine-wife, fat and dark as a spider. Her face had been pretty once, but it was lost now in pallid dough, and only looked out, fugitive, when she smiled. Her eyes were a bawd's, darting and sly, while her fingers moved among the coins, sorting them into piles.

I stood across from her, asking for her husband, while my eyes got themselves used to the dimness. She shrugged, saying he was upstairs, abed with an ague; her voice was soft and warm as a Tuscan night, caressing-low, and sibilant on the English.

I looked about me, sipping the cool red wine she gave me from the opened cask, feeling with my fingers the fragile stem and the gentle swell of the blown goblet. We have not these glasses in England, but they are common as dirt in the Italian lands. The noon crowd had not come in yet, and the little round tables were empty, but for one. Two Franciscan friars sat there, their gray-clad backs hiding whoever sat opposite, their horny bare feet filthy among the clean rushes of the floor, for the wine-wife kept a fresh, neat house. I looked at her, questioning with my eyes. She shrugged again. 'They had the price,' she said, holding out her hand for my coin.

These friars are a main nuisance of London; the order is grown so debased since its early days. The poor saint of Assisi must be spinning in his grave by now!

I watched these two as they bent close in converse, like plotting thieves they were; I noticed she had served them in round clay bowls, like leech-bowls. For none can trust these men, though there may be some new saints among them, for all we know. One moved, leaning back to tip his bowl-dregs into his mouth. I saw between them then a fair youth with golden hair and a face of antique beauty such as the old Greeks sang; his cheeks were as smooth as a girl's, he was not above eighteen. I sighed. A new-come student, I thought, from some outland place, Ireland, perhaps; they are after his jewels. For he blazed with them in the half-dark, arm-rings and a gold collar, massive, studded with rubies; I had seen such great collars in Ireland, on their many kings; it is not the fashion here.

As I watched, the other monk moved his hand, sliding it up under the youth's tunic. He jumped up as if he were stung, upsetting his stool and backing against the wall. He was tall almost to touch the ceiling, but gangly as a colt. I almost smiled at his face, for all my sympathy; it looked as though he had found a scorpion in his soup or bitten the half of a worm in his apple.

I am not over-big, or brave either, but I know my way around. I took up my blackthorn stick, which I had leaned against the counter (I am never without it in the London streets), and walked over to that table, saying, 'Out. Be on your way.' One, he whose hand had usurped, fled out the door, but the other was slower. I saw a bulge above his rope girdle under his robe, and heard a chinking that was not all beads and crucifix; I ran after him into the street. At the corner I caught him up, grabbing the stuff of his robe and holding on. My pulling loosened the stolen purse and it fell onto the cobbles. 'Pick it up, boy—quick!' I cried to the young fellow, seeing from the corner of my eye that he had followed. 'Pick it up!' I cried again, for a crowd was collecting. He did so, stooping awkwardly from his great height, staring still. I raised my stout stick and beat that friar about the shoulders, he raising his arms to protect; his face had a rat's look, cheap and evil. 'Go it, man! ... Lay it on, Master!' I heard from all sides. I did so, for these bad monks get my temper up; they should have been outlawed long ago.

A barrister came up, taking his time, holding up his blue-and-green sergeant's gown from the dirt of the street, like a great lady crossing a puddle. He put out his hand to take my stick. 'Lose yourself, scum,' he said to the friar in a weary, flat tone. I let go the monk's robe, and he was gone before you could say Rich Pope.

The barrister took out a little book. 'Your name?'

'Geoffrey Chaucer.' I answered, and showed him the half of the King's Custom seal I carried.

'No matter, Master Chaucer,' he said. 'You will be fined. Friar-beating is still an offense. King's Court on Monday next.' He snapped shut the little charge-book, and walked away through the crowd. I saw as he went that his face was as weary as his voice, though he was young still. Some of these sergeants are as jaded-wise as any venal priest; their calling hardens them.

'Let me pay the fine,' said the fair youth, at my elbow. 'It was for my sake that you did it....' I heard his voice for the first time; quaint-sounding it was and lilting. Ah, a Singer, I thought. Welsh. There are not many of them about London outside hired folk, but this one was full rich, it was plain to see. He smiled. I saw his face was not beautiful as I had thought;

its lines were too strong-marked for that, and the length from high-set cheekbone to jaw too long. But he had a goodly look, and pride under. 'Do you know,' said he, still smiling, 'how many times I had near lost my purse this forenoon? Twenty— at least—but I caught them at it. I had been warned ... but holy folk—I had not thought it of them...'

'Holy folk!' I said, and spat into the dust. 'Dregs and dirt! Thieves all—or worse.... I'll pay my own fine, I enjoyed it. But you may buy me a drink if you will. The wine I left must be warm by now.'

So back into the shop we went, the young bedizened tower beside me, he stooping to go beneath the door-lintel. I got two stemmed glasses, brimming, from the wine-wife, and she questioning me with raised brows. 'I am fined, but no matter—a few good licks I got ...' I grinned at her, and she smiling back, a transformation. I looked at her, thinking, sweet Christ, she cannot be forty even, and the nymph long gone, buried in that lump of flesh; it is the way of these women of the southern lands. My Criseyde, too, I thought—shall I make her fat in the epilogue, and casting sheep's eyes at all men, after her fall? Ah, no, I told myself—it is too cynical, it will never go, and none will buy it.

I went back to the table where the boy still stood, shy and dignified, not sitting before his elders. Laughter bubbled wry in my throat; I am barely thirty! 'Please sit, sir,' I said, and seated myself as well. 'A lesson learned,' I said, and raised my glass. 'Let's drink to it and speak no more ... Trust none in this town—the gray friars least of all...' He looked shocked but drank with me.

After a moment he said, shy again, 'I know you, Master Chaucer. I have read your works ... all I could lay hands on. I got my English from them,' he finished, proud. I smiled. 'Oh, I do not have the sound right yet——' he added. 'But I will get it. I have only been in London one morning ... but the writing of it I have fairly now—after a whole summer's study.'

'There are many English spellings,' I said. 'Mine is the London-kind.'

'Well—London is where I will be,' said he. 'In my country, too, there are different speech-ways. You have only to cross a mountain to hear another tongue, almost...'

'What country is that?' I asked, although I knew.

'The English call it Wales,' he said. 'But that is from the old German and means 'foreigner'—and we are not that, of course, to each other. At home, we mostly call it Cymry-land...'

I asked him how it was spelled in English and shook my head, trying it over on my tongue. The nearest I could get to the sound was Cumberland, but that was not quite right. It is a subtle language, Welsh.

I asked his name, and he answered, smiling, 'I am called Owen ap Griffith Fychan ap Griffith ap Llewellyn ap Owen ap Griffith—and a string more, going back into the mists ... long as your arm it is, my name, and would take a day to say it. It is the Welsh way.' And so I knew he had a pedigree, like a very king, or better. Indeed, I learned later, he was rich as old Croesus and descended from the three great princely houses of Wales, but I did not know that then, of course. I knew only that he wore an emperor's ransom on his back and had high-bred courtesies. I liked him from the first, a fine warm youth.

He told me he awaited a friend, there in the wine-shop, long overdue. 'Perhaps I have mistook the place ... or maybe there are no lodgings to be had...' For the friend, he said, had gone hunting a place for them among the various inns. 'He is my brother-in-law,' young Owen said, 'or will be ... For we will study law and the humanities together here at Westminster— and he will this next year marry my sister...' I saw him much pleased with himself that he had made play with the English words, and smiled appreciatively, though, truth to tell, the joke was not over-funny. Still, thought I, he is very young, and the young love riddles.

The place was filling up; it was always popular with the students, for its foreignness, and its good wine and scrubbed tables. My new friend had a look of worry. 'Do you think,' he said, anxious, 'that Rob has been waylaid...? He carried several purses...' I shook my head, thinking to reassure him, though it might well be so, but just then the young man walked in. He was not so raw as some, for he had brought a burly fellow along, armed with a pike; we saw him pay the man off at the door.

He found us quickly in the crowd, for, as I have said, this Owen glittered with gold, even in the gloom. 'I am as dry as old Cato,' he cried gaily. 'How does one get a drink in this place?'

I offered to shoulder my way to the counter, being an old customer. It was none so easy either by now; the crowd was getting boisterous. To my surprise I saw beside the wine-wife a young face, her daughter, eyes downcast, making change, while the mother dispensed the wine. I looked at her curiously, for I had only glimpsed her before in the shadows of the upper solar, when I sat at chess or talk with Messer Vitelli. It must have been her first venture into the shop, too; I saw her thin cheeks were pink at the sly words she heard. All the young men crowding about were staring and nudging each other, their manners forgot. It was a cruel thing to do to a young maid, convent-bred; I tried to read the mother's face, but it was bland as milk. Was she offering her girl to the highest bidder? Messer Vitelli must be ill indeed; I knew he doted on this girl, his only child. I shrugged it off; it was none of my business, though I felt pity, for the child was fair.

The two youths at my table were speaking Welsh; they broke off for politeness as I brought the wine, the newcomer thanking me in right good Oxford speech, only a little different from our Londonese. He was called Robert Pulestan and looked to be wealthy, too, from his dress, fashionable and rich with velvet and fur. He was about twenty, well made and middling tall; his features were neat and fine, and he sported a little beard trimmed to a point, the latest court look. He had had no luck with lodgings, he said; the Inns were full up, those that did not look flea-ridden. He had finally put money down on a place in the Chepe, but it was a filthy hovel, dark and dank, he said, his nose wrinkling. I laughed. 'They are all alike,' I said. 'One is worse than the next.... However, I know a man who is putting up four new ones, right here in Fetter's Lane. Maybe I can help. He owes me a favor...'

'We will pay right well,' said this Robert, eagerly. I nodded sagely. 'You will have to,' I said, 'through the nose...' They laughed, both, and we drank to it. I did, in fact, pull a string or two and got them in, though the nearest finished still did not have a roof. I went with them to see the landlord, after we left the wine-shop; he was a chancery clerk named John de Tamworth; the Inns are all kept by Westminster people, it is how they augment their earnings.

I saw the two youths into their new lodgings; a whole floor they had, smelling of fresh-hewn wood and shavings and open still to the sky. De Tamworth said the roof slates would go on tomorrow. 'For these guildmen are very independent,' he said. 'One must wait on their pleasure.' It is a true saying, that; the Guilds are becoming more powerful every week. The walks and grounds of the inn were fine, though, and planted already; in spring there would be a pretty garden. And De Tamworth kept a good table; he was known for it, having another inn in Chancery Lane.

Owen looked up at the sky, cloudless, as he stood there in his bedroom. 'Let us pray it does not rain till tomorrow,' he said, smiling.

Pulestan looked at him, frowning. 'We must go now and get you some proper clothes. You are got up like a barbarian. No one wears those gold bib-things here.... I have word of a good tailor....'

'I must stop back at the wine-shop,' Owen said. 'I have not fee'ed the barmaid...' So he had noticed her!

'She will not be there now,' I said. 'Besides, it would not be fitting. She is the daughter of the house, and a convent maid as well. She was helping out only, her father being sick upstairs....'

'So—she will be a nun, too...?' said Owen softly, his face a puzzle to me.

'Oh, no,' said I. 'I think not ... but it is the way of the Italians ... she will learn a little, reading, maybe, and some woman-knowledge. And then, too,' I went on, for I knew Vitelli, 'he would keep her out of London and its hazards, until such time as she is wed....'

He was silent, Owen; I could not read his thoughts; in some ways he was old for his age.

'Cheer up, man!' said Robert, hearty. 'She is not the only penny in the London streets ... you have only to look....'

TWO

Philippa was angry at the fine. Not angry with me, though she felt I was foolish to involve myself in an unknown Welshman's quarrel (I have explained that Owen has commissioned from my scribe copies of all my works, which will bring me a nice profit, but she does not trust the Welsh and insists I demand advance monies!). No, she is uncommon angry at our laws, and truth to say, the fines are becoming ridiculous; one can hardly sneeze without being charged for it! But the royal exchequer is always low, and money must come from somewhere; each year the poll tax goes up too, I cannot see how the poorer fellows can pay it at all. But that is another story, and a harsher one that will lead us to bad times sooner or later, if it is not halted somehow.

I must make a comedy one day of the fining, for sure. There are fines for dressing too richly and on the wrong days; fines for eating certain foods or for drinking cow's milk in summer; fines for quarreling with your wife and for shouting at your servants; fines for throwing ordure out of the wrong window or for stepping in it on the lane! To name a few only.

But the king's revenues really swell from students in the Inns. Besides the fines for cutting lectures, or booing and cat-calling, there is one that fills the royal coffers. The members are fined a whopping sum for having women in their rooms; now think you, these students here are green lads up from the country, however rich. They have never seen such charmers as our expensive London whores; many of the girls have retired already on their quick-earned wealth! The bawdy-houses are run like rabbit hutches, pallets all in a row and crowded each to the next; the independent whores have husbands or fathers at home and cannot work there; the walks and gardens are blustery-cold in most months; so the inns do a booming business, if unlawful. Mostly the fellows just add the fines on to their lodge fees and shrug it off. There is lately, too, another fine, which would be funny were it not so disgraceful. By now so many newborn babes have been left on the bachelor doorsteps that there is a right high fine upon them, too! Sometimes there are lawsuits over paternity, but such are mainly fruitless, for who can tell? Mostly they just accept the fine; it is another hazard of woman-trafficking. Being courtly bred in the main, the youths cannot drown the foundlings like kittens, so, in turn, they dump them, with a gratuity, at the door of some monastery or other. Lately the holy men have grumbled and sued for some monies from Westminster; they say they are getting crowded, the houses of God, with these orphans that cannot pay their way. And so it goes, a farce indeed, but sad under. I ache for the poor little unwanted creatures and ponder often their uneasy fates.

When next I saw young Owen, I almost passed him by, though I had appointment with him, in the matter of these books he had bespoken me. We were meeting in that same Purple Grotto where I first encountered him; I had brought an apprentice-scribe along, to carry the books. I had not realized there were so many; some, even, that I no longer liked, creatures from a green pen, but Owen had asked for them all. So here I was, books, prentice-boy, and all, and I could not find my patron. He rose from a table, smiling a little, to take my arm. I must have gaped, for he laughed aloud, and said, 'Well—you heard Rob ... I have been to the tailor....'

I could see nothing of the boy in him, or the overdressed Welsh mountaineer either, though it had been a bare six weeks agone. Here stood a very man of fashion, but larger-than-life, as it were. As I remember him after, he had always this look, Owen, a look of having come from some other where, a place where they grew other, larger beings. It was in part his great size, of course—but something other there was also. I fancied, in my romancing way, that it was destiny's mark upon him, though I could not tell then which way life would bend him.

I saw he had shaved, and he saw me looking. 'It was too soft, my beard,' he said, passing his hand over his chin. 'I must wait a bit, to be in the fashion.' But in all else he mirrored the latest conceits, even to the new liripipe, a silly headdress if I ever saw one. On him, though, it had a rakish air, almost charming, for he wore the foolish long tube wrapped round his head, turbanwise, like a Turk; folk mostly let it hang, like the trunk of an

elephant-beast, misplaced. He wore, too, the new shorter tunic;
I hoped it would not come in, for my own legs are something
spindly. I much admired his cloak, though, velvet plush of an
amber color; I saw, with a little shock, that his eyes matched.
One does not often see yellow eyes on humans, though our
white tabby has them.

I seldom run on like this about clothes; my own are mostly
ink-stained after a week. But I resolved to get this tailor's
name; I had a fleeting thought to so please my Phil, who loves
finery. It came to nothing, though, for I forgot, as usual. Ah,
well—it is my nature to go drab. She must put up with me as I
am, poor Philippa.

Young Owen had found out the amount of my friar-beating
fine, a whopper it was, and had added it onto the monies for
my books. He was main insistent, so I took it; one cannot protest forever, and I had made the gesture at least. Besides, it
would sweeten Philippa; she likes none that I fancy. Even
Gower, a fine poet, and well born, too, she cannot stomach; she
says he has a mouth like a haddock. Well, that is beside the
point. I have this failing often, my mind darting; my critics
point it out, too. I must use more discipline. Well, all skills
must be learned, and God willing, I have time still.

The shop was empty, save for us; I could see no sign of Vitelli or his lady, though a heap of change-coins lay upon the
counter beside a row of glasses. I went to the stair door which
led to the upper rooms, closed now, and knocked. There was a
little silence, and then a rustle, and the door opened a crack.
'We are closed, Master Chaucer,' whispered the wine-wife, in
her soft accented speech. I must have looked my amazement,
for she said, after a moment, 'Help yourself to wine, then, and
your friend ... but shut the door, if you please. We want no
custom now....' So saying, she vanished, closing the stair door
behind her. I shrugged and got the wine, shutting the shop
door after.

'They are busy abovestairs,' I said. 'We must serve ourselves.'

An hour at least we must have spent there; three glasses of
wine apiece and much good converse. Owen examined the
manuscripts, pronouncing them fair copies, though he some-

times questioned a phrase or a spelling. Mostly they were the scribe's errors; one cannot find good ones these days, and they are charging more and more for their service, these fellows, mostly unfrocked priests or worse, with no pride in their work. But one or two mistakes were mine, and I had to grin and admit it. Owen had hawk eyes, yellow though they might be, and could read a whole page at a glance and take the meaning clear. I am careless, sometimes, when I write in Latin, for I am rusty, mostly using English, as I do. Owen found a place where I had given Vergil's goddess a 'partridge's wings' (the Latin for 'partridge' is right like to the word for 'rapid,' but no matter, I should have caught it). He chuckled slyly and corrected it; I saw too, he could write a good hand, a true paragon, this youth. He shamed me, and I said so. He looked at me gravely and shook his head. 'But I have not genius, Master Chaucer,' he said, 'and it flames here, in your pages. What is a little trick of memory to that?' Though I knew it was his youth that talked, or maybe the wine, still was I much pleased, for none has ever spoke me so.

I thought to take my leave then, for some business or other was sure to be waiting, and half rose, when the stair door burst open and a slender girl rushed like a blind thing across the room. She held a square of thin stuff about her face, veiling it, but I saw it was the daughter of the house and put out my hand to stop her. 'A priest——' she cried, near sobbing. 'A priest ... I must fetch him to my father....'

'I will go, madonna,' I heard from Owen. 'Where is the nearest church ...?'

'In Vintry Lane, round the first bend to the left,' I said. 'The little chapel, rose-brick ... Father Oswald. Hurry!'

I held the girl in my arms; she was boned like a bird, small and delicate, and shaking now with her weeping. 'Get you upstairs, little one,' I said. 'Go to your poor father. He is bad, then ...?'

'Oh, sire,' she whispered. 'I doubt not he is gone already....' And she signed herself. The veil slipped and I saw her face; all swollen it was and tear-stained, smudged, childlike, from her hands. They were black with dust, and she looked down at them, puzzled. 'Oh ...' she sighed, shakily, and almost she laughed. 'I have been putting charcoal on the brazier, but we could not warm him....'

'I will mind the shop,' I said. 'Go you up now to him....'

It was not long before I heard feet on the cobbles; through the window I saw Owen running before to fling open the shop door. I sank to my knees as the little acolyte passed through, bearing the sacred pyx on a velvet cushion. He was about ten, maybe, but skinny and small; one of those foundlings I spoke of earlier, perhaps. His eyes were solemn with importance, and there were buttery crumbs around his mouth; he had been interrupted at his dinner. Behind him came Father Oswald, fat as any burgher, his surplice slipping to show a wine stain, old, on his habit; it was a poor parish. He bore the crucifix before him, stretched out at arm's length, and I signed myself. I saw, too, from the corner of my eye, that Owen did not kneel but bowed his head only; was he a Lollard then? They are as plentiful as rats here in London, but he had only lately come.

He thought to open the stair door, though, which I had not. Father Oswald nearly collided with the small pyx-bearer, where he stopped short in the doorway; I saw a look of impatience quiver across the priest's face.

The little one fumbled under his white robe, the cushioned pyx wobbling precariously in his other hand; he drew out a censer and shook it hard, turning round, before he disappeared up the stairway. The perfume rose strong; I almost coughed. Owen looked at me slyly, wrinkling his nose. 'Cheap stuff...' he whispered.

'It is only a little church,' I said, in some reproof. One must be seemly in the presence of death; of course, the Welshman had not known the Lombard, it was all one to him. Still, respect for Holy Church was bred in me. I thought to myself: Ah-hah—the barbarian is showing!

We waited, listening to the low murmur from abovestairs; in a little, the priest and the priest's boy came down, holding up their skirts now and moving faster; I guessed they were hungry still. I stood in their path. 'Is he——?' Father Oswald's eye rested on me briefly.

'He made a good end,' he said. 'He rests now in the arms of Jesus.' And he sketched a cross-sign quickly in the air and vanished through the door, the small boy at his heels, clutching the cushion and pyx as he ran to catch up.

We left some silver to pay for our wine, putting the coins down carefully so they would not chink in that still house of death, and left together, carrying the books between us.

'You did not kneel, Owen ap Griffith,' I said. 'Perhaps you are Lollard?' I walked beside him, thinking to help him with his burden, my books.

He hailed a boy with a cart, though, slipping him a small coin and directing him to his lodgings. '... just there, at the street's end. The Sign of the Unicorn.' The boy tugged at his forelock and pushed the cart on before us. Owen turned to me. 'Lollard——' he said. 'What is that?'

I nearly laughed but remembered he was still new here. 'In London,' I said, 'it is every other person you will meet.... Have you never heard them preaching at the street corners or haranguing in the taverns? Plain-dressed fellows they are, and will have no buttons to their clothes, and carry wooden crosses, or none at all....'

He looked thoughtful. 'I have seen such—and heard them, too ... but have not listened, in truth. I thought they were a breed of London eccentric....'

I chuckled. 'And so they are ... and most of them harmless enough. They follow Master Wycliffe, a mild-mannered man, he that has Englished the Scriptures. All manner of men have some liking for him—the duke, for one ... Lancaster. And the younger Edward's bride, the Fair Joan, even attends his meetings, with the young Richard, their son.... She has a Bible, they say, all fair writ in his own hand, Wycliffe's, and in good round English....'

'I should like to see that Bible,' he said, 'for I am much interested in all manner of theology and myth....'

I was main shocked. 'Holy Writ is no myth!' I cried. 'That is not Lollardy even, but heresy!' I made to cross myself, but checked it. I would not want to be taken for a foreigner in the street; we English are not a flaunting sort, like Lombards or Spaniards. Still, I made the sign in my heart, to ward off his words.

Owen spoke in sweet reasonableness. 'I had not meant to

offend, Master Chaucer. But you are a man of letters.... Surely you see something of myth is there. It is only made up in men's minds, after all, like all faiths, and not even written down in the beginning either. Look you,' he spoke, turning to face me, earnestness in his eye, 'if I tell you somewhat, and you tell another, and he, in his turn, tells the story, too, does it not change a little in the telling, even in such short space? What of tales that are handed down from generation to generation? Those that started in the mists of antiquity, as religions have done.... Must they not have added and subtracted, those old men? And embroidered, too, for the excitement of it? They were only human, after all.'

'Christ was more than human ... or so I have been taught,' I said stoutly.

'Many great men have somewhat more ... you yourself have it, in your genius. And the bards have it, and some great leaders of thought. But no man is a god....'

'Then are you worse than Lollard,' I said, fingering the crucifix under my shirt. 'For they are Christians all....'

He had been earnest, Owen, but now his eyes were gay. 'Well, I am Welsh, after all, and we are foreigners and pagan....'

I knew he mocked me, this great stripling, but I am not proud and pressed my point still. 'Yet you were main shocked when I beat the bad friar with my stick....'

'Well,' he said, 'my mother taught me respect for all such.... At home they rank just under the bards, and above the minstrel-folk.'

It was outrageous talk, but I could not help but smile. 'Your bards—what are they, in truth?' For I had heard much of these men but knew little.

'A bard——' he began, thoughtfully. 'Well, old Homer was one, and the Italian Dante ... and you, sir, are another....'

'Now do you blaspheme indeed, young Owen,' said I. But I was pleased, under.

'If you will come to my father's house in Sycharth,' he went on, 'you will sit beside the great Julius and write poems all the day——'

'I cannot sing, though,' I broke in, catching his mood, and

gay now myself. 'And at the harp I am all thumbs....'

'It does not matter,' he answered airily. 'There are those who will do your harping. You will have books by the hundred, and ink, and sharpened quills.... And no wool-stamping, either, and no running about the streets to earn your monies....'

'What of Philippa, my wife?' I said.

'She will live in the women's rooms, with my mother and sister and all their ladies.'

'She will not like that,' I said, laughing and shaking my head. 'She has been her own mistress these several years now. At any rate, we are used to warming each other in one bed.'

'Oh,' he said, his eyes dancing, 'we find means for that in Wales, too!'

He was a fine youth, in spite of his strange beliefs; humorous and wise he was, beyond his years. We fell to talking of poetry and verse; he said he would English, as best he could, one poet that they called the Welsh Ovid so that I might read his work. 'For he is much like you yourself,' he said. 'He writes of nature's ways, of women, and love—but in a homely wise, and does not follow the fashion....'

'It is not that I *do* not follow,' said I. 'But that I *cannot*....'

'Do not play the fool with me, Master Chaucer. I have read you with much care. You write as you please, and the devil take the folk who do not like it!'

I had thought myself a good court poet, but when I looked into my heart, as he bade me by his words, I saw it was not so. I am stubborn and selfish in my scribbling.

He read my thoughts, for he said then, 'You serve yourself, Master Chaucer—and your art. There are no better masters.' We had been standing in his inn courtyard, pacing a little as we talked, the painted sign creaking above our heads. 'Will you take dinner with me here, Master?' said Owen. 'They serve a good rich pasty and duck stuffed with oranges....'

My mouth watered, for it was well past my mealtime. I patted my stomach. 'I will get fat, and Phil will scold. I take bread and cheese only at midday as a rule—but just this once....'

He chuckled and led the way. 'They have a middling good ale too—or maybe you prefer wine....' He turned back, leaning close, and frowning a little in thought. 'What is her name?'

I was a bit startled, and stared at him. 'My wife?'

'No, no——' he said, impatient. 'The maiden of the wine-shop. She has an antique Roman look....'

'Well, they are Italians, after all,' said. 'Her name is Raimunde, I think. Messer Vitelli—rest his soul—had no son and named her after himself.'

'Raimunde...' he said, trying it out on his tongue. 'It has a pretty sound....'

THREE

I had thought that now that I had a title as Comptroller, I would bide all my time at Aldgate. But, no, off I went again, out of the country. I had been sent on many missions before, both as merchant and diplomat, and even served once under poor dead Prince Lionel as a knight at arms! I do not know one end of a lance from the other, in a manner of speaking, but then there was not much fighting in France, except at Crécy, and I was too young, thank Jesus. For in spite of all the glory, there were many who did not come back, and who more likely than craven Geoffrey!

This time it was a diplomatic mission and secret; I was forbidden even to tell Philippa. For all the hush-hush, she guessed it anyway, as might anyone in London without too much wax in his ears. The Prince of Wales, that some called the Black Prince, Edward, had died finally of his long ailment (another hush-hush, but who does not know it for the French disease?), and his little son, Richard, was now the heir to the throne. Now, royalty will always try to marry off its heirs, even though they be but ten years, poor mites, if so be they can find good marriage portions and a suitable royal child. My delegation was a kind of feeler to the French court. There was a daughter of Valois, little Marie, hardly more than an infant; it was thought to sue for her hand if the climate looked right. I was to go with another, Sir John Burley, the captain of Calais. I knew this man from an earlier mission and looked forward to seeing him and the pretty fortressed Calais town, too; I did not relish a Channel crossing in December, it is true, but one does not say no to royalty.

Royalty, I say. It was Alice Perrers who briefed me on my mission and gave me gifts for the little Marie. A cage of singing birds I carried, and a silken pillow for her head, worked with the arms of England and France in gold thread. A doll dressed in robes of state, with real hair, flaxen, and blue glass eyes, and many more gifts, including a miniature painting no bigger than your palm, the likeness of young Richard. This woman, Alice, was more than the king's mistress; she formed the spearhead of one of the most powerful factions in the land. She opposed the Black Prince while he was alive and now had full sway over the ailing old king. It was easy to see how she did it, though many whispered witchcraft; I think he loved her merry humors that made him laugh and forget his woes and burdens of state. There were no long faces at court while Dame Alice held sway. She was small and slight as a child, with a triangular face and small mouth, upturned at the corners. Her eyes were huge and black, ringed round with some Eastern paint to make them larger still. Pretty and sparkling as a jewel she was, with her shining black hair bound up in a net of emeralds; the weight of her hair seemed to pull back her little head, and it tilted proudly on her long white neck. She wore green always, she named it the color of constancy, though she had a husband, too, somewhere out of sight. Her enemies called her upstart, a weaver's daughter, but that could not be; she had been lady-in-waiting to the queen, like my own Phil, and only knights' daughters, or better, may serve a queen. I liked Dame Alice well; she had a goodly wit and daring tongue, and her morals were her own.

As I took leave of the lady, with a page to carry all she had burdened me with, she reached out her little hand and gave me something. I saw it was a tiny purse, cunningly embroidered with her emblem, the daisy. 'Wear it round your neck, Master Chaucer,' she said. 'You have complained long of seasickness and writ about it too.... Inside is a charm against the sea.' Her lips curved in a wicked small smile. 'For I am a witch, you know....' She waved me away and turned to the old king, who smiled against the pillows where he lay. As I backed out of their presences, I heard her laughter rise, gay and wild, with a sharp, hysteric edge.

The witch-charm did not work; I was pea-green and weak all the way across the Channel. Our boats were designed not to sink and seldom do, but they are shaped like deep bowls and bob about like corks on the choppy water. It took me a whole day at Calais to get my land legs back.

It was a weary tussle, that matchmaking mission, too tedious to remember now. Suffice it to say negotiations went on all that winter and into the spring, and still no result. The young king, Charles, I saw only once, and nearly choked on my ceremonial wine. He had been a goodly and fair youth, with curly hair and a well-turned leg; folk had named them, he and his beautiful girl queen, Isabeau, like Venus and Adonis, unsurpassed for comeliness in all Christendom. I remember his eyes, of a sweet lightness, that rested on her only, Isabeau, and would not go from her face; wild in love with her he was, and plain for all to see, a rarity in high places. Now, a bare four years after, I saw him sprawled upon his throne, those same eyes vacant as the sky, and his royal clothes filthy and torn, the hose all dark with wet where he could not hold his water. He seemed not to know anyone, either, or that which passed before him, his mouth ever smiling, loose-lipped and slobbery. I had heard nothing of this, only that he was ailing somewhat; later, Burley told me the poor young king had run mad in the forest of Le Mans, attacking his brother and wounding five men; he had never gained his reason either, though some days were better than others. I was told this day, as I saw him, he was in his better health. God save him, the poor hinny!

The queen received in our later visits, sitting beside the king's brother, the Duke of Orleans, upon twin thrones. His hand rested in her lap, and his fingers played idly with her rings, drawing them on and off; he yawned from boredom, too, behind his other hand. Or perhaps it was from lack of sleep; I had heard the gossip, that they two roistered all the night hours through. He is her lover, or so it is said, and sure they seemed on terms of great intimacy at all times. They, too, are a handsome pair, the duke more vulpine than his brother but of a fine elegance, and she, Isabeau, having a beauty to take the breath away. White she is as milk, dazzling fair, and tall for a woman, a queen indeed to look at. I could not like them, though; their hearts show in their haughty faces, brittle as glass those hearts. But I am fanciful, as I have said, and moved by the young king's plight as well.

I reported back to Dame Alice, having achieved nothing but a stalemate. A decision was impossible; the French wanted our English town of Calais dismounted of arms and rendered harmless, and the English side refused to accept Marie's dowry (it was twelve towns of Aquitaine, which seemed a bit greedy to me, but I did not make the terms I offered). Poor old King Edward looked worse, if possible, hardly able to raise his head from his bed. There were no less than twelve physicians in attendance, and the smell of blood from the leech-bowls was rank; Dame Alice carried a pomander-ball, which she held to the king's nose and her own in turn. Once, while one of the statelier of us ambassadors was expounding something or the other, I heard the king whisper feebly in Alice's ear, 'Oh, I am sick—so sick....'

She bent and kissed him quickly, saying, 'Nonsense, my dearest lord. You will be up, tomorrow maybe, and riding to the hounds!'

'In May?' he asked, but smiling now.

'Well, we will go a-hawking then ...' she said.

After, one sobersides said to me as we left their presence, 'That bad wench! She ought to be exhorting the poor king to look to the state of his soul.... Hawking! He will hawk no more!' And he sniffed, angrily. 'There is not a priest even in those rooms....'

But I thought, privately, that the king had good fortune indeed in that Dame Alice. He would die kindlier for her and without melancholy. If she had not true love, she had at least a kind heart for that old man. And it is not every man who can smile as he lies mortally ill. But there are many who hate Dame Alice for her power.

I had been bade stand by to go back to France, but before the month was out the little Marie of France had died. All the remaining English envoys took ship for home after that, their mission over. Thank God I was not among them, for they were set upon by pirates in the Channel and murdered, all, their ship sunk, too. Philippa gave a gold pyx to St. Martin's, the church where I had used to go as a small child, in gratitude for my escape.

I was glad, also, to be home, in truth; the French court, for all its look of luxury, is ill-kept and shabby where it does not show, the chambers drafty and the floors full dirty. And England, in Maytime, is beautiful beyond thinking on; even in the London streets new green decorates all the houses, and the flower-sellers are out in droves, the whole smelling like heaven, fresh and sweet. And the sky is blue, the sun overhead; even the rain, which comes nearly every afternoon, seems meant for washing only. We Londoners turn up our faces to it, so good it is to feel, soft, with a caress in it, and only lasts a moment or two, before the yellow sun comes out again. I have ever loved London in the spring.

Young Owen had sent me, in my absence, his own Englishing of that Welsh poet he so admired, Dafydd ap Gwilym, which I take to be in our London tongue, David Williams. I read these poems with much enjoyment; there were only three, but I suppose they are fair hard to translate. I have no way to tell how good a job Owen had done, knowing nothing of the Welsh tongue, but for sure the thoughts of the poet are there for all to see. Fresh as new paint he is, this David; there is none like him to my knowledge. He writes of homely things and nothing of the false court conceits; of love and coupling, most pagan it is, and I have hid it from Phil, for she would call it indecent; other moments though, the poet soars suddenly and takes the breath from you. A pity he did not write in Latin, for all the world. His work will die, like mine, I suppose, for that it is writ in the vulgar tongue. Ah, well, we must be as we are, we can do no other. And at least I have had the pleasure of reading him; and some there are who have read me, too. Owen says David is revered all over Wales, even now that he is in his grave. I could ask for nothing better from my own country.

This Owen is making his mark here at Westminster. In more ways than one. His master at law, Sir David Hanmer, another Welshman, calls him the most brilliant law scholar of all; they say, too, that Owen confounds his masters in the lecture halls with his ready questions, of pith and moment, and with his prodigious brain, in the way that the young Abélard had done, in his early days, so long ago in Paris. No monk is he, though, Owen; nor, of course, was Abélard, in truth, when it came to the point. Owen has not matched that scandal yet of Héloïse and all that followed, but he is still young; we must give him time. There are already a dozen naughty stories going round about our Owen, and he not yet dry behind the ears, in a manner of speaking.

Most are purely made up, as tales will be told about one who catches the imagination for his foreignness or some such thing, like the story that he is a warlock and descended from old Merlin. They say he does all by some dark magic, his quick learning, and other things, too. But then the Welsh are always suspect, even those poor working folk who slave among us for half-pennies. I give little credence to any of these fables, but it seems the most unlikely one of all is a truth, as happens more often than not.

I have told about the foundlings left at the rich young men's doors; it was told that just the other day Owen and his fellow-lodger, that Robert Pulestan, who would be his brother-in-law, opened their door on the way to their first lecture in the early morn and near fell over a large basket, woven in the country way. In it, wrapped as one, were two babes, as like as peas in a pod, looking to be not a day old even. There was no letter, for like as not she who put them there could not write, but the wrapping was pinned about with Owen's best gold brooch-pin. It had been missing for many months; he had thought it lost and forgot it. What is more, when the babes opened their eyes upon being lifted, it was seen that those eyes were yellow as amber. Indeed, they looked, both, to have been stamped out by Owen in his own coin, which is of course the gist of the tale; two little images they were, of Owen, in small. Phil told me the story first; I cannot think how it came to her ears—we live main far from Fetter's Lane. But goodwives gossip, too, and this was too good to go by unnoticed, I suppose. I counted on my fingers and shook my head; he would have had to father them his first night in London-town!

However, when next we met, Owen and I, on some business (he had sent ordering more copies of a work of mine, for May-gifts, he said), I found means to repeat the tale, slyly and with no little laughter, thinking to hear him protest it. He said, though, that it was all true and that he was right sure, also, who the mother was. It is a story, that, out of an Italian bawd-book; the reverse of the usual dilemma. He had looked high and low for the girl, he said, for some months; she had disappeared soon after he had known her. 'She was a girl from Kent,' he said, 'young and new to whoring. I found her fair and would have seen her again....' He had sent the babes, boy-children they were, to his mother in Wales. 'She will rear them for me, along with my brother's bastards and my father's....' I marveled; it is not the English way, except among royalty. Of course, I was forgetting that he *was* royalty or something that passed for it, there in his own country.

I asked suddenly, 'And have you named them, the babes?'

'Surely,' he said, looking high-nosed, 'they are my firstborn ... Evan ab Owen and Tudor ab Owen, princely names.'

I chuckled, under, at his lordly manner, this sprig of Wales; he was full man now to the sight, his awkwardness almost vanished. I saw his beard had come in well; he wore it carefully trimmed, forked like my own, but something fuller, and more gold than his hair. It was not the most followed fashion, and I was flattered, telling myself that he copied me. It was not so, of course, he but went with his own whim in this matter; after a while, he commanding so much attention in the Holborn inns, folk said I copied him! Philippa was indignant and said I should tell all that I made that beard-fashion. I could not very well wear a placard, though! Besides, it was our only likeness, this huge golden youth and I, little round Geoffrey, that passed unnoticed in a crowd.

FOUR

In June, the old king died at Sheen Castle, with none but his confessors around him, save for Alice Perrers. The story goes that, seeing him lying dead and knowing herself now without favour and, in a sort, penniless, she quickly stripped the stiffening royal fingers of their rings and fled. I do not believe it; I myself had seen three of his rings upon her hand a year ago. Many jewels she had of him and monies, too; in afteryears she came often to court, when all the scandal had blown over. She lived with her husband, a prosperous squire, and they were both respected London dwellers, rearing a family and sporting a coat of arms as well. It was oblivion, of a sort, for Dame Alice, but perhaps she was tired of intrigue. Except for the monk of St. Albans, who wrote cruelly about her in his *Historie*, folk forgot her and left her past alone. And that monk, as all knew, was her great enemy, she having stripped him long ago of power. So the grapes were sour in his mouth, poor mean churchman, and his writing not much believed. It was poor stuff at any rate; he had not an ounce of talent.

The day King Edward died was the day of his jubilee, the celebration of all his great victories; a bitter thought, that, for the hero of Crécy was not much mourned. Those who had gathered in the streets for the free wine and to see the parade and the mummers turned away in disappointment, and some, I saw, made the sign of the evil eye. It was a widespread rude belief that Edward had died from witchcraft, Alice's or some other. Sure, he had gone down sadly in his last years, a dotard or worse, and his wits scarce about him. Men whispered that John of Gaunt, as the Duke of Lancaster was called, had used his influence on the dying king, his father, to grant him half little Richard's kingdom. This was not quite the case, though by royal decree the duke's Lancaster holdings, and they were vast, were declared a Palatinate's empire, which meant, in effect, that the Crown revenues supported them, making Gaunt as powerful as a monarch. It is a point of law and tedious to go into, but many thought a witch had helped

Gaunt to it. Or a warlock maybe, for some of the ignorant named Master Wycliffe, the Lollard, warlock, and worse. And often had Gaunt helped that man. Myself, I think it was from honest reverence for his teaching; the commons, though, have ever hated Gaunt for his high-nosed ways. They even call Gaunt and Alice conspirators, lovers as well. I doubt me if those two have ever met!

A fortnight after his death the king was buried with great pomp in the Abbey, beside his queen, who had gone before him. The great Westminster building was lit with a thousand candles; it was bright as noon. The crowd that had lined up for the jubilee was out again; there was no free wine, but most folk love a good cry near as well.

I saw Owen in the crowd, not crying, but laughing, or so it seemed. I stood by the side of the street where the great cortège wound by, awesome in purple and gold, jewels and plumes; Owen was on a balcony above one of the inns, not his own. He was at some little distance from me and separated by the procession. When the king passed by, in effigy, lying proud and golden on his bier, I saw Owen pull off his black scholar's cap and bow his head; there was a figure beside him, slender and small, her face veiled. When the king's effigy had passed, I could see, over the foot mourners behind it, that Owen reached out to pull her close, twitching aside the veiling from her lifted face. Then came the procession on horseback, endless, and blocking my view. When all had passed, finally, the balcony was empty. I saw it was not an inn at all, the house where he had sat; the sign had been removed from over the door and the front new-painted like a private dwelling. I made note of it in my head, to inquire who lived there, for I am curious as an old crone, but I forgot. For that night came a summons from the Duke of Lancaster and a commission for some coronation verses.

The little new king would be crowned on July 16; there was not much time to spare. I was hard put to it to versify at all and kept scratching out mistakes, for the days, and nights, too, rang with the sound of hammer and saw; they were putting up scaffolding, for benches all along the route he would take to his crowning, a long road, and winding through the inner city, right under my windows.

The whole of London, it seemed, was readying itself, in some manner, for the crowning of the little Richard. Engineers, inventors, smiths, sculptors, carvers—all were preparing the marvels that would greet him on his progress through the streets. Minstrels were hired to teach the townsfolk their songs and words, for there were all kinds of entertainments planned as well. His uncle, the great duke, John of Gaunt and Lancaster, was in charge of most of these arrangements, for he headed the Committee of Claims that decided who should serve in what capacities during the coronation ceremony and the banquet. It was a touchy task indeed, for it involved pedigree and politics, and none must be slighted; one could not envy him, he was bound to make some enemies.

I was to ride in the procession the day before the ceremony; indeed, so many of us citizens were a part of it, one wondered who its spectators would be! Even my little son Lewis, just a year younger than Richard himself, would march with the boys, wearing the little king's livery, and Philippa would ride in the great coach with the queen mother's ladies. My friend John Gower had writ some verses, too; he said all us poets would be read aloud in a masque at the banquet, the masque to be prepared by some of the more favored Westminster students. So you see, everybody and his brother was joining to do honor to the little new king. Myself, I had not much to do, once my verses were finished, for I wore my official city robe and badge, but Philippa was in a state of distraction, for the seamstresses were all over-burdened, and she had to have two new dresses, one for each day. I could not see why, in fact, for she had not been to court for some time, and no one would recognize her best gowns, which were main fine. She looked at me with great scorn, though, when I mentioned this; I had violated some sort of women's mystery. Old as the hills it is, this rule; whatever the occasion, a woman must have a new dress for it.

In the end, I saw much of the procession, for my place came at the end, with other city officials, and I watched as it passed and joined them in my turn. It was a gorgeous thing; one would never have known there was poverty in the realm. And indeed, this day there was not, for the conduits ran with wine, and there were vendors at every corner, giving away their good things to eat; they had been paid, of course, privately, by the royal exchequer. Some folks were drunk already, before the parade began, one could tell by the red faces and blurry voices; they could not fall down in the gutter, though, they were too tightly packed for that. Those who could afford it sat on the tiers of benches put up so hastily; I hoped they were sturdy-built, for sure they were loaded with human flesh that day, and all in finery, too, a brave sight.

The churchmen came first, scarlet and white, in their tall bishops' hats, and then the nobles, my Duke of Lancaster glittering golden among them, looking like an effigy already; his face had always a chiseled look. The little king-to-be rode on a great white horse too big for him; a slim beautiful boy, looking grave and a little scared. My own Lewis marched sturdily with the other pages, grinning and out of step. They would go early to bed, all, that night, for it was a long slow way, right through the whole city.

Philippa, so fine I near did not know her, waved and smiled beside her sister in the big open coach. The queen mother, that had been called the Fair Maid of Kent, looked like a pig's bladder in her pale-blue satin, so fat she had grown; her smile was still dazzling, though, beneath her too-bright hair, and the people cheered her, for she was a great favorite always.

There were many great wonders devised by the guilds to do honor to the little Richard: play castles erected for the occasion, plaster saints with movable heads, lions and leopards that roared through mouths that opened by wires, a dragon with iron scales that breathed forth fire, and much else of marvelous invention. The best, though, to my mind, was the goldsmiths' angel, that leaned down from a tower to place a crown upon the young lad's head as he rode under. Cunningly devised she was, of some metal, with every joint moving; I could not figure how it was done. He lost his royal composure then, Richard, laughing with delight like any boy and clapping his hands. 'Look at the little love——' and 'Sweet lad——' could be heard from the crowd, and they cheered him roundly, some of the women weeping, too, as women will, for this heavy-burdened youth. He was much loved by his subjects that day, the pretty little boy.

The ceremony next day in Westminister Abbey included mass, a sermon, the taking of the royal oath, the presentation to and acceptance by the people, the blessing, the anointing, the robing, vesting and arming, the enthronement, the crowning, the offering, the confession, the absolution, and finally the drama of the new king's champion, in full armor, at the Abbey doors, offering mortal combat to any opposition. It lasted seven hours; I myself near fainted, and I just a spectator. Philippa clucked at my side, commiserating with the little boy, so white and spent, looking as insubstantial as an angel in his snowy robes with his hair all loose on his shoulders. Our own Lewis, who had marched yesterday, was still lying exhausted in his bed. But young Richard, for all his frail looks, bore himself nobly till the end. He swayed then and looked almost to fall; his tutor, Simon Burley, swooped him up in his arms and carried him out of the Abbey, home to rest before the banquet. As they came past us down the aisle, the big man striding like a conqueror with the boy limp in his arms, I saw that Richard had fallen asleep. One of the ceremonial slippers, worn first by Edward the Confessor, fell off the small foot, a bad omen, some said. I say simply that the shoes had been made for a grown man, after all, and were far too big, naturally.

The nap must have done him good, Richard, or perhaps they had fed him some reviving drug, for at the banquet which followed Richard created four new earls; speaking the words in a strong clear childish treble that rang through the hall. One of the new earls was a boy his own age, Thomas Mowbray, and a murmur went up from all as the two little children smiled at each other and gave the ceremonial kiss of peace.

There was another boy-child present, too, and seated near the king. This was the Duke of Lancaster's heir, Henry, a sturdy, substantial ten-year-old, big for his age. Once, from my place well below the salt, I saw Richard, his cheeks bright red from excitement and the unaccustomed wine, lean over to his cousin, young Henry, laughing. He reached up and took the heavy crown, crusted with jewels, from his own head and offered it to the other. Henry took it, trying it on and quickly taking it off; it was plain to see he thought it far too heavy. A comic little mime show for sure, with one of the royal tutors scolding behind the throne.

The masque that came after was a fine, fair spectacle, with tapestries hung to represent Jerusalem and twenty girls representing the Virgins of Jerusalem singing a song in praise of the new king. Philippa nudged me hard and whispered, 'Virgins! Your Owen's wench has a bun in the oven already!'

I looked at her, startled. I never knew where she got these homely country expressions. She was not even English-born and had never lived outside a city. Also, her fund of gossip was amazing; where did she get it? She did not even know 'my' Owen. 'Which one?' I whispered, in my turn, for I was curious.

'Third from the left, in the front row,' she hissed. 'They had not the decency to hide her belly behind some flat ones.'

I scanned the young girl-faces, all chosen for their beauty. With a little shock I saw the one Phil meant. It was the wine-shop daughter, that I had seen last the day of her father's death; I had wondered, fleetingly, what had become of her, the wine-shop being closed now for months. Having been alerted, I fancied I could see a tiny bulge beneath her girdle, though I think, in truth, it was not noticeable at all. This Owen had a way with him, for sure, if Phil's words were to be believed. The girl was no common whore, but a respectable merchant's daughter. Still, I remembered the wine-wife, her mother, and the sly bawd's eyes of her. Poor child, I thought, she is spoiled now, and who will wed her after? Still, she looked right happy, in the line of girls, her dark eyes shining as I had never seen them and her cheeks soft and round as an apricot-fruit.

Then began the verses for the masque, and I listening closely for my own. The first mum-show was of shepherds on a hill; all dressed in goatskins and their feet wrapped in rags, and they mimed wonder at a marvel of a star that rose above their heads. And very well done the star was, and moved slowly across the painted sky. From where I sat I could not even see the wires. The words, read by someone behind the tapestry, unseen, were of the portent of a child born to greatness, that would be a great king and lead his subjects to glory, and even peace. It was a shameful stealing of the Bible tale and blasphemous, I thought, but it was in Latin, so not all understood. I thought it main silly, too, for sure in Jerusalem there was Hebrew spoke in those days. I wondered who had writ it and looked about for Gower, thinking to surprise a guilt look on his face. I could not find him, though, in the crowd; Phil knows some Latin and thought it was my work, turning to scold with a look of shock, but I shook my head. 'I did not write it,' I whispered. There was much applause at the end, though, for it was a pretty pageant, and none but us, perhaps, found it amiss. The churchmen, all, were beaming amiably at their places at the high table. I say all, but I got a glimpse of Master Wycliffe in the shadows, long-faced; one thing about the Lollards, they like their religion unsullied.

My verses, too, were took, in some sort, from the Bible, for the theme of the masque was 'Great Days of Jerusalem.' Some songs came before, and dancing, and a mock battle fought between two mountebanks, one tiny and one huge and padded out more with wolfskins. This was David and Goliath, and the mummers very comical, the Goliath cowering in terror, his great jowls shaking, as he fled from the little strutting David.

And then I heard my own words, but from one unseen and, strangely, on a keening, high wail that sent goose pimples down my arms. Like the cry of some wild sea bird it was, and a shock. Then silence, suddenly, and another shock, for on came the mummer of that voice, an ancient, bent and withered, fluttering with rags and white-bearded to the waist, feeling his way before him with a stick. A mouse might have squeaked in the silence and be heard plain, but for the remorseless tap-tap of that stick. It was the prophet Nathan, of Israel, as I had writ him, but I had not writ him blind. And blind he was, one felt it with horror and pity; I do not know how he did it, the mummer, it was more than the stick that told. His eyes, large and shining, were opened wide; one knew he saw things we did not see. And then the voice began again, low, low, but all heard it; my verses, but better in the telling. He spoke of the child-king, beautiful as Absalom and wise as Solomon, that would grace the realm of Israel (all knew it, of course, for England and sweet Richard), and the voice rose slowly, high and piercing-sweet as he prophesied of peace and plenty, and rising higher still and wild again, his long arms reaching upward. At the end, the prophet shook with convulsions, terrible to see, and foam even appeared upon his lips and beard, as the old prophets were described in the Bible. A sight of awe and terror, truly, and wondrous real. When they carried him off, all unconscious from his ecstasy, the whole company, after a stunned moment, stamped their feet and cheered for that show-man. I got a glimpse of little Richard; he had climbed upon the table to see better and was clapping his hands and smiling wide, though his child's eyes streamed tears, like all the others in that vast hall. Then on came the mummer to take his bow, stepping light, and no stick now. He snatched off his beard and wig and sank, courtly, to one knee, facing his king. His hair was yellow-amber as he shook it loose; as he raised his head, I saw it was the Welsh Owen, hard though it was to credit. He might have made a fine living at it, mumming, had he need to. And so I told him later, when he came among us to take his seat, neat and court-dressed.

'Well,' he said, speaking in his own voice, pleasant and lilting, 'I have spent all my life among them—mummers and minstrels, bards and singers ... it is no wonder I have picked it up....'

I saw the little king come forward then, from his place, toward where we sat, two of his tutors hurrying behind him. We all rose and fell right away to our knees, of course, but Richard cried, impatient, 'You may rise.' And the wave of his small hand was so lordly that nearly I smiled. We rose and stood, shuffling, as he walked up close to Owen, peering up into his face, so far above him.

Owen smiled at him, liking what he saw. 'We could talk better, your Majesty,' he said, 'if I kneeled. I am something tall.'

'It is true,' said Richard, frowning with seriousness. 'Did you drink cow's milk—to grow on?' And he looked about him, that little despot, waiting. And it came, of course, the laughter, chuckles, deep, from all the men, and little polite tittering from the ladies.

'No, sire,' answered Owen. 'In my country it is ale.'

'I would like that better,' said Richard, looking to where his mother sat. She smiled and shook her finger, playful. Owen bowed to her, and I saw the red creep up from the low bosom of her gown; his look must have had favor in it, and she is not too old to be moved still.

The little king stared upward into Owen's face. 'And what country is that?'

'I am Owen ap Griffith, Prince of Wales.'

A gasp went up from all the company then, for this was the title that had been the little king's before he was crowned. But Richard's face was screwed up, thinking. 'The heir to England is called that,' he said. 'Would you have my kingdom then?'

'No, sire,' said Owen, laughing. 'It is an old Welsh title—I have a mort of others, too. Prince of Powys, Gwynneth, and Deheubarth, to name a few....'

'Then,' cried the little king, delighted, 'you have more even than I to remember!'

'In my country, yes. I found it a nuisance when I was young.'

'You are not very old now,' said Richard, looking at him square. 'How many years have you?'

'Eighteen, today. It is my birthday.'

'My crowning day!' cried Richard. 'Come and sit at my table then, and we will drink to it. I like young people about me....'

The Sire de Gasquelin came forward then, another tutor, and plucked at Richard's sleeve. 'Sire, I think you have had enough wine for one day....'

The boy looked to his mother, asking, and she waved her hand. 'One more will not hurt him, De Gasquelin. He has had hard going ... and done right well, too....'

As they moved back toward the dais, the tall Welshman and the slight golden child, I heard Richard say, eagerness coloring his words, 'How did you do it—the foam, sir?'

'My secret,' said Owen. 'Call it Welsh witchcraft....'

FIVE

I am a natural-born homebody and like nothing better than to nest among my inkwells and papers, raising my head only to look out my own window onto my own particular length of the yellow-brown Thames. But, alas, I am committed to the king's business and must go where I am sent. I say alas, but Philippa chides me, insisting that I love to take my leave of her and flit to foreign parts. This is not so, for she is welcome to come along, there are monies aplenty, but she will not. She says all countries outside England are filthy, even her own Flanders. I do not notice this, but then perhaps I am not overclean; I often forget to wash the ink stains from my fingers, even at table, and eat the ink along with my meat!'

Perhaps, in truth, I am a liar, too, like all my writer-sort; when I am away from home, I enjoy it too, in the main, there is so much to see. And once one has weathered the Channel and got past the green-sickness, the Continent is like another world, so beautiful and strange. Crossing the Alps in July is like journeying in Paradise; I had done it once before in winter weather on a business trip to Florence; one toe is blue still from the frostbite. But this time I was going to Milan, my joyful thoughts running ahead of me, for it is a heaven for scribblers and readers, too, that city; they say there are upwards of fifty scribes there, all careful professionals, used to copying manuscripts. Think of all the books that must be there by now; one has only to hunt them out!

We left England in May, Sir Edward de Berkeley and I, with a full retinue of sixteen men, on a mission to the court of Milan, to 'discuss certain affairs touching the expedition of the king's war.' For a fact, we were going a-begging. One of the richest men in Europe, Bernabò Visconti, ruled in Milan; he had an English son-in-law, a Sir John Hawkwood, said to be a brilliant general. So we were killing two birds with one stone, as it were, financial and military. The war was that same old war with France, chronic by now, and on again now that the marriage negotiations had gone for naught. In truth I doubt

England could exist without this French war; kingdoms must have their games, too, like men. The little king, Richard, of course, knows nothing of it all; he is ruled by his uncles and tutors, his mother, too, and sits all day at his studies, or so they say.

So we two, De Berkeley and I, are to sweeten this powerful pair, Visconti and his Hawkwood son-in-law; I am assigned, of course, to the Italian, not being a military man, and then I speak the tongue a little, too. I look forward to meeting him, though he is much feared as a tyrant; I am of too small consequence to be in any danger from his willful wrath. And, tyrant or no, he has the name of loving literature and art. The great Francis Petrarch, rest his poet's soul, lived eight years in the Visconti palace and was the godfather of Bernabò's little son, Marco.

Milan is a city of surpassing beauty, built on a green plain and crisscrossed by canals. The walls of Milan look to be bathed in the sunset glow, for they are built of a rosy brick that is found nowhere else. As we rode in through the gates, it was plain to see that Visconti loved civic order, too. I have never seen such a city! Everything new, even the gutters. The streets were all paved with flat stones, smooth to the horses' hooves; there were no beggars about, and no thieves either; I can spot a footpad anywhere, after London, and I say there were none. But perhaps the jails are full, or the gibbets—who knows?

We passed the street of the booksellers, a tantalizing glimpse only I got, for we could not stop, but must report to Visconti first thing; I saw little shops, their fronts open, and stalls in the street, piled high with all manner of manuscripts, old scrolls from antiquity even! I cannot wait to get back to it, and have marked out the location in my head.

We went straight to the Visconti palace, all travel-stained as we were; we were searched at the gates and my notebook and charcoal taken away. There is nothing in it of treason, only some comments I made to myself on the journey; still, it is a wearisome thing, I will not get it back till it is deciphered. Which may be a long time, for I have scribbled in haste, on horseback, and carelessly. De Berkeley's sword was confiscated;

his face was black with wrath when we were shown to our quarters.

We were given a chamber large enough for a regiment, with a marble bath set into the floor and steps leading down. There is a hidden system that pipes the water in and drains it out, and all the fixtures are gold! The bath women are black Nubians; their skin has the purplish glow of ripe plums. I tried not to stare. We have not this custom in England, of women bath-attendants, and I was in some unease, shy of my plump body and thin legs. De Berkeley, though, pinched buttocks with a will, his bad humor forgotten.

They had a trick I must remember to tell Philippa; baskets of hot coals were lowered, hissing, into the water, and steam rose. It was too hot to step into at first, but wondrous refreshing to our aching joints; of course we have not so many servants at home, but perhaps it could be managed, in a sort.

The great hall of the Visconti palace took our breath away, so magnificent it was and so grand. We have nothing like it in England, not even the beautiful Savoy palace of the Duke of Lancaster. For one thing it is roofed in blue and gold, cunningly carved and painted, and arching like the sky, and all about the walls are painted great heroes of antiquity, Hector and Aeneas—and the French Charlemagne as well—in scenes of battle and glory and of a surpassing beauty. The artist was a man by the name of Giotto; we have none such in England, or in France even. I could not take my eyes away.

It is vast enough, the hall, for a regiment; though we were quite a number of petitioners waiting and watching the empty throne, still we could not fill a corner of it. I heard a voice, low, behind me. 'Are you following me, Master Chaucer, or is it the other way around?' I turned, and my mouth fell open. It was our Owen, all got up Italian style in blue and gold satin that matched the palace. I must have stared still, for Owen laughed and said, 'It is the summer and there are no lectures at Westminster. I am buying some treasures for my father's house in Wales—some of this same artist and some others, too. One must have the Bernabò seal upon all bills of sale ... so I am here, waiting, too.... I know your errand—the same old war! No wonder the poor commons groan and cast black looks. It is *their* pocket that will furnish all, in the long run....'

I sighed and shook my head sadly but said nothing. After all, I am paid for my work. I thought better to change the subject; many learned youths are hotheads and afire to change the world; I saw the look in his eye of argument and eagerness and would not bite. I said mildly, 'The Duke Visconti—have you seen the man?'

'Ah,' he said, his eyes crinkling, 'and you have not? Let me prepare you! It is a bull in velvet, Bernabò.... I trust you have no papers about you?'

'My mission is in my head mostly,' I said. 'But why? Is it that he dislikes documents?'

'One cannot tell, in truth,' said Owen. 'But yesterday there was an emissary from the Pope.... Our Bernabò is no respecter of the clergy—he even disregards excommunication, going his own way in spite of it.... Yesterday the Pope's ambassador was made to eat all his papers, for Bernabò did not like their contents. There were twenty-six pages, and all the wax seals, too!'

I looked my disbelief, but Owen swore the tale was true; he thought it very merry, but I was main shocked. The Holy Father is titular head of all Christendom and sacrosanct, too, by virtue of his office. An upsetter of values, this Bernabò, and one to vaunt his powers; I dread such natures and always have, being a coward.

Owen read my thoughts, for he said, 'The Duke of Visconti is cruel only to his peers and those mighty above him. He has a great heart for the poor and lowly and reveres genius, too, as you may see by his surroundings....' And Owen waved his hand at all the gorgeous wonders of that hall, glowing like gems set in wall and ceiling. I looked again, eyes upturned, lost to that beauty; my neck got a crick in it before Visconti entered and we all fell to our knees. Indeed, I think my knees grew calluses that day, for we had been told to remain so until our turn came round; many of the petitioners were lengthy speechmakers and spoke some dialect of the country as well, so I could not even understand them, though I knew court Italian, of course.

It was a fine show, though; the duke bellowed and stamped, his neck reddening, while the ambassadors cringed and groveled, touching their foreheads to the floor before them. I could not get Owen's words out of my head and smiled within me as I watched. For the Duke Bernabò Visconti was a bull indeed, thickset, with legs like tree trunks in their silk hose, and a chest measuring two at least of any other man's. He had no neck either, his head rising massive from his burly shoulders; thick, curly lips and flaring nostrils he had, and big black eyes that looked to pop out any moment. I saw, though, that when he listened, those eyes were keen as a knife blade; it is a thinking bull, I said to myself.

Owen's turn came before mine. I had noticed he knelt on one knee only, in courtly-wise, and changed knees several times while the duke glared hot at him and waited. When his name was called, Owen rose, brushing the dust from his knees, and came forward, taking his time, to stand before Visconti's dais. He did not have to look up to the duke even then but faced him square; I had not imagined his height, Owen. He took a sheaf of papers from under his cloak, frowning as he flipped them over; finding the last page of all, he handed it to the duke. 'It is an order for some paintings and such. . . . Just your seal I need—you need not trouble yourself to read it, sire. . . .'

The duke's popeyes stabbed at him. 'I read everything!' he shouted. 'Think you, then, that I cannot?'

'Oh, no, sire,' said Owen, slow and smiling. 'The world knows you most learned. . . . It is just that it is such boredom to wait while you do it—so many pages, and all nothing but figures. . . .' And he yawned delicately, putting his hand up to mask it. A gasp rose then from all the kneeling court, and the duke purpled to match his royal velvet. 'Sire,' said Owen, smiling wide, his yellow eyes a-glint and alive, 'I would as lief *eat* them, if you please. . . . It is well past my lunching time already. . . .'

The duke stared, and Owen gave him stare for stare, not smiling now. It was a long moment and I held my breath. Then suddenly the duke threw back his bull's head and laughed, long and loud, so that the hall rang with it. When he stopped, Owen tore off a page-corner that he held and offered it to the duke, his face all grave and earnest. 'Will you join me, sire?'

The duke bellowed then, sputtering and slapping his leg, tears of laughter coming to his eyes. 'I marked your knavery before, sirrah.... You are a whoreson Welshman, for sure....'

'That I am not,' said Owen. 'For my mother is descended from the rulers of Rome.... Helen she is, named for her Latin forebearers.'

'Then are we kinsmen, Master Owen, for I myself,' said Visconti, 'am come down from those twins that founded Rome....'

Owen's left eyebrow shot up; it was a trick he had, and looked bird-quizzical and comic, too. 'Surely not,' he said, 'from Romulus and Remus? For they were suckled by wolves, and took in wolf-looks with the milk.... For sure your beginnings must be farther back yet—in ancient Crete and the Minos-kings....'

'The bull-kings, you are saying ... I take your meaning.' He wore no smile, Visconti, and I could not read his face. 'Take care, young Welshman. Do not go too far....'

'Do we not all, sire,' said Owen, 'take our looks, and valor, too, from some beast? I have thought often, what if men walked on all fours once, coming down from the trees, or crawling out of the ocean, even?'

'It is a darkling thought——' answered the duke, frowning, but smiling after. 'But do not say it in front of churchmen—or they will have your head. They will have it we are sprung from God....'

'Yes,' said Owen, spreading out his hands. 'But which one? The ancients worshiped many—none human. Boars, wolves, horses, and bulls, too'—and he shot his eyebrow high again, looking at the duke sidelong. 'And even the Christ they likened to a lamb....'

'For sure, sirrah,' said Visconti, 'you are not come from that one—or any you have spoke.... I see you a great cat upon a mountain, all yellow against the sky, and waiting slow to pounce.'

Owen bowed low. 'I give you thanks, Sire Visconti, for the lion is king among us animals....'

The duke shook his head. 'It is not so in Milan,' he said.

'And well I know it,' answered Owen, laughing now. 'So,

Minos, what say you? Shall I eat my papers or no?'

'No, for I will sign. ... I like you well, lion of Wales. ...' And, beckoning Owen to him, he kissed him full on both cheeks, the kiss of courtesy. Then he took up the papers and a pen and signed, not troubling to scan them even. 'What is this seal?' he asked, squinting at it. 'I cannot make it out. ...'

'It is the dragon of Wales,' said Owen. 'Another beast, but mythical and no worry to a bull-king. ...'

I caught my breath at this, but the duke took it fair and grinning wide. Owen heard my gasp and turned. 'Have you met yon man of genius?' he said to Visconti. '*There* is nothing of animal at all, but pure soul in his writings. ...'

I felt my neck go red, for I am not used to such lavish words, and said, dropping to my knees again, 'Except I be a mouse or squirrel nibbling away at words that others have writ ... I am a translator only, sire ... Geoffrey Chaucer, on King Richard's business——' And I bowed, from my lowly spot, though I nearly toppled; it was main hard to manage on my sore knees.

'I have read your works, Master,' said the duke, looking at me keen out of his bulging eyeballs; almost I thought him ready to charge! 'You are too modest—or too fearful!' said Visconti. 'For from what other did you translate your "Parliament of Fowles"?'

I was some flustered, in truth, for I did not know how the mighty would look upon this little piece of fun-poking; I meant it for a harmless bit of fooling, but who could tell with high folk?

'It is a rare comical poem, Master,' said Visconti. 'But is it true? We have not parliaments here and do not know their workings. Besides, you have not finished it. ...'

'Sire, that is its one claim to veracity. For as you say "unfinished," so do the English people cry "an end!"'

'You are no coward, Geoffrey Chaucer,' said the duke. 'Though, being a tyrant, I will scoff at parliaments, it might not be so were your own monarch sitting here.'

'Oh, sire,' I answered, 'King Richard is but upwards of ten years. For sure he has fallen asleep at many a government session!'

'And so you are safe—for now!' He looked at me for a moment, thinking. 'But you said you are come on the king's business. . . .'

I nodded. 'On the business of his kingdom. . . .' I could not forbear a smile. 'On the business of Parliament. . . .'

'Ha!' cried the duke. 'And so the right hand knows not what the left does! A true diplomat you are, for sure, Master Chaucer. . . . Well, let us have it—spit it out!'

'Sire,' I said, 'it is private—for your ears only. . . . I beg privy audience at your convenience.'

'It is war or money or both,' he said. 'But never mind, you please me, sirrah, like your Welsh friend. . . . Tomorrow at first light!' And he turned away, fixing his stare upon the next suppliant. I groaned inwardly; how I hate to get up in the morning!

'Cheer up, man,' said Owen, taking my arm and steering me through the company. 'Either go to bed early or do not sleep at all . . . it is the only way. Will you take meat with me now in my quarters? I have the apartments that were once Francis Petrarch's.'

'Petrarch's!' I cried, on fire to set foot where the great poet had lived and loved. 'The duke shows you much favor,' I said, for I was main awed.

'Oh, he has not lent the place to me,' said Owen. 'It is the highest rent on Milan's books. None has been able to afford it since the poet died. . . .'

He spoke in high good humor and carelessly, loud for anyone to hear. There shows the barbarian Welshman again, I thought. We English speak soft of money, if at all. And still, he was a gentleman, one could see.

SIX

Petrarch's former home was in the west part of the town, near to the Vercellina gate; it was the upper floor of a graceful little building such as the Italian masons do so well, with a kind of gallery, iron-railed, and all open to a view of the distant Alps. It was above a bookshop, which made my avid heart beat faster from the first. Later I spent many happy hours browsing there below, for the owner got to know me and let me be; upstairs, too, became my second home in Milan.

It was a small apartment only, but Owen had filled it to the brim with all manner of furnishings; hangings, and statues, lamps and books. I had never seen such crowded quarters; in England we are more austere, owning only that which cannot be done without. Great nobles, of course, like John of Gaunt, have many treasures, but then, too, they have palaces to house them. Here, one must gather up one's skirts so as not to topple something precious off its perch. There were all manner of chairs, too, and cushioned; at home we mostly sit on backless benches. Though it seemed cluttered at first, still it was main comfortable, once one had grown used to it.

He had crowded the place with people, too, Owen. There was his man who opened the door to us and disappeared after; I assumed he was a sort of chamber-valet. There was a cook I never saw who produced food fit for the gods. There was his young mistress, Raimunde of the wine-shop, with her mother, too, and her twins by Owen. My eyebrows near fled up into my hairline at this, remembering those twins he had sired before, and Owen laughed. 'Yes,' he said, 'my offspring come in pairs, it seems—the better to people Wales!' Fat healthy babes they were, too, rosy and laughing, and bearing, as before, the unmistakable stamp of Owen. The grandmother, she who had been the wine-wife, bore them in, one on each arm, and tumbled them out upon the floor, where they squirmed and crawled over each other like puppies. It was hot, and their only garments were little shirts stopping at their waists; I saw that they too were boys and asked their names. 'David ab Owen and Rhys ab Owen,' I was told, though the names sounded a little different in the Welsh.

The shy, small Raimunde had disappeared; I thought the lady had even grown in stature. The almond-pale face was tinted now, but delicately, with some Eastern paints, and the large eyes made larger in the way of the Saracens, too, with a thin black line drawn round. Her brows were plucked into the arching shape that was coming into fashion, and her clothes were banquet-fine, though it was not much past noon. I thought her overdone, and it saddened me; I had been much taken with her fawnlike person, all vanished now.

Her soft southern speech was gone, too, and her English was as unaccented as my own. Indeed, she had all the bearing and grace of a highborn lady, flirtatious looks and small head-tossings; the very picture of a court creature, mannered and sprightly. Somewhat was awry, though, in that portrait; I could not put my finger on it, and it teased my mind.

Her babes, too, she had no eye for; although once she bent over them, dangling her jeweled crucifix for them to play with, snatching it away as one toys with kittens, and showing her little white teeth in a curving smile. When their nurse came to take them for their feeding (another member of that teeming household!), she did not leave off her conversation even, though Owen tossed them, crowing, into the air, and tickled them to make them laugh. The wine-wife-grandmother left us, too, for some shadowy parts and did not come back; I guessed that she, with the wet-nurse, had most of the rearing of the boys.

The table was laid and all made ready; there was a delicious smell from somewhere, making my mouth water, for it was late. 'Call Master Nathan from his books or whatever——' said Owen to his manservant, and I saw there were four places set out. Sweet Jesus, I thought, and there is yet another living here!

Presently there came a courtly gentleman, richly dressed but all in black; he had a long, Italianate face, something sad, though when he smiled I saw his dark eyes were fine and kindling-warm. 'Here is another bookworm like yourself, Master Geoffrey,' said Owen. 'Though he peruses a different sort of manuscript ... a doctor-surgeon he is and forever study-ing—body-humors and physics, and alchemy, too....'

'Ah, no,' said the gentleman, shaking his head, 'not that—not alchemy. For it is a waste of time, like the search for the Philosophers' Stone....'

Owen laughed. 'I would not set you off, Master Nathan ... else will our pasty grow cold.' He turned to me. 'Here before you is a great man of medicine and its lore—versed in all the

Eastern knowledge he is, and much of his own learning, too. I fetched him for the bearing of my sons, for I do not trust the midwives ... and I have kept him by me for his friendship and to pick his brains. Greek I am learning from him—and the Hebrew tongue also.... Gentlemen, know one another. This is Master Chaucer of England and the greatest poet of that place ... and this is the physician Nathan ben Arran.'

I almost gasped, putting two and two together. The fellow was a Jew! I had never been so close to one before, except by accident in the street. And now I must sit at meat with him. I was main embarrassed for Owen, that ignorant Welshman, and did not know where to look.

The food was delectable, clear broth, colored red and ice-cold with a subtle taste, little prawns, cold, too, served on lettuces, a hot pasty, and all manner of fruits and comfits to follow. Even so, it was a horrid meal; I could not eat for the sight of the Jew opposite (at least they had seated me there, and not beside him!). That man had strange tastes, though his manners were better than one would expect; he had a separate set of dishes and would not eat the prawns or pasty. Indeed, he ate little—soup, and bread, without butter, and a half of a pear—and drank no wine, explaining that he could not work after, for the wine went to his head and made him drowsy. They spoke throughout, Owen and he, in courtly wise, and Raimunde, too, did not refrain from making eyes at the Jew and cooing at him like a very pigeon. I could no more speak than eat; I was not angry, but puzzled and outraged. As we lingered over our wine, the man Nathan rose, excusing himself that he had much to do before sunset.

When he had left and the door closed behind him, I burst out, uncontained. 'God's nails, man! Are you so deeply in his debt? Perhaps King Richard will help—I will have a word. It is a disgrace, for a fact!'

Owen stared at me, a little line between his brows. 'I do not take your meaning, master....'

'You need not have him at your table, you know ...' I stammered. 'It is not done....'

'Nathan?' said Owen, his eyebrows shooting up. 'Why not? He is my friend....'

'Well,' I said, reasonably, 'you are Welsh and do not under-stand, perhaps....' He disconcerted me, Owen, with his stare, and his doxy, too, turned astonished eyes towards me. I was on a sudden shy of what I had to say, though I knew not why. 'Well,' I said, finally, 'the man is a Jew, is he not?'

There was a little silence. Owen's face, always too long for a youth, looked old as a mountain and hard as a mountain, too. Though it was hot still, cold crept over me; I have been always craven and I thought, in that long moment: What have I said? Have I impugned his Welshness? One never knows with these outlanders, civil though he has been.

But then he spoke, all the strangeness vanished from him, and his manner mild again. Spreading his hands in a kind of shrug, he said, 'And was he not a Jew, also—your Jesus?'

I crossed myself, though I do this seldom, just in case the Christ or His Mother had heard. 'He was the Son of God,' I said.

'He was the son of Jews,' said Owen, flashing fire, 'and descended from the Jewish David—on both sides. It is writ so in the Scriptures, for I have read them, all. In later years men saw Him good and called the goodness God—that is all.'

If I dared, I would have made the evil eye sign then. But I did not. I swallowed my ire and took my leave as soon as it was decent. I did not even look into the inviting dark of the downstairs bookshop but hurried back to my quarters to pace the marble floor. I avoided De Berkeley's conversation, pleading a headache, and went early to bed, just after sunset. I did not sleep a wink all night.

SEVEN

The next dawning I waited in vain for the Duke Visconti; after an hour word was brought me that he would see me at supper. For once I was glad of a despot's whim, for my head felt as though it had been axed and I reeled where I stood;

perhaps Visconti too had slept ill!

A I stumbled out into the early sunlight, blinking, I felt a plucking at my sleeve; it was Owen's manservant, with a letter. It was short, bidding me meet him at a cookshop near the west wall; '... for sure you have not yet broken fast—and the cook there has many treasures, besides good English ale. My man will bring you there.' It was autocratic and put my back up, for why should I do this Welshman's bidding? But then I bethought me of little King Richard; he was much taken with this Owen, after that masque-play at the coronation feast, and sent often for him, to hear stories told and watch him act out parts. So prudence won, and I swallowed my pride and followed to the cookshop.

The ale was as good as promised, and there was bread and brawn, too, English style; the cook had lived in London once and even spoke Londonese. After, I felt much renewed, and the pounding in my head died down to a dull ache, though I felt it still. Owen was bright as the morning, barbered and combed, talking fresh of this and that as though it were noon; of course he was not much above half my years, a thing I often forgot. I answered shortly, for me; partly because I was yet bemused from my sleepless night, and in part from a strange unease. I do not often feel such wise; in my small way, I am a confident person, letting folk take me as I am. So I could not understand myself, and it made me quiet.

After we had eaten our fill and drunk another mug of ale, Owen pulled me to my feet, saying that he had a fine surprise for me. 'In back it is,' he said, with a nice gaiety, his face all aglow with its youth and its after-shave oiling. 'The cook is a favorite with all the scribes of Milan. I promised you some treasures ... see for yourself!'

He spoke true, for in a room behind were piled all manner of books and scrolls, a delight to behold; the student scribes brought their wares here to this cook-man, and he ran a thriving business on the side. I was soon lost to everything else, dipping into book after book, like a fat bee tasting spring flowers. I pounced suddenly, grabbing. 'Here,' I cried, 'here is another copy of *Il Filostroto*, that I have taken my Criseyde tale from!'

'Oh,' said Owen, 'one of poor Giovanni Boccaccio's forgotten poems....'

'Boccaccio?' I said. 'Oh, no—this is Petrarch's own. Unsigned, to be sure, but I have it on good authority....'

'No,' said Owen. 'I have a signed manuscript, got by Bernabò's own scribe from Boccaccio before he died——'

I was minded to argue, for I had heard that same Boccaccio lecture in Florence three years before, and he was a learned pedant, no more. But I thought better of it and instead asked mildly if I might see the signed one.

'But certainly,' said Owen. 'Though it is writ in a hasty hand, probably his own, and is hard to follow.'

We spent some little time in that hidden bookshop, and I struck several happy bargains and was much pleased with myself. As I tucked my purchases under my arm, Owen handed me another book, all wrapped and tied, so that I could not see the title.

'Promise that you will read it, at least to the halfway mark,' he said. 'It is a good copy in a fair hand, though the sense is poorly set down, unlike Boccaccio's. But there is somewhat to be learned from this bad writing here'—and he tapped it—'if you will persevere.'

I was curious and promised to read it at first leisure. 'Probably this afternoon,' I said, 'for I have nothing else to do till supper.'

'Good,' said Owen. 'I will see you then, for I, too, am bid to sup. The bull-duke likes my face, it seems—or perhaps my mistress's.' And he laughed a little, saying, 'He saw her in the market yesterday as he rode through. I was told he asked her name, and her protector....'

De Berkeley was out and I had the apartment to myself, settling down straightaway for a good read. It was cool for Milan, a little breeze coming through the windows and ruffling my pages. I dipped into one after another book, finally putting all aside and taking up the gift from Owen to unwrap it. Upon the title page were writ the words *The Jew of Venice*. Ah-ha, I thought, and so he would teach me a lesson, Owen. It must be the work of some Jewish scribe, extolling all the virtues of his race. For sure they exist, those virtues, as they do in all men; but must I have my nose rubbed in them?

I turned the pages idly, then stopped, suddenly caught by a phrase. It was not as I thought. Here was the picture set down of a very devil, greedy, sly, evil, and ugly too, covered with warts, humpbacked, and with a twisted leg as well! It was sickening to read, so unreal as it was, but I could not stop, for the grisly tale gripped me. It was of a gentleman of that same city, a noble merchant (a paradox, for sure, for there is none such, but let it go), mostly good, fair, and handsome, with a well-turned leg. I made a little face as I read, for I found the gentleman as tasteless as curds. He had suffered losses, business-wise, and went to the evil Jew in his smelly ghetto to borrow monies for his next venture, a shipping deal. The Jew is set down all scraping and bowing, but spitting when the merchant's back is turned, so vile he is. When asked what interest he will charge, the Jew answers, 'A pound of flesh!' It was like a joke one hears in the street, and writ down in sober thought; I had no stomach for the rest of it, skipping to the end. Of course the merchant ships were sunk and the Jew demanded his payment; it is taken to law, and a youthful angel-lawyer (almost one could see the halo!) confounds the Jew and he is led off in chains and cursing in Hebrew, to rot in some doge's dungeon. What trash! I turned the pages, looking for a signature, and almost missed it. But on the back was writ very small the letter *P* for Petrarch, as the master always signed!

My mind was in great turmoil; I had thought to rest before the duke's supper party, but again I tossed upon my couch, unable to resolve my painful thoughts.

'... well—and it may be a forgery, after all,' said Owen, as we sat at wine that supper evening. 'Who is to know if the great man wrote it, or some other?'

'But,' I said, twisting my glass round in my fingers, 'it is so badly done, with no skill at all....'

'Genius flies out the window when scurrilous passions enter,' said Owen, like a very schoolmaster. 'Look you,' he said, bending closer toward me and speaking low. 'That same master, our Petrarch, he was in debt for years to a moneylender in the Jewish quarter.... He would not pay—and his debts mounted ever higher, and his hatreds with them. When, in desperation, after six years, the Jew brought suit, the great Petrarch, having the ducal ear, had the man's property confiscated, and the man, with all his family, driven out of the city. That piece I gave you was writ, or so it is said, to justify those acts. . . .'

I sat in stunned dismay, for Petrarch was ever a name of magic to my ears; I had supposed him a man of genius and above all petty motives of revenge or hate. And, creeping cold within me, too, came something else I could not put a name to. But Owen named it for me.

'And so you see, Master Chaucer, to what lengths it can drive —this aversion for one's fellow creatures. Even men of genius are affected by it—*in*fected, rather—and debased. Even the high-minded Petrarch—even. . . .' And he bent his yellow eyes upon me; I fancied, in the strangeness of my feelings, all this way and that, that I saw a mocking light in them.

I burst out, 'But—perhaps this one, this Jew he writes of, perhaps he *was* a scurvy fellow and a cheat!'

'Perhaps,' said Owen, still with that odd light deep within his eyes, 'but there never lived such a one as is pictured in these pages. Admit it, man. . . .'

'It is exaggeration, for sure,' I said, 'and a grotesque portrait. But yet, not every Jew-man is fine and noble, either.'

'Nor any other man,' said Owen. 'We are all unlike—and all kin, too, by our natures. . . .'

'Well, I trust,' said I, with some bridling, for I was main tired of this Welsh sprig's lecturing, 'I trust I write so . . . for so I understand the human nature, also. . . .'

Owen smiled, a trifle nastily, I thought, and pointed his overlong forefinger at me. 'Yet did you, Master Chaucer, sit unwilling at meat and silent, writhing in distemper, across from the good Nathan—it was plain to see. . . .'

I did not fancy his description of me, though it was apt, and funny, too, almost to make me smile, though I forebore. After a moment I said, 'I have been taught from a boy that these Jew-people put our Saviour on the Cross. . . .'

'Not so,' said Owen, shaking his head, 'for they were a sub-ject people, the Hebrews, and had not the power. It was the Romans did it. And it is beside the point anyway—for whatever, Nathan was not there. Nor any other of his people living now. Nor the descendants of those old crucifying Romans, that we sit among tonight—and that you do not shun. . . .'

I was silent then, and thinking, for I saw that he spoke sense. And, for sure, the fellow had not asked to be born a Jew and scorned! Nor no man can order his birth, high or low. I was dizzy with these thoughts, darting, and Owen not speaking, sipping his wine.

'Well,' I said finally, 'I will beg this Nathan's pardon—what time you will lead me to him—for I own myself wrong in the matter of this man. . . .'

Owen raised his hand. 'No—you need not. Most like he has not noticed it; he is used to it, after all. . . .'

I said, but slowly, and puzzling it out, 'It is that I did not put myself in his shoes. . . .'

'How could you?' said Owen, smiling. 'You are English, after all. And the English hate foreign things, all . . . Flemings, Lombards—and Welsh, too. How often,' said he, his yellow eyes a-crinkle, 'have you dubbed me barbarian in your thought?'

'Never——' said I, but I lied.

'Well, here we sit, anyway,' said Owen. 'It is a matter of degree only. A Jew is stronger stuff to stomach . . . but I yet have faith in you, Man of Genius!'

I thought he mocked and looked at him hard, but his eyes were earnest and his mouth most grave. I was happy to see the little Raimunde come toward us, skirting the long low tables. She carried something wrapped in silk, and small. 'Look——' she said, smiling delight. 'Look what the duke has given me—all gold and marked with his crest!' In the silk napkin there lay a delicate circlet, cunningly wrought of twisted yellow gold, thin as wire, and dangling from it a bangle bearing the Bernabò crest. It was somewhat larger than wrist size, an arm-ring perhaps.

Owen took it up, frowning. 'You cannot wear this!' he cried. 'It is a slave-anklet, borrowed from the Saracen custom. All the duke's concubines wear them—he has thirty-five. . . . Would you be the thirty-sixth?'

And he took her hand, pulling her down beside him, she

tossing her head and making a little face, pouting. 'It is a pretty thing ... and must I give it back?'

'No, for I will.' And Owen took the bauble in his long, strong fingers, bending and shaping the pliable stuff into a passable likeness of a toy dagger. When he had finished, he whistled to him a little page who had been standing near, goggle-eyed. 'Take this to the duke, your master—with my compliments!' The page took it, looking scared.

We could not see the duke's face, for he sat half the hall away, with the dancing-floor in between. But we saw that he beckoned someone, giving an order. When the servant returned, bearing a state cushion, the duke got to his feet, heavily, and came toward us behind his man. I stumbled to my feet hastily, bowing low, but Owen did not rise and lounged at ease upon his chair, his arm about his lady's waist. The manservant stood before him, holding out the cushion. 'The duke's compliments,' he said. Upon the cushion lay a bright dagger, ruby-studded, its point looking evilly sharp. Owen reached out and took it, turning it about. Then he rose, bowing slightly. 'Thank you,' he said, looking at the duke.

'It is a better weapon than the one you gave,' said the duke. 'You may need it....'

'Ah, no,' said Owen, 'for in Wales we do not stick bulls....' And he bowed again. 'But I will keep it anyway. It will come in handy for cutting up my meat ... sometimes beef is tough....'

Again there was that little savage silence between those men, while I quaked in my shoes, and I heard a hound scratch somewhere. Then Duke Bernabò bellowed loud, laughter to make you jump, and, stepping forward, embraced Owen. 'We are brothers, Lion of Wales,' he said, 'all unlike as we are. I only sought to do your lady honor.'

'Ah, there we are!' cried Owen. 'It is custom comes between us ... I did not understand. In Wales, and England, too, ankle-rings are not worn. Although we sometimes tether cows so—when they are to be serviced.'

'By the bull, eh?' said the duke, laughing again. 'Your wit is something heavy—but let it go....'

'The hour is late,' said Owen, laughing too. 'Try me another time.'

'I'll take you at your word, Sir Welshman, for I like you well. . . .'

And indeed, Owen was summoned often to that duke's side, oftener than I, though I had business with him; I think Bernabò enjoyed the crossing of swords, as it were. There were not many would dare it, in a tyrant's domain.

As for me, I managed to beg some little monies for England's war-waging, or at least the promise, so I counted my visit profitable.

I spent many hours, too, with Owen, in cookshops, and bookstalls, and in his house, too. For he was very hospitable and made me welcome while he was there.

Back he went, though, for the fall term at Westminster, before my business with the duke was finished. I missed him after, and the Jew Nathan too, for he went also, in Owen's train; we had had much pleasant converse.

I grew to like him well, Nathan, in spite of his race; he was a learned man and with a fine wit. And never again did I cross the London street when I saw a Jew coming or twitch aside my cloak to avoid contact. I even, in later years, let my Thames Street house to a Jew-family that had the price, though I was much criticized for it. It does not do to practice intolerance, for all are equal, as I have found. And many good Jews there are, of upright hearts and fair-mindedness; if I had a daughter, though, I would not have her marry one.

EIGHT

I bethought myself often of Owen's quick words about the French war and taxation and the poor people paying for it all, in the end. I would not listen in Milan, for I hate all manner of word-strife and contention, but in the years that followed I had to listen, and to many mouths as well, for the citizenry of London were becoming more and more outraged at the hated poll taxes. These were main unfair, taxing every person for the same sum, a whole shilling finally, at the third levy! I could afford it, and Philippa, too, but what of her housemaids, that earned little more in a year? What of the apprentices, unpaid, and the freedmen of the shires, scraping their barren wages to make ends meet? What of the vast unfree that had to work twice their time to have the price from their overlords? And the list went on and on. The government enjoined, in a lordly way, that the richer would pay for the poor—but who could enforce it? The rich do not stay rich by giving away their monies.

It was more complicated than this, and the people's grievances were many, but the poll tax, especially the third and highest one, brought all to a head, and Hades broke loose all over the realm before all was ended.

Hindsight is easy, as all men know. Few of us foresaw in the year of 1378 what might happen in the next three years. We go about under a cloud of our own concerns, for the most part. I heard the hedge-priests haranguing at the street corners, but I shut my ears and listened only to the verses that buzzed in my head. The groups of two and three that gathered in the lower taverns and even under Aldgate, where I lived, grew more numerous by the month; I was aware of this in a vague sort of way, as of a nuisance added to the London streets, but I did not see its import.

I have been trying to sort it all out in my head—how it began and progressed, what causes there were, and all the rest—that time, so brief, so raging, that men call now, all over England, the Hurling Time, the time of the revolt.

For ten years the war with France had gone on, a weary and unprofitable business, as I have said. Though England never lost a battle, she gained nothing and her French possessions dissolved into thin air; it was diplomatic failure and mismanagement by the nobles, and many were hated heartily for it. Duke John of Gaunt was always unpopular and, unjustly I thought, was blamed for much of the nonsuccess. When he and other nobles were a-waging their useless wars, the French fleet sailed up the Thames and burned Gravesend. The people of the south there had their homes burned and looted, and their women slaughtered or carried off; the nobility, who did not suffer at all, behind their fortified walls, did nothing to help them, and feeling ran high against all the 'high-noses,' as they were called. On top of this, free labor had been oppressed by the Statute of Laborers, and wages had been kept low, while the unfree were worse treated than cattle. And then they, the free and unfree, were asked to foot the bill for the conquests that had conquered nothing and for the defenses that were useless against the invaders! I simplify, but it is tedious long to explain, and that is the true gist of it.

The poor preachers, Lollards all, had for years now been more than outspoken in their criticism of the clergy and nobles alike; sometimes their language was enough to curl your hair. But now came a different breed of preacher-man, all over London and in the shires, too. They were plentiful as locusts and for the most part as much of a plague, for they were wild-eyed and dirty and speaking some of the thicker dialects, so that it was hard to follow them. Plain it was, though, that they, all, preached not warning and denunciation, but out-and-out sedition.

One of these men had by now a name that was whispered over all England; the nobles, too, recognized his power, and he had been jailed many times. Still, one heard of him everywhere, but soft, in the streets and stews, and even in the remoter villages. Up and down the countryside his words were repeated. 'Thus and thus says John Ball—and it is true,' went the whisper. I myself would not go to hear him, resisting for months; I did not want to hear persuasive treason, for my life and its profits were tied up, all, with the government, and the noble persons, too. Often and often did Owen try to lure me, for 'he is a great man, and a thinker of power, a speaker of simple truth, unadorned,' he said. Still I would not hear him, even though all London turned out below my windows.

My Phil, though, I could not turn from her purpose, once she was determined, and it was ever so. I was main struck that she would take to the man, for always had she been a courtier-lady and, like me, lived upon the nobles' bounty. 'You *will* come—little Geoffrey,' she hissed, 'for the mad priest speaks true.' I took umbrage, for I am none so little as that, she herself is half a head shorter. But I never would quarrel with her, my Phil, for one cannot win such a battle.

He was speaking a little ways outside the gate, to avoid the authorities; the city officials winked at him so long as he was not within, for many, in their hearts, held with him and against the high-noses. The crowds were pouring through the gate since dawn, making our house that was perched above ring with their noise; some even had gathered the night before, to get the best places. There was a cotter's hut in that meeting-place, with a flat roof of slates, and he had climbed upon it, John Ball, to be seen by all.

Mad priest, Phil had called him, but even from my far place in the crowd I could see he was none such. His habit was patched but clean, of a gray wadmal-stuff, girded up over bare feet and legs. He had a mild face and quiet manner, standing quite still, a stocky man upwards of forty, holding up his hand for silence. When he spoke, his voice was low and his words full of reason; low and calm he spoke, but all heard, for not a skirt rustled. He did not wave his arms about or flash his eyes, but like a rock he stood and spoke as one man to another.

'My good people,' he said, 'good men and women of London-town. Things cannot go well in England. Things cannot go well. They can never go well until all property is held in common. They can never go well until there are neither villeins nor gentlemen. They can never go well until there is naught but one united people. What gain have we poor from those that are raised over us? What advantage comes from those lords that we call masters? You know, good people, that there is none ... Do those lords above us deserve to be above us? How is it that they hold us in servitude? What grounds are there? What right have they? We are all descended from the same father and mother—Adam and Eve. The nobles' claim to be more truly lords than we rests on one thing only.... It rests on their power. Their power to force us to labor for them. Their power to force us to produce for them. To produce for them that they may spend....'

There was more of the same, simple words and straightfor-ward. They were pure treason, of course, and a chill went down my spine to hear them, but Phil, beside me, had tears in her eyes, and clapped her hands wildly at the end, with all the others. He climbed down, John Ball, helped by those just under him, and his face still mild, with a little smile upon it. One gave him a drink from a water-bottle, and another man climbed up onto the roof-top. I saw it was another winked-at one, he that was called by all, Edmund Outlaw. He was another breed, tall and thin, with a lantern jaw and eyes set deep so that they looked like black burning holes. He was missing an ear, and a long scar ran down his left cheek, an old brand mark, *F* for Felon. All knew his story. He had in his villein's childhood, upon the manor where he was bound from birth, stolen, at the yearly lord's feast, a loaf of white bread from the high-noses' table. It was done on a dare, as boys will, but they took his ear for it and branded him too; he was eight years old. There were many such tales in our land, sad and wrong, and all pity those unfortunates. This man had run away, joining a group of tumblers that go about at fairs and such, entertaining the crowds and living by their wits. But he was a Lollard thinker, too, this Edmund Outlaw, and went about with John Ball now, sharing the hedges he slept under, his crusts of bread, and his jail-cells, too. He held up his arms, enjoining silence, for the folk had cheered him. His voice, when he spoke, was strong and full, trained to be heard above fair-noise, and he spoke, as it were, in enigmas, at least to me. But the people cheered each sentence wildly, throwing their hats into the air. I cannot remember it all, or word for word, but something of it I can repeat.

Owen said after that these words were parts of letters sent all over the shires by those stirring up revolt; though the words were veiled in metaphor, still the folk knew the meanings.

'John Sheep bids John Nameless and John the Miller and John Carter to beware of guile and stand together in God's name.... He bids Piers Plowman to go to his work and chastise well Hob the Robber [which I took to mean Robert Hales, the treasurer and collector of the poll-tax, but I may be wrong]. Take with you John Trueman and all his fellows ... look you shape to one head and no more [Did this mean there was a leader already? Was it John Ball or some other? I was all disquieted, for sure the crowd understood all and took each meaning clear]. The mills of God grind exceeding small ... and so has John the Miller, he has ground small, small, small. Look you the mill go aright with four sails, and the post stand in steadfastness. We have right with might to back it ... we have will with skill to give it effect.... Make a good end of that you have begun. For if the end be well, all is well.... Falseness and guile have reigned too long. Truth has been set under a lock.... Sin fares as wild flood.... True love is away.... God give redress, for now is the time!' At this last his voice rose high and wild and the black pits of his eyes streamed tears. The people wept too, swaying and moaning, and some of the women fainted. And Edmund the Outlaw ended up, when he had calmed them, 'John Ball has rung your bell! Sing with me—sing it with me—all together ... "When Adam delved and Eve span, who was then the gentleman?"' And they sang this song or chant over and over. It was the first time I had heard it, but certainly not the last. All England rang to it before the year was out.

I am a craven-heart, so I did not see the holocaust close to, but holed up in my house and was forgot, thank Jesus. For once I ruled on Philippa, too, and kept her by me. When the mobs from Kent and Essex poured through Aldgate, our house above trembled and I did too, but none thought to seek us out for robbery or worse. From our windows, peeping, we saw the beautiful Savoy palace of the duke's all flaming through the night; by morning it was destroyed, and others, too. Many lost their lives, beheaded, and throats cut, all flung anyhow in the streets. The rebels, inflamed with hatred for the foreigner, killed all the Flemings and Lombards they could find, blaming them for the loss of trade. The jails were thrown open and the freed prisoners mingled with the poor from city and shire, and the mob ran riot, looting and burning, seeking out the nobles and the law-folk and collectors. My official garb and seals of office would have sealed my doom had I been abroad, as they did for many another.

The insurrection was put down by the bravery and grace of the fourteen-year-old Richard, but I cannot tell that story, for I hid in cowardly wise while my little king rode out to meet the rebels. But I have no shame, for at least I am alive to tell another tale or two.

BOOK III

GOD'S POOR

Told by Lady Margaret Hanmer

of Flintshire in Wales, later wife

to Owen

ONE

Word of the rebellion had not spread to Wales; even the border, where I lived, was quiet in the spring of 1381. We had all heard of the good priest John Ball, of course; there are no good priests but Lollard priests, to my mind, for I came early to question churchly teachings. I had been brought up by men, in a way, except for Nurse, my mother having died at my birth; I thought like a man, and more so than my brothers even, for I loved learning from a child, and Dada had got us a tutor that was a follower of the great Wycliffe. The folk all round about whispered the words of that John Ball and hummed the little song, 'When Adam delved and Eve span ... who was then the gentleman...?' But, as I say, we had no real knowledge of how far the insurrection had come in England.

Even the London-folk must not have known all, for Dada would never have sent for me if he had foreseen. I must explain that Dada is mostly in London, whereas we, my brothers and I, live on our manor in Wales. Dada is Sir David Hanmer, judge in the Court of King's Bench, one of the highest positions in the land; it is a great honor, truly, for a Welshman, and all Wales feels much pride. I was greatly thrilled to be summoned to London, for I had not seen my father for near a twelvemonth; besides, I was about to become a lady-in-waiting to the new queen!

She was not yet queen, Anne, the girl from Bohemia, but she was contracted to marry Richard the following winter, and the Queen-Mother Joan was rounding up ladies for her against her arrival. The queen-mother had only attendants of her own age about her, old as the hills, forty maybe, and, being a kind soul, wished the young Anne to have companions in her new country. I had come to London once before, for the coronation, and was bid to supper too, so the lady queen remembered me. I had been only eleven then, and prettier; I hoped the queen-mother would not find me too tall. I practiced every day walking with my knees bent under my long gown, but it did not do much good; I was still higher than my brothers, even the oldest.

I am fifteen now, just Anne's age, and marriageable myself. I am called beautiful, but it is not so; there are always some who will say that about an heiress. My hair only satisfies me; it is long and thick and of a good color, pale gold, almost silver. But my eyebrows are dark and my eyes gray, so nothing matches, though my face is passable otherwise, and there is a dimple in my cheek if I remember to smile in the proper way. There is much to remember if a maid is to be thought fair, Nurse tells me. The dimple, for one, and to look sidelong, instead of straight, at gentlemen, to slouch and bend the knees (only if you are too tall, of course), and to poke the stomach out. This last is impossible, as I have none, not even a hint; I look very silly so, as if I were about to do a backbend, like a mountebank! I have tried them all, these beauty tricks, but without much success. My tutor, Morris Stove, says a maiden as learned as I has no need for frivolous accomplishments, and frowns upon them, while Nurse scolds abovestairs. So I am torn between the two, one might say. For of course I should like to have everything—what girl would not?

I do have everything, truly, that money can buy, for Dada is very rich and I am his only daughter. Morris Stove says good Christians do not need to go in furred surcoats and jeweled girdles; he is right, of course, but I cannot disappoint Dada either. He had spared no expense for my court journey; I had a whole wagon filled with trunks, just for my clothes alone! And all new, for I had grown again this last year and nothing fit; the maids had been sewing for weeks.

Nurse was not going with me, to my delight; I have outgrown her, and her rude country tongue embarrasses me. Instead, there would be my very own tiring-maid, a village girl I had known all my life, and as excited as I was myself, and with us a distant cousin of my mother's, widowed, and too poor to be strict.

We left at first light on an early June morning; it would be a fair day, one could see, but the air was still heavy and damp, the dew sparkling the grasses, and at the last moment I had one of my choking fits. Nurse went scurrying for my medicine, a nasty brew that did not help anyway; I took it to please her. I get these attacks sometimes, from the weather perhaps, or from excitement, and wheeze and cough, my breath coming short, until they subside. This fit was not so bad and soon over. I was still gasping a little, but I said, 'It has passed ... Let's go now. Dada said we must get an early start....'

'Oh, no, little Madam,' Nurse said, from somewhere around my chest and looking up at me, clucking like a wet hen. 'Hurry-head, flurry-head! Where is the charm I gave you against the choke-and-spit?' I have said her tongue was rough.

'I lost it,' I answered, lying. It was an evil-smelling God-knows-what, all sewn up in a piece of silk. I had thrown it into the latrine.

'I knew it,' she said, nodding. 'Here is another, on a string. ... Put it around your neck—so!' And she flung it over my head, knocking my head-veil awry, and poked the messy wad down my dress. 'Next to your chest,' she said. 'Protect you from the Derfel-spell, it will....' Nurse is from the hills; up there they think everything bad comes from Derfel; they are very ignorant.

I was exasperated and opened my mouth to argue, but I saw Morris Stove put his finger to his lips and shake his head gently, looking at Nurse. I looked down at her, too, and saw there were tears in her eyes, and she trying to hold them back. I bent quickly, a hard lump coming in my throat, and kissed her cheek; it was soft and slack as trodden moss. She is getting old, I thought. Ane when will I see her again? And the tears pricked behind my own eyelids then, for sorrow, and a little shame, too, for that I had been happy to be rid of her.

Morris Stove and my three brothers rode with us a little way, as far as the next village. From there on we would be on our own, with two pages from our house as escort. When we said farewell, my brothers acted distant and a little bored, as though I went to London every day; of course, they would be going to Oxford, all, in the autumn, and that is farther still. John, the youngest, gave me a shamefaced kiss, but the others waved only. Morris Stove gave me a little book, written in his own hand in Welsh, *The Gospel According to John*, and a small wooden cross. I hung it on my belt to please him, though it looked all wrong beside my embroidered purse, being so plain. 'Be a good Christian,' he said, taking my hand. 'Do not let the court fripperies turn your head. Remember God's poor. . . .'

We were three days and nights on the road, for the mule-wagon with my finery slowed us up. Each night we stopped at a different abbey, to sup and sleep; Dada had forbidden us the inns, nests of robbers he said they were. The convents were mostly plain fare and hard pallets, but one was wealthy; all the nuns wore velvet habits sewn with pearls and ate off silver trenchers, drinking wine from the French lands. One nun, the prettiest, had painted cheeks, I swear! I shuddered to think what Morris Stove would say! Well, he would never know, and we could not shun their hospitality, after all.

After the first day, Aunt Janet (she was not really my aunt, as I have said, but I knew nothing else to call her and do her honor) swooned in the saddle when her horse shied at a chicken that ran across its path. She had been afraid of the poor beast all along, being timorous by nature and not accustomed to riding either; she was a good soul, Aunt Janet, and kind to me as well, though her face was like a sheep's under her old-fashioned wimple, and she told her beads every hour in bad Latin. We had, after, to put her in the wagon to ride with all the trunks piled round. It slowed us up some, I can tell you, for she weighed a good fifteen stone, and the mules had to strain. But Branwen and I were free-er to giggle and gossip with her in the back of us, Branwen being my maid, a round, laughing damsel with red country cheeks. And so we came in sight of London, with the two pages riding before.

It was hot, and I had taken off my rich furred surcoat, folding it under me, where the saddle chafed my legs. My blue gown was as simple as a shift; I had taken off the hanging sleeves, too, not caring if I freckled for once, and Nurse not by to say me nay.

We saw the smoke from far off, hanging in the air like a black cloud and smelling, too. From far, too, we saw the crowd about Aldgate; it might have been a fair-day, but I knew somehow that it was not. 'Ride ahead,' I said to the pages. As they set spur to their horses, one of them turned and gave me a

strange look, cruel and sly, with a smile under. We never saw
them again; they were boys hired just that spring from an English manor lord, a border neighbor. If they had been our own
Welsh, they would never have run away.

'Sweet Jesus,' whispered Branwen, bringing her mount close
to mine. 'What is abroad here, Miss Maggie?' For, coming
closer, we could hear rumbling and shouting ahead, and a
rough-dressed man crossed the road, lurching and swaying,
carrying something round on a long pole. He stumbled into a
ditch and lay still; we thought he was dead. But as we came
nearer we smelled the stale wine, sourish, strong on the air,
and the round thing rolled off the pole into the dust. Branwen
gave a little strangled cry and clutched me hard, so that I near
overbalanced. It was a severed head, bruised and swollen, its
long hair matted in the blackened blood, and the teeth bared
in a grin, horrible to see.

'Be quiet, Branwen!' I hissed, looking behind to see if Aunt
Janet had caught sight of the grisly thing in the road. Most like
she had not, for she held the end of her trailing wimple across
her face against the rotten wine-smell; I saw, then, that more
men were stumbling onto the road just behind the wagon,
carrying the same long poles with their pitiful souvenirs. Off in
the fields a knot of people moiled and shrieked. I could not see
so far, but I thought it must be the place of execution. I am a
noblewoman, after all, so I straightened in the saddle, clench-
ing my teeth and swallowing hard so as not to vomit. 'Be quiet,'
I said again to Branwen, for she was beginning to whimper like
a hurt puppy.

'Oh, Miss Maggie, can we not turn back? Let's turn back,
do!'

'We cannot,' I said. 'Don't look now—there are others behind us and running to catch up.... Go smartly, they have
knives, and I think they are drunken too....'

We spurred our horses to a canter, and I turned, beckoning
to the wagon-driver to hurry. He was simple, and waved back
at me, grinning. I cursed the day we had brought him; there
were better brains on the manor, but poor Crazy Gib was a
praying Lollard, and Morris Stove had persuaded me. Looking
back, I saw the ruffians had near come abreast of the wagon

and were reaching out hands to grab its sides. But Crazy Gib
nodded and smiled at them, raising aloft his wooden cross.
They fell back then, waving their trophy-heads, and he shook
rein, the wagon clattered close behind us now; he was not so
crazy after all. Did they fear the New Cross then, those wild
drunken men? At any rate, they were far behind now, and we
coming close to the gates of London.

Branwen was still making those little hiccoughing sounds; I
jabbed her hard with my elbow, not slowing my pace, and said
low and harsh in a voice not like my own, and surprising me,
'Stop that now! If you do not—I will throw you off into the
road and leave you there.... I mean it!' She stopped then,
round startled eyes looking reproachfully at me, for I had been
more friend than mistress always.

The din from inside the city walls was dreadful to hear, a
muffled roar, crackling noises, not identifiable, and over all the
high terrified whinny of horses. Outside the gate, someone
stood on a cart, waving his arms about and shouting to the
crowd, and they cheering; we could not hear the words. Above
the gate was a row of heads stuck on lances; most were like the
one we had seen close to, matted hair and black blood, but one
had a bishop's miter jammed down over it, nothing showing
but a long, sparse white beard. Beside it, another wore the
silken judges' hood, the white all muddy and torn; my heart
gave a great lurch, but the hair and beard were coal-black—
not Dada then! Though I streamed with sweat beneath the
thin stuff of my gown, still I was clammy-cold, stiff with terror;
they had gone mad, all, for sure, in London-town!

There was no turning back, for the road behind us now
swarmed with folk, all headed, too, for Aldgate. They sang as
they went, but again I could not tell the words. But Crazy Gib,
behind us, sang too—something about 'mills grinding small.'
The gates stood open, and none guarding them, for all were
listening to the fellow on the cart; I thought to make a dash
through and gave signal to Branwen. But from the crowd's
edge a man ran out, catching both our bridles and holding on.
He was no more than a boy, really, and his face not evil, close
to, but my heart hammered against my ribs, and I clutched up
the little wood cross, my parting gift; beside me I heard Bran-

wen hiccup again. More came to join the boy, surrounding us. The fumes of wine rose strong, making my gorge rise. They were peasants all, one could tell from their shock heads and wadmal-wear, but not like our tenants at home; these were thin as weeds and ragged, filthy with old, crusted dirt, and covered with festering sores. 'God's poor!' I thought, my mind going back to Morris Stove's words, and you should see these hellish scarecrows, you clean, decent scholar! But I pushed that thought away, for it was not noble, or Christian either; the marks of oppression and ill-use were upon them, poor souls, and yet I feared, and rightly. The boy's hand, where it held my bridle, was brown with dried blood, and there were sticky round spots upon his leather apron, blood too, but fresher.

'Here's a pretty pair,' one shouted next to him; on his forehead was a raw, red welt, shaped roughly in the letter *N*. Newgate, I thought; they have let out the prisons. And the face under had the jail-pallor, like old cheese.

'This one is mine!' cried the boy at my horse's head. 'I like the hair ... gold as the rich monks' plate....'

'The other is a better armful, lad——' said the jailbird, looking up at Branwen, lewd. She gave a little bird-shriek.

The man who had been haranguing the mob jumped down from the cart, quick, a swarthy fellow, broad, red in the face. 'Commons be not rapists!' he shouted, pulling the two away from their places, and squinting up at us. 'Where be you bound, wenches?' For he took me to be a village maid, so plain did I go in my blue, with my hair in a loose single braid behind.

Under its swagger and bluster his face looked kind; I wet my dry lips with my tongue and answered somehow, though I did not think the words would come. 'We go to the Queen Mother Joan, at Windsor ... to serve her....'

'She be at Tower now, the Fair Maid'—for that was how she was known for many years now, in all the realm, the Fair Maid of Kent, for all she was so old—'with her own sweet Richard-boy....' I had to strain to understand, for he spoke the speech of the southern parts, blurry and thick; I knew the king's English only, being Welsh. I saw his eyes go to my hands, and flinched within; they were too white for a servant's. But he only looked for a long moment, silent, then reached out to take my cross, turning it about in his big hairy hand. 'A lady——' he said. 'And with John Ball's own token. . . . How come you by it?'

'I am of the New Learning,' I said. 'In Wales we are many. . . .'

'Wales, is it . . .?' he said. 'There be good fellows in Wales. . . .' And he whipped out from under his clothing something that glittered in the sunlight. 'And will you spit upon this gaud then, lady?'

It was another cross, heavy and ornate, with jewels set in and wrought of gold; upon it hung the agonized Christ, cunningly painted with the great wound in his side, and the bright blood trickling. I had not before been called upon to do this, though I had been taught that good Christians must spit upon all Popish symbols. I hesitated; the man watched, holding out the painted cross, Some of those nearest had heard and moved in closer, ringing us round. The smell from them was awful, sour and unwashed, God forgive me for thinking it! I swayed where I sat; the man's eyes were on me, steady and unwinking, waiting. And though I did not look, I felt those other eyes, too, hostile. I gathered saliva and spit, though it was not much, my mouth being so dry; beside me I heard Branwen gasp, and the scarecrows gathered round me gave a ragged sort of cheer. He who had held the gilt cross spat too and handed it round; the hawking and spitting was enough to turn your stomach as all vented their pent rage upon the thing. After, they hacked at it with axes and ground it into the mud; just so had they done with those folk who answered wrong, I knew within, and shuddered.

My savior, for so I thought him to be, that burly one still holding my wooden cross, now gave it back and smiled, gap-toothed. 'Myself will take you to barge for Tower,' he said. 'None will harm you, little lady-Lollard, while Jack Strawe is about. Jack Strawe, he be the leader of the Essex-men, and none says him nay. . . . Who be these others with you?' And he looked at Branwen, trembling visibly atop her mount. 'Be her Lollard?' he asked, jerking his thumb at her.

'Yes——' I stammered. 'Yes—she, too....' And I kicked her ankle viciously where it hung close to mine; she gasped again, it must have hurt. But it was better than death, after all, and I would beg her pardon later, if God granted us whole skins.

'Wait,' said Jack Strawe, holding up his hand and walking to the wagon behind. Crazy Gib stood up in his seat, grinning wild and holding his own plain cross aloft; he understood more than I had credited. But poor Aunt Janet had swooned again, her fat legs in their decent woolen stockings all sprawled, showing her under-kirtle and more besides, a line of blue-white flesh, pitiful, at her thigh. Her poor sheep's face wore a look of fright still, though she was still as still, and in her slack hands was twined her string of Popish beads, giving all away. 'I am converting her,' I said. 'She is old, but she will learn ... and she is poor——' I added quickly. 'A poor widow lady, living on charity, that cannot pay her poll-tax ... she hopes to get it from the lady-queen, for a charity—if so be I can get her there....'

The burly man came back to stand beside me. 'Jack Strawe believes you, lady ... Jack Strawe goes by his heart....' And he hit himself in the chest hard, with a stern look round. 'Make way,' he cried. 'Make way for Jack Strawe and the Lollard-lady!'

He who was branded from Newgate ran up, grabbing Jack by the arm and holding on. 'What of them coffers in the cart? Commons have pickings there, for sure....'

'Commons be not thieves either,' said Jack Strawe, drawing himself up; lordly, he looked too in his rags, for a wonder, with a look of pride on his homely red face. 'Commons come only for their own. Commons want charters only. We be not thieves!'

And all that tattered smelly mob cheered then, stamping their feet. 'Not thieves! Not thieves!' they chanted. 'Rights only! Rights for the commons! The commons and King Richard!'

'Make way!' shouted Jack Strawe. 'The Lollard-lady goes to the king and his mother! She'll put in a word for commons! Let us pass!'

And the mob fell back, cheering me now; so touch-and-go is

their temper. I let out a breath, shaky, and guided my horse forward. Jack Strawe turned at the gate, under the dreadful heads that grinned above, and raised his hand, fisted. 'John Ball hath rung his bell!'

And the crowd answered, with one voice, 'John Ball hath rung his bell!' And then, as we passed through Aldgate, I heard, behind, a reedy boy's voice raised, 'When Adam delved and Eve span ... who was then the gentleman?' And all joined in that song, behind, as we rode over the cobbles into London-town.

TWO

We were silent, all, as we went upriver, the sights of the London streets still graven deep upon our eyes; Branwen, even, did not sob, and Aunt Janet, up from her swoon, looked half-crazed, her beads slipping through her fingers, and her fear-dry lips mouthing her prayers; I hoped she could not be seen from the shore.

Jack Strawe, good as his word, had led us through the wreckage and right down to the Thames, and had commandeered a barge; a rotten thing it was, and we stood in water up to our ankles, but it did not sink, and for sure we were lucky to have anything at all. The rebel army had taken all the boats, even the pleasure barges were filled with ragged savages, men and women, sprawling drunken among the velvet cushions, or coupling shamelessly in the sight of all. For I saw now that it *was* an army, truly; there were thousands upon thousands in the streets and more across the river and at Mile End. None other but rebels were to be seen, except for the poor hacked and headless dead, and some starveling children that clustered round the corpses, curious; I had seen one, a little girl, snatch a buckled shoe from a lifeless foot and run, dodging Jack Strawe's men, into an alley. I wondered why she wanted it; it was too large, and only one, no use to her. Perhaps it was the gilt glitter of the buckle.

We had seen, too, the beautiful Savoy Palace, a smoking ruin; after we passed, a whole wall crumbled and fell into the street, just where we had ridden a moment before; it sent up a cloud of choking dust that clung to our clothes and our hair and clogged our nostrils. When I looked back, I saw that only a marble fireplace still stood, its mantel sheared off, all that was left of that splendid house. The Templars' Inn was razed, too, and nothing left at all; those knights had always been remembered with hatred for their cruelty and greed.

Many of the other Inns of Court were burned and gutted; in front of one, a huge bonfire flamed high, and folk leaped and shouted. I trembled to think what it might be, for I could not tell, but Jack Strawe raised his fist and cried, 'The filthy tax-lists—devil take them!' So I knew it was just paper, after all.

I cannot tell the sights even, like nightmare it was and in the white light of day obscene; rubble and charred wood and pieces of bodies all mixed together. They had slaughtered all the foreign persons they could find, dragging them out of their houses where they hid and beheading the men on the spot. They did not seem to have harmed the women or the children, for we saw none dead, only wretched mourners huddled in front of their burned-out hovels. The rebels, you see, both country peasants and the city-bred, hated foreign folk; they blamed them for their loss of trade, especially the Flemish weavers, who worked for a pittance and undercut the English workers, and the Lombard merchants, that prospered in the wine trade. At one street-turning, we saw a great heap of bodies, headless, their clothes mostly stripped from them, and, picking over them like so many crows, their women, all in dusty black, sorting out their poor dead. Two little boys, not long out of the nursery by the looks of them, dragged a mutilated body from the pile, each tugging at a leg; the mother bore the head, a round lump with blood oozing through, in her wrapped skirt front. She turned to look at us as we passed; a black hood covered all except her face, bloodless as dark ivory, with great burning black eyes. She cursed us, all, taking us for rebels; it was in the Lombard tongue, like Latin, but softer, so I understood, my blood running cold in my veins.

The Street of the Jews was gone, nothing left but some

blackened wood, and no bodies even; perhaps they had got away. I knew the place from the broken words scrawled on the bits of wood, scurrilous words and hateful, damning those poor folk who had lived there. I remembered that only the better sort could write, students and some merchants maybe, and wondered how they could have been so low, seeing they were not ignorant. Jack Strawe, too, and all his men, cursed and spat at those ruins; I forbore, from cowardice, to say that our Saviour had been one of those they cursed.

Students-of-law, too, we saw dead in the street, still in their black gowns, for none coveted that wear. There were no nobles dead; for sure they were barricaded, all, somewhere out of sight. I saw a few corpses, though, in the parti-color of the serjeants-at-law, and two in the judges' red; my heart knocked wildly then, against my ribs, for I feared each moment to come upon my father, dead in the street. But the destruction thinned out as we came Thames-side; only drunken peasants, men and women, lay in the waterfront lanes. All the wine-shops had been looted, of course, and the food-stalls as well, and the wretched poor folk, so long deprived, had gorged themselves, abusing their shrunken stomachs. Pools of vomit were everywhere, and worse besides; I was glad my horse, not I, had to walk in it.

As we neared Tower Wharf, I saw that none manned the gates; there had been a mort of smart-liveried squires, and soldiers, too, when last I had seen it. There were rough-clad peasants all about, armed with picks and axes; a woman, even, I saw, laughing among them, her skirt girdled up to show her legs, and a kitchen-knife, rusty, thrust through her belt. Jack Strawe came close, whispering, 'The password, Lady——' he said. 'Tell them—"John Ball hath rung his bell."'

For he did not disembark with us, but kept the barge with his men; I guessed he thought it too good a thing to lose. So I went first, and holding my head up well, though I was scared as a rabbit, and spoke the words in a voice that never shook; truly it is hard to fathom where these reserves of courage come from. Not from God, surely, for I had not thought once to pray.

They let us through, but surly they were, and the woman spat after us; when we were well inside the gate, Aunt Janet swooned again, and Crazy Gib had to carry her. He was a strong lad, for all his lack of wit; he had to be, as I have said. Below the Tower there was a knot of soldiers, wearing the king's white hart badge, and more inside the hall, but I thought they, all, wore the same sullen, waiting look of the peasants outside.

I had been used to seeing smart, neat looks and straight backs when last I had been inside this same Tower courtyard, and in all the palaces of the English king; here, though, was nothing in order, and none looked our way or bespoke us even. Like an ill-run Border manor it was, and set my back up; one must be high-nosed with them, it is the same at home. I straightened my back in the saddle and called for one to dismount me, snapping my fingers as I had seen my brothers do. One, lounging against a wall, looked at me, lazy, picking his teeth with a straw but not budging. I drew my horse closer to him and drew my brows together too, for I was angered. I scowled down at him, and he laughed, spitting out the straw. 'Snap me no snaps, wench, nor no scowls neither—I am not your man ... though you might be worth a shilling if the night was dark enough....' My jaw dropped; I had forgot how plain I went, in my gown stripped of its sleeves and my tumbled hair, with my ankles muddied from the barge-bilge. It was soldier-talk and ugly; I reminded myself how the maidens of Christ's poor must put up with it every day, and held my tongue, turning from him.

To another I said, milder, but in a cold voice still, 'Will you dismount me, sirrah? ... I am the Lady Margaret Hanmer of Flintshire, to wait upon the queen-mother ... I am expected.'

He came running then, an armor-bearer by the looks of him, younger than I, with no spurs yet and a face as freckled as a thrush egg; he pulled off his cap and looked up at me, round-eyed as he took me in. I said to him sharply, 'There is trouble in the streets ... had you not heard! Do you think I came here on a cloud, escorted by angels?'

'Indeed, Lady,' he said, 'I did not mean to stare ... It is just that I wonder how you came here at all. They say London is rebel-held, and all is flames and murder...'

'It is a long story,' I said, 'and I mean to tell it once only——
Will you help me down from this beast? For there are insolent
eyes watching and I cannot manage my skirts....' I had
thought nothing of letting them fly above my head earlier,
when I jumped down to get into the barge, driven by haste
and terror, but here in the Tower yard I must act the noblewoman, even if I did not look it. Besides, my knees were something weak.

He blushed then, all over his freckles, the poor youth, for his
lack of manners, and at the thought of the leg-show too, I
guess.

He helped me down then, and very neatly we did it between
us, my skirts all gathered seemly, and no more than an ankle
showing either, as I flung my leg across the saddle and slipped
down, holding onto his arm. 'Someday,' I said, for I am used to
my brothers and always speak my mind to boys, 'I will invent
some better dress for riding astride—a skirt for each leg, may
be....'

He looked at me as if my wits had left, that I should think of
such things at this dire moment, and I laughed a little, shakily.
'I have come through Hades, sure—but it is behind me now.
Will you take me to the Lady Joan, sir? I did not catch your
name....'

He had not given it, and he blushed redder than ever, feeling like a churl, as I had meant him to. I was angry with all
males that moment for what the soldier had said to me.

'I am called Robin, Lady ... Robin Bevan.' And he dropped
to one knee.

'Oh, get up, you silly,' I said. 'There are worse things than
lack of manners today....'

Coming close and whispering, he said, 'I will report the soldier, Lady. I am a squire, and they will listen.'

'Who is "they"?'

'Well, the king ... if he—*when* he comes back——'

'Comes back? Where is he then—the king?'

'Sh-h-h, Lady. Come inside ... follow me.' But before he
turned to lead the way, I did not miss the leap of fear in his
eyes or his hand that fingered the little silver cross at his throat.

I followed him through a small side door and a dark passage

smelling of damp; we came into the great hall. More men-at-arms idled there, a group playing at dice even; they stared at us incuriously and went back to their game. They were too few for a king's service and I looked at Robin, questions in my eyes.

'Sh-h-h, Lady.' He led me to a small room off that was used to store arms; I saw a stack of bows in a corner, and some lances without tips. 'They are not with us—those soldiers,' he whispered. 'Many, even, have gone over to the rebels, taking their arms....' His voice dropped lower, and broke in the middle, the way boys' voices sound when they are growing. Any other time I would have laughed. 'We are prisoners here —all....'

'But where is everybody?' I asked. 'Where is the king?'

'He has gone out to meet with the rebels.... They have sent him—his uncles....'

Dear God, I thought, and he is a boy only. Do they mean to sacrifice him then? I said nothing and waited only.

Robin swallowed; I could tell his throat was dry, and fear still stood behind his eyes. 'That is what they wanted—the rebels. Wat Tyler—he is the leader—or one of them, there are a few leaders, or so they say ... they will treat with none but the king himself....'

'Was he frightened, do you think?' I whispered, fear creeping in me too now.

'Oh, Lady, you cannot doubt it.... Last night he stood long upon the battlements alone. When he came down his face was pale as curds. And this morning he could eat no breakfast. They say he took some ale only—and vomited it up.'

'When did he go?'

'Lady, I think it has been more than two hours now ... and the meeting was at Mile End only—not much more than a mile away....'

'He had an escort...?'

'Oh, yes—twenty maybe were with him. Sir Aubrey de Vere bore Richard's sword ... and some others rode out too—I have forgot.' His speckled round face was shiny with sweat, and his throat worked like a bird's. 'Lady—your father, Sir David—he rode out with the king...'

'My father ... then he is alive!' I began now to tremble in earnest—for relief, and quick upon its heels, the clutch of fear again.

'Oh, Robin,' I gasped, 'you have not seen what I have seen! So many heads—on walls—and carried like prizes on poles through the streets! And some wore miters and some the judges' hoods.... I have been so afraid....'

'No—no ...' he said, taking my hand, 'he is safe—your father ... or was——' Suddenly he dropped my hand, as if it burned him. 'Oh, Lady, forgive me. I had forgot my manners....'

'Don't be a lack-wit,' I said. 'This is no time for ceremony ... and you are no varlet either—you are as good as I am, if it comes to that! In Wales we are not so bound by pridefulness; I am "Lady" by accident only. And you may call me Margaret, for we are friends now....' I managed a smile, though a shaky one. 'For sure you have noble blood anyway—you have named yourself squire....'

'My father is Third Master of the Wardrobe,' he said, looking proud. 'He has the charge of King Richard's hose....'

I nearly smiled, even through my worry. We do not swink and swank in such wise at home; there we have servants to do such work and they are paid a proper wage. But I would not wound him, Robin, for he took comfort, like all the English, in such vanities. I said gravely, 'So you see, you are nobler than I. My father was but lately knighted for his law-service. We are rich only.' He looked shocked; of course the English nobles, especially the petty ones, think talk of money is beneath them. I could see, behind his mask of courtesy, the thought, 'Welsh upstart!'

'The Lady Joan ... his mother—can you not take me to her?'

'They are abovestairs—in her chamber. I will lead you—but they will not let me in, for they suspect everyone....'

'Nonsense,' I said, taking his hand firmly. 'You are with me....'

We mounted some stairs, winding, and came onto a small landing; a huge door stood there, shut tight. I scratched at it, as we do at home, but none answered. There was noise within, like animals scurrying. I knocked; still no one opened. 'Use

your dagger-hilt,' I said to Robin. 'Rap smartly, or they will
not hear.'

He did as I bade him, but like a woodpecker it sounded
only, and I snatched the dagger from him, pounding hard
upon the heavy door. The scurrying stopped; I could smell the
fear on the other side. Raising my voice, I cried, 'Let me in! I
am the Lady Margaret of Wales!'

My voice is loud when I wish, but it is a maiden's, after all,
and harmless. I heard the bolt as it slid back, rasping, and the
door opened a crack. Yellow eyes looked at me, cat-colored,
over a white beard. 'I cannot stand here all day!' I hissed. 'Let
me in! You can see I am not armed!' I still held the dagger,
upraised, and handed it quickly to the boy Robin. 'It was for
knocking only,' I said, little laugh bubbles popping in my
throat; I am always plagued by the comic side at odd moments,
sometimes in chapel even. I saw that yellow-eyes' lips curved
above his whiskers, too; I looked at him sharply as he opened
full the door and passed me in. In God's name, who was this
mountebank? The beard was stuck on only, for the glue was
not yet dry; he wore a kind of wadmal robe, long to the floor,
like a begging friar. I wondered if he went on stilts under; he
was the tallest person I had yet seen, outside of myself.

'I am Owen ap Griffith, Lady——' Welsh! What was he doing here, in the queen's chamber? His arm in the flowing robe
gestured to the right. 'She is there, yonder—the lady queen.
Forgive me that I do not take you to her ... there is haste ...'
His look went to Robin, drawn in small behind me, and it was
a prince's look; Robin stepped forward, almost bowing. 'The
queen is there,' said yellow-eyes. 'And now, you must excuse,
Lady——' He turned to a small table where some odd objects
were laid out; I had a glimpse of a paint-pot, and stared still,
not moving. I saw with horror that the tall one took up a razor,
its long blade catching the light wickedly; he advanced to a
boy who stood waiting, and, taking his chin in one hand, with
the other began to shave the hair from the boy's head. It was
raw-red as carrots, the hair, and the scalp blue-white where it
showed from the first shaving. The face under was full of fury
and getting red with it, redder than the hair. I thought I heard
him curse, that boy, and the Welshman laugh; it was all most

odd, for sure, but I had no time to puzzle it out, for I must go to the lady-queen. She had seen me by now; her bright-gold hair showed above her ladies' heads where they stood in a little circling knot around her bed.

Like a clutch of geese they were, gabbling, but they fell quiet as I came near; I knew they stared at my disarray. I curtseyed low to the Lady Joan as I had been taught. 'I am Margaret Hanmer, Lady.... You sent for me, true, but I am come at a bad time. I wish I could go elsewhere, but——'

She stared, too, the Lady Joan, her eyes round as marbles and bluer than her satin bedgown; I saw that once she might have taken your breath away. Fair Maid of Kent they had called her, and some did still, though her cheeks were like dough that is rising, floured, and she looked to burst from her clothes any minute. Painted she was, thick, and red and white, with no eyebrows at all, but her mouth was like a rosebud still, and her smile showed perfect teeth and a sunny nature. She won me from the start, for she held out her hand, dimpled and glittering with rings, and bade me rise. She pulled me to her and kissed my cheek; close to she smelled of violets, and I saw that tears had made little runnels through the powder; I knew her sick with fearing for her son, poor lady, but still she spoke to me, and warm and kind. 'You have grown into a beauty, child—what eyes! Like smoke they are, so dark against that hair. Never let them pluck your brows either, it is an original look ... charming....' And she tilted her head to one side, studying, for all the world as though she had nothing on her mind to but appraise my points; it is the measure of her charm, for so, I have found, she is to all.

But then I saw her take in my sorry state, my gown all dark at the armpits where I had sweated in the heat and in my terror, my dirty feet, and my hair that was like a nesting-place for mice. 'What have they done to you, little Margaret ... what have they done, those dreadful creatures?'

'Oh, madame——' I said. 'I am unhurt ... though I have seen sights——' I wet my lips; they were cracked and I could taste the dust on them, a burnt taste, nasty. 'Is there water, madame? I am very thirsty....'

'You shall have wine,' she said, and signing for one of her

ladies to fetch it. I gulped it down, choking; it was strong and tepid, and I would rather have had water.

'Lady,' I said, when I had drunk, 'there was one Jack Strawe that befriended me ... very kind he was and brought me here by barge....'

'Jack Strawe!' she cried, putting her hand to her throat. 'He is one of the worst ruffians.... They say he has butchered half London!'

'Well, Lady——' I said, stubborn. 'To me he was kind, and let none harm me—nor would he let the mob have Branwen either or—— Oh, sweet Saviour,' I cried suddenly. 'Aunt Janet and the rest! I have left them behind me in the courtyard! Oh, Christ forgive me ...!' And I made to dash for the door. The Lady Joan cried out, stopping me. 'Someone will fetch them—stay here where it is safe! How many are they—those folk you brought with you?'

'My mother's cousin, Aunt Janet, Branwen, and Crazy Gib— just three,' I said. 'The pages fled at the first sign of trouble....'

They were found, unmolested, in the courtyard, but not before they had been robbed of the two riding-horses, the other horse, and the wagon with its full coffers. Now was I shamed indeed; I, who had thought myself too full-grown to need a nurse! Nurse would never have let a robber near, unless she lay dead upon the flagstones; she is little, but loud. Worse still, I had left my poor charges to fend for themselves; I was not fit to be called a noblewoman, much less a Christian! And now here we were, with no more than the clothes we stood up in, and sorry indeed they were by now. With rosy Branwen pale and whimpering, Aunt Janet with not many more wits about her than Gib, and Dada facing the rebels with the little king, I could hope for nothing but that the stone floor would swallow me in my misery. But of course it did not, nor ever will. We must always stand and face what comes, God help us.

And I was in no worse case than any in that room, for sure. We were all in the lap of Jesus, as the good Morris Stove said always. But I admit I did not think of him then, Morris Stove, or Jesus either. I thought only of myself, and Dada, and the king.

THREE

Poor Lady Joan! I had only Dada to worry about as the hour wore on and the royal party did not return; besides the little king, her other sons, too, were in that retinue facing the rebels. She had been married before, and these two were her first-born of that marriage, Thomas Holland, Earl of Kent, and John Holland, Marshall of England. To be sure, they were grown men and had fought in wars besides, but the rebel army now numbered more than one hundred thousand, or so it was said, and the king's people some twenty only; they were at the mercy of a mob, which, like a cat, may jump any which way.

Even in her distracted and pitiful state, the queen-mother gave orders that a change of clothes should be found for me, and water to wash with and combs and veilings for my hair; I looked in short time almost presentable. Branwen, too, got some of her color back and left off trembling, for I bade her tire my tangled hair, and with something to do, she was almost her old self again. Aunt Janet was put to bed on a pallet in the little alcove behind the queen's bed; there was a small altar there for private prayers. I knew the queen was sympathetic to the New Learning, but in older people you will always find it so; habits are ingrained, and they *will* tell their beads, though it is forbidden. At any rate, there was a hanging covering the place, so poor Aunt Janet was out of our sight; a good thing, for just to look at her in her witless terror could infect us all. We were bad enough as it was, for one of the queen's ladies, an Irish noblewoman, kept on humming low an air from her country; we have one at home much like it and I knew it for a death-dirge. Each time the Lady Joan shushed her, she would leave off for a bit, wringing her hands, and then begin all over again. The other ladies, the English ones, were all tight-lipped and looked angry, but I saw it was masks they wore only, to cover their secret fears.

As we sat waiting in our unease, there rose a little clamor in a corner; we had been all in a hush, as underwater creatures or folk in a dream. I heard a voice, like my brothers' at play-war,

but shriller, and a crash of something metal on the stone floor.
'I will not! I will not hide—I will stay and fight....' And
under was a choking sob, childish. It was the shaven-headed
boy, beating helpless fists at the tall Welshman. That man put
the fists away from him, easily, like removing a scratching cat
from his clothes, and came to the queen-mother.

'Lady,' he said, standing before her, 'give me leave to drug
him—he will not play his part....'

The lady-queen rose, all motherly and anxious, and went to
the boy, drawing him close. 'Henry,' she scolded, low, 'you
must go now.... Be a man, Henry. You are near fifteen....'

'I am a man!' he shouted, more child then ever. 'I am
stronger than Richard. I can carry a man's lance.... Why
could I not go to put down the rebels? I can do it better!'

'Henry,' she said. 'Have sense. They will kill you on sight.
You are your father's son ... Richard is king. They will listen
to him ... if God is good....' And the poor lady sketched a
cross-sign in the air.

'I am more king than he!'

'You are not.' And she spoke firm. 'You are Duke John's son,
that they seek to kill. They have burned his palace and killed
all his serving-people. Doubt you that they will spare his heir?
Have sense!'

So this was Henry of Lancaster, the Duke John of Gaunt's
son, he they hated most of all for his wealth and power! The
boy was a fool, as well as unpleasant.

'Henry,' said the Lady Joan, shaking him a little, 'you will
go with Owen the Welshman. He will take you to Hereford—
to your stepmother and your sisters, where you will be safe.
You will ride before him and wear the invalid's smock, and
you will feign weakness and the plague....'

'The pox, Lady,' said the Welshman. 'It is easier—and just
as feared.'

'I will not!' screamed the boy. 'I will not—he is not even a
knight!'

'He can buy and sell you and your father, too, and his face is
not known to the angry people. You will go with him—and be
grateful—and not put us all in peril.' She spoke quietly, but to
command, and even that angry boy listened, the runnels of

tears drying on his red cheeks. 'Else we will open your jaws and force down poppy-juice. It is bitter, Henry, and will make you sick later.... Will you go ...?'

'I will go, madame,' he said, his eyes lowered. 'But,' he whispered, 'he should not have shaved my head....'

'They would have known you by your red hair, Henry, and it will grow. It is a poor price to pay for your life, after all....'

The Welshman with the yellow eyes came close, bearing a little pot and a brush. 'Hold still, Lord Henry. We must paint on the pock-marks....' And, like an ungainly tiring-woman, peering in concentration, he carefully dotted the sullen boy-face. He stepped back to survey his work, then dabbed his fore-finger in another color, and smeared the whole round his eyes, a dark-blue shadow; for all the world like a poor fever-patient he looked then, that Henry, in his ugly unbleached smock, bald as a gosling and the red spots looking angry and horrid.

The Welshman, Owen, set down the pot and, hitching up his long monk's gown, wiped his fingers, sticky with the paint, on his hose beneath. 'Madame,' he said to the queen, and smil-ing, 'take heart, all will be well ... the commons love your Dickon, as do we all. He will come back safe—and with his honor, too—I promise it—and I am descended from old Mer-lin, remember?' The queen smiled back, for a wonder, through her worry; I saw it was an old joke between them. He bent his cat eyes on me then and said, 'I am the court fool, Lady Mar-garet, though I am something tall for it....'

The queen took his hand and said quickly, 'Never say it—you are our savior. He saved your father's life but yesterday, child, with his mummery!'

I was all at sea but said, and my heart in it, 'I am grateful, sir——'

'It was a little thing, and we two bawds together, acting out parts——' My father! When I looked close, I saw he was young, above the white beard; the lines of age, too, were painted on, like the pock-marks I had witnessed in the making. 'But now—we must be off with this wild cockerel,' he said, wry, and gazing down at the sorry sight of the heir of great Lan-caster. 'Lord Henry, you must go limp in my arms and speak not at all ... and groan a little from time to time....' The pale eyes flashed once at him, like lights behind a skull-lantern, and I saw the fists were clenched, but Henry said nothing and let himself be gathered up in the Welshman's arms. Fury burned in him, though, you could almost feel its heat: I would not like to be on the wrong side of that red fellow's temper! I wished him a safe haven, though, for all that I did not like him; I did not want my father's benefactor to suffer for this little churl.

'God keep you, sire,' I whispered to that Owen, and he smiling small.

'My wits will keep me, Lady, and our Welsh magic,' he answered, his face going grave. 'There is no God abroad this day.'

His words shocked me, but they made a sort of sense, after the sights I had seen; I put the thought aside, to ponder on another time. I stared at him blankly. 'Your beard has come unstuck,' I said; it sounded stupid, but was all I could think of.

He laughed then and said, 'If you will wet your finger and put it to my chin, and press the beard for a moment ... I am encumbered with this heavy royal load....' I licked my finger, for there was no water near, and did it, and the beard stuck; one could have sworn he was a begging friar. 'Thanks for the kiss, Lady,' he whispered. 'I will not wash for a fortnight.'

I turned bright red then, cursing myself for it, but I could not help smiling. It was a long moment; I heard the queen-mother say, 'Go quick now, sweet Owen....'

At the door he turned and said, 'I leave you Master Nathan, for guard. Watch well, my Nathan ...' and they were gone through the doorway.

I saw then the man he meant; indeed he was the only one in the chamber, except for Crazy Gib. It was he who had fetched up Aunt Janet and the rest, I remembered now. He was of goodly bearing, slight but strong, in his middle years, dark-bearded, and with a foreign look. Though that may have come from the turban he wore, Saracen-wise, with a great jewel set in at his forehead. His eyes were larger than English eyes, or Welsh either, for that matter; there was wisdom in them and live brightness, with an old sadness under. I thought on his name, out of a Bible tale—was he then a Jew? I had never seen one; I turned away my eyes lest he should think I stared.

'Are there no guards then at all, madame?' I spoke to the queen-mother and she answered, low, 'Not here—but below in the courtyard are some few left ... if they have not joined the rebels....' Her voice trailed off, and I felt her tremble where her arm pressed mine.

'There is Robin—that led me here to you—and for sure there are others, too, madame, that are loyal still....' I spoke to soothe her, for she was our lodestar, but even I did not believe my own words.

'I fear most for the archbishop. It is his head they have demanded first of all, along with the Treasurer, Hales, and Duke John—but he is safe in Scotland, John, God be praised....'

'And where are those others, madame ... have they escaped?'

'We thought to smuggle them out—in those same monks' clothes that Lord Owen wore—but they were recognized and brought back, though none harmed them. There is nowhere to hide, if——' She swallowed, and I saw a small pulse beating in her throat; I pressed her hand, hard. She went on. 'My Lord Archbishop Sudbury is in the chapel, saying mass—the others with him.... He is praying for all our souls, if——'

'Madame,' I said, 'there are weapons here ... I for one can wield a sword—or an ax, even, if it is not too heavy....' And I pointed to the ancient swords crossed, ornament-wise, upon the wall, and the old battle-axes from Crusader days.

She smiled a little and looked her unbelief. 'I have been raised with boys only,' I said, 'and no girl-folk round to play at dolls. They—my brothers—have taught me long ago to handle swords ... and I am not bad at it either. At least my arm is long, and I am tall to chop down-wise....'

She shuddered, making a little face, but said only, 'Let us pray there will be no need. For I fear those old knives are blunter than churn-paddles by now. They are for show only.'

For want of something to do and to look brave amid all that unspoken fear, I went to the far wall and, reaching up, took down a long sword with a jeweled hilt. Its partner came with it, for they were insecurely fastened, clattering like an alarum bell on the stones and sending up a cloud of dust. The one I held was weighty, near breaking my arm, but with two hands I could lift it.

The ladies were all twittering like magpies now, to see a maid behave so; at least I had taken them out of their benumbed state. I turned to face them. 'Come, let us all lift them down ... we are not made of wax, we women, and dull as they are, they are better than plowshares and shovels—which is most of what the rebel army carries....'

One flew to get a cloth for the dust, and the others pulled stools over and reached down those tarnished blades. It was a comic sight, all those fine-dressed women in their billowing skirts and wimples slashing down and thrusting, giggling like girls; I hoped for grace to tell the silly story later.

The boy Robin made to show those ladies how to parry and trust, pointing out that these old swords were double-edged; he must have learned just weeks before; he had all the knowledge there, in the front of his mind. We were almost gay; the queen-mother, even, waving a great rusty blade to saw the air.

Presently that Nathan came forward, shy, showing us the curved knife he wore at his belt. 'It is of Eastern work,' he said, 'and will cut through wood as though it were butter....' And then he said, smiling faintly, his teeth showing white against his sun-dark skin, 'And I have my lancets, too....' He was a doctor then; I had not been wrong to see his wisdom in his eyes.

We sank down soon, on cushions or chairs, breathless and warm from our unwonted exercise, and a little cheered as well. Action is always better, be it ever so foolish. The Irish lady left off her humming and brewed a tisane; it was black and bitter, made from a root they grow there in her land, and hardly fit to drink. Hot it was, though, and welcome; fear makes dry mouths.

It was getting on for noon, and still no word from the king's party; I switched aside the hangings from the eastern window, but there was nothing to be seen along the road, not even a dust cloud. There was nothing for it but to wait. The cups and dishes were all in a mess, and none came from the kitchen to clear away, though we rang the kitchen gong. I had the feeling, cold within, that there was no one there belowstairs, save for those few in the chapel, and the surly soldiers in the courtyard.

I could feel the flush creeping up my neck, and the breath short in my chest, for so does it always when I am in dread and idle to think on it. I said, 'Lady, let me go down with these cups and the beaker—Robin will come too, surely. We will be quiet ... none will hear....' She looked something startled, for such is not a lady's task, but nodded. Perhaps she knew that soon I would pace the floor and wring my hands, else.

'Branwen,' I said, 'gather up these things. Between us we can manage.'

'Oh, Lady, no!' she cried. 'I cannot. I am too afeared ... I do not know this place....'

'You will come—or I will send you from me ... out of the walls!' And coming close, I whispered, fierce, 'You are Welsh— had you forgot? You are no craven like these dithering English. Besides, I need you by me.' And I laid my cheek against hers, briefly. She looked shamed then, and wiped away her tears.

The stairs in that tower-place were winding, all, and steep. It was all we could do to bear the trays and watch our footing, Robin going before. I wondered how the poor serving-folk managed it every day. Finally we reach the bottom, seeing no one. 'This way,' said Robin, and we followed, close to the wall, and coming out into a long passage.

The great kitchens were empty, and echoed our footfalls. The fires were cold, no spits turning, though a huge kettle hung above the hearth, full, and still warm. I smelled a faint smell of herbs and onions; my mouth watered, and I realized I was hungry. 'Robin,' I said, 'there is food about somewhere ... even a little bread. Where is the larder?'

We found a store of cheeses and honey, though the meat hung raw from the hooks. I broke off a bit of honeycomb; it tasted like food from heaven. We began piling baskets with the produce, all we could find, to take to that upper chamber with us, when there came a loud clashing outside the castle; steel rang on stone, and a thumping sound, and voices like angry growling.

'Oh, Lady, let us fly!' cried Branwen. For once I did not chide her, and Robin said nothing either. We stopped our pillaging and hurried back down the long hall to the stairs.

We had barely gone four turnings when we heard the doors below burst open and feet upon the flags of the hall floor. 'For Jesus' sake, hurry!' Robin's voice had a sob in it. 'They are coming for the archbishop....'

Already there were sounds upon the lower stairs. 'In here—quick!' And Robin pulled us into a small chamber and shut the door. There was no bolt upon it; this must be the room where the churchmen changed their vestments and prepared for the mass. Under the sounds of running feet, below the muffled shouting, we could hear a chanting, ghostlike. God save us, would they drag the poor fellow from the altar? My fingers tightened; I realized I was still clutching my basket of food. I set it down upon the floor and wiped my hands on my dress front, for they were sweating.

The noises were close now; there must be many ruffians upon the stairs. I heard Branwen hiccough beside me, and gripped her arm for silence. We were next door to the chapel itself, for sure; we heard the heavy doors burst open, and the chanting, suddenly louder, broke off. There was another door, small, beside the one we had entered by. I crept over to it and tried it; it gave and I opened it just a crack. I could see the priest in his robes, backed up now against the altar, his arms stretched out in the shape of a cross, and another man, kneeling. I had just a glimpse of that man's face, terrified, and then they were upon him. The little altarboy dropped the pyx and ran to hide behind the archbishop.

It was a wordless mob, like beasts they were, and perhaps not so very many; I was confused and could not tell. I saw them drag the churchman from the altar, though; rough peasants they were, in rags, and not soldiers, so I knew the Tower was being stormed by the rebels. The archbishop's miter fell off; under his tonsure his hair showed thin and white, and his face pitiful, gray and wrinkled as a nut. I remembered he was an old man. He was their oppressor and I knew it, yet could I not bear to see him stripped of his dignity and treated so. He might have been any ancient grandfather.

The altarboy still clutched his master's robe as they dragged him across the stone floor. At the door he reached out and grabbed the carved pillar, holding on. One of the men pulled him loose and flung him hard into a corner, where he lay still, like a crumpled doll; his head must have struck the stone wall.

None came into that little room where we watched. The whole beast-mob followed after its victims. We heard them all the way down those stairs, feet like hooves and a thudding, too, as though they dragged a corpse already; I prayed in my heart that it was so.

We heard them leave and the silence after, the dying away of the shouting; they were outside the castle. We listened a moment to make sure, then started for the stairs again. 'Wait,' I whispered, 'the acolyte....'

We ran inside the chapel. All the prayer-benches were over-turned, the gold altar-things smashed upon the floor, and glass from the windows scattered about, like bits of rainbows where we trod. Only the Christ-figure still hung upon the wall, its painted agony garish beneath the thorn-crown, the wound in its breast gaping to show the bleeding heart.

Beneath lay the little altarboy, still as stone. He could not have been more than nine years of age. His eyes stared upward, blue, and the blue veins showed delicate at his temple. There was not a bruise or a drop of blood on him, but he was dead. I closed the staring eyes with my hand, gently, as I had seen the death-women do at home, and we left him there, under the image he had served.

FOUR

They beheaded the old Archbishop Sudbury, the Treasurer, Hales, and John Legge, a sergeant-at-arms, that day upon Tower Hill; along with them, too, a poor friar. We watched from the upper window of the queen's chamber as they were led, stumbling, to their deaths. My heart turned over when I saw that friar, for he was tall and straight. When his cowl fell back, though, his hair showed black below the tonsure; I knew then that the golden Welshman had got away, and gave thanks, silently. The Lady Joan said even she did not know the name of the luckless friar, save that he was an adherent of the hated Duke John.

We could not see the actual executions, for the Hill was too far distant, but four times we heard the wordless shouting, cheering each dread deed; upon our knees we prayed aloud to drown it out. Still at our prayers we heard the crashing of the gates below, and an uproar of voices and great clattering noises in the hall. We had barely time to get to our feet before the chamber door burst open and a ragged horde poured through, filling the room. All was confusion; grimy faces, wild, with eyes that rolled whitely in them, and an angry growling sound like animals preying. I saw Robin lunging with a sword and someone knocking it from his hand, his face all surprise; I held a heavy sword myself, not remembering how I had come by it, but swinging it hard at a grinning face and missing, falling backward against a wall. Master Nathan's scimitar bit through a neck, horrifyingly; the head fell over, hanging by a thread, and the blood pumped thick in an arc, spattering him before he went down under their cudgels.

The Lady Joan lay sprawled upon her bed, a little knot of rebels standing over her. I pushed through them, angry, clearing a path with my weapon. There was a face close to mine, a woman's, fat and sweating. She was the one I had seen earlier at the gate below. 'The white whore!' she shrieked. 'Jack Strawe's whore!' I struck her face full with my sword-hilt and saw the mark it left, sickened at myself, before she fell. Someone wrested the weapon from me, pinning both my arms from behind.

I could not move but watched, helpless. The hangings were pulled down, and all the furnishings toppled over; feathers fell like snow where the pillows had been slashed, and even the mattress had a great gash in it. I gasped to see the queen-mother; her bodice was torn open, right down to the waist, and the large globes of her breasts gleamed white against the purple bed covering. 'There's good milking here, our queen's a fair old cow even yet....' And one leaned over, cupping her breasts. 'Give us a kiss, sweeting——' I saw that she had fainted, poor lady, and did not hear, for a mercy; she was the most royal lady in the land!

Someone shouldered past, pulling away those about the queen and flinging them aside as if they were bundles of old clothes; I heard a voice I knew, an Essex voice. 'Shame!' it cried, loud. 'Commons be not filthy dogs! Commons be men!' And he wrapped the lady-queen about with a fallen hanging, covering her, and peering hard into her face. 'She be swooned only, poor lady ... and a good thing, for Jack Strawe'll kill that one that harms our little king's mum ... with his own hands, Jack Strawe'll kill him....'

'Master Strawe,' I said, from behind him. He whirled round and saw me. He had little pig eyes and a lumpy face, but like one of God's own angels he looked to me that moment. 'Why, 'tis the Lollard lady! Let her go! She be as fine as any of us ... she be on our side. Her'll put in a word for commons with the little king....'

They loosed me then, and I asked quickly, 'Where is he—the king?'

'He be signing charters ... commons have won all.... All that we asked he has granted....'

'Then why have you come here—to kill and to pillage?'

His face looked dark then, and I saw his frightening side. 'The king has granted us those traitors' heads—Sudbury, Hales, Legge. And the bad duke, too ... John of Gaunt shall suffer....'

I was aghast. That could not be! The Duke John was Richard's favorite uncle ... and those others, too—they were high court figures. Richard, poor little boy—he must have been playing for time, hoping they could get away. Well, they did not, I thought grimly—except for the duke.

It was all or nothing, and I would not be despised for a coward. I had the man's ear, and I would speak. 'Take your men away,' I said. 'Look what they have done to their king's property! They will pay for it! They have mishandled the queen-mother and frightened her sick! Her bed is all torn apart—what did they think to find there?'

'Commons want naught but their rights,' he said, stubborn. 'The duke's head we want—as we were promised....'

'It does not lie in the Lady Joan's bed,' I said with scorn.

'Nor among the feather pillows, or behind the wall-hangings! It is on his head—in Scotland!'

'We think he is here,' Jack Strawe said. 'And we will find him—and his redheaded brat as well....'

'He is not here either, Henry of Lancaster,' I said, hoping I spoke true and that Owen had got him well away.

'But search we will,' he said grimly.

'Master,' I said, and I pleaded, believing him kind, 'give us leave to go from here. We are all women, save for one boy, and my poor half-wit. Our doctor is fallen already.... You would not slaughter innocents?'

'Lollard-lady,' he said, 'there is that same barge outside the Water Gate, a-waiting ... if so be you can handle it amongst yourselves—for commons have no time for succoring royalty....'

I looked for young Robin, beckoning. Those who pinioned him let go, at a sign from their leader Strawe; he was a sorry sight, all torn and with blood upon him, but he said the blood was not his own, and but for a dazed look seemed still unhurt.

'They will let us go, Robin,' I whispered. 'But quickly, before they change heart ... Where?'

'The Wardrobe is closest—just downriver. And it is well fortified.'

'Well, hurry,' I said. 'Rouse all who are unharmed....'

While Jack Strawe held his men in check, we scurried about, taking what we could gather from under those hostile eyes, cloaks, and a jewel or two snatched up in haste; the Irish lady had her small spaniel under her arm, whimpering low.

'Robin,' I said, 'you must make shift to carry the Lady Joan. Gib is strong, he can help you....'

I ran to where the doctor, Master Nathan, still lay upon the floor. He was bruised about the face, and a great lump was swelling at his temple, but his eyes were quick and lively. 'Leave me,' he whispered. 'I cannot stand ... they have smashed my knee....'

'I will not,' I hissed. 'We need a doctor.... Branwen and I can support you between us. You must hop on the good leg, and so we will manage.'

And manage we did, under those scorning looks. None

helped us, but they let us go and did not hinder us, and somehow we got aboard, all. Robin and Gib, breathless from their royal burden, had to return for Aunt Janet, staggering, for she was heavier still, and in her swoon yet. When they laid her on the deck she woke and in her terror began to scream, over and over, senselessly, like a dog that howls at the moon.

Master Nathan, white from the pain of his leg and the strain of hobbling on it, spoke from the corner where he lay. 'You must slap her smartly across the face. It is the only way to break the shock....'

I did so, praying inwardly for forgiveness; she stopped suddenly and was still as a stone, so that I bent to feel if her heart still beat. Master Nathan's lips curved small and he said, 'She needs a drug, but for now it will do....'

The queen-mother was moaning soft, calling for her son. 'Dickon—oh, my Dickon....' Any other time my heart would have been wrung with pity, but now there was no time for it. None of all that company knew how to pole a barge, not even Robin. Truly, these English are of an exasperating ignorance!

I showed him the way to hold the long pole and where to find holds for it in the muddy shallows, keeping close in to shore; many and many a time I had poled for sport in our own streams at home. It was something harder now, of course, with all those souls aboard and the barge riding deep. Our arms ached mightily, even with Gib helping; indeed, I grew hoarse with giving orders, for the poor witless one oftener than not would pull the other way.

We made it, though, to where we were bound, for it was not far. And none too soon either, for the barge was sinking fast; we waded knee deep in the water as we struggled to shore, and after, when we looked back, there was nothing left of our craft to be seen. Only the long pole, discarded, floated in to the shore.

The Wardrobe was a small mansion in Carter Lane, close to St. Paul's. It had been built to house goods for export, by some king or other, long ago, and was very strong, like a fortress. It was used nowadays as a royal residence, but it was a small place, as I have said, and scantily furnished; there was one couch only, and not near enough chairs to go around. We counted ourselves lucky, though, for the rebels had not come near that part of town; there was not even a smell of smoke in the air.

Best of all, there was a kitchen, with a hearth and a spit and kettle, and two loyal cooks, looking shocked and running to serve us. I had never thought to eat eels, for they looked nasty things always, to my mind, but I ate them that day and with relish. There had been a great catch of them that morning, fresh out of the Thames; they squirmed darkly in a dozen tubs on the scullery floor. I turned away my eyes and swallowed the hot cooked morsels, and drank the eel soup too. It put some heart in me, for I had had nothing since daybreak and my breakfast beer.

Indeed, we all revived somewhat, with the food and the feeling of safety in that place. Master Nathan lay on some cushions and instructed those hale ones of us, so that we might succor the sick. Actually, the ladies were mostly just nerve-shattered, and a strong wine stopped their shaking, though the Lady Joan could not leave off her weeping, and Aunt Janet lay in a coma still.

Master Nathan himself was sore hurt, though; his knee was smashed to a jelly and impossible to look upon without retching. We bound it up, though, Branwen and I, smeared over with a smelly salve that he had ordered from the head cook. It would heal, he said, but not to walk straight, for the tendons were split and the knee would never again bend. 'I go with luck, though, Damsel Margaret,' he said, and his eyes deep pools. 'Most of my kind hop headless into eternity—after these last days. . . .'

'Are you then a Lombard, sire? Or——' I spoke shyly, for I did not know the proper word for his people.

'We are called Jews, but among ourselves we are Israelites.'

'I know,' I said eagerly. 'It is the same with us. They call us Welsh, the Saxon word for "foreigner" . . . but we are the oldest race of these islands. We are the Cymry.'

'You are a good damsel,' he said. 'And wise beyond your years, with much heart. . . . You do not fear us then—my people?'

I spoke low and only for his ears. 'I have been taught that our Saviour was of your people.'

'Ah, yes,' he said. 'Your Jesus. In our tongue he is called Yeshua and honored for a holy prophet....'

'But you do not believe he was the Son of God?'

He shrugged a little, smiling, and spread his hands. 'So are we all—all sons of God....' And, still smiling small, he turned aside his head and slept. The salve upon his knee must have had some drug-thing in it.

I still sat beside him for a moment, thinking on his words. It was a better creed than ours. But stern, and without mercy. For if we are, as he said, all His sons, then why do we hate and fear? Why do we kill? I sighed then, rousing myself, for I could not think it through. I was tired still, and knew myself, in that moment, young. Young and ignorant, though wrapped about in pride as I had always been.

FIVE

The dreadful day wore on; hard it was to believe the hour was not much past noon when the little king rode in, unharmed. I could have sworn we had been waiting a full week.

Though we watched for him on the water side, it was by the postern gate that he came, riding west from Aldgate. They looked to be in procession, he and his lords, for they moved full slow and surrounded on all sides by folk on foot. At first I feared the mob had taken them prisoners, but it was plain as they came close that it was a peaceful and even merry throng. They sang and clapped their hands, and when Richard dismounted, the whole great mob of them knelt; it looked to be hundreds of folk.

All of us there in that Royal Wardrobe were of a mind to kneel also, in thanks for his deliverance, but the queen-mother enjoined us to keep countenance before the commons and not betray our feelings.

I had not seen the king since his crowning, when he was no

more than a child; he had grown now into a fine-boned youth,
middling tall and with a face as glowing fair as an image on an
altarpiece. I did not dwell upon him, though; my eyes went
looking for Dada behind him. When I caught sight of him,
smaller and grayer than I remembered, I flew into his arms,
tears running like rain down my face. I had not known how
greatly I had feared.

He patted my shoulder in that awkward way men have with
weeping womenfolk, and I laughed to see him so, dashing away
the wet drops with the back of my hand. It had been only
months, but I had grown again. I was near a head taller than
my father. Even in my distracted state it crossed my mind that
if I did not stop soon I would be like a freak at a fair.

I heard the Lady Joan behind me, speaking fair words to my
father and taking both his hands. 'Sir David,' she said, 'your
daughter is as brave as she is beautiful. She has been our
touchstone——' Her voice broke, and she kissed me quickly; I
felt her lips tremble.

'Your son does not want for courage either, madame,' said
Dada quietly. 'Look at him now.'

We all turned then to see Richard, extending his slim hand
most royally for the nearest of his kneeling subjects to kiss. 'I
am your king,' he said. 'You shall have your charters—and all
that I have promised. Only be patient and wait for me—I shall
come soon. But now my lady mother wants comforting ... she
has been sorely tried this day.' A cheer went up for that golden
lad, and above their ragged persons the poor sad dirty faces of
the crowd shone as though they looked upon the sun.

Inside the walls, the Lady Joan took her son's head between
her hands, looking deep into his eyes. 'Oh, Dickon, Dickon—I
had thought that you were lost!'

'There is nothing to fear, Mother,' said Richard. His voice
was clear and high, and of a peculiar sweetness. He spoke too,
with great calm in a youth; only a little flush on the cheekbones betrayed his inner excitement. 'Mother, they love me ...
they worship me as their true king. They want their rights only
... and what they want has reason. Too long have the poor
suffered in our realm. I shall give them their charters, signed,
and they will go away in peace....'

I saw, behind him, two nobles in their middle years exchange glances, darkly, and one of them shook his head, a bare
movement but I caught it. How simple could this Richard be?
We were almost of an age, he and I, and I a country girl; yet
did I know the many factions at war within this kingdom of
his, and the greed upon greed that had fostered all this present
discord. Complex it was, for sure, too complex for me to
fathom. But a hint of it I could feel wherever I walked in this
England. Be sure these high-nosed nobles would give nothing
but for their own gain. Honor is an empty word among them, a
thing for tournaments and show. Of course I was my father's
daughter, and he the most learned lawyer in the land. Also was
I a woman, and wary of men's games by nature. Still did my
heart go out to Richard, that boy-knight shining with his own
bright faith.

Richard was full of fair words for the rebel leader, Wat
Tyler. This man had got his name, as so many of the English
do, from his occupation; he was a tiler of roofs by trade,
though some said he had once taken up arms and knew the use
of weaponry. None knew his beginnings; he had had the benefit of some schooling, certainly, for he spoke well and with
some eloquence. Most like he had been taught by a good parish
priest in his own county. My father also spoke him well,
though guardedly. He named him a man of goodly bearing, a
natural leader. 'But,' he said, privately, 'I do not trust the fellow. He is using the people's wrongs to further his own aims.
He means to be a power in the land, and to subvert the state.'

The king spent the afternoon with his clerks, signing the
charters they had drawn up, granting the people freedom from
the hated poll-tax and fair wages for labor given. Hundreds
were given out and hundreds of folk went home bearing them
with joy. Many of the insurgents remained, though, charters or
no. For while Richard signed and sealed, mobs murdered and
looted. It was said that there was not one street in London
where no dead bodies lay. The jails had been thrown open,
criminals took advantage of the anarchy to kidnap and demand ransom, debtors to murder creditors, and those with old
scores to settle them by dagger thrusts. We heard the hideous

cries and the tumult in the streets all day and all night, while
we cowered within our walls.

Not all of Richard's retinue had returned with him: his half-
brothers, the Hollands, had disappeared. When the queen-
mother asked for them, Richard said, almost gaily, 'Oh, they
ran away!'

'Dickon, they could not! They are seasoned warriors!'

'Well, Mother,' he answered sweetly, 'they are commoners,
after all!'

My father said he thought that, upon seeing the great multi-
tude at Mile End, they had ridden off for help. If so, they did
not bring it, then or at any time during the insurrection. It is a
mystery still; for sure those two were not captured or harmed
in any way, for they were often at court in later years.

I did not miss the mother's face, though, saddened by her
youngest son's royal words, before she turned away.

I marked the faces of those who had accompanied the king;
they had to my mind a crafty look, as though they had meant a
shrewdness that had not come off. Except for Dada, of course,
and the De Veres. Sir Sir Aubrey de Vere was the oldest man
among them, upwards of eighty, but with a bluff and open red
face that belied his years; his grandson, Robert de Vere, I eyed
with much interest, for he was the king's favorite friend. He
was about nineteen, I would think, and very handsome, in the
king's own fair-faced way. Fresh-cheeked he was, with fine
straight features and lips as red as a maiden's. Looking closer, I
saw with a little shock that they were painted! I had not seen
that fashion before, but then I had not been to court for near
five years.

'Where is Owen?' asked Richard, looking about him. 'I
thought to find him here——' His face changed then, a flickering look of fright upon it. 'They did not take him—with Sudbury and the rest?'

'No, sweeting,' said his mother quickly. 'He is safe away by
now, for sure, or we would have heard.... No, Owen tried to
lead the archbishop out, in poor-friar garb, but they were recognized and had to flee back inside the Tower.... They took
Sudbury and the others in the chapel there—at prayer. But
Owen was not with them....'

'Where is he then ...?'

'At Hereford, maybe, by now—with your cousin, Henry of Derby....'

She told the story quickly of the painting and the play-acting. Richard's face was alive with glee, and malice, too; when she came to the head-shaving he laughed aloud. 'Oh, Mother, if I could have seen Hank's face! I would almost have missed the rebel-meeting for that!' It *had* been comic, and I felt myself smiling; Richard, looking about him, saw my face and stayed a moment upon it, we two smiling together.

'Owen is so droll ... when he is not a Greek god from Olympus....' He looked at Robert de Vere, a sidelong look and something sly. 'Do you not think him beautiful, Rob?'

There was a little silence. 'He is too tall.'

'Ah ... but all is in proportion, I think.' The little silence between them held again; then Richard gave a little laugh and pointed a long finger at me. 'We must mate him with this damsel here ... they would make a new race of giants between them.'

I felt my face go red, but curtseyed low, as Nurse had taught me. Richard came toward me. 'You are new here. What is your name, Damsel Goddess?'

'I am Margaret Hanmer, sire.'

'Ah ... I like your father well ... I think I shall like you too. I like pretty people about me ...' he said, moving away. Then he turned back, coming closer and speaking low. 'Robbie does not. He is jealous. He wants me to admire none but him....'

'Oh, but, sire,' I said, quickly, 'he is much handsomer than the other one ... than Owen!'

'You think so?' he said, drawling the words. 'Then shall we marry you to Robert?'

'Oh, no, sire!' Then I spoke quick, all in confusion. 'I mean —well, I am not ready to marry yet.... I am barely fifteen!'

'I am fourteen only ... but I am to marry in the winter. Think you it is too young?' His eyes had a strange glint; I could not read them.

I answered, 'Not for a king—no.'

'It is an honest answer.' He studied my face for a moment. 'Are you clever as well as beautiful?'

I smiled. 'My brothers do not think me either.'

'What are they like?'

'They are—just boys, like any other.'

'Not like kings?'

'No, sire....' I smiled again. 'But then I have only seen one....'

He laughed and lifted his hand to raise me up. 'I could wish the Lady Anne to be just like you.'

I looked down at him. 'But not so tall, surely?'

'Oh, no,' he said gravely. 'For then I would refuse her, dowry and all.'

'Well, that is an honest answer, too,' I said. 'I hope, for her sake, she is a little dumpling.'

'And if she is, I will tell her a witch from Wales said it.'

'She will not have far to look then, for I am to be in her train.'

'God's nails!' he cried, in mock terror. 'Then I shall see you about often!'

'I am afraid so, sire—casting spells.'

'I doubt it not.' His face lit up. 'You are much like him—like Owen....' He looked on a sudden shy. 'I have never jested with a girl before....'

'Well,' I said, at a loss, 'perhaps they have been afraid of you, sire....'

'No,' he said. 'I have been afraid of them....'

I moved close and touched his hand; Nurse would have fallen dead at my presumption. And very low I said, 'Sire, I wish you may like her well, the Princess Anne....'

'I wish it too ... and thank you, Margaret of Wales. You have made me forget what waits me there—outside....'

I stared at him. 'Surely they will not send you again!'

He nodded. 'They send me to parley at Smithfield Market—tomorrow. It seems the rebels are not satisfied with the promises and the charters. They want more heads to roll ... rich men and lords. And we know they have sent a large force to the border to search for my uncle of Gaunt.'

'They will not find him,' I said quickly. 'He will be well inside Scotland.'

'I pray so,' said Richard. 'But I am guilty of those other

deaths—Sudbury and the rest.... I answered yes as everyone
told me to do. But I never doubted they would get away while
we held the rebels in talk.'

'None blames you, sire,' I said. 'There was no choice left to
you.'

'Still must I do penance all my days.... They were my subjects, too.'

There was a look upon him that should not be upon a boy; I
saw how he would look, Richard, when he was old.

We were a small force there in the Wardrobe, though some
lords and burgesses had joined us, including the mayor of
London, Master Walworth. All were much alarmed at the
murders in the city; they had thought the rebels would be
satisfied with the executions of the hated archbishop and other
scapegoats. But no, it looked as if things might worsen; reports
had it that Wat Tyler, Jack Strawe, and the preacher John
Ball were still in the town, and that thirty thousand of the
rebel army yet remained. These did not even ask for charters,
but plotted to overthrow the government entirely.

I had lost track of time, but there was a scribe who recorded
that it was Friday, the fourteenth of June. The night came;
none slept more than fitfully, though it was black dark, for we
were afraid to light candles, fearful of attracting the attention
of the roving bands that roamed the streets.

The next morning, Saturday, brought no change, and no
news came. There was constant discussion among the men; all
knew now that they must fight or be massacred. But all the
city's nobles and merchants, the rebels' targets, were scattered
in other places like this one, shuttered and locked in. How
could they get together, where could they muster, who should
lead them, how strike back, when the insurgents were everywhere? There was no answer.

Still there came to the Wardrobe gates those gentler peasants
begging for charters; the king and his clerks issued them all
morning, as many as could be written, signed, and sealed.
They hoped thus to thin the rebel ranks a little, for those who
received the charters went back to their counties satisfied. It
was a drop in the bucket, though, when one considered thirty
thousand!

Occasionally a spy of the government forces got through to us; the news was always dreadful, more murders, more riots, and a general lawlessness. One reported that Tyler had boasted that in four days all the laws of England would be his laws. He would seize the king, force him to agree to a general massacre of the governing classes, including the churchmen, just as he had agreed to the death of Sudbury and the others. Then the leaders would demand a new kind of government, with no upper class between the king and the commons. If Richard did not agree, he would be killed, and Tyler himself would become king. Indeed, it was said that Tyler thought himself king already. Who in London had his power? It was a fearful thought.

Many of those about us were against letting Richard go to the parley at Smithfield; my father said the risk was too great, and the queen-mother broke down, weeping. Richard, holding her in his arms and weeping too, said tremulously, 'Mother, it is the only way....'

A vote was taken, and it was settled that he must go, but with as strong a force as could be mustered. Mayor Walworth sent out spies to bring word to the loyal Londoners to be ready, if there was need to fight. We could only hope they would get through to enough of the strongholds.

The queen-mother, sobbing, begged leave to go to Westminster Abbey and pray for her son's life. 'We shall all go, Mother,' said Richard. 'So many of us—surely God will hear!'

It was difficult to count how many of us there were on that pilgrimage, but a scribe later listed our number at two hundred. All followed Richard to Westminster, even us women-folk, except for Aunt Janet, who had not yet wakened, and Master Nathan, who could not walk.

We set out at three in the afternoon; The Abbey was not far away. The abbot and the monks from that place, seeing our procession, came halfway to meet us. They were clothed as for a high mass, richly robed, except for their feet, which were bare. Though I am of the New Learning and against all churchly pomp and show, yet was I moved by the sight. The abbot bore a large gold cross; Richard dismounted and, kneeling, kissed the cross. Even from where I rode, far behind, I could see, in the slanting sunlight, that his face was wet with tears. Behind him, several of his lords jostled one another to be first to kiss the cross after him. I had noticed these men before; they were the kind of sly fawners, whispering behind their hands, that give a whole court a bad name. Dada and I exchanged glances, grim. In Wales such creatures would not be trusted to polish the silver!

The abbot asked us to pray for the soul of Sir Richard Imworth; he had taken refuge that very morning at the shrine of St. Edward the Confessor, beseeching the saint to preserve him from his enemies. He had many, as all knew, for he was the governor of Marshalsea Prison and a notoriously cruel oppressor and torturer. The commons had dragged him from the shrine and beheaded him. Though he was a great sinner, the violation of the sanctuary is counted greater. Myself, I think God makes no such distinctions. But the pious among us crossed themselves in horror at the deed.

The king went first to that very shrine, St. Edward's, where he remained a wearisome time while the rest of us sat horse in the afternoon heat. He then proceeded to a little chapel and knelt before an image of Christ's mother. I could not see or hear, but after I read in a chronicle that he beseeched the Virgin for a miracle. We of the New Learning do not hold with miracles. But, if I should ever be tempted to such a belief, it would have been that day of the Smithfield parley.

SIX

Many chroniclers have written of that fateful Saturday at Smithfield Market. To hear them tell of it you would think they had been there, but they were not. Neither was I, but my father was, and it is his account that I will follow.

First I must explain why that place was agreed on by both sides. It was just outside the city wall, not far from Aldersgate; if all went wrong for the king's party it might be possible to withdraw back through this gate. On the other hand, it was the largest flat area anywhere near; Wat Tyler could range his people in battle formation there and have room to maneuver. He must have seen many a tournament there in his time.

The royal party went straight to Smithfield from their vigil at the Abbey; the queen-mother and her ladies were bolted back inside the Wardrobe, to wait with trembling limbs and fast-beating hearts.

The doughty old warrior, Sir Aubrey de Vere, rode out first, bearing the king's banner, and beside him his grandson, the comely Rob with the truce flag. The king rode directly behind, on a tall white destrier far too big for him, so he could be seen well by all. He wore a purple robe embroidered with the leopards of England and the lilies of France (for he was liege-lord of the French lands of Bordeaux). On his head was a thin gold circlet, his long hair showing paler gold beneath it. He looked very serious, very pale, and very young; to his poorer subjects, ranged under their rough-clad leaders, he must have looked, in his beauty and splendor, like an angel sent down from heaven. It was his only advantage.

For, against the small band of nobles in their robes of state, there stood upwards of thirty thousand men made desperate by privation and near-slavery. Moreover, many of these were veterans of Crécy and Poitiers, and bore in their bow-arms the long-bows that had won those battles. With this army, too, were the Lollard priests under John Ball; I believe that it was this good monk that had persuaded Tyler to parley. It makes no sense otherwise, for London and the Londoners were at the mercy of the rebels, and as things stood, all those with the king could have been butchered at any time.

My father said that, as they sat horse, facing the rebel army, some hundred or so paces away, one of these monks rode toward them, holding high a scrap of white cloth; as he neared their party, Dada and those nearest heard the king gasp. It was the Welshman, Owen, still in his mummer garb; with his back to the rebels, he put finger to his lips. 'Tyler will come to you, sire,' he whispered, 'but take care not to make a false move. Grant everything he asks, for if you provoke him in any way, he will sign to his followers to seize you....' So saying, he rode back to the rebel ranks.

All knew, in the king's party, that this Owen had smuggled out the heir of Lancaster just yestermorn, yet here he was, among the rebels, spying for his king! It was such seemingly impossible feats which gave rise later to the feeling among the English that this man was possessed of magic powers; of course, he had simply ridden hard, accomplished his mission, and thought fast.

But since this Owen was there, on the other side, he heard many things; I am able, therefore, to write down something of Tyler's words as well.

And so, between Dada's account and Owen's, I have pieced together my narrative; it is as true an account as any have writ of those bewildering, sad, and fateful events.

Wat Tyler, awaiting the arrival of the king, addressed his army in these words, or something near: 'We have nothing so far. The king's charters are worth little if anything. The time has come for us to act! Let us sack this great city, this rich London. Let us do it now—before the other county commons arrive. For they are on the way, with seasoned warriors at their head. If we do not take first—they will take all! For they have learned this thing in war. And they have learned, too, to put no faith in the promises of the high-noses.' Thus did he urge that the king's charters were worthless, and the king's words false. Though many believed him, some did not, and there was muttering in the ranks. Then Tyler saw the king arrive on the scene and went on to say, 'Look—there is the king. I intend to go over and speak to him. Do not move unless I sign to you. But if I sign—come across and kill everybody, except the king. Do the king no harm. He is young, he will do what we want. We will take him with us all over England, and thus become lords of the land.' And he showed them the sign, the fist clenched and the right thumb pointing down to the earth. Dada says that was the sign the old Romans gave to dispatch a fallen gladiator, though how this man knew it is a mystery. Many things about this man are mysteries, indeed, for here was a leader who had risen against oppression and in the cause of freedom, now urging his people to sack a city, to murder, and to oppress in turn! Of course, he was in too deep now, and events had come too far; it was kill or be killed. And then

again, few men can resist the taste of power; like honeyed wine
it is, sweet and strong.

But after Owen, in monk's guise, had returned, no move was
made. It was about five o'clock but still bright, for it was summer. The mounts of the king's party pawed the ground and
shuffled, as though their nerves, too, were touched. And across
the field one could see the bowmen fingering their arrows and
smoothing the feathered tips. And still Wat Tyler did not
come, and no move was made, each side facing the other, with
unease in between.

'Does he want an invitation?' said Rob de Vere, his face
flushing and his hands tightening on the reins.

'Well,' said Richard, 'perhaps he does ... we must not offend
him ... perhaps it is proper in these circumstances. After all,
there is no precedent....' And he smiled a wan smile.

'Your Grace,' said Mayor Walworth, 'I will go and ask him
in your name.'

'No,' said my father. 'You must not. You wear armor beneath
your robes, I can hear it clank. It would not do if they heard.
... Let me go, sire. They can have nothing much against me,
after all, except my judge's scarlet—and I do not go in law-
robes today....'

And so my father rode across to where the leader sat. He said
after that he was in much fear, for all the bows were raised as
he rode and pointed straight at him. Tyler sat as still as stone
and as haughty as an effigy.

'Master Tyler——' my father began. The leader stopped
him with a wave of the hand, imperious as Caesar. 'How dare
you address me without dismounting?'

'I am a knight,' said Dada, brave as brave. 'I dismount before my king only.' There was a little silence, prickly and cruel,
while each pair of eyes held, man to man, as if bound by a
ribbon of light. My father has Medusa-stared many a felon in
the dock, and nobles among them; his eyes are gray, like mine,
but with steel under.

The other man's gaze shifted first; he shrugged a tiny shrug
and said, 'It may be a different story come tomorrow....' My
father waited still.

'Well, speak, then,' said Wat Tyler in a flat voice.

'We wait the parley,' said Dada. 'The king urges you to come at once——'

Wat Tyler pulled on the reins so that his little horse rose, pawing the air, and thus raised above father, replied, 'It is your business to hurry, not mine. Go back to your king. I will come when I please!'

Dada rode back to the king's side. None had heard the exchange; when Dada repeated it, Walworth swore a great oath and made as if to ride forward. 'Wait,' said the king. 'We must not provoke him.'

From the rebel ranks, while both sides waited, a tailor spoke, addressing Wat Tyler. 'My lord,' said he, 'what of my bill for the sixty quilted surcoats I supplied—who's going to pay that? I'm owed thirty marks, and not a penny have I seen....' And Tyler answered, cool as cool, 'Be easy—you will be well paid this nightfall. Stick close to me—it is the only pledge you need.' I repeat these words as Owen told them later; it was clear that Tyler and most of the leaders were confident of the outcome.

And confident he looked, too, when at last he rode toward the king, taking his time, and reining in his beast so that it paced in a mincing gait, creating a look of mock and insult. He was followed by his standard-bearer and a small retinue; his archers stood behind him at the ready, awaiting his signal. He moved his mount close to the king's, very close, so that they were near touching, and reaching out his hand, he took the king's, shaking it hard and long, without ceremony; a gasp went up from all the king's people, for here in England the king's person is held almost sacred. Besides, the king was a boy still, delicately made, and under all his poise, white with strain; the man Tyler was large-framed and even heavy, strong as all the poorer sort must be in this world to survive it. It must have been a strange and awkward sight, like a great mastiff confronting a quivering-nerved brachet-hound. And Tyler said, 'Brother, cheer up!' Another gasp. 'Brother, cheer up, for you will have forty thousand more commons in the next fortnight, and we will be good companions all. Forty thousand more are coming—from all the counties....'

Richard said, sitting straight in the saddle and showing no

surprise or offense, but in great mildness, 'But that is what this parley is all about. What more is it that you want? Why do you not go home to your counties?'

Tyler's face grew very grim and dark, and all the jocularity vanished from it. Leaning close to the little king, he said, jerking his head to his rear, 'Do you see those men over there?'

'Yes,' said the king, still calm. 'Why do you ask?'

'I say so because they are all under my command and have sworn to do what I want.'

'Very well,' said Richard. 'I have no objection to that.' It sounds a silly answer, but thus was it reported, and I suppose Richard could think of nothing else; for sure he was trying hard not to incense the rebel leader.

But Wat Tyler was, on his part, trying to pick a quarrel; he wanted to give the signal he had promised, but as yet the king would give him no pretext. Wat Tyler said, 'And do you think, King, that the people over there, and as many more in London, and all under my orders, should leave you thus without having your charters?'

'Certainly not,' said Richard. 'They shall have them. I have given many already; and all shall have them, each section, each county.... And now, my friend, go back and ask your people to leave London quietly. For it is our intention that each village and town shall have its charter, as I have promised.'

Then Tyler swore a 'great oath'; it must have been shocking, for Dada would not tell it me, nor has any other writ it. He shouted that his people would never go home with these same charters. They wanted far more than the indemnity and freedom promised in them. He then proceeded to list demands so outrageous that he was sure no king on earth would ever grant them; it is clear he wanted to start a pitched battle. Among the things he asked were all the church's property confiscated and given to the commons; this would be a third, at least, of all the wealth of England, my father said. And he demanded the abolishing of all classes and the death of all the nobility. The lords about him grew restive, for it angered them; Richard, that fourteen-year-old, held forth his hand. 'Calm yourselves,' he said to his lords. 'All this is reason.' He spoke in a pleasant voice and easily, telling Tyler that all those demands would be met. Let him go back and tell his people and take them home. Tyler did not go. He sat his horse, his face unchanging.

None knew what to do. The plan of the king's party had failed. In spite of all the concessions made, the tempers held in check, and the king's fair words, Tyler was still here before them, his huge army still in battle array, his archers ready for the word. They waited, the lords and the rebels.

For Tyler, too, did not know what to do. All his wild demands, all his insolence, had provoked nothing. He had no excuse to give the sign. The young king's pleasant manner and the charming grace of his concessions made it impossible for the leader to swing the mob against him. Tyler suddenly grew thirsty; he snapped his fingers, calling for a drink. One of his followers ran back to the other side; he fetched up panting, bearing a flagon of water. Wat took a drink and spat it out quickly, making a face. 'I wanted beer, you dolt!' And off sprinted the poor fellow again. 'Well,' cried Wat, with a coarse guffaw, 'the water will do to rinse my mouth; there is a taste like scum from all the French wine I have drunk lately.... Do you find wine dries the tongue up furry-like, King?' And he slapped Richard on the back hard, almost unseating him.

'I cannot say,' said Richard, when he had recovered from the hearty blow. 'My wine is watered always.'

'Ah, brother, when you come with us we will give you all the wine you want—neat!' Then came running the man with a great tankard, foaming. 'Ah-h-h ... good English beer!' cried Wat. 'But first I shall swill out my fur mouth.' And so saying, he did it, spitting again and again and making vulgar noises; my father saw that some of the spittle had hit the king's sleeve, but still Richard did not move and even kept a pleasant countenance. This little king was known to be so fastidious that he went apart behind a hanging to blow his nose!

All the king's party watched as Tyler drank long of the beer, flinging the tankard from him after and wiping his mouth on his sleeve. Some of the foam still clung to his beard, running down onto his surcoat; the king's face gave a little spasm. I myself would have retched; I cannot abide smeary mouths and careless eaters. I am reminded of the hog sties at home and the dripping snouts from which I averted my eyes as I rode past.

There was an esquire, named Ralph Standish, nearby, bearing the king's sword; apparently he, too, was much reviled by Tyler's boorish ways and could no longer contain himself. He shouted, 'Go back to Kent, you swine! You are nothing but a robber—and they know you there ... three times have they jailed you for it—I know that face!' He was a Kentish nobleman, that Standish; perhaps he spoke true, for Tyler wheeled upon him and seemed to see him for the first time.

'Ha,' said Wat, 'so you are here! Give me your dagger!'

'I won't,' said Standish. 'Why should I?'

Tyler's face was black with malice. 'Give it over!'

The king said, low, 'You had better give it to him.' Standish stood reluctant for a bit, then pulled the dagger from the hilt at his belt and tossed it over with his left hand, the right still holding the king's sword.

Tyler caught the dagger deftly in one hand, without scratching himself even, but his eyes looked two daggers at the esquire. 'Now give me your sword,' he demanded.

'I cannot,' said Standish. 'It is the king's.'

Wat Tyler began playing with the dagger, tossing it from hand to hand and high into the air, as if he played a boy's game, his mouth stretched wide in a wolfish grin. None knew what he would do next. He rode a few paces off and turned, beckoning to Standish. 'Come here,' he commanded. 'Come close.'

Tyler's henchmen were drawn in close beside him now, and Standish, quite sensibly, feared to go near. The king said, 'Ralph, go—for all our sakes. You have my sword. I give you leave to use it as your own.'

Whereupon Standish rode up to the waiting Tyler. Tyler ordered his sword-bearer to behead Standish. Standish then lifted the king's sword, and spoke boldly. 'If any strike at me, I shall strike back. I have the king's sword! Do you imagine I will bow my neck to your ruffian? Let him try it!'

Tyler's sword-bearer made no move, for in all probability he did not know how to use a sword; it takes some skill. But Tyler, furious, raised the esquire's own dagger and tried to stab him with it, Standish parrying the thrust with the sword.

Wat, in a rage, shouted, 'By God, I will not eat again till I have your head!' At this, Mayor Walworth rode forward and grabbed the bridle of Tyler's mount. 'How dare you, sirrah— in the king's presence!'

'I owe the king no respect!' shouted Tyler, beside himself.

Walworth replied hotly, 'Fellow, watch your words—you presume beyond endurance!'

'What is it to you?' screamed Wat, and struck at the mayor's stomach savagely with his dagger. The armor beneath Walworth's robes turned aside the point. The king, at last losing some of his control, cried, 'Arrest him—someone! Arrest him!'

But Walworth took the gamble which made him famous after. He drew his broadsword, shouting, 'You stinking scoundrel!' He struck Wat a hard blow downward on the shoulder, and then another. Wat reeled in the saddle; Ralph Standish, stepping forward, ran him through with the king's sword. Wat must have been a man of truly great strength, for the sword blow had obviously touched a vital spot; blood gushed from his wounds, so that he looked like a painted man, and his horse, too, was red with it. But he spurred his beast, crying loud to the commons to avenge him. The horse carried him some four paces only; he fell to the ground half dead.

The rebel army, too far away to comprehend the happenings, saw the flash of the sword and cries went up in joy that their leader was being knighted. When they saw him fall from the horse, though, and the king's retinue close in on him like a pack of dogs on the fox, they knew that something dreadful had happened. Owen, standing among them, said that the whole crowd was stunned, unable to believe that Tyler could be undone, all in a minute. Then the cry went up, 'Our captain is dead! Our leader has been slain!' From all sides came the frenzied cries, 'Let us stand together ... Let us die with him.... Let us loose our arrows and avenge him! Come—let us put all the high-noses to death. To battle, men!' And they ranged themselves again into battle array, each archer with his bow before him. They began to bend their bows and shoot.

The clash had come; the king had tried to avoid it, and Tyler had finally brought it on, but Wat himself had been its first victim. It looked now as though the king would be the second. The arrows were beginning to fly; the little band of nobles was hopelessly outnumbered, and no help had arrived from the city. Only a miracle could turn the tide of events.

And a miracle did. But a man-made one, or king-made, as it turned out. Richard, fourteen years old, frail-boned and white-faced, took command. Perhaps he remembered the old tales of his famous father, the Black Prince; perhaps he was touched that day by the strength that comes to the hopeless; it is not clear how it happened, but happen it did. Richard was more king that day than ever in all his sad reign.

He turned to his lords and said, in a voice new with command, 'Stay here. Let no one follow me.' Then he rode forward, unarmed, to face the mad throng of desperate men. His voice, reedy and clear, could be heard all over the field. 'Sirs— what is it you require? I am your captain. I am your king! Quiet yourselves!' The mob surged forward, surrounding him, looking up at the young face, so beautiful, so delicate, so fearless. Straight in the saddle he sat, looking down and saying, 'Do not be sad over the death of your leader, for I will go with you as your captain. Follow me—follow me into the open fields and you shall have all you desire!'

And he began to move his horse out of the square and into the country parts beyond. At this point a few of his nobles spurred on, against his orders, to go with him, wherever it led, my father, Standish, Walworth, and the two De Veres; the other cowards melted away, as rats are said to leave a ship that is sinking, none seeing them go.

The commons followed after; Owen said after it was touch and go whether they would turn on the king and kill him or agree to go home with their charters. Without Tyler to lead them, they were lost and divided. The king was indeed in great peril; he looked, said Owen, like a gilded lamb among lean and hungry wolves.

At the sacred well of St. Agnes, just north of the market, Walworth turned back, whispering that he would summon Sir Robert Knollys, waiting with his forces in the city.

It is difficult to tell the rest of the day's events, for my father was with the king. So no one knows exactly how Walworth obtained the severed head of Wat Tyler, or how Sir Robert

Knollys, with his seven thousand troops, got so quickly out of the city. But, bearing the dripping head of their leader, came Walworth, with Knollys and his fighting force.

The city forces numbered only a fraction of the rebel army, but when the commons saw the head of their leader high above them, they were utterly undone. They began throwing down their axes and clubs, swords and bows; some ran away into the standing corn of the fields and hid. Those left cried to the king for mercy, begging he forgive them their misdeeds.

Without Tyler, who for three days had made them masters of London, they became a poor rustic rabble. Sir Robert Knollys was all for a general massacre; he was a veteran peasant-slayer, having fought against the Jacquerie uprising in France. But Richard, heady with his first taste of command, forbade it. 'My people,' he said to the cowering peasantry, 'throw down your arms, all ... there will be no slaughter ... go your ways in peace. ...'

So Richard was a king that day both brave and merciful. The great Peasants' Revolt was over; the noisy riot ended in a muffled whimper.

I myself heard Richard's words, as he returned to his mother in the Wardrobe. She threw herself into his arms, too distraught to speak, poor lady. He kissed her with great tenderness, and said, 'Lady Mother, be happy—for today I have recovered the crown that I had lost.'

And so he had, for now—poor beautiful Richard.

SEVEN

The aftermath of the revolt makes me shudder still to tell, though there were those who felt the rebels had been too leniently treated. True, there was no general massacre of the peasantry, and only the leaders suffered; still it was horrible to think upon those deaths. The priest John Ball I had been brought up to revere, and the man Jack Strawe had been kind to me; the day they were drawn and quartered I had the worst

choking fit I ever remember, gasping for breath and thinking
to die of it, even my fingertips turning blue. The physician,
Master Nathan, saved me, lighting a brazier and throwing
upon the coals a pinch of some pungent-smelling stuff; when I
inhaled it as he bade me, the choking subsided. Like magic it
was and quickly done; he said it was an herb from the Eastern
lands, rare and precious. He said these fits are caused by mist
and damp, and so they have been in the past for me; this day
of the executions, though, was bright and beautiful, with a
blinding brilliant sun, so it is a mystery to me still.

King Richard, too, was ill that day, and could not attend the
death-showings. With him it was different, vomiting and purg-
ing; poison was suspected and the cook jailed, in that quick
English cruelty inherited from the Normans. That poor cook
died under torture, but Richard recovered and was as good as
new. I privately think that both of us were sick at heart, in our
different ways; Richard wanted amnesty for all the rebels, having promised it in his own words, but he was overruled by the
lords who advised him, and his uncles, too, for he was a minor
still, of course, and a king in name only. Later, when he had
power, Richard showed himself cruel, too; in the main it was
toward his peers and such traitorous lords, and never to the
poor wretches of the commonalty. Revenge it was, perhaps, for
the strictures placed upon him by all the nobility in his early
years. Or perhaps he held them dear in his memory, those commons who had loved him and hailed him as their leader. I
thought upon it often, in after years, for I grew to have much
affection for the young Richard; with all his faults, and they
were many, he was a lovesome king. We Welsh, both high and
low, have a strong sense of justice, and Richard was much
maligned, and worse, in the end—by his own kind.

One benefit only the commons gained from their rising; the
hated poll-tax was never tried again. Otherwise the peasants
lived much as before, still starving, often as not, still unfree,
still bowed under the yoke of their English overlords. By November of that year the rising was forgotten as if it had never
been. And in the next year's January, the king was married in
the greatest pomp and splendor yet seen in the realm; the price
of the bride's dress would have fed a whole county for a year.

She was no little dumpling, the Princess Anne of Bohemia, as I had wished on Richard in jest, but a handsome, well-made girl of a quick grace and proud carriage like a spirited filly, and a quick mind as well, as learned as any judge. Her pictures do not her justice, they are insipid and silly in the court mold; I cannot describe her either, but while she was queen she set the fashion in all things. Even her wall-eye was much admired, and many a court maiden wore an addled look trying to imitate it!

I shall never forget that wedding day or the masque that followed it. The bride did not wear red with flowing hair, as is done in Wales, but went all in cloth of silver, and on her head she wore a covering headdress, silver, too, and all the hair hid beneath it; a crescent moon topped it, with a little winking diamond at each point for stars. On the Lady Anne it looked piquant, but later it was copied all over the kingdom and resembled nothing more than a pair of horns; most women, wearing this hennin, would have been better at chewing a cud! Richard, glittering with gems beside her and royally robed, stole shy side-glances while the Bishop's Latin droned; it was his first look at her, for they had been betrothed by proxy, as the custom went. I hoped that he liked what he saw.

The royal pair sat side by side at the feast, eating little of the fanciful concoctions that were set before them; there was much wine served them, too, each one different to complement each new dish. I think it went to their heads somewhat, for her cheeks were red as fire, and from time to time she leaned her hot face against the maiden's at her left, as if to cool it. This damsel, with her arm entwined in Anne's, had been reared with her from childhood and they were friends most fond; Agnes was her name, and her duchy I have forgot, an unpronounceable name it had. But they dressed as twins always, those two, but in different colours, and even resembled each other, too, being quick and merry, though Agnes' eyes were straight as dies.

Beside the king sat Rob de Vere, who had borne the marriage ring; he, it was plain, was already drunken before the feast was well away. He swayed in his seat and would not answer the king's low privy words. When they led the royal couple to their chamber, and the ribald words began rising all round them, and they walking wooden, like puppets on a string, Rob drained his goblet and set it down, staring after them. I saw his fingers tighten on the goblet's stem, the knuckles white. The slender glass broke, suddenly, cutting his hand. I think not many saw, for attention was all on the young royal pair, but the Lady Agnes saw; she moved quickly to his side, wrapping a napkin round the hand and whispering to him, low. She smiled and fondled his hand, for they were very free in their ways, these girls from the great Continent; his face did not lighten, though, and his eyes were sullen still. I guessed he was thinking of his own marriage, put off for years and due now within a fortnight. The De Veres were male-barren and Rob was the last of the stock; he would be expected to get an heir and quickly. I knew the girl, a lumpish, dull-eyed creature, rich, from the North Country; it would be no enviable task.

Owen of Wales I had not seen in all those months that followed the rising; Dada said he had gone back to his own manor to see to his holdings and to pay his death-duties, for his father had died suddenly in a fall from a horse. Dada had nothing but good words for this young gentleman, naming him clever beyond any in the realm, with a turn for any kind of learning you might think of. Dada set great store by this, being no mean scholar himself. I was most curious about him now, Owen. Since I had been at court, I had heard all the gossip; they said Owen, who was only upwards of twenty years, had fathered brats by the dozen, by as many women. This, of course, one could not credit; the English always slander the Welsh. I knew he kept a mistress; the Princess Anne (I must remember she is now queen and get used to it) had told me this, and she is always right with her tales; though how she knows I cannot tell, she has been in England a bare fortnight! The girl is a Lombard wench, not noble, but of a decent merchant family and has been with Owen several years and borne him sons. This is no scandal, of course, for what English youth does not do the same, if he can afford it? De Vere does not keep a woman, but the gossips, sniggering, give him other, darker vices, an idle court, after all, with nothing much to pass the time but the telling of tales.

Still, I looked hard for Owen; I could not believe he would not appear at the marriage-feast. He was close to the king and owed him homage as well, Richard being his liege-lord. I thought I saw him at the second table's end, among a little knot of students, noisy. When he turned, I smiled and raised my hand to wave; too late I saw it was not he, though much like. I felt like a lack-wit, for the unknown youth grinned lewdly, almost smacking his lips, and bowing from the waist. His companions laughed loud, making free talk, though I was too far away to hear it; I turned away, blushing, and pretended to be busy with my dish of savory. And very glad I was when they snuffed out the candles for the masque, for all those youths' eyes were on me for my boldness.

I had seen other court masques, of course, and the traveling mummer-shows at home in the market-squares, but this was like none of them. For the fair-day shows are very vulgar and funny with songs and rude jokes, even when they are about the lives of the saints, and the masques are pretty things about gods and goddesses, mostly in French and sung to lute music. This one was as real as real; one could swear, almost, that the story was happening before the eyes. The piece was put on by some of the Westminster students, the cleverest, and was writ by Geoffrey Chaucer in London English! A gasp went up at the first words, for the feeling of naturalness was a shock. But very soon all in the hall were silent, listening, for the story was cunningly told, like life itself unfolding, a wonder to look on. There were no choruses in the background, no pretty boys or girls posing against a painted cloth; instead there was Criseyde in her chamber, like any well-appointed room, and she bored and idle and looking out of the window as a parade of soldiers passed by. And so it began, the tale of Troilus and Criseyde, a true love story; I hung on the words, engrossed, and wept at the end at her faithlessness.

The Troilus I did not much like; he was one of that strutting sort of youth, all muscles and teeth, that thinks too well of himself, and waved his arms about too much, sawing the air. Criseyde, though, was lovely, small and delicate as a wood-nymph, in her simple girdled Greek robe. This was no dressed-up boy, for her voice was all woman, clear and full; nor no whore neither, she had all the airs and graces of a highborn lady. Her high-dressed hair was black and her eyes dark; her bare arms, too, were not white but the color of one of our Welsh hill-maidens', sun-kissed. There was something odd in her speech too, a foreign sound, though I could not place it. It came upon me suddenly that this must be the Lombard, Owen's woman; I blushed in the dark, hotly, for no reason. It was no business of mine, after all; I barely knew the man.

I recognized him in the masque, though, even in his toga and sandals and clipped, curling hair. He took the part of Criseyde's uncle, a Greek nobleman; he had not age enough for it, but no matter, one might swear he was the very man. Worldly and wise he was, with much wit and a beckoning air, and in this guise he made, as it were, the story to happen. For that uncle, Pandarus, he was called, in subtle words and ways, and like a sweet serpent, caused Criseyde to fall in love with her Troilus and the tragedy to thus unfold. Like playing God he was, and so did his manner appear also; for he is taller than any man. I do believe, and straighter, with a voice now thundering, now dropping low, and his eyes flashing yellow fire. It was a cruel story, as cruel-sweet as life, but I did not think of that then but listened hard with the rest, feeling it all within me.

After, the candles being relit, the floor was cleared for dancing; I had many partners, for word always gets about when one is rich, and I was nearly new to court besides. Also, I had all the steps right, being quick to learn; Anne had brought these new dances to England, very complex they were, with intricate patterns, and many had not mastered them. Some of my partners I had to teach, laughing, and some hands I slapped. For much wine had flowed that night, and there were bold lads reaching for whatever they could grab hold of.

We are not meant to refuse any in the dance, for all present were highborn and equal, but one time I would have feigned illness, if I dared. For that youth that earlier I had took for Owen appeared to claim me, staggering a little. He took my hand to kiss, but turned the palm up and put his mouth to it, flicking it with his tongue. It tickled and was wet; besides, in our country it is a rude sign, or so I have heard, of something further. I snatched my hand away and looked up at him, scowling; he laughed. I saw, close to, he was not very like. Tall he was, for sure, like Owen, but something thicker, and squarer about the jaw.

'You waved at me, damsel, did you not? And beckoned me with your smile. . . .'

'I took you for someone else, sir. . . . And now pray excuse me, I am feeling faint. . . .' I heard a sound behind me like a hiss, and looked round to see Owen himself, frowning at the other and shaking his head.

'This is my brother, Tudor, Lady Margaret—in his cups. . . . Forgive him if he offends. The Lady Margaret Hanmer of Flintshire, Tudor! And beg her pardon, if you please, for I see in her face that you have displeased her. . . .'

Tudor pulled at his forelock sheepishly, bowing and scraping jerkily, a parody of a rough yokel from the wheatfields and speaking a crude sort of back-hills Welsh, asking not to be punished. 'Don't take off m'hands, Lady . . .' he whined. Truly, this family must have mummer blood, all!

'More your tongue, like!' I answered, in the same dialect. We all laughed then, my not wanting to be a spoilsport. Besides, now that I knew the young man a true Welshman, I felt easier.

'Get you gone, churl!' cried Owen, in the king's English, like a very Norman high-nose. And off slunk the brother, play-cringing.

'Will you dance with me, Moon Maiden?' It was a delicate compliment; I was dressed in palest gray, for the feast fell on my mother's death-day. I had seen earlier in the mirror how the color lightened my eyes to silver. I took his hand.

'I am clumsy,' he said. 'But I know the steps. . . .'

He was not, for all his size. But I recognized some kinship here, for I speak in such wise myself; I think all too-large creatures like ourselves deprecate our persons, feeling them too much, even of a good thing! My eyes sent him a message, shy.

'Shall I call you Diana?' he asked, close to my ear. 'You are slender and straight as one of her arrows. . . .' Sweet Jesus, I thought, I am not even bending my back in the fashion; Nurse's words went all for naught! I tried it earnestly, the graceful sway, poking my stomach out and frowning in concentration. Just then the dance brought us together and my rounded stomach pressed against him, somewhere low and hard. I drew back quickly, fire-veins running down my legs. He missed the next step, recovering it quickly; then looking down at me most grave, he said, 'The touch was pleasant—but it is a silly posture-fashion.... I would rather you did not look pregnant till you are.'

The fire ran upward then, coloring me from the neck up in a dark hot blush; it was my night for it! The dance then took us apart, and I was able to cool off, bending my thoughts upon the steps, most tricky. Most like none had mastered this measure, for all the dancers dropped away, and we two whirled alone upon the marble floor. The music stopped, and there was a little noise of clapping hands; Owen bowed to me, and then to the swimming sea of faces, watching. I curtseyed low, feeling all elbows; I was not used to all those eyes upon me.

Grateful I was when the music struck up again, another tune. 'I am breathless, sir,' I said. 'The last measure was as energetic as a country jig-hop.'

'Shall we find an empty corner then, Lady?' asked Owen, threading me deftly through the moving partners. There were no sitting places, the tables and benches had been taken away; the few chairs were filled with those too old to dance. 'The night air is frosty, but there are none abroad there.... Will you walk with me a little outside in the courtyard? I have a cloak here—behind the scenes....' And he drew me with him through a little door behind a hanging. It was just under the musician's gallery and was the place where they had dressed for the masque. It was close and small, untidy as a rabbit-pen, with an odd smell I could not identify. I looked at him, wrinkling my nose; he laughed. 'It is a mixture,' he explained. 'Paint ... and glue ... and unwashed wig-hair. And the sweat-sour smell of fear, too, a little....'

'Fear ...?' I asked, looking puzzled.

'Excitement, apprehension.... The true mummers that take their living from it—they call it stage-fright, for they play upon a raised platform that they call a stage.'

I nodded. 'I can credit it, for sure I myself would swoon from it—if I were called upon to face so many....'

'I think not, Lady,' he said, 'for I have heard reports of your courage among the street-rebels....'

'There are different kinds of bravery,' I said.

'Many,' said Owen. And where I stood against the wall, he place a hand, with an easy grace, on each side of me against the wall, so hemming me in, and leaning very close, looking intent into my eyes.

'And are you not afeared of me, then? For there are a mort of stories round the court—that I am wizard—that I know Merlin's magic....'

I stared back at him unblinking, and did not shrink within even, but said boldly, 'There is another sort of tale that I have heard, Sir Countryman....'

'I doubt it not,' he said, still standing so. 'For there is not much that I care to hide ... and folk imagine, like the bards, a hundred verses, where one would serve to sing the song....' He was telling me something, but I did not know what; I lowered my eyes to hide the question in them and said nothing.

Inches from my ear he said then, 'You have not told me yet what I shall call you.... Diana? Or ... Artemis, perhaps?'

'My brothers call me Maggie,' I said, smiling small.

'There is a tiny dimple beside your mouth,' he whispered. So *some* at least of Nurse's teaching I had not forgot! 'But,' he said, persistent, 'I do not wish to be as your brothers.... In my own family the women mostly Romanize their names, for pride. Yours then would be—Margareta.... But it does not suit you. For it brings to mind a dusky Latin damsel....'

My look went past him to a tumbled heap upon the floor, apricot-colored, diaphanous; I had seen *her* dusky limbs glimmering through its folds in the masque-playing. A terrible black fury rose bursting to my temples; never had I felt such before, but I knew it for jealousy and was much angered with myself, hoping it did not show. 'I do not like any of your names,' I said, prim as prim. 'They have a heathen sound....'

'The Old Welsh is "Marred" ... but that is heathen, too.'

'Well, let it go for now,' I said. 'What does it matter any-

how? We are strangers, after all.' My words sounded peevish
even to me; I wished that I could swallow them. I went on,
moving restively between his hands, 'It is too warm here ...
and the smell....'

'Forgive me, Lady,' he said, taking away his hands and moving back. 'We had come to fetch a cloak.... I forgot.' He
moved to a chest that stood in the middle of the room, lifting
the lid and rummaging within. I followed; as I passed the
crumpled apricot gown upon the floor, I gave it a little kick,
vicious. He raised his eyes just then and I saw he saw.

'She played well, Criseyde——' I said. 'I should have liked to
tell her so. Where is she?'

'She is not received at court,' he said quietly. 'I have sent her
home.' Home. The word hung in the air between us. He
stooped and picked up the gown, smoothing it out into folds
and laying it upon a bench. I could not bear to see his hands
upon it.

To still the beating thing within my chest, I said, 'Well, I
cannot wait while you tidy up for all. There must be others to
do such work.'

'You are right,' he said, looking at me strangely, and for a
long moment. 'Come, Marred——' he said, putting a fur cloak
about my shoulders. 'Come, little heathen....'

EIGHT

I remembered long his kiss upon my lips, cool in the icy air and
warming to fever-flame, and our bodies pressed close on all
their lengths under the fur cloak. The night was bright, for the
moon was full and much snow lay upon the ground, creating a
changeling noonday; we heard a group of horsemen ride out,
the iron of their horses' shoes ringing loud against the hard-
packed ice of the drawbridge. I recall wondering where they
were bound in such a hurry, and Owen answered, as though I
had spoke my thought, 'It is nothing, little silver-eyes ... the

hour is late. Some earl, half-drunken, racing his henchmen home.'

We spoke little and kissed long and burned within that cloak, leaning against a parapet, ice-covered, and not feeling the cold. I had not been kissed before in all my days; these were not the wild, wet, clumsy lips of the boys at home, not the snatched fondlings of a fair-day, or the romping, blindfold games that children play, sniggering in the dark. Later, in my bed alone, I remembered, in anguish, that he had much practice, Owen.

He left me at the little door that opened onto the stairway leading to the ladies' bower where I slept; I climbed the steps on shaking legs. Inside, I stood a moment, a stranger to this warm, firelit chamber and the soft girlish snorings from the pallets spread upon the floor, and thankful that none was awake to see me. Though I felt as changed and shaken as a Derfel-bride, my breasts all swollen and aching and a sticky wet between my legs, yet was I a maid still. I lifted trembling hands to my head, surprised to find my hair fast-braided under my veil-coif; even my dress was girdled and seemly. I did not remember tying it; perhaps he had.

He had said that he was going away—out of the country on some business that he did not name. I would not see him for a month at least, but he would send me word.

Day after day passed by and no word came; night after night I lay unsleeping on my pallet, with the soft breathing woman-sounds around me and the fire flickering low. For the court stayed long in that place, and the festivities stretched into weeks, and we queen's ladies must attend the new queen through it all.

I was like a pining, molting bird; I hardly heard the whispering that went round. As in a dream I learned it; the midwives were not satisfied with the condition of the royal wedding sheets the first night, or for a fortnight after. Richard looked white and wan at his high seat, and beside him Anne laughed feverishly, her good eye beginning to turn outward too. Dimly I thought: Poor royal pair, to be hawk-watched so!

On a bright morning, with a thaw setting in and the icicles dripping at the windows, my father rode up from the City; I saw him from our chamber and ran down into the courtyard, for I had not spoke with him since the day of Richard's wedding. He was all mud-splashed, for the roads were a melted, churning mess, but he wore a look like a cat that still has the cream upon its whiskers.

After the stableboy had taken his horse and a page had drawn off his muddy boots and another brought him a breakfast tankard, he stretched his legs out, groaning. 'Ah, lass,' he said, 'my bones are none so young as they were ... they feel the damp....' I clucked at him, naming his talk nonsense, but, counting up, I knew it for the truth; he had had two childless wives before our mother.

'Look you, Dada,' I said, for I was always main Welsh when I talked to him, 'look you, not a day over fifty shows on you....'

He turned to look at me then, his eyes crinkling. 'And how old do you think I am then? You are fifteen, and your brothers not much more—one foot in the grave I have not yet....'

'Oh, Dada,' I said, laughing, 'a head for figures I have not!'

'That is plain,' he said, stern. 'But let it pass.... I did not ride all the way here, slipping and sloshing, to talk of birthdays. See here, Maggie—are we private here? And can the queen spare you for a bit?'

'Oh, for sure, Father. She has eighteen others....'

'And what do you say to a wedding day of your own?'

My heart leaped like a startled hare; I knew it was time for him to think of such things, but I was not ready. He had been an indulgent father and had passed up all my suitors, though many girl-children are betrothed almost before they can walk.

'I have a contract here,' said my father. 'And the letter that came with it ... from the Italian lands....' He paused, watching me closely.

I stared at him, wondering. I knew no Latin men, nor had any seen me, that I knew of. 'Oh, Dada,' I cried, low, 'you have promised not to wed me to a foreign man—long ago you promised it!' And I began to twist my hands, one upon another, distracted.

'Leave off the wringing of your hands, girl,' he said. 'This is no foreigner, at all, at all.... It is Owen ap Griffith, that styles himself the Prince of Wales....'

'Owen ...' I said, on a breath let out. 'But you said from the Italian lands....'

'He is there on business,' replied my father. 'I thought you knew. He says here'—and he glanced down at the paper he held—'he says he thinks you agree well, you two.'

Agree well! And that is what he calls it! I could not control the flush that rose up from my neck.

'You are coloring,' said Dada, smiling sly. 'And are you then feverish, girl? This thaw——'

'Oh, Dada,' I said, 'leave off—and do not tease me! It is my life we are talking of——' For my mind was in a turmoil, to and fro. And I was blowing hot and cold, my mind hearing only 'He has business there—in the Italian lands.'

'It is a finer contract than I could have hoped for,' said Dada, reading it. 'Even with your looks ... he is asking no dowry at all, at all ... only that you consent to marry in a place called Dolgelly, in the hills. He has a fondness for the place, it seems, and for the priest there, that was his tutor long ago.... Of course, he has holdings all over Wales ... the richest man in all the Cymry-land, he is. And in England, too, perhaps. I doubt not he could match Lancaster—or the Percys, even!' And almost he rubbed his hands in glee, like any usurer—my father!

I felt my face setting hard, my brows drawing down. 'I will not marry him,' I said.

My father's eyes were round as marbles. 'But why? He is not only rich, but the most learned youth in this realm—and of a gentle nature, I know him well. And they call him handsome— myself I take no note of such things. He could have his pick of any girl in Wales—or Europe even, and they jumping at it!'

'I am not any girl—I am myself! And I will not have him!' And I burst into a storm of weeping, covering my face with my hands and sobbing loud.

'Hush, girl——' My father took me by the shoulders, shaking me a little. 'Do you want the whole palace to hear? Leave off now, sweeting....' And he patted me awkwardly. 'Now tell me what ails you?'

I was sniffling and hiccoughing like a very serving-wench, like my own Branwen, who has had no gentle training, and I felt shame at myself. It took a little, but I stopped, dashing away my tears and looking at him straight. Then quiet, I said, 'Owen ... we could—agree well ... but—he keeps a mistress.'

My father stared still. 'Well, what would you? He is twenty-two and lusty. I cannot marry you to a monk!' And Dada put his hand beneath my chin and lifted it, making me meet his eye. 'Have sense, girl! You were not reared by the nuns either! What man does not, if he has blood in him and sap.... I my-self——' And he broke off. Now it was my turn to stare. 'Well, girl,' he said, blustering a little, 'think ... your mother has been dead these dozen years and more. Would you have me sleep in a cold bed always?' I still did not speak; I was shamed but stubborn. And he had spoiled me, too, Dada.

He got a little angry then and spoke hard at me. 'Would you have a Richard, then—or De Vere?'

I glanced over my shoulder, quickly. 'Father—sh-h-h-h!'

'Or Henry of Lancaster? He is younger ... and mayhap a green boy still. Gaunt sued me for your hand four years ago, but I would not have him. He is a good match, too, but I cannot like the boy.... Vile of temper he is and would not use you well....'

'Oh, Father, no! Oh, no!'

'Well, that is past anyway, for Gaunt has betrothed him al-ready ... right out of her convent he snatched her, the poor lass. Pretty as an image too she is, little Mary de Bohun....'

There was a little moment between us, then I swallowed hard and said, 'I am sorry, Father. Only give me a little time ... a little time, Dada, to think on it....'

'He does not want an answer now,' said my father. 'If you had only listened a moment, you would have heard all. My consent only he wanted, and to make known his wishes in the matter, as a nobleman should do. It is your answer he waits for. And he wants to see you first and ask you to your face if you will have him.' I was shamed indeed now, and tears pricked behind my eyelids. 'Well, don't cry, lass. The storm is over, surely?'

'Dada,' I said, 'when—when will he come back from—from there?'

'Oh,' he said briskly and clearing his throat. 'It may be any day now. He writes as though he is already on his way....'

'I would have had him write me ...' I whispered, small.

'Then would I be angered—your father.' He peered at me close. 'And how well do you know him, Miss Bean Pole?'

I smiled. It was his jest-name for me, though it was long since he had said it. 'I—encountered him a few times only. At the rising, when he went as a begging monk to save that Lancaster Henry——' I saw he smiled, and smiled, too, both of us knowing he was of no monkish nature. 'And at the wedding we danced ... and he—praised my gown. That is all,' I lied.

'Well, you have taken his eye, it seems,' he said dryly. 'On your knees you should be, thanking....'

'Oh, Dada,' I said, laughing now. 'And who is marrying him —you or I?'

And so he knew my mind, and so did I. And in my heart I went upon my knees—not thanking, but rejoicing. I washed my hair every morning and put camomile brew upon it for the shine; cucumber paste, too, I wore to bed on nose and cheeks for the freckles, though one can hardly see them, in truth, in the winter. And sing at my lady-tasks I did also, though I left off if any came near; they call us Welsh *singers*, but it is not so with me. I cannot keep to the melody.

Only when I thought of the Lombard, in the dark secret places of my being, did I gnash my teeth and groan. Silently. I *would* have him—and I would scratch her eyes out, could I but meet her face-to-face. Poison, even, I thought on, like a demon-lady. I trembled with hate, born of love.

Now that I knew he would come, and soon, I worried that I would not still please him, dressing up like a peacock, even in the early hours of morning, sometimes changing my gown four and even five times each day. I took Branwen to task if a hair was out of place, for she had the tiring of it; scold her like a fishwife I did, and she not knowing why. For of course I did not breathe a word till all was settled.

The young queen called me to her one day while we sat listening to some new verses; her lips curved and her eyes danced with mischief; one of them of course looking off past my shoulder, as it ever did, an odd sight, but somehow charming. 'You look as though someone had lit a candle inside you!' And she shook her finger at me. 'Now tell me, miss, what has come about, for I am your queen!'

'It is a secret ... but I will tell you first of all—I promise. And,' I went on, to change the topic, 'you yourself are mightily changed from the sad looks of these last weeks ... and will *you* tell *me*?'

'I will,' she said, 'but bend close, for it is a very state secret. And also you must swear never to tell anyone....'

And under cover of the minstrels' song, she whispered that the midwives were finally satisfied. 'Oh, God, madame. I am so happy for you! When will it be?' In spite of her warning my voice rose.

She put her finger to my lips. 'Sh-h-h....' And she gave a little laugh. 'It is not that—never think it! And Jesus knows if it will ever be ... but at least they have the proof now that I am no longer virgin....'

'Well ... in time ...' I said.

She stared. 'How green a Welsh-girl are you then?' she said, looking at me strangely. I felt the hot blood begin to creep into my cheeks. 'Oh, do not blush!' she said, tossing her head. 'All the court knows about Richard ... one way or another....' She looked for a moment pensive, then smiled again. 'And I do not care! I have foxed the old dames anyway—and now they will leave us alone and stop snooping. Listen——' And she leaned even closer. 'I took a pig's bladder filled with blood into the great bed last night, along with a sharp needle....' And she made a jabbing gesture with her hand. 'It did the trick! I think they will preserve those sheets in the Abbey!' She laughed again, a sound like glass breaking. 'You are shocked. ... Well, Richard is gentle and good, sweeter than any other prince, and I love him.... Now at least they will blame *me* and call me barren....'

I took her in my arms, for all she was my queen. 'I think,' I whispered, 'you are the noblest lady in the world....'

A week went by, and still no Owen; I was much distraught, for we were packing to remove to Sheen Palace, in the country.

'At last,' Queen Anne said, sighing, 'we can shake the dust of this gloomy old stone heap. . . .'

'Oh, madame, I do not find it gloomy!' I was surprised; Windsor is well-appointed and comfortable. 'The courtyard at least is beautiful.'

She looked at me strangely. 'It is naught but a keep,' she said scornfully. 'No hedges or paths or lovers' walks. . . .'

'Oh, well, it is still winter, after all——' I replied, and turned my head aside to hide the dreaming look upon my face.

We rode out next morning; I wore my oldest gown and cloak, for the sky was gray and promised rain. We all gasped in wonder when the queen's horse was led out; it bore the strangest saddle, high-backed and with stirrups of mismatched lengths. Also her groom had put it on wrong, and many of the ladies giggled, liking to see her Bohemian servant put down for once; they were an overbearing sort and not much liked by the English-born.

When Anne appeared, we stared again; she wore a gown of narrow cut and a close-fitting quilted surcoat, slit at the sides. Very becoming it was, but hardly suitable; the skirt was not full enough for a lively dance step, let alone going astride a wide horse's back! But while our mouths hung open like lackwits', she stepped nimbly, first one foot, then the other, onto the stirrups, exactly as though they were stairs, and seated herself sideways! So I surmised that the saddle was not put on wrong, but a new fashion from her own country. She sat very straight; it was a piquant posture and quite graceful, but looked precarious. I prayed silently to heaven that she would not fall off.

Richard rode up then and walked his horse all round her, examining and exclaiming. Suddenly he clapped his hands, smiling like the sun. 'How clever!' And turning to us all, he said, 'Have I not the most inventive of ladies?'

'Oh, Dickon,' she exclaimed, 'I did not invent it! You do me too much honor!' But the fond smiles they exchanged showed plain to all the great accord they felt for each other.

Richard promised to order a round dozen more of these new sidesaddles for the best horsewomen. 'But,' he cried, 'we must have a competition . . . and they will be the prizes!'

Privately I thought it not so much of a much, for I noticed Anne must hold her horse to a sedate pace; to gallop would be disaster. I foresaw a long and wearisome ride.

And, for sure it was; we had not gone a ten-mile when the first drops began to fall. There were riders bearing a canopy to shelter the king and queen, and the queen-mother was in a covered litter, but the rest of us were sodden within minutes. There were no inns along the way, no shelter at all except the great trees, which reached their branches over the road above us; very little good did we get of them anyway, since they were still not in leaf.

There was no storm, thank Jesus, and no lightning to fright us; just a steady gray curtain of rain, chill and wretched. My cloak was a thick wool, close-woven, and with a great hood; the shepherds at home make them, for they are often out all night, unsheltered, hunting a lost sheep. They are coated with some sheep-fat, and the water runs off, so I was better off than the rest of our party; my feet only were soaked, and my gloved hands that held the reins. The smell, though, wool and animal fat combined, and strong in the wet, was making my stomach heave, and I wished myself anywhere but that endless-seeming road.

We had come in sight at last of Sheen; smoke curled in thin spirals from the chimneys, though it was still too far to be more than a speck on the horizon. We heard through the rain a pounding behind us, loud. I turned; it was one horseman only and coming on at a fast gallop. He caught up to us and, passing all the train behind, rode up to where I went, behind the litter. It was Owen, and my heart jumped to nearly unseat me. He wore a Welsh sheep-mantle, twin to mine, but with the hood thrown back; his hair was dark-plastered to his cheeks and neck, for it had grown out since the masque, and his eyelashes were matted together like little spikes. He looked just like a statue in my father's garden, a Roman river-god it was, dug up from old, old times. Nurse used to hurry me past, for it was naked, in the antique way, but still I had seen; I blushed at the thought, under my hood.

He drew rein beside me, pulling his mount to match our slow pace. He took my gloved hand and, turning back the cuff, kissed my wrist; it was a seemly touch of courtesy, but still it burned deep.

'It has stopped raining,' he said, 'and I cannot see your silver eyes beneath that ugly hood....' I threw it back; he was right, and it was clearing ahead. 'I galloped hard to bring you the sun,' he said, smiling. 'You are more beautiful than I remembered, even,' he whispered. 'I had thought it was the moonlight, flattering....' I threw him a sharp look and saw he jested; I smiled too. 'The dimple, though,' he said, 'is just the same—lopsided....'

He road ahead then to pay his respects to the royal pair and the Lady Joan in her litter; there was much talk and marveling at his speed, for he had been one hour only on the road to our four. Arriving at Windsor too late, he had spurred on to be with me, though only I knew it, happiness churning within me like water on the boil.

He rode the rest of the way beside me, talking of this and that, things of no moment, till we crossed the moat at Sheen Palace. 'When you have dried out and changed your gown,' he said, 'walk with me a little in the garden. It will be solid underfoot by then, in this sun, and it may be we will find a bit of green, even, blooming just for us. An hour then...?'

There was no green of course, for it was February still; the hedges were thorny and the paths treacherous with mudholes. Yet did I wear my best mantle, a black velvet, ermine-trimmed. My hair I had loosened from its braid and tied behind with little black ribbons, for it was damp still from the wet journey. He took my hands and stood away, looking up me and down, nodding. 'You know how to dress,' he said. 'Few women do.' It was an odd compliment, but I liked it. From my first choosing of clothes I have known that rich dark colors become me most, though Dada calls it too old a look for a maiden.

We walked a little, silently, he guiding me through the dry places as though I were an unbroke horse that might shy; I smiled to myself, remembering that my brothers would have pushed me in, like as not, and I not watchful for the potholes. Truly, it is a sweet thing to be handled so, and new to me as well.

'You have spoke with your father?' he asked finally. I nodded.

'Marred,' he said, and slowly, choosing his words. 'I am twenty-two ... I have not thought much on marriage. My father, while he lived, never pressed me to it, for we, my brother Tudor and I, have lands and manors enough without a bride-dowry to swell them.... And then, too, I have not known before a woman I might want in such wise, for a lifetime....' He threw me a side-glance, quizzical. 'There have not been so many as the court would have it either, though some few there have been ... and four sons I have—two sets of twins they are, who bide with my mother in Sycharth. I would have you know this, for I take pride in these my boys and will do them honor while I live....'

I had not expected such candor and I could find no words.

He went on, saying, 'You moved my heart, Marred, when first I saw you at the Tower chamber-door ... all in your disarray like any byre-maid ... but a queen's courage in your eyes....'

'I was frighted half to death,' I said, with a smile.

'I know,' he said.

'And also,' I said, my words rushing upon each other, 'I have none too many virtues either ... willful I am and of a vile temper sometimes——'

'I know,' he said. 'You are human, like us all. I would not wed a goddess, though it is pleasant that she looks like one....'

'You speak me fair, sir,' I said, very low. 'But you need not— for I love you and cannot hide it....' And then I melted, all my composure gone, and hot tears sprang and ran unchecked, and I sobbed in anguish. 'I love you—but I will not share you....'

He took me by the shoulders then, looking hard into my crumpled face. 'I would not ask it, Marred, sweet.... Listen, dearest, I have taken her away, back to her own country....'

I stared at him, then, the tears drying. 'And do you use all women so—to throw away when you have found another?'

His face went still as stone for a moment, as though I had slapped it. Then slowly he said, 'I—do not think so, truly. I would not wish to be such a one, man or woman.... But—we are all different, Marred. She is not you, nor you, she. I think she has been a-weary of me for many months now—bored with the English damp and the English chill as well—for she cannot appear at court, a merchant's daughter only she is and not welcome among the fine ladies. Wales, too, she hated; I sent her there for safety during the rising. My mother gave her much courtesy, but she is melancholy, Mother, and no joy or converse to be had from her.... Raimunde, that is her name——'

'Pretty,' I said, but hating its sound on his lips.

'Raimunde pined for Italy and the Milan court....'

'She is received there then?' I asked sharply.

He smiled a little smile, difficult to read. 'She is received into the Duke Bernabò's harem, which she has long desired....'

I was puzzled, for I did not know the word. 'Is that some women's order?' I asked. 'A convent...?'

He laughed, shortly. 'You might call it that....' Then his face was grave again and even a little stern. 'I will be honest with you. She has gone to be the duke's concubine....' I drew breath, greatly shocked. 'Do not look so,' he said. 'She will like it there, among all the other girls. She is a lightsome person, loving gaiety and little talk and easy graces. It was plain to see—after a short while. I blamed myself, for that I had debauched her. I took her from her father's house, after he died, and her mother with her; his affairs had been left in sad bankruptcy and they were glad of it....'

'I think you were kind,' I whispered fiercely.

'Well, I wanted her,' he said simply, each word striking a blow upon my heart.

He drew me to him and said, 'Listen well, little Marred. I have wanted others, too, in the same easy way, and they coming easily to me, for the silver and the gowns. But you I want in all ways, for as many years as I can see. You I want for lady—and for wife.'

'And you love me?' I asked, tremulous.

'Did I not say the word, then? ... It means so many things. ... Yes, I love you. I love you well....' His eyes held a look strange to me, that I was to see often in them—a look somehow inward, turned in to himself. 'Only once did I love before you ... long ago, and I a boy only. She was not noble, but of peasant stock. I would have wed her, not caring how many said me nay—but she would not have me....'

'She would not?' I asked, wondering. 'Where is she now?'

'She died—by her own hand,' he said, 'betrayed by another....'

'Oh, Jesus keep her ...' I whispered in pity. 'What was she like, poor damsel ...?'

'She was much like you,' he said. 'Pale and silver-gilt ... tall....'

I was much moved. 'I will pray for her....'

'She is dead only,' he said, his yellow eyes looking into mine, a strange hard look. 'Save your prayers for those who suffer ... they are many....'

It was an odd thought, and disquieting, to pass from lover to beloved on a betrothal-day.

But that was Owen, my husband, as I knew him all my days.

BOOK IV

THE RED DRAGON

Told by Griffith Lloyd, Owen's bard

ONE

Never will I forget my first sight of the Lady Margaret of Wales, Owen's bride. Tall and straight she was, and beautiful, and lit up the dim little church of St. Sulien's like a thousand candles.

Lovely, laughing women there are all over Wales, and more in the great world beyond, and I have seen them. None to match her have I seen, though, then or after. The heart speaks once only.

Though Owen was descended from the three great princely strains of the Cymry and his coffers overflowed with the wealth of an emperor, yet was no more made of that marriage day than any petty house of the gentry might run to. King Richard and his new queen would have come; indeed the Lady Helen, Owen's mother, vowed, weeping, that they had begged, both, for an invitation. That is not to be taken for a fact, of course, for that lady has gone sadly awry in her wits since Lord Griffith met his death.

There was next of kin only in the little church, apart from myself and the miller Iestyn; strange choices both, some would say, but that is Owen. Still was it filled to overflowing, St. Sulien's, and the courtyard, too, and the roads lined, all, for miles about. For that family is honored greatly by all the poor villagers, for its grace and mercy to those beneath it; even though the manor-house has been closed these several years, still do the folks have long memories.

Bards and minstrels crowded the yard; old Iolo had been bid first to do him honor, but refused to step inside the church. Pagan and stubborn has he been all his days, Iolo, and living in the past; some of the younger bards had carried him there in an armchair, and he sat at state, like a very chieftain, outside the church door, in his robes marked with old Druid signs, or what passes for them nowadays.

It was a simple ceremony, too, with no pomp or show, for the

Lady Margaret is a Lollard, or so they say. Instead of a ring to bind his vows, Owen clasped about the bride's waist an antique warrior's belt, cunningly wrought of little shields chained together, with the center large one representing the old red dragon sign of Wales. He had dug it up somewhere, and said it was from Arthur's time or before; polished it was, though, and gleaming bright in the dim church, looking like gold but yellower. Later I found that it *was* gold, and the dragon made of rubies, set in; the lady wore a king's ransom, for sure, and another was at home, for she was very narrow-waisted, and the belt had been cut to size.

Inside the church, beside Owen's mother, stood his four bastard sons, still not much more than babies, but richly dressed, and their fair hair done up lovingly, by the grandmother's hand, into cherub curls. I could not help but muse upon the young bride's thoughts, for delicate and tender she was as a young shoot, no mistake, and it is not all bastards who are honored so. She stooped and kissed them after, though, each one in turn, and her sweet eyes loving upon them.

When the wedded couple came out, walking arm in arm, cheers and clapping filled the air, and some of the minstrels put hand to lute and struck up a lively air, known to all the folk, and the cotter-people began to fall in behind the wedding-party. There would be dancing and feasting all day upon the manor green, and each was dressed in his best and scrubbed and shining. The couple had not reached their horses, tethered a little ways off, when a strange thing happened, strange and something unpleasant. The bride, smiling, had just turned away; a clod of earth and manure struck her in the back of the head, spattering her red head-veil. It had been aimed at her face, for I saw the throw. Quickly I ran, catching the culprit and pinning him by the arms; a fool I felt too, for he was not above six years or seven at the most, and his little arms like sticks on him. A face black and scowling as an imp of Satan he had, though, and hill-Welsh filth coming out of his mouth. He was alone, or so it seemed, though the near folk said a woman had been standing there beside him; no sign of her now was there, though, and he answering nothing when he was asked. A hill-woman they said she was, queer-dressed in the old way, with glass beads sewn all about her skirts and feet bare as the day she was born. One said she put the clod into the boy's hand and whispered low, before she vanished.

A little knot of people had gathered round; Owen pushed his way through them and stooped before the boy, looking level into his eyes. 'What is your name, boy?' he asked, grave but kind.

'Rhys,' he said, looking down at the ground. 'Rhys Gethin.'

Someone cried, 'Rhys the Savage!' And another, 'A savage for sure—steals chickens and eats them raw!' And a woman made the sign of the evil eye.

'A small savage it is, for sure,' said Owen, smiling small. 'Look at me, Rhys.... Do you hold me Lord?'

The boy shook his head, the long hair wild about his face. 'We have no lords up there—where I come from. But,' he said, bold and his black eyes angry, 'I am of your house ... my mother told me. It is my mother should walk where she walks!' And he pointed to the Lady Margaret where she stood white-faced and still. A gasp went up from all sides, and I looked at him close. Nothing of Owen's house had he, in face or color; pure old Celt he was, small-boned, red-brown of skin, and black of hair, showing already the flattish nose and jutting lips that mark the race. There are still a few of them about in the hills, living in caves like animals and worshiping old gods; some say they were here before the early Britons even.

Owen still stayed there, low, looking intently at his face. 'The lady you struck is my wife,' he said. 'And I do not know your mother....'

'She knew you once!' cried the boy. 'All your lords she knew——' And he used an obscene word; old Welsh it was, but close enough that all understood. 'All the lords and lordlings she knew ... good Griffith and Bad Vaughan—Red Howell—and the gold ones, Tudor and Owen.... She said it, she herself, many times. I am of your house!'

I saw Owen turn and look at his brother, Tudor, a strange look; Tudor's lip curved, sheepish, and he shrugged. Owen bent his look again upon the boy. 'Then, little Rhys, if you are of my house, you must come and live in it....' There was another gasp, and a stunned silence after, at those words. 'Loose him, Griffith Lloyd,' Owen said to me. 'He will be quiet now.... Rhys Gethin, go to your mother. Ask her leave. And if she gives it, come when you will ... but within the next fortnight, for we leave for another manor, two mountains away.' And he held up two fingers. 'If you have anything you want by you, you must bring it, too....'

The boy shook his head. 'There is nothing ... oh—my bow!'

'Is it a good bow?' asked Owen.

'I made it myself!'

'Then bring it. Go along now....' The boy still stood, not moving. Owen rose. 'Go along—what is it?'

The boy wet his lips; after a moment he said, 'Lord Owen—I have a wolf cub—almost tame he is....'

'No,' said Owen gravely, shaking his head. 'Noble houses do not harbor wild animals now. That was in the ancient days only. I will give you a hound-puppy....' The boy stared, then snatched up Owen's hand, and held his dark cheek to it for a little moment. Then he was gone, darting away into the trees like a small black shadow.

The feasting was good and the dancing better; Owen had ordered a great platform built, with fine wood floor, smooth to the feet, and the minstrels sat near, playing all the old country tunes and, later, some of the newest from court. Owen and his lady led the dancing, and very well they did it, though I noticed she breathed heavily after some of the more boisterous rounds. She had taken off the smirched head-veil and put on a garment new to me, a kind of sleeveless mantle of some thin stuff, dark blue; it turned the bride-gown beneath to purple. Against the dark richness her red sleeves flamed and the ruby dragon shone like a sun. Her flowing hair, like a sheet of paler gold, was held back by a purple ribbon. It was a new and outlandish fashion, from the English court, I guessed, or from France or Italy, but it became her well. Never again, though, did I see her go in red; the Lady wore black and white, creams and silver-grays, without ornament and of a flowing line; it was the Lollard in her, perhaps, for they go plain always. She never needed ornament, though, the Lady Margaret; she was a jewel of herself.

Old Iolo came forward after the dancing, with the Druid

bands and the bowl of blood; it is a custom hereabouts, to
honor the Druid wedding-rites. Owen bore Iolo much love and
would have done it to please him, but the Lady shook her
head. 'I cannot countenance it, sir. It is against my beliefs....'

'Oh, Marred, come——' said Owen. 'It is such a little thing
to please the greatest bard of the land.... It means nothing, an
old custom only.'

But again she shook her head. 'I cannot....' She could be
stubborn, my Lady, my heart's life.

He was my kinsman, Iolo, and I knew him well; I saw the
dark red creep up to cover his face, almost purple it showed
against the red of beard and hair. He was old then, and
would live much longer; even on his death-day and feeble as a
newborn babe, he trembled with choler. He glared at her out
of his fierce old eyes; for a moment I thought he would strike
her. She reddened too, but stood her ground, giving him look
for look. Then he said, and shrugging, 'Ah, well, it is no
matter. The Druid marriage is for another lady, and later. Another and more beautiful....' And he turned away and took
his seat again, not looking at her.

'You have offended him, sweet,' whispered Owen, in his
lady's ear.

Her face was troubled, for she had a kind nature always. 'I
am sorry, Owen. I feel strongly ... I could not....' She looked
up at him suddenly. 'What did he mean, another lady...?'

'Oh, some nonsense only,' said Owen, smiling broad. 'Some
bardic nonsense—to spite you....'

He would not take up his harp, though, Iolo, sitting stern in
his ancient hard majesty, though all the folk begged him, and I
knew he had spent hours preparing a eulogy for the dead Lord
Griffith, Owen's father.

All the other bards came forward to give of their best, sweet
songs of the Cymry, known to all, and I myself did something
new of my own; well received it was, though I say it myself,
and Owen gave me a gold arm-ring. But still Iolo sat, unmoved
and unmoving.

'Owen, Lord,' said Lady Margaret, low, 'shall I ask him?
Shall I go upon my knees and ask him, begging his pardon?
Perhaps——'

'Go upon your knees you shall not,' said Owen, laughing. 'He is an old bad boy only ... but we shall go together, and you ask him nicely....'

'Revered sir,' she said, standing before the old tyrant. 'Will you not honor us with one song.... I beg you—for the whole vast world rings with the name of Iolo Goch the great ... and I have never had the pleasure.... Please—for me and for my father and brothers, who are not from these parts....'

He looked up at her; the furious glare changed slowly to a sly look, like a bad child planning mischief. He rose and said, 'I will play ... but first I must kiss the bride ... a bargain?'

She came forward, blushing a little, thinking to receive the kiss of courtesy or an old man's dry smack. He seized her and bent her back, kissing her full and hard on the lips. A long, long moment it was, and he still with his mouth planted, and his old hand, hard as horn from the harp strings, fumbling in her bosom. Owen stepped forward then, parting them, and taking the lady about the waist. His face was set in hard lines and I knew him angry, but he laughed and said, 'Iolo—that is kiss enough for a hundred songs.... Did you think to bed the bride first? Get you now to your harp and finger it instead!' So saying, he walked his lady back to their high seats.

Iolo came forward then, shambling like an old man, for show, and I brought his harp to him. He bowed before the couple, hand over his heart, as is the bardic way; something insolent there was in it, though, a sly old devil he is, my kinsman, genius and all.

'Play then,' said Owen, again in the lordly custom. 'And,' he added, 'it had better be good!'

It was, of course. Not good, but great, one of the greatest eulogies ever played or sung; there was not a dry eye in the whole crowd, even the Hanmer in-laws wept, though they had not known the Lord Griffith even. Old-fashioned it was, and the sentiments tawdry as dead flowers; but genius worked in it, leavening the flat dough. Greatest of the great was he always, Iolo; none other can match him.

When most of the folk had gone home, happy and drunk, and the soft grays of twilight crept all about, Owen called me to him, bidding me fetch my small harp. 'Oh, God save me, Owen, I cannot follow Iolo!'

'No, not that am I asking ... not a bardic song ... enough of that have we had anyway by now. Play us a Latin love-song, Abélard, maybe——'

I took my little harp, a pretty thing it is, and a new fashion; something between harp and lute it is, and tuneful above both. I ran my fingers over the strings to get the feel. 'Shall I Welsh it?' I asked.

'No, give us the Latin, for we all here know some of the words....'

I gave them the beautiful 'Pervigilium Veneris' of two centuries agone:

> With the strange cry of swans the pools are shrill:
> The nightingale beneath the poplar shade
> Singeth, as though remembering the passion,
> Forgetful of the pain.
> She sings, I hold my peace:
> For when will come my spring?

I do not know if any of my hearers wept; I did not care. My heart within me wept unseen, for this was my cry of love.

TWO

Next day the hill-boy, Rhys, came down from his wooded lair, bearing his small hand-made bow and a bundle of fox-skins, red and silver. They were not cured properly and stank, the dark blood still staining the undersides, but Owen took them gravely, thanking him. 'We shall have to find suitable clothes for you, Master Rhys; all who live in houses must dress as befits their rank. Will you wear my livery then and serve as a page? You are something older than the other noble boys of my manor. I cannot put you in the nursery....'

'What is ... page?' asked Rhys, wrinkling his forehead.

'Well, you will do errands ... small tasks ... all noble boys serve thus. Later you will learn weaponry and to sit a horse....'

'I can ride horses now ... and I have my bow.' He looked suspicious still.

'Well, the hill-ponies are too small to count. I meant chargers. And long-bows—and a sword, too, when it is time....'

'A sword? Like that?' And he pointed to the dagger at Owen's belt.

'No, that is a knife for cutting meat at table. You shall have one of those, too. A sword is long and very sharp....'

The small dark face lit. 'Oh, I will like that!'

'Good,' said Owen. 'But first we must clean you up.' And he whistled a manservant to him. 'This is Rhys ab—well, we do not know ... Rhys of the hills, let us say ... Scrub him up, skin, hair, lice and all ... and give him a page's gear....' And off went that young savage, scowling black, for he shied always at a strange face; indeed he was never tamed, truly, black of heart and deed he was to the end of his days, though true, in his way, to the house he claimed.

He never made page, though he wore Owen's green with the small red dragon badge; set at work with the animals, to care for them and keep them, he practiced shooting with his bow into a clutch of hens or a pen of swine. Beaten for it, he would not utter cry, but turned and bit the hand that held the rod. He could not learn his letters, either to write or speak, even the simplest, or to pour the table wine, or to hold the napkin. Friendly was he to none, save Owen himself. Only battle songs moved him; his dark face shone at a war saga, and his feet moved to the march. In truth he never learned the ways of civilization. Except for one sort; he was quick at all weaponry, alert to all the arts of war. In time he served us well, and all Wales owes him honor. But in his childish days he was the wolf-cub always.

He could not endure the manor ways; three times he tried it, living within walls, and three times gave up, fleeing back into the hills. The last time, when he was twelve, he disappeared, we thought forever. Much later, he returned, at Welsh need and for love of Owen. But that story comes later.

My story is of Owen and his house; of his children and his

kinsmen, his minstrels and his bards, and of his lady that
headed them all. It was a huge household; the little country
manor at Dolgelly could not hold it. After two weeks spent in
celebration, we removed, all, to Sycharth, the great goodly
manor that had been Owen's birthplace. Long and low and
modern it was, in the Italian style, rambling over much of an
acre. There was a moat and a drawbridge, but I never remember the bridge drawn; open house and open hearth kept
Owen, wherever he was, and a welcome set out for all.

I remember the day we arrived there at Sycharth; Owen,
twinkling, called all the house-folk to him, and made much
teasing ceremony with his lady, solemnly handing over the
great keys to her. There must have been well over a dozen—
bakehouse, scullery, chapel, smokehouse, and all the rest. And
each weighing a good weight in itself; foolish they looked
hanging in a bunch from her girdle and pulling it low upon
her hips.

'Oh,' she said, and laughing gay, 'I shall go lopsided from
this day! Heavy they are—and how shall I know which from
which?'

'That is your business,' said Owen airily. 'And now we shall
call you Argylwyddes!'

'A heavy name,' she said, 'and what does it signify?'

'I guess it is not used much in those border parts where you
come from, half-English they are there.... But it is our word
for "lady of the manor" or maybe "keeper of the keys." ...'

'The French is prettier,' she said. 'Châtelaine....'

'But not so solemn-sounding, little Argylwyddes....'

It was a merriness between them, and now and then he
called her by it, bowing and hand over his heart, in jest. Much
later, and the household grown with growing children, and she
moving in dignity about it, the title stuck, somehow, and many
addressed her so.

She wore the great keys at her waist, the Lady Margaret,
from that day, heavy as they were. And heavy were the responsibilities for that slip of a girl, too, in that huge and burgeoning household. The Lady Helen, Owen's mother, was
little help, for she was much given to melancholy and sometimes kept all day to her bed, weeping. When she was up and

about, she was not much better, for she was fumbling and forgetful, her wits addling more each day. Margaret's kinswoman,
her Aunt Janet, was the Lady Helen's twin in all things; like
withered babies they were, in Margaret's care, one thin, one
fat.

Branwen, though, her maid that had come from home with
her, was capable and strong, a merry creature, too. And when
the Lady Margaret was pregnant for the first time, she sent for
her old nurse. A tiny thing she was, but a staunch rock to lean
upon. She stayed like a small shadow by Margaret's side, stern
and bristling, and with a rough tongue and hard hand to rule
the maidservants. She filled a need, Nurse, worth her weight in
gold she was; Margaret was gentle and never scolded, Nurse
making up for it and keeping discipline like a battle commander.

Twin daughters she had and two days and nights in hard
labor, paying for her narrow elegance. The Israelite attended
her, the physician Master Nathan, for Owen would have no
midwife, naming them superstitious bunglers. Owen, too,
stayed by her side through it all, against custom, and scandaliz-
ing the older folk. After, Margaret said, smiling wan and white-
lipped, 'Oh, Owen, it seems you can make nothing but twins—
can you not try half as hard next time?'

'Oh, Marred, sorry I am . . . so hard for you it was. . . .' Owen
was white, too, and glistening with sweat, as though he had
brought them forth himself.

She smiled again. 'I jested only, sweet my lord . . .' and turning her head upon the pillow, she fell asleep.

Pretty mites they were, the little twin girls, like as two peas
in a pod, and blue-eyed and flaxen-fair. They were christened
Margaret and Janet, the vicar of St. Suliens coming over the
two mountains to sprinkle the little faces and murmur Latin.
There were festivities for a week, dancing and harping, and
games played upon the green, for it was spring, to celebrate the
birth of Owen's first true-born children, though they were
daughters only.

Tudor, big and shamefaced, came to the Lady Margaret, laying upon her lap another set of twins, girls also, and of his own
making. 'Their mother is dead,' he said, 'and will you have the

care of them, for a mercy, Sister Marred?' They were fair babes too, big and rosy, with black hair and eyes.

'I will and gladly,' she said, but biting her lip to keep from smiling, 'if so be we can find so many wet-nurses....'

He did not smile, Tudor, though all the company laughed, but said, most earnest, gazing down at the little kicking bundles, 'Their names are Gwynneth and Gwenllian.'

'Which is which?' asked Owen.

Tudor scratched his head, frowning. 'I have forgot.... Oh, yes—Gwynneth has a mole beside her ear!'

'Ah, yes, I see it,' said the Lady Margaret, most grave.

'They will be good girls,' said Tudor. 'Their mother was a princess.'

Owen laughed loud, clapping his brother upon the shoulder. 'Tudor will bed with none but princesses.... Where, then, shall we find you a wife, brother?'

I guessed it had been a daughter of one of the hill-chieftains; they are many in these parts, all styling themselves kings. Wild and proud they are, and loving their freedom and the old ways; not Christian even are they but rear their sons to pillage and loot and give their daughters in barter. I wonder how much Tudor had paid.

So now there were eight children of that house; nine if you counted the doubtful Rhys of the hills.

There was much traveling about the countryside, and even farther, that spring and summer, to show off the new daughters. I think it was an excuse, though, for Owen always loved to seek out new places, and old, too. And the Lady Margaret was hardy, for all her fragile looks. Near a year did they spend from home, while the fine weather held, going first to Robert Pulestan, nearby, that was married to Owen's sister, Laura. Then on to Flintshire, Margaret's home, where the gurgling babies were solemnly dowered with rich portions, lands and goods. 'Leave some for your sons,' cried Owen. 'And for your sons' sons!'

'There is plenty for all!' cried the Judge Hanmer, his thin face flushed with wine and goodwill; he had much love for Owen, naming him executor of his estate when he himself should die. I saw much strangeness in this, for he had hale sons and hearty, almost grown now. They cheered with the rest, though, David Hanmer and young John; I remembered that they had no law-lore nor any love for it either, and so perhaps were glad to be rid of the burden. After, long after, the border English whispered that the Hanmers were all held by witchcraft, Owen's. It was a dark word that plagued him all his life, but ever would he swell the rumors, laughing, and calling upon Merlin and the dark fairies of the hills.

There came to Owen at the Hanmer manor a messenger from the English king, sweating he was and tired to drop from the saddle, for he had ridden hard, and thrusting a packet at Lord Owen, with the royal seals dangling from it. 'Bring wine and meat,' said Owen. 'Wine first'—with a sharp glance at the courier's drawn face. No more than a lad he was, and the man's heart not yet strong in him. I have thought often and often on this cruel practice; Norman it is and foreign to our Welsh ways that takes these boys and trains them to the fast saddle, wearing them out and killing them, like as not, before they are twenty.

When the lad was at ease and a little color coming back into him from the mulled wine, Owen broke the seals, carrying the royal letter to the fire-hearth, for it was evening. He read, frowning, and gave a short laugh, harsh. 'Our Dickon is going to war,' he said. 'Scotland, this time. They push at him again....'

'I do not take your meaning, sweet——' said Margaret.

'Well,' he said, drawling out the words, 'Richard needs pushing.... He has no stomach for war and war-play, which it is more like to be.... Nor have I either,' he said, sighing, 'if the truth be told ... but I am commanded to his side—commanded to take up my knighthood, too.... Well, the one I cannot avoid, he is my liege-lord ... but the knight's plume and all the rest—no, I will not!' And he held his nose, laughing. 'A stinking plague on all these Norman nuisances! I think I am not compelled....' And he turned to Sir David. 'What says the law, Sire Father?'

'You are within your rights, but——'

'Good. No buts then.' Owen's eyes crinkled like a cat's, and his lips twitched thinly. 'I shall say I cannot afford it....'

And all laughed then loud, except the Lady Margaret. 'Oh,

my lord—do not go ... you will be killed!'

'In Dickon's wars?' laughed Owen, putting an arm about her. 'I shall come to no harm. He wants me for a mountebank —to cheer him with my foolery and my magic. Like as not I shall not even see a battle....'

'Oh, do not go! Write ... say I am sick ... tell him I am with child——'

'Sweetheart, even Dickon will not accept me as nursemaid! I must go—it will not be for long. Richard will not endure the discomfort of winter quarters.... I shall be back before it is born....'

'*It*! Oh, Owen!'

'Well, Marred, I do not know the creature yet to do it honor ... no more than a seed it is, for sure....' And he tipped her head up and laid a kiss, light, on her closed eyes.

'It will be a son,' she said, angry a little she was, my sweet lady. 'It will be a son. I feel him kick already ... and he is sitting high. Nurse says it is a sure sign....'

'Sure sign of what?' teased Owen.

'Of a boy.' She was earnest and would not smile, though he pulled at her hair and tried to stop her mouth with kissing.

'A girl is carried lower ... Look—how high it is!'

'I can see nothing,' he said, pretending, for she was so slight that even an egg would show. 'I care not what it is, Marred. Except no changeling.... Give me no changeling....'

He left soon after, Owen, taking road for London and the king and thence to the Scottish Wars, the lady standing straight and proud and not weeping till he was out of sight around the bending road. Owen had left me with her as protector, and for a comfort with my songs, for she never could like Iolo; we took leave next day of her father and brothers, going back to Sycharth before the autumn chill set in.

I think she worked too hard, my lady, to keep from thinking, and strained her small strength, for the child was born early; a boy it was, as she had promised, but something small and puny. The old women muttered that it would not live for Owen's return. 'He will live,' said the doctor, Nathan, washing his hands. 'Just keep him warm, and do not wrap his legs but leave them free....'

'I shall call him Griffith,' she said, her small hand grasping mine to pull me down to her ear. 'It is Owen's father's name, but'—and she whispered low—'it is yours, too, dear friend....' And she smiled at me. So sweet she was, my lady, and I with my heart breaking within me.

When Owen came back, without a scratch on him, as he said, Margaret was mending fast and the babe, too, out of danger, though he was red and shriveled still. Owen bent over his lady where she lay with the child beside her and, still in his outer cloak, smelling of wet and snow, folded her in his arms and covered her face with kisses.

'Will you not greet your son?' she said, all rosy and laughing.

'I do not know him as well as you, sweetheart,' said Owen, looking down at the baby, who had set up a squalling from being crushed. After a moment, he said, 'He has good lungs, our son....'

'He is beautiful,' she said, patting the child and trying to quiet it. Owen reached out his hand for the babe and its little fist closed on a finger. It stopped its wailing, looking surprised. 'Ah,' said Owen, bending his look upon it, 'he's wondering who I may be. Well, we will get acquainted later, sirrah....' The child stared up at him, solemn as a judge. He laughed. 'It is Sir David to the life!'

'But he will call *you* Dada!' she cried.

'Never!' said Owen. 'I forbid it!'

She pouted, but in a merry fashion; I had never seen her so, and feeling shy, I left them.

I had much fondness for this firstborn of the lady; always I remembered the night of his birth, living it over and over again upon my bed alone, or beside the fire as I tried out the notes of a new song.

She had a hard time of it always, my sweet lady; all her birthings caused her great pain and travail. I think that with a midwife she would have died, for their skill is small, unless the patient be a very breeding cow, wide in the girth. That night, and Owen away at the wars, she cried out for him, over and over, hour after dreadful hour. Nathan came at last to me, where I waited, sick and frightened, in the hall below, and

asked me to come to her. 'You are near his size and shape ...
mayhap she will take heart, thinking he is near ...'

I stood beside her, awkward; she strained toward me in the
half dark, her pain-blind eyes searching, her hand grasping at
mine, slippery with sweat. 'Owen ... Owen ... my love....' I
took her in my arms, and she holding me in a grip that took
my breath; and so was the child drawn out of her, on one great
sobbing cry. After, she fell asleep, and I still holding her, my
arms growing numb with her sweet weight. She never spoke of it
after, and for sure, I told myself, she never knew. Yet had she
called him Griffith.

THREE

Owen told us tales of Richard's court, its fopperies and conceits, its gossip and its intrigue. Strange to my ears was this
world, as though it belonged upon a far star, and I shook my
head in wonder. Margaret listened, with the new babe, still
sickly, in her lap, wrapped warm against the winter nights,
while the other children squabbled happily among the hound-
puppies at our feet. Starved for news she was, Margaret, for she
knew them all, the queen and her ladies, young Richard and
his lightsome squires; her eyes danced, sparking silver in the
firelight, and her little laugh rippled out; now and again she
sighed. When Owen told of the Scottish trip, the whole court
in its hundreds, removing there to the wilds—horses, coffers,
musicians, pastry-cooks all going along, and the great wagons
near breaking from the weight of them all—she clapped her
hands, delighted. And true it was that Owen made them live,
those people and those happenings; better than any minstrel
was he, and made us laugh to hold our sides.

'Oh, Owen,' she cried, 'and Anne was there, in Scotland—
with her ladies, all! I too might have gone to war. You were a
churl to leave me behind!'

'The Lady Anne was not with child,' he said, with a soft
look, rebuking. 'Nor ever like to be ...' he added, low.

I saw the look then that passed between them, secret and something sly, before she said, 'And Rob de Vere—what of him? Is he still beside the king?'

'He and two new ones ... Bushy and Bagot, lords both, and newly created, but common as dirt under, and fair-freaks for sure....' And he rose, mincing on little feet, his elbows at his sides, and gesturing from loose wrists. One could see the lace and ribbons and smell the perfume too; here in Wales it is only the lesser sort of pages that go about so.

Old Iolo in his corner gave a rough sound in his throat and twanged a harp-string. 'Catamites!' he said, and spat into the fire, so that it hissed. ' 'Twas how the barbarians took Rome, all rotten from within, she was, at the end ... and Greece, too—that was once a pattern for the ages...'

'Not so simple as that was it, old pagan,' said Owen lightly. 'And not so bad yet is Richard's court....' He bent toward Margaret, saying under his breath, though I heard, 'But true it is ... some of it is rubbing off on Richard....'

She shook her head, sad and serious she was as an old dame clucking in a corner, and Owen laughed. 'The poor boy,' she said, 'he was a goodly youth once....'

'And so he is still,' said Owen. 'And only a little womanish around the edges.... It will not hurt England ... to have a—gentle king....'

There was a little silence. 'But tell me of the wars,' said Margaret. 'But softly, and not to frighten the children....'

Owen smiled. 'Nothing to frighten was there at all, not from where we sat. The castles of Scotland are near as fine as England's.'

'There were no battles then?'

'Oh, there were some, and some of the rougher knights went forth into the mists, and some few came back dead....'

'But you would not....'

He shrugged. 'Not if I could avoid it. It was not my war....' He smiled broad then, remembering. 'Lancaster went, thought....'

'The redheaded Henry? One would expect it ... so angry he was always....'

'Yes,' said Owen, 'and angrier now that he is grown. I think his gentle mother fed him thistles, or perhaps the pretty Swynford did it for spite. . . . He has married her, by the way.'

'Who—Gaunt?' Margaret's eyes were round. 'But she is a commoner!'

'Richard gave them permission. He has legitimized their bastards, too. They are called Beaufort now, with lands and titles to match, and much wealth. He has created much bad blood among his nobles by this, Richard. It was the act of a despot. . . .'

'She is very beautiful, Katharine Swynford,' said Margaret, wistful. 'I saw her once. . . .'

'I thought her overblown,' said Owen. 'Besides you, Marred, she is a blown rose.'

'Oh, Owen——' She laughed, protesting. But I knew her pleased, under. 'But he was not hurt in the wars—that angry Henry?'

'Not he,' said Owen. 'He came striding in—to the morning court in all its finery, the Lady Anne feeding Richard comfits from her hand—clank-clank in his armor, mud up to the waist, face redder than his hair and hair standing on end. Thud-thud-thud—on the floor at Richard's feet—he threw them, the poor shaggy Scots' heads, three of them, dripping blood.'

She shuddered, covering her face with her hands.

'That is just what Richard did!' cried Owen. 'And he called for someone to take them away. "Take the horrid things out!"' shrilled Owen in cruel maiden-mimicry. '"They are messing up my floor!"'

Shocked we all were at the show; he was our king, after all. But still we laughed till it hurt. Owen's face straightened then, and he said, 'Even so . . . it was like throwing down a gauntlet. For Richard was stung—and would have us go next morning in our turn—into the moors at sunup. Covered with plate he was, Richard, and surrounded by knights and esquires. Still, he did go. It was our only brush with the enemy. . . .'

'You also!' cried Margaret. 'And you never told me!'

'It was not much of a much,' he said. 'The Lady Anne gave us flamingo feathers to wear in our helms—from her favorite bird they were—and she acting as though we went to tourney for fun.... We waited long for the fellows to appear, it seemed all morning, so that we wearied in the saddle and sweated under our armor. Then suddenly, they rode out, yelling, from the low crags. Half-naked they were, with dried animal hides above their bare legs, showing bluish from the cold. One came straight at me. The horse was trained to war and would not back up—there was nothing for it, I had to put my sword out. It went into him, and he fell off his mount—dead he was, I guess, for it pierced his middle, but the sword was not tempered well, and it broke off. Nothing but a stump, jagged, left in my hand, and nowhere to go...'

'What happened?' whispered Margaret, on a breath.

'I stabbed with it, over and over again. I do not know if it ever hit a mark. The mist was too thick by then to see even a foot before your face. It was a nightmare, unremembered, like all battles. We outnumbered them, I guess ... they faded away at the end. And we came back, heroes ...' He laughed, harshly. 'Richard tried to knight me, after ... he was excited as a boy at play and surprised at his winning, too.... 'Out! I cried. 'Out, Dickon. I'll be no knight!' And so he gave over. Well,' he said heavily, 'that was it ... that was our battle. We came home after, with all our train.' And now he slumped in his chair, his big frame looking old, on a sudden, and sad. He ever could make pictures with his body, Owen, more telling-real than any song. 'I do not relish fighting without a cause ... and killing.' He sighed then, and held out his hand to Margaret. 'And our own cousin Celts, too, for so I know them to be ... the Scots.'

That was Owen's tale; old Iolo has it somewhat differently, and of course, his song is the one that will live, says Owen wryly. In that magnificent ode, our Owen is the greatest warrior the world has yet seen, mowing down fierce enemies with no more than a broken stump, and none can withstand.... By the hundreds they flee from the famous Knight of the Flamingo! Life and poetry are far apart, the old poetry anyway. There is a newer style coming in, with simpler words and shorter sentences, to let the truth shine through. Owen is kind enough to call me its leader, this New Bardry; I can only hope to do some justice by it before I am gone from this world.

Owen was restive all that winter, pettish and sharp as I had never seen him. If I did not know him so well, I would have thought him jealous of the new babe. For I saw his look upon him as he lay sleeping in his cradle, a look hard to read. He slammed down the book he was reading, too, when the poor small Griffith began his wailing, and strode blackly from the room. He wailed often and long, and did not grow, and the Lady Margaret gave him all her time, Owen flinging at her that she neglected the other children, and she weeping after. Owen spent much time from home, too, riding hard among his lands or climbing lonely upon a hill. Once, when the hoofbeats were hard upon the packed earth, and we listened, all, to the sound as it faded into the distance, the Lady Helen spoke, his mother. Mostly she mumbled or sang sad songs, low, and did not answer when she was spoken to, but this day was she bright and sharp as a fresh-minted coin. Nodding sagely, she said, 'So did his father ride from me, often and often, and I weeping sore ... so did he stay from me, and I not knowing where ... it is the blood will out, the dark blood of the Powys....' And Margaret cast anguished eyes upon her and held the babe close, clutching, until he cried again, waking.

One morning, and the thaw setting in, melting the snow and making it run off the rooftree with a sound like a little rushing river, we sat at ale and bread, Margaret, as always, dandling the little Griffith before the hearth-fire. She would not eat, though Owen buttered a slice of fine white bread and brought it to her; she said, gazing anxiously down, that the babe had caught a cold during the night. True as she said, the small nose was red and running, and the lips were chapped, a pitiful sight. 'We will fetch Nathan to him,' said Owen. 'It is nothing ... meanwhile let us wipe his nose ...' And, so saying, in a gesture rare from him, he took out his own face-cloth and gently dabbed at the small face. The child woke, screaming.

'Oh—Jesus,' cried Margaret softly, 'he is turning blue!' For Griffith was yelling now at the top of his lungs, hiccoughing and choking, eyes squeezed tight shut and the little fisted hands beating the air.

'It is temper only,' said Owen, taking the baby and turning him upside down, shaking him; the child stopped crying and stared at him, the color coming back into his face. Margaret ran to Owen and snatched the child, so that he set up a fresh wailing, thin and fretful.

'Poor sweeting, did the big bad man fright you? Big, rough man! Mother will hold you. Mother won't let him get you.... There ... there!' She jounced him up and down on her lap, crooning, and still he wailed. She fumbled in the pocket of her gown and brought out a small piece of honeycomb, saved over from the summer, sticky and dark, and thrust it to his lips. He stopped crying and sucked on it greedily, then jerked away his head, and threw it up, soiling his mother and himself.

'Margaret, for God Almighty's sake, have I not told you to leave off stuffing him with sweets!' said Owen, impatient now and angry. 'Babies cannot stomach such things! Where is his nurse?'

'Her milk does not agree with him. We are giving him cow's milk.'

'Can she not take him from you at least? And clean him up? You spend too much time with this boy, Margaret. Such gentleness you never showed the twins....'

Margaret, stung, cried out, 'I was a good mother to them always—but they are not sick ... never were they sick as my little Griffith ...'

'Then let Nathan tend him! And listen to what he tells you! You make him sicker with your fawning and coddling——' He broke off suddenly. 'There is a sour smell in this room!' And he strode to the window, flinging open the shutters. The day flooded in, bright and beautiful, with a moist hint of spring.

'Oh, God, Owen,' she cried. 'You will kill him in this wind!'

'The fresh air never killed anyone,' he said, exasperated. 'You will kill yourself with worry. Leave us, madame. I will call Nathan to you....' And he turned on his heel, stiff, and went to the door, summoning a page. 'Get you inside——' he said, turning back, but his voice was kinder. 'Get you inside, my dear, and clean him up ... and rest. You have had no sleep this last week of nights. Rest a little.' She still stood, staring numbly. He raised his voice, sharp. 'Go now—leave us. Before he howls again——' And he turned his back, his face dark with his dark mood. And not a word did she say, but bent her head and left the hall, pressing the child's round small head to her shoulder.

Owen let out a breath, loud. He walked to the open window, sniffing. 'It smells of spring—not baby!' And he laughed shortly and clapped me on the shoulder. 'Will you ride with me, Griffith the grown? I have a mind to see the hills, and they running with the first floods ...'

As we waited for the saddling, Owen said, brooding, 'I cannot bear to see her so! Forever with this one runt-child she is, cozening and tickling. She will not heed the doctor either, but tips out the potions he brings, when he is not looking, and feeds him her own sticky sweets—or sometimes it is a lump of bloody liver crammed in his mouth or hot broth spooned in and it running down....' And he made a face, disgusted. 'Look you, Griffith, night after night she spends beside his cradle, if he so much as rustles in his sleep! She will not call his nurse or any to help her. If he cries, she takes him up and brings him into the bed to lie between us. And I, too—I cannot sleep for fear I will turn over and crush him ... and so it has gone since his birth. God forgive me, I cannot like him for it!'

'It is not the little one's fault, Owen,' I said, finally.

'No,' he said, 'you are right ... to be angry with a babe! My wits are going from me!' And he shook his head as if to clear it. 'No, it is she ... it is Marred that angers me!'

'She is afraid for him,' I said.

'There is no need ... he will mend. Nothing is wrong with the babe, Nathan said it—a little colic, a distemper....'

'She will get over it,' I said. 'Women are like that when a child is weak or sickly ... I mind me your mother when Tudor was born, and I a child myself only, and visiting. He was small and puny, though hard it is to credit now—she was forever coddling and cosseting....'

'Sweet Jesus!' he hissed, reddening. 'And I should hope she will never go my mother's way! ... Mother was ever a fool.'

'She will not. It will pass.'

He gave me a keen look that pierced; there was a little silence. 'Ah, here are our mounts,' he said, stabbing his toe into the stirrup and swinging up, whistling to his horse softly.

We headed out on the straight road to old Dinas Brân, the

air sweet as new wine, and a little breeze sharpening it; after a bit we flung back our hoods, for it was close on noon and almost hot, for a wonder.

'I mind how we rode this way ... long ago it was, and Tudor with us.... Is it still there, do you think—the House of the Snake?' Owen asked. I said I supposed so, I had heard nothing. 'And she is dead by now, I am thinking,' said Owen, musing, 'the lady named for a witch, the Lady Morgan. Beautiful she was as a goddess, but old even then ...'

'Not so old as that,' I said. 'It is not ten years ...'

'I asked Iolo about that lady—just a little while ago it was— and I remembering suddenly,' said Owen. 'He never answered —but looked at me strangely, a sly look; you know how he can be, as if he knew a secret—the old devil!'

'And said nothing?'

'Nothing sensible. Just something like, "Ah—so you have come to it at last!" And something about the old Powys blood will out, or some such ... full of old Druid nonsense he is, and likes to play the cryptic. I know not why we endure him, but for his art....' And he shook his head, laughing.

It was still there, we saw it ahead of us, from far away, flat-roofed, with conical mountain of Brân behind it, dark against the sky. I thought to ride on, but Owen drew rein at the low entrance, leaning from his horse to peer beneath the roof. He gave a little short laugh and said, 'Strange—before, when I was a boy and we came here, I thought it vast, this place, and with an antique magnificence.... I see now it is small and shabby—crude too, like the work of children——'

'The cave behind is very old,' I said, remembering, 'and this built on in recent times....'

'I cannot recall the cave,' said Owen. 'Only the Lady Morgan ...' And he dismounted slowly, as in a dream, and walked into the place, past the snake-columns with the faded, flaking paint. I followed, almost against my will; the place had a faint repugnance for me, yet was I drawn to it in spite of myself, and Owen, too.

Inside was a close smell, musty and with a hint of earth and mold; cobwebs lay in the corners, but the earth floor was swept clean under the rude altars, and the goddess-image, Epona on her horse, was free of dust, for I touched it, curious. It was old, so old; the stone was pitted, and the features of the face almost worn away. 'Where has she come from, do you think?' mused Owen, beside me. 'Perhaps the Roman legions brought her ... or she may be older still, from the time the first Cymry-folk set foot on our shores.... Strange—most of these little statues are wood; I myself have one at home that I stole from a shrine in the forest ...' There was an eager note in his voice, and I knew he coveted it; Owen was forever collecting such things, the older and uglier, the better; full of a sense of history was Owen, always. He put out his two hands to lift it, but small as it was, it was too heavy. He shook his head, laughing. 'Well, I cannot steal this one, it seems....' He still stood and studied it, walking round to look at it from all sides. 'It is too heavy for an earth-stone ... it must have been carved from a piece of fallen star ...' I stared at him, shocked. 'Oh, there are many such stones ...' he said. 'I myself saw one fall, in a field, making a deep crater in the earth. When I ran to see it, I found it just such a stone, rough and pitted from its swift long journey through the sky ...' I stared still; my thoughts had never run on such things. 'Look you,' he said, seeing my face. 'I think it may work ...' And he drew his dagger from his belt and laid the blade flat against the stone. There was a tiny click, and when he took away his hand, it stayed there, held by the stone. He drew his breath, excited. 'It draws the metal, do you see? There are such stones deep in our own earth. At the bottom of a dry riverbed you will find them, or in the bowels of a mountain where there is a cave-fissure ... they are not so powerful as this, they will hold a needle only, but—one can see how the ancients worked their magic, for it does look like magic-work, does it not? There is a natural explanation for all such things —witchcraft, the Sight, all these wonders—if one could be have the time to search it out....'

I thought to myself: Oh, Owen, never will there be time enough for you to do all these things you long to do—a lifetime is not enough, for a man so delving, so eager to know all. I think he divined my thoughts, for he bent a curious look on me, and spoke; always had he this mind probing, a secret of his own.

He said, 'Old friend, say it. All the knowledge in the world
—sought out for a lifetime and stored together—will not add
up to the magic of one perfect song. . . .' And his eyes seemed to
turn into himself, and he was silent long. Then he said, 'And I
am the more bereft, for I cannot make a song . . . or any other
thing that lives, like this carving even'—and he slapped its side
and pulled his dagger away, sheathing it. 'And so I must search
always—to find a little here and there . . .'

We entered the cave proper then, stooping, for both of us
had grown since the other time; there was no spotted fur hanging at the entrance now, but inside there was a rushlight burning, resin-soaked, for the smell caught in the nostrils. We could
see the walls; closer to us they were than we had thought, and
covered with painted symbols, the paint still fresh-garish, for no
sun came here. We drew breath in wonder, both, for the work
was of another age, and the signs not known to us, lost in the
mists of time. There was Epona again, but wearing a flounced
skirt and a diadem; her breasts were bare. The gods were all
woman-gods; one suckled twin babes, another had a huge fertile belly, and little baleful eyes, a third was covered with
breasts, like the dugs of a sow; I counted upwards of twenty.
On a far wall was painted a goddess, cross-legged, with six
arms, writhing like snakes; the rushlight did not reach so far,
and in the dim, it looked real, like a monster, and I felt the
flesh creep on me. Owen pointed upward, at the ceiling, silently. I looked; across the whole width was a picture of a huge
woman, her feet apart, each foot planted among hundreds of
tiny men, two armies at war. Her face was fierce and horrible,
the mouth dripping blood, and a horned helmet on her head.
'It is the war-goddess, Morrighen,' whispered Owen. 'I have
seen her likeness before, but on a bit of pottery in an old grave,
and small-graven to strain the eyes.'

A large altar was there, hollowed out in the middle and dark-
stained with old, old blood. Behind it on the wall was painted
a huge single staring eye, black-ringed, with a red center. 'The
secret symbol of the Mother,' whispered Owen. 'In ancient days
no man could look upon it, but that he turned to stone. . . .' I
crossed myself, and he laughed, but shakily. 'She has no power
anymore. . . . The woman-gods do not live any longer—except

here, perhaps, in this timeless place—though perhaps the Virgin-worship ...' And he rubbed his chin, thinking. Now was I truly shocked, for I am a Christian true, and it was blasphemy he spoke; yet such was his hold on me, then as ever, that I said nothing. Owen was like the star-rock; he drew men to him as the stone drew steel.

We stayed awhile, quiet and awed; as we turned to leave, Owen put out his hand to touch one of the painted walls. The color came off, powdery, onto his finger, a deep dark purple. 'Curious,' he said, 'what manner of coloring did they use, those old image-makers?' I said perhaps it was a chalk-stuff, colored with plant-dyes, and he nodded. 'Well, it is not used anymore, this cave, that is evident, though someone keeps the rushlight burning and sweeps the floor...'

'Whoever it is,' I said, eyeing the cobwebby corners as we passed through the wooden house, 'she is not a good housekeeper...'

I heard him laugh as he walked ahead of me, out into the sunlight. 'And here, I think, she is—the housekeeper....'

I looked where he pointed, halfway up the hill to the old fortress of Dinas Brân. A girl was coming down, leaping from hummock to crag, as surefooted as a hill-pony; she carried a short broom such as one sees at cottage hearth-sides. The wind caught the edge of the upper garment she wore, flinging it out and exposing a breast; she saw us staring and caught the cloth together with her free hand, though her look was bold still. As she came closer, I saw that she was beautiful.

She called out to us, pure Old Welsh it was, with the bardic cadence that is hardly ever heard anymore, even in the songs. 'Who are you? What do you want?'

Owen answered, the words difficult on his tongue and a little slow, that we had hoped to see the Lady Morgan.

'She is blind now and does not come down from the Ladies' Tower anymore,' said the girl. 'I am her granddaughter. I am Lowri.'

Owen caught his breath. 'I have seen you, too, then ... a little maid you were when I was last here in this place....'

She looked at him as a man looks, hard and direct. 'I do not remember.'

'Will she greet us, do you think,' said Owen, 'if we go up there?' And he gestured to the ruined castle. She shook her head. 'Not today. She is resting today. She rests most days—except when we sacrifice.'

He smiled. 'What do you sacrifice?'

She looked at him, a cool look. 'It is a mystery.'

He laughed again. 'But not to you.'

'Of course not,' she said, tossing her head. 'I am a priestess.' I saw then that she was very young. Beautiful she was, but strange, as strange as the clothes she wore. Her short skirt was full above her bare feet; a dark-red color it was, and made in flounces like the skirt of the Epona painting. The upper garment reached only to the waist and was split in front and without fastenings; each time she breathed, one caught a glimpse of white flesh, whiter than snow. She clanked and jingled with gold, her arms covered with bangles, long strings of gold beads wrapped round her throat; from her ears hung large gold rings, almost covered by her hair, which was worn loose and flowing. It, too, was a red color, but brighter than her dress, the color seen sometimes on a leaf in the autumn. Her skin was very white and her eyes were blue. They were set in a slant, upwards at the outer corners, wild-animal eyes. There was a wild-animal look about her altogether, to my mind, though every smallest gesture and movement was almost ritualized, as in some kind of dance. Owen followed her about as she tidied up the place, talking to her, a teasing note in his voice; I had never heard him thus before.

'It is swept clean already,' he said. 'Do you come every day?'

'When I can,' she answered, blowing at a speck of dust on the Epona statue. She peered at it close, unsatisfied, and picked up the tail of her dress to dust it; we saw she wore nothing beneath.

'Are you *her* priestess?' asked Owen.

'Of course not,' she said, scornful. 'She is only a little goddess.'

He smiled. 'You serve the Mother then?'

She flashed a look at him, then nodded.

'I have forgot her name ... Diis, is it? Dia?'

'We do not say her name. It is forbidden.' And she put her finger to her lips as if to make sure.

'Who is "we"?'

'There are many priestesses up there ... in the castle. I am the highest, though, after my grandmother. When she dies, I will be The Lady.'

'And your mother?'

Her lips came together, tight. 'I am not allowed to speak of her. She ran away—to live with a man ...' Her voice sounded frightened.

'And so she cannot be a priestess now...?'

'Oh, no!' she said, shocked. 'She cannot ever come back, even....'

'Was the man she ran away with your father?'

'How am I to know?' she asked. 'She never said.'

'You remember her then....' Owen was not teasing now; his voice was gentle.

'A little ... I think. It is very long ago.' Her face was shut in again; she turned away and went through the cave-opening. We saw the light dip; she must have been checking it. She came back, holding the edges of her garment together, with both hands. She had left the broom inside; perhaps she would sweep the cave-floor later. 'Go now,' she said. 'It is time for afternoon prayer.'

'When can we come again?' asked Owen, softly.

She shrugged. 'I cannot tell when The Lady will receive you. She does not often speak to strangers. Perhaps ... next week.'

'Tell her it is Owen, Prince of Wales, and the bard, her kinsman....'

'I will tell her,' she said, her face expressionless.

Owen stepped forward, putting his hand under her chin to lift it and looking into her eyes. 'Do you never smile?'

She drew back, out of his reach. 'When there is something to smile at.' She stood for a moment, then walked back into the cave without another word.

'Whew!' said Owen, laughing a little and shaking his head. 'It is a rare bird, that! ... But beautiful as Circe. The most beautiful damsel I have yet seen....'

He was silent as we rode away. Then he said, looking up at

the hill where she had run down, 'She ought not to dress in
that shameless way outside the castle. Any goatherd might take
her as she passes.'

'Perhaps one has,' I said, lightly.

He threw me a look sharp as a knife, but said nothing. We
rode for home.

FOUR

Two more children were born to Owen that year; one, a boy,
of the Lady Margaret, and christened Meredith. The other was
a girl and not christened at all, but dedicated in some dark
and doubtful rite to the Mother, with none but women by.
The girl Lowri carried the child in secret and brought her
forth in secret, too; it was a precept of that cult she served. No
man would be their master, those women of Dinas Brân, nor
know their mysteries. They gave themselves, like goddesses, in
divine contempt, to get girl-children to rear up in the old way.
Thank God these cults have died out, or nearly; they could
turn the world upside down!

I had known that Owen wanted the girl, from the first; fair
women ever went to his head like strong wine, a family weakness. He did not bring her under his roof, though, as his father
had sometimes done, to shame his lady before the house-folk. I
was not in his confidence either; he rode out alone, after that
first time, saying he went on 'manor business.' In the end I got
it out of old Iolo; one could see he was dying to tell.

Old Iolo named himself that Lowri's grandsire, though I
privately think he was not sure, and boasted. He married
them, in the old Druid rites, for the girl would not come to
Owen otherwise; those rites are not binding anymore, of
course; the Church's way is all, nowadays. But I guess it meant
something to the girl, or to her lady grandmother, the High
Priestess. There was another ceremony, too, Iolo said, looking
sly; he called it the Sacrifice, something to do with slaughtering
a lamb and sprinkling its blood on the earth to make it fruit-

ful, a nasty business, like all those old customs. But, thinking about it later, I took odds, privately, that Owen did it as much to satisfy his curiosity as his itch; these antique rites fascinated him as all old things did. Strange, for his mind looked ever forward, leagues ahead of other men. I mind, though, he said once that only in the past could one find the future; I never understood him, of course; I am only a poor bard.

At any rate, they were not together long; he tired of her soon, or perhaps she of him, and the Lady Margaret none the wiser and happy to have him back at home.

Their next child was a girl, Catherine, and beautiful as an angel.

'But,' said the physician Nathan, after, washing his hands, 'there will be no more, Lady ... something has gone amiss there, inside you. I have taken it out, and you will be as good as new ... but you will bear no more ...' He looked at her where she lay, her gray eyes wide, and the tiny babe upon her arm, and his own dark eyes softened. 'It is just as well,' he said. 'You had not the strength for it anyway ...'

She smiled. 'And I just now thinking that the birthing was easier this time ...'

'You felt nothing then—at the end?'

She shook her head, weakly. 'Nothing.'

'Good,' he said. 'It was the strongest poppy-juice I could brew. You will most like sleep the sun round ... and when you wake, call your women and do not stir—or you will break the stitches ...' But she had drifted off and did not hear.

As for us all, in that household, we went about awed, feeling that a miracle had happened there. For Nathan, finding that the birth was something awry, and the child would not come forth, and fearing to lose both lives, had cut into the womb and drawn out the living child. It was, he said, the very way that the great Julius Caesar had been born; he had studied it, Nathan, from charts in old books, but this was the only time he had done this thing. Owen had held the bowl and the knives and sopped up the blood with cloths, straight as a poplar till it was done and his face unmoving; when it was seen to be accomplished and that both mother and child would live, that big man fell over in a faint like a giddy damsel. I remembered that, as a child, he was ever sick at the sight of blood, though he hid it well; Owen will never make a warrior.

It was a burgeoning household; even with the deaths of the two old women, Owen's mother, Helen, and Margaret's aunt, that followed upon each other as if seeking company in the grave, that manor was full to overflowing. For there were Margaret's five children, and the four boys that Owen had earlier sired, Tudor's twins, and another of his, little Efa, still an infant. It was a mystery, that; none knew who the mother had been, but for sure the child was of this Powys house, the very image of Tudor she was. A lay brother had brought her over from Valle Crucis, saying she had been left there, in the laundry room, upon a pile of new-washed clothes. Wrapped in a nun's veil she was, and a note pinned on, telling her name, Efa ap Tudor, it said, and a prayer writ out in Latin. The lay brother shook his head to any questions, but one of Margaret's maidservants, that had used to work for the Valle Crucis nuns, had an answer. One of those same nuns, she said, had disappeared months ago without a trace; they had hushed it up and never mentioned her name after. And so, said the serving-maid, looking wise, 'twas one more nun gone to the bad, and this was the fruit of her sins.

Margaret bade her be quiet, saying, 'Would you throw the first stone?'

The slut blanched, for she had three brats of her own and no husband. She took the meaning clear, for Margaret read Scripture lessons every Saturday for the house folk out of a Bible that was Welshed by her Lollard tutor. 'But,' said the slut, cringing, 'a nun is different...'

'No different,' said Margaret. 'A human also, she is, and bound by unnatural vows. Besides, you do not know.... Get back to your work!'

She took the babe up. 'A pretty thing she is, for sure ... of an age with our little Catherine, and near as like as sisters....' And so the little Efa stayed and slept in the same cradle with Catherine. Tudor, though, scratched his head and said he could not remember; his face was so comical that even the Lady Margaret laughed, though one could see she was shocked, under.

They thrived, all; even the sickly Griffith grew apace, sturdy of limb and with a quick and lively mind, though he inherited his mother's shortness of breath. Nathan named it asthma, a disease known to the ancient Greeks, and said, looking grave, that there was no cure. And so Margaret cosseted him, on the sly, against Owen's orders; the boy knew he was favored, and sometimes whined, sometimes looked smug, and created small enmities that served him ill in later life. It was a shame, that, for Griffith was, in some ways, the most forward of the lot, learning his letters in a baby lisp and counting up sums on his chubby fingers.

Besides the children, there were always relatives a-visiting, too, for Owen's house had never a latch to the door, as the saying goes. Sometimes his sister Laura came to stay, for her man, Robert, was often away from home; he had taken up his knighthood and owed service to King Richard. This Laura was a beautiful woman, something stately, and there were many years between her and the Lady Margaret; she was apt to usurp the housekeeping, trying to run things her way. Most of us were glad to see the back of her as she rode for home, for her ways were something strict and overbearing; she would make a formidable old lady.

The Hanmer brothers were in and out a good deal, for they much admired Owen and were all at sea themselves in their estate affairs. John fathered a girl-child on one of the serving maids, or at least she said so, and he did not deny it. He could not take the daughter home, for he was much afraid of his wife, a rich widow and a shrew. And so there was another child to rear, for Margaret claimed kinship and would not let her be brought up a servant's by-blow; they called her Olwen.

And then there were my own daughters; I am no monk and found solace, and some pleasure, too, in their Lombard mother's arms. I would have married her, I believe, since I could not have the wife of my friend; St. Paul has said 'tis better to marry than to burn, though he may not have meant it in such wise. She died, though, my children's mother, after the second birth, and so I have burned all my life, God help me. I brought the girls to my Lady Margaret, telling their sad story and begging them a place with her. Her eyes leaped briefly in a way I could not read; surprise there was and almost, I thought, chagrin. But my love for Margaret colors all my perceptions, and, too, hope dies hard. In my darker moods I read her look as shock that any woman would have me; I am almost hairless already, at thirty, and repel myself sometimes.

At any rate she took the children and with love; the eldest, Megolin, is a good girl, pretty and docile; the baby, Sibli, is ugly and small, dark as a Moor like her mother, but of a lively intelligence. Even in the cradle her eyes were bright and knowing, and at two she could finger the harp and make her own little tunes.

I have not counted them up, but with all the children, visitors, bards, and minstrels, it was a city of itself, there at Sycharth. It was not quite the way that Iolo sung it: Prince Owen and his thousands of retainers, like a chieftain of old times, and his bounty flowing to all; but something there was in his song of truth, indeed. And peaceful and pastoral those days; days that will never come again in my time.

Boarhounds and bratchet-hounds and their puppies lived there too, each child with his favorite, and the maids forever sweeping up and scolding. House cats stayed mostly in the kitchens, for they like comfort and to take their pick of food scraps, and do not care to be caught up and fondled. Pet rabbits were kept outdoors, and ponies in the stables; still was it a hazard to walk there with one's head in the clouds, so easy was it to tread upon a poor squealing creature. Order of a sort there was always, though, because of my lady, when Owen was not about, the animals were limited to the children's quarters. He himself liked them about; his favorite boarhound followed him everywhere; second of his name he was, Cabal, and himself old already, for his sire had long since died. This Cabal was the saddest of beings; when he was left behind and Owen out from home, he stood droop-eared in a corner, facing the wall, and from time to time bumped his head mournfully and gently against the stone, and whimpered softly in his throat. It grieved Margaret, and she tried to tempt him with marrowbones and sweetmeats, but he only looked at her dolefully and went back to his head-thumping. Owen said that, like an aging human, his wits were failing him. But Owen's step he knew,

and would run to the door, stumbling and shambling, to greet
him, and all the small offspring swarming after.

One spring day, when Margaret's youngest was nearing two
and toddling, Owen rode up; he had been away a full week.
Before him on the saddle was a fair little maid, his image in
little, a sight that would make a fair-show. She was wrapped in
his green mantle, and her face showing only, but there was a
shine upon it, rare to see, the eyes in her alive as two birds
about to take flight. He carried her into the hall, astride his
shoulders, the mantle falling anyhow behind, and her small
hands clutching his hair to hold on. He set her down among
the hounds, big and little, that leaped up or tumbled at his
feet, and she looked down upon them with pure delight and
clapped her hands together, stooping quick to touch and pet
and laughing as they licked her hands. It was a charming picture, the child so small and brightly beautiful, among the innocent and playing creatures of God. She cannot have been
much above three, but already were her movements sure and
full of a quick grace; I saw, with a little shock, that she wore
the strange dress of the ladies of Dinas Brân, the flounced red
skirt and little bodice, with baubles dangling at her ears and
beads about her little neck, and the small feet bare under, and
stained red with Eastern henna dye. Owen looked down upon
her, and in his face was love, naked for all to see. A sudden
quiet fell then, and he, sensing it, looked up. There stood the
Lady Margaret in the doorway, and her features straight and
stern as I had never seen them, like marble they were, beautiful and cold, and the eyes steel as a sword blade.

He took a step toward her, lifting the child, and drawing her
along by the hand. 'They have called her Morgan——' he began, but she cut him off, my lady. A thing never in my life I
had seen her do.

'I'll have no more of your bastards in my care,' she said, and
her sweet voice harsh with passion. 'I'll have no more!'

There was a little silence, and I saw the child look up at the
lady, so tall above her in her flowing skirt, its folds gathered up
in a hand where the knuckles showed white bone beneath, so
hard her clutch upon the cloth.

'Oh, Lady,' she said, the little thing, and without a childish

lisp, 'oh, Lady, I will take care of the bastards. Which are
they?' And she stooped again to the puppies; plain it was that
she thought the name a breed of dog. 'Lady,' she said again,
and very earnest, 'I have no pets at all but snakes ... and I
cannot love them, though Lowri pinched me sore, and the
Blind One scolded...'

There was a small silence, and the Lady Margaret bent her
head into her hands and sobbed, not caring that all heard. The
child Morgan ran to her then, pulling at her skirt. 'Oh, Lady
dear, they did not bite, the snakes, for their fangs were drawn!
Do not fret ... it was just that they wiggled and felt cold....'
And Margaret looked down then upon the upturned face, the
track of her tears showing, but a soft curve to her lips. The
child gave a sort of breath-catch and said, 'Oh, Lady, so beautiful you are ... none of the Tower ladies are so. They scowl
always and hold their faces so.' And she made a face of stone,
old and stern it looked, and the brows drawn together in a
straight line. It was comical, and Margaret smiled, putting her
hand out then and laying it upon the small head.

'Wipe off that horrid look, little one,' she said. 'Those ladies
are a cruel sort, for sure.'

'Oh, no, not cruel,' said Morgan. 'But they are very religious.'

Margaret shook her head. 'Not so,' she said. 'Jesus wants no
hard faces about him.'

'Who is Jesus?' asked the child. 'They did not name him ...
or any man-god at all.'

I could not read her face, Margaret's, but it was passing sad.
She put out her arms and gathered the child to her. 'And will
you kiss me, pretty one?'

After, Morgan said, most grave. 'That was my second kiss of
all my life—and'—she looked at Owen, his own mocking
charm upon her face—'yours was the sweeter, Lady....'

'Little witch,' said Owen, laughing, 'of course. My lips are
not so soft ...' And he turned and looked at Margaret, a long
look.

'Meredith,' called the lady, to the corner where he watched
round-eyed. 'Meredith, my darling, will you take this little
Morgan and show her the ponies?' The little boy came forward

then and took the other's hand. 'And tell her there are no bastards here.... I have made a mistake ... puppies only, and kittens, and the like....' The children left the hall; from the back they walked like a pair of twins.

'Oh, Owen,' cried Margaret. 'I must love her—for Jesus' sake ... and for that she is your living image, too. But why did you do it ... why?'

'I do not know. Forgive me, Marred.'

'Who is the mother?'

'She is dead. She hung herself by an old belt they called Myfanwy's. Perhaps it had some meaning for her ... she was crazed, at the end. Her name was Lowri.'

'That one who pinched the child ... her mother?'

'I think she did not know,' he said heavily. 'I do not know the right of it ... and only now I heard from Iolo that there was a child at all. I have not seen the girl for a long, long time.... The little Morgan was born when our Meredith was. But there was no doctor there—only those unhappy women with their strange wild ways. They dosed her perhaps with some filth of their concoction, or did not wash, or such. The birth went well, but after, the girl Lowri took a fiery fever and near died. Her wits left her when she recovered.... I am sad to near it, for she was a fair, wild damsel, and it is my guilt ...'

'And I all unsuspecting ...' murmured Margaret, bowing her head. 'Have there been others ... other women?'

He shook his head. 'None. I swear it.'

She was still for a moment. Then very low she said, 'Was she—so very fair...?'

'Strange and sweetly made—yes,' said Owen. 'Like a pretty thing made some other where—like a statue dug up from a foreign soil ... or a vase shaped lovingly ... or a picture that was painted with rare skill. She was a thing I wanted....' He lowered his head; I had never seen him shamed before in all my days. 'Men are not gods,' he said.

'Nor women either,' said Margaret. 'I know ... but I am sick with jealousy.'

'It is you I love,' he said simply and looking at her straight.

'Truly?'

'Truly—and for always.'

She came forward into his arms, and they stood so, clasped, for a long moment. She looked up at him, her face all wet with tears again. 'I must pray for myself, for I hate her, Lowri, even dead....'

'Pray for her, too, if you must pray ... and for the wits of her that vanished—where? And for the little daughter ... and for me ... and for all that walk the world. You have your faith, and I would not take it from you. We are all different. Myself, I can—question only. It is my way. But still I love you dear, my Marred....' And then I saw he wept too, and turned away, my own heart weeping for us all, and for our frailties that are all we have.

FIVE

Event followed event in the years after; even in Wales, where we get it late, came the sad news that Richard's queen, that Anne that Margaret loved, had died of the plague at Sheen Castle. At home here we all wept for her, and the English, too, for she was much beloved; they had called her the 'good' queen, for all her gay frivolity. And Richard, wild with grief, had razed that pretty castle of Sheen to the ground, for that it had harbored death for her. And so he had loved her dearly, in his way. The English were shocked at the destruction of that lovely place; some called it the most beautiful in the realm. But Owen and Nathan, too, said Richard was wiser than he knew; they said that all plague-places should be burned and nothing left, for the infection lingers in the very walls.

Owen and Margaret went to the funeral of state at Westminster, and with them her father, that had been king's justice and close to Richard. Owen said, on his return, shaking his head, that Richard was in bad straits; he was setting all the nobles against him, for he had grown very high-handed and too royal for those wealthy men of power. There were many plotting factions about him and much unrest, though the commons still loved Richard, remembering his courage as a boy in

the great Peasants' Revolt. Also, as Owen said wryly, Richard
put on a good show, princely and rich with color; the English
love romance, though they miss the glory of the Black Prince,
of course. Richard would rather die than fight, and the English
would rather fight than eat. So someday, Owen says, they will
hate him for his peace, though they profit by it.

He has no heirs either, Richard, a sore point in all the kingdom. They urge him and urge him to marry again and beget a
king, but he puts them off. He says he cannot forget his Anne
so soon, and that there is plenty of time; he is not much above
twenty.

I am not much of a historian; my knowledge is second- and
sometimes even third-hand, and besides, I am easily befuddled,
being a poet by nature. Still, I will tell it as I remember, the
passing of those years. We had a little flurry of our own; our
Owen, Tudor, Robert Pulestan, and both the young Hanmers
testified in a lawsuit. Silly it was, said Owen, over who had the
right to bear certain arms, for who could care. Yet did those
two men care who contested it; if it had not been for Richard,
that man of peace, they would have come to blows, and much
innocent blood shed, and for no more than a colored device
upon a shield! This is how it was, as I have read it.

Richard, Lord Scrope of Bolton in Wensleydale, and Robert
Grosvenor, of Hulme and Allostock in the county of Chester,
both had fought in the Scottish campaign and both displayed
'azure, a bend or' on their coat of arms. Richard referred it to a
court of chivalry, and in one way or another, the suit went on
for more than five years, as such law matters often do. Scrope
had the word of all the English nobles, many of those who
opposed Richard's ways, but Grosvenor had his county and the
near marches of our own Wales. Among others, Owen, Lord of
'Glendore,' testified that Grosvenor had borne those arms in
Scotland, and that in all the counties round about Chester
they were known to be his. His brother, 'Tudyr de Glyndore'
(the English spell anyhow and to their own purpose!), did so
also. I must explain that the Welsh spelling is Glyn Dwr and
that it derives from a property of Owen's in the glen of the Dee
River, where later he built a magnificent dwelling.

Strange to say, among the witnesses on the other side was the

famous English bard Geoffrey Chaucer, who was an old friend of
Owen's. Owen said that he called out when he spied Chaucer,
'Ah, God, now will we lose all! For never will my Geoffrey
show his face if it be not in a winning cause!' He was sorry
after, for he remembered that Chaucer hid in his Aldgate
house while the rebellion raged below. 'And who could wish
him other?' asked Owen. 'Poets are not warriors, and if genius
be not saved, what has the earth left to its credit?' At any rate,
he was right, for Scrope won the case, and Grosvenor sulked in
his holdings and chalked up a grievance against England.

But the incident made Owen think of those works of Chaucer that he had translated into Welsh; he dug them out one
day, asking me to set them to the harp. They were great poems,
in their way, lively and clean, and fresh as a mountain wind a-
blowing, but they refused to do my will. They would not go to
music, though I tried hard, to please Owen. Too much pith
there was in the words, and too much comment under. In the
end, I devised a kind of strumming, tinkling counterpoint, involved and difficult, and sometimes sounding strident, and
would speak the words against that strange background. It did
not go down well with my Welsh audiences, especially the
other bards, who shook their heads and pulled long faces. The
minstrel folk, though, made much use of it, capering and
dancing to those little rhymes. Owen did it best of all, for he
could always get the wit in and the irony, and still not lose the
heart.

A year or two went by, and word came that Richard had
decided, or nearly, on a bride, and a great shock to all it was
too. For he had settled on a princess of France, a child not yet
five years of age. It would be many a year before she was ripe
for bearing. But the French king Charles, the mad one, invited
Owen to send a daughter to the French court to be a lady to
that child-queen when she should marry Richard. Owen, reading the letter, made comment that he hoped that poor king was
in one of his lucid moments, for such an invitation could not
be ignored. 'Send the nearest in age,' the letter went, 'for then
they can grow together, along with some other princesses that
will be in the child Isabelle's train.'

Owen folded the letter. 'I shall take Morgan,' he said.

Margaret raised wide eyes. 'But she is——'

'It is all one to him, bastard or no,' said Owen, smiling. 'Wales is not true princedom, alas ... they will not care, and who is to tell, anyway? It will be a good thing for her, Morgan. She is bright and healthy, big for her age. She will learn courtly manners and the language, and English, too, later. And you would not spare one of your true-born, this I know.'

'Well, the twins are not of an age ... too old they are already...'

'Yes——' said Owen, smiling. 'Nearly eight they are, and doddering....'

She laughed, Margaret, but then her face changed. 'Will they be kind to her there ... in that Valois court? I have heard dreadful tales...'

'I have thought of that.... Poor Charles has fits and is sunk in melancholy, and his queen lies with his brother....'

Margaret gasped. 'Isabeau—with Orléans? This I did not know. I knew her infamous, or so says all the world....'

'Perhaps she has cause. Who are we to judge? It cannot be an easy life ... hers. At any rate, Isabeau plays canny politics and may have need of Welsh monies sometime.... Besides, it is the Duchess Valentine, Louis of Orléans' wife, who has the care of all the court children, and she is as kind and good, almost, as you, Marred. But let us go to France and bring Morgan there. You have seen little of the world, and sister Laura will take our brood for a time, and gladly....'

'Oh, Owen, could we?' Her face shone. 'And my French I will practice every day...'

And so they went and were away a year, in that court and in Calais and in Florence, which is in Italy. And sore I missed them both, for sister Laura is no substitute. Though, to her credit, I must add that she is musical. And so at least I made my verses, set them to music, and sang them. They were love songs mostly, and Lady Laura thought them made for her. So some accord there was, and both of us flattered, in our different ways.

They returned, and Owen much excited; for in Florence he had met with a Lombard architect—the name I have forgot—and they had drawn up plans for a new manor in his Glyn Dwr holdings, which the English call Glendower. I saw the plans but could not understand them, all lines and numbers they were, and figures added up. Owen said it was to be modeled on the ancient Greek houses, with open roofs and porticos, and all manner of buildings joined by passages, colonnaded. I shook my head, for I could feel already the chill of our Welsh winters in such a place, made for a sunny clime. 'You are an old stick-in-the-mud, friend Griffith,' said Owen, laughing at my stubborn looks. 'But you will see ... all will be glazed, in the latest manner. And the glass holds out the wind, if it is securely set in ... and lets in the sun to warm and light us!'

'The drawing is beautiful,' said Margaret, 'like a pleasure palace it will be, for sure ... and none like it in the world....' And so I gave over. None of my business was it anyway; I am growing old already and crusty. So does life deal with unhappy ones.

The Lady Margaret had changed a little; she was Ceres now, and no longer Diana, deep-bosomed she was and stately. When she wore her bridal belt of the Red Dragon, I saw that new links had been set in. 'I shall soon wear all your old gold, Owen,' she said, looking down at herself ruefully.

'And why not?' said he. 'It was made for a goddess full grown—and you are not yet that....' He loved her still, and so did I.

They had all the news from those far places, too. Sad I was to hear of the death of little Mary de Bohun, Henry of Lancaster's young wife; she died soon after Richard's Anne, but not from plague. Margaret said it was from too much child-bearing, and wore her out. Seven children she bore in as many years, and of that seventh she died. Her age was twenty-three. But now Lancaster had heirs aplenty; only the first boy-child died; there were four others, and two little girls as well, for knightly pawns. 'I fear that house,' said Owen. 'I fear the House of Lancaster. Close to the throne it is, and Gaunt's ambitions rubbed off on his red son....'

'But Mortimer is closer,' said Margaret. 'If Richard should die without issue, there is the Mortimer heir.'

'Henry of Lancaster bears much ill will to Richard, from their earliest days. I saw it long ago—when I was at court.

That red Henry ever thought himself the stronger and the more deserving, resenting his king-cousin.'

'And Richard?' she asked.

'Richard makes many mistakes. Laughed at him then when they were boys ... discounts him now, forgiving all his plotting —for their cousinship. He will make one mistake too many, Dickon—I can see it plain.'

'Then you have the Sight, like Merlin?' teased Margaret.

For once Owen did not jest but said heavily, 'No. There is no such thing. But plain it is to see if one looks hard and long. Dickon is high-handed, gay, extravagant; he plays the despot. But it is play. He rages, but he is gentle under. His favorites are ill-chosen, and he flaunts them besides—and they are much hated. And then his French marriage—even the commons, who love Richard well, are muttering against it. A child—and a French child!'

Margaret, for all her new womanly looks, sounded shy and girlish. She said, low, and her eyes downcast, 'I think ... I knew Anne well, and she has told me something—a secret thing between us it was ... but here I will say it. Richard loved her well, but even she—he never——' She stopped, growing red.

'He never lay with her. I know. For Nathan was her doctor for some trifling ailment and examined her. Anne was not barren. But she was virgin still.'

There was a little silence, then Margaret said, 'Poor Richard. I will pray for him.'

'Pray hard, sweet Christian, pray hard and long. Perhaps it will help.'

Tudor spoke then; he had said nothing before. 'You both dwell too much on this king. I saw him once only and I never met him and I like it not. He is an Englishman—who cares? And he is only a man, even if a half-one....'

Owen laughed. 'And you, Tudor, brother, are a whole Welshman, that is for sure....'

Tudor laughed with him, and a little glint came into his eye. 'What of that Isabeau? What of the French queen? Is she as beautiful as they say?'

'She is too fat,' said Owen, 'and growing fatter every day. And her teeth are dark from sweetmeats, the paint an inch thick upon her cheeks.... But, yes, she is beautiful. Of an evil beauty, like that strange flower from the southern lands ... the one that swallows living things....'

'And she swallows men, then?' asked Tudor, laughing. 'Still, from the talk of her ... it would be a sweet death.'

They talked then of other things, the Valois court, and the poor mad king that ruled it—when he could. 'It is Isabeau that makes the policies,' said Owen. 'But times there are when he is as sane as any, Charles. And then is he consulted, and his answers wiser than most.' He sighed. 'I have seen him in his melancholy moments only, when the sickness takes him in that way. Hard it is to credit the tales of his raging ... when they must chain him to his bed.'

Tudor spoke. 'I have heard that once, in the forest of Le Mans, he ran at his brother, Louis of Orléans, who had ridden out to meet him, brandishing a sword. And that it took five men to subdue him, and all sore wounded in the process.'

Owen nodded. 'That was the first time it took him, the madness. Perhaps he had learned of his brother's liaison with his wife, and the knowledge drove him wild.... Nathan thinks, though, that it is a result of that disease that the Italians call the Saracen, the French call the Italian, and the English call the French sickness....'

Tudor laughed, making a rude gesture; Margaret looked away, her white skin showing pink. 'He has, I think, the face of a saint,' she said.

'And so the French, his subjects, call him, for they pity him as an innocent, afflicted by God,' said Owen. 'They love him well, their king. And Isabeau they hate. Pelt her with filth and shout filth, too, at her when she rides abroad. She must go in a covered litter always.'

Margaret smiled a little. 'Our Morgan is a wise child. The little maid looked up at the queen, when she was presented, bold as bold, and said, in the French she had picked up already, 'But she is the Morrighen of the cave-roof!' I took the meaning, for Owen had told me of that warrior image, so horrid and wicked, dripping blood. But when the queen asked, "Who is that?" the little Morgan answered with a sweet smile, "A goddess, Lady." And so was Isabeau pleased, for she loves

flattery, even from a babe. She spoke her fair, Morgan, calling
her a beauty and a charmer that lived up to her witch namesake.'

'And she is friend already to Richard's betrothed, Isabelle,'
said Owen. 'That is a fair little maid, and no resemblance to
her mother.'

'All those little princesses are fair,' said Margaret. 'But
shamefully neglected they are, their clothes spotted and
stained, torn even, and their hair uncombed. Only on Isabelle,
that will be a queen, have they spent a half crown even.
Shameful it is to see! They are babies still, and Isabeau not so
much as glancing at them, and carrying around an ugly little
dwarf like a doll to play with, all dressed in cloth of gold and
stuffed with comfits....'

'It is an evil custom, that,' said Owen, shaking his head. 'All
the royalty of Europe have it, this cosseting of poor freaks and
fools. Richard, at least, will have none such about. He is sensi-
tive to beauty ... and to pity, too, Dickon ...'

And so the talk came back to him, the English king; Tudor
left the company, bored, but I felt a stirring within me, and a
song that worked in my head. It turned out I never wrote
it—yet was it written, later, much later.

SIX

The years went by, so slow it seemed, so slow; looking back,
they were no more than a snap of the fingers, or so it seems.
The children of Owen's house grew and were no longer children, but lads and maidens. That Rhys of the hills, so darkly
troublesome, so mysterious and wild, was gone, back to where
he came from, and none sorry to see him go; he was not made
for houses. Owen's oldest girls, Janet and Margaret, who was
always called Maggie, were betrothed and married to goodly
knights of Wales. Maggie married a distant kinsman of Owen's
mother, Helen, who had holdings in the Deheubarth, in southern Wales, and lived on his manor there. Janet married closer

to home, a Sir John de Croft, knight; half-Norman he was, and a friend to Rob Pulestan, our Laura's husband. They lived at the Dolgelly manor, her dowry portion, and came a-visiting to show off her firstborn, christened William. But there were now two maidens gone from the house, or three, really, Morgan being now at Richard's court in the train of his little queen Isabelle. Still, Rhys Dhu of Cardigan, kinsman of old Iolo, hearing of the Lady Margaret's kindness, sent his own mother-less daughter, Elliw, to be reared among our maidens. They were pretty damsels, all, close in age, chattering and twittering like birds, and a sweet sight to behold in their light dresses and flowing hair. My own Sibli grew out of her baby ugliness, though she was plainer than the others, sharper of nose and with a sallow-colored skin. A beautiful voice she had, though, to sing, and much skill at harping and upon the lute, making her own songs. Though there are no woman bards, some of her songs are sung still, and she was called, by the people, the Small Bird. The boy-children went off to Oxford, one by one, to study there, so, in a way, it was a house of maidens.

The Lady Margaret taught them to sew and spin, and to embroider lovely tapestries, and I taught them the harp and lute, though some among them were all thumbs. Owen was forever finding likely damsels among the low folk of the coun-tryside to swell the coterie; they were like the ladies-in-waiting at a court, performing small useful light tasks and learning skills along with the others. Latin, too, they had, and some other learning; the Lady Margaret had sent for her own child-hood tutor, Morris Stove. He taught them Scripture, too, of the New Learning kind, out of his own Wycliffe Bible. Owen, though, insisted they learn about all the religions of man (he called them mythologies!). So the Latin poets that they read took care of the classic gods of the ancients, and the physician Nathan gave lessons in the old Bible tales of the Jews, and I was summoned to tell of our own Welsh gods, and of the angry Saxon ones, too. So he said they could choose, and Margaret was scandalized, but Owen laughed and said they would choose hers anyway, for plain to see it was that all those dam-sels adored the lady of the house.

Owen even brought back tales of other customs and other

worshipings, for he traveled much those years, going as far as the Indies and Cathay. Beautiful hard, smooth wood he brought back from those places, called teak, like dark ivory, and marble from Italy, and began the building of his new Glendower House. Folk used to gather in groups, giggling, to watch the workmen, for it was so unlike any other house they had ever seen. Like a city it would be, without walls, except low ones made of that same wood, and many low buildings joined by open passages and interspersed with open spaces that would be courtyards, walks, and parklands. It took two years to finish and was a sight of wonder, so fair it was and graceful in the valley.

Iolo was growing ever weaker and could not play much anymore, though he criticized all my songs as though I were still a novice. I was bald as an egg, with strange bumps upon my head that I had never known were there. Owen said there was an Eastern science based on these bumps, and that all men had them, all different, under the hair. He put my hand to his own head to push through the thick hair and feel them. It gave me no comfort, though, for I knew I looked strange; no eyebrows had I either, but jutting crags above my eyes where the hair had once grown, and no face hair either, or indeed anywhere. I felt myself the victim of an unknown disease and wondered in what other way it would take me later. Would I lose fingernails, too, and the nails from my toes? Would my skin peel off and my teeth fall?

Owen had taken to dressing in his own style; copied from the ancients it was, with something of the Greeks and Romans and something of our own old chieftains. He wore his hair long to the shoulders, still a tawny, tarnished gold it was, and straight as rain, and bound about his brow a thin iron circlet he had dug up somewhere; he called it the Crown of Eliseg. Short tunics and mantles in summer he wore, with bare legs in sandals, and in the cold months mantles of spotted lynx or red fox pelts. He wore a little beard, trimmed to a point, though the fashion was coming in for shaven faces. Sometimes he parted the beard, making two points; many of the minstrels copied him, but only him did it become—it was not an easy look to achieve.

Upon his manor house roofs were two that were glazed and open to the sky. The women's quarters, on an upper floor, had this, and sunlight flooded the place, even in winter, warming it and making all gay and bright. Another building, smaller, he had built, where the physician Nathan dwelt, with hearth at hand for heating his potions, and all manner of herbs drying above it; all the equipment of his trade was here, and shelves, too, full of his heavy books that he studied from constantly. Many of these had he found in the Orient, for he had gone there with Owen; he said they were far advanced of us in those countries, where medicine lore was concerned.

On the upper floor of this same building, the roof was again open to the sky, with glass upon it, too. Here were all manner of instruments for star-studying; there were long rods with tiny holes at one end and a larger at the other, triangles and squares, glassed over, a great crystal ball, and a model of the moon and the stars and the earth. Maps, too, were there, strange markings upon them, and old and rubbed away in spots; found in far-flung places they had been, when some other wise men had perhaps known more. Owen and Nathan pondered over them but could not fathom their meaning. They were not maps of earthly places, that was clear. Had the ancients then been able to journey through the skies, had they the means to fly to other worlds? Owen said, shaking his head, that he did not think so, that surely such an event would have come down to us, at least in myth, as the story of the Great Flood did, that is in the Bible, and indeed in all the lore of peoples everywhere. No, he said he thought they had some instruments or some knowledge, some learning, that had been lost long ago. And he sighed, a great sigh, and sad. 'It will have to be done over again ... But I have not the mind for it, try as I will ...' And Nathan, smiling, said he could not think it through either, or understand the markings. Even the writings upon these maps were unknown, though Owen said that upon the pyramids of Egypt there were similar symbols. Someday one would find the secret of this unknown tongue, and with it all the knowledge, they said. But still they pored over them, straining their eyes, and still they read the stars, through their odd instruments. It looked like magic to eyes like mine, and so it did to others, later; men called Owen, always, those that were his enemies, the Welsh Magician.

Still did he travel out with pick and shovel and trowel, to dig for his own peculiar treasure, too, in the old burial mounds. Broken bits of pots he brought back, and the two of them would sit upon the floor, with all that old mess, and try to fit them together, the pieces. When they managed to fit piece to piece, to make what looked like, maybe, half a vase, they almost wept for joy, counting the day well spent. Nathan was another such seeker of knowledge; the two looked to grow old together, playing with their strange toys. Once I came upon them, and Owen holding a bit of blackened metal. 'This is a spear-point,' he said, 'from the men of long ages ago, though the wood of the spear is rotted away ... I found another such once—when I was a boy, and my tutor Iorweth fitted it onto a lance. It only needed sharpening. . . .' And so did life go in our Wales, with singers of song, and seekers of the ages, and sweet golden damsels light-footed on the green and flowering ground, and my lady among them all, serene and beautiful. And I only weeping for my love, not knowing that all would go, all vanish.

The news from England was never good; plots and counter-plots there were at the court, and murder and execution, and treason everywhere. The Lord Henry of Lancaster, called Bol-ingbroke, and the king's cousin, rode up to London with a lord called Thomas Mowbray; upon Brentford Bridge those two had a great falling-out. None knows what caused it, but each called the other traitor. Owen said that Henry must have ac-cused Mowbray for the murder of the king's uncle of Glouces-ter in Calais, for it must have been his orders, at least, that did the deed. Lord Henry confronted the king with it, and Mow-bray accused Henry of some other deed. The king appointed a day and a court to hear them both. The whole court hearing got out of hand, and the two nobles near came to blows; Rich-ard then appointed a day that they should fight it out—to the death! It is a Norman custom, that, to prove justice by the force of your arms and your bodily strength; it has never caught on much here in Wales, thank Jesus. Only on the border lands does this justice prevail sometimes—but they are half-English anyway.

They came, both knights, to the tourney, the death tourney, all armored, even to their horses. Henry had even begun to ride toward his opponent, lance forward, when Richard flung down his royal glove—a sign to cease. At the end he could not go through with it—Richard is, as I have said, a man of peace. But he dealt out cruel punishment of his own; he banished Mowbray from the realm forever. Henry, his cousin, he hit with a lighter rod; banished for ten years he was, and a month only to put his affairs in order. 'That was his first mistake, Dickon's,' said Owen to his lady when the news came.

'Should Richard then have let them fight?' cried Margaret, flashing.

'No——' said Owen, slowly and looking intent. 'For then Henry would have won ... he is the better knight. But never should Dickon have shown him leniency ... he will regret it....'

'He could not kill him!' cried Margaret. 'He could not kill his cousin!'

'He killed his uncle, did he not?' She stared. 'Whose orders, think you, cut off Gloucester's life? The hands that strangled may have been Mowbray's, but never would he have dared without Richard's consent!'

'Ah, Christ!' she cried, her head in her hands. 'He was a wicked man and a bad uncle—but how could Richard——?'

But Owen did not comfort her, but only looked into the fire; upon his face that look he gets sometimes, turned inward. Finally he said, 'Kings must keep their thrones ... if they want them. Dickon may lose all through this gesture of kindness. Lancaster has powerful friends in France and Burgundy ... Brittany, too. And he has other nobles in England that will join with him, too, against Richard. Richard has made many enemies among them, you have seen that. The people love him, but his peers do not.... Margaret'—it was not often that he addressed her so, calling her his own Welsh Marred— 'Margaret, Lady, I must go to France. I must spy out the land there. For Dickon is friend to me—and to all Welshmen. It is not always so with English kings....'

And so he journeyed again, Owen, to those parts of France where Bolingbroke had gone. Never would any suspect Owen of partisanship to any; he was known as such another as the Duc de Berry, the old Frenchman, who loved all manner of art and artifacts, both ancient and modern, and with wealth enough to buy wherever he might hunt his beloved objects out.

He was so long gone that the Lady Margaret pined; one night as I played soft upon the lute to her alone in that solar chamber under the stars, and they shining bright, she looked at me, shy, and asked if I thought it possible that Owen might dally with the Queen of France, that notorious seductress, Isabeau. 'For he lied when he said she was not beautiful ... the most spectacular beauty of France she is, and perhaps of the world, for all her evil ways...'

I answered, and meaning it, though I had not seen that lady queen, that truly I did not think so. 'For Owen would not want that which all men have had or may have. Only the rare does Owen love, like you, Lady. Only that which is for him alone ...' And I looked at her, my heart showing.

'Good friend,' she said, 'sweet Griffith, you have courtesy ... true it is that I do not believe it either ... but so many months have passed. There cannot be so much of spying, surely...'

I answered that I thought he would have stopped, too, at Richard's court, in the Tower of London, to report to him, and to see how his Morgan had grown.

I could have bit my tongue out, for she looked at me strange. 'Morgan——' she said, musing. 'Morgan has much of Owen about her, the coloring, and the eyes ... but something else, too, she has ...' And she reached over to me, staying with her hand my touch upon the lute, so that all was silent. 'Tell me, good friend—you knew Morgan's mother, I think she that was called Lowri and was one of the Dinas Brân women...'

'Not to say "know," Lady,' said I. 'I saw her once only and never spoke with her at all. I never knew that Owen saw her after....'

'I believe you, Griffith Lloyd, for you have said it. And yet—the woman in me asks you—how did she look? Fair ... very fair?'

'Oh, no, Lady,' I said quickly and speaking from somewhere
deep, 'I—did not like her face ... wild it was, like an animal's.
And like an animal's—without expression ... still it was, and
carven in its lines, and no human pity upon the features, no
smile to soften it, and no softness in the eyes either. Sweetly
made she was, and graceful as a cat. Beautiful, yes, as a cat is
beautiful.' And then I thought again and said, to be fair, 'But,
Lady, I never came to know her ... and I think she had been
reared that way, to wear a priestess look. No other beings had
she seen at all—except those strange women. And so perhaps
that is why, to me, she, too, was strange....'

'Owen loves strange things ...' and her voice trailed off into
stillness.

'But only for their strangeness, and not for always,' I said.
'Have you not seen his collection of old diggings? And in that
cave where we saw her, Lowri, he wanted also the little stone
image of Epona. Wanted it even more, I think, save that he
could not lift it. And ugly as sin it was, that image, and would
make you shudder....'

There was a small silence. Then she said, 'Oh, Griffith, I am
main jealous. It is my sin. I cannot bear to think of him with
another....'

'Lady,' I said, 'I understand you well. For such is my nature,
too....' And in the starlight I felt the flush upon my face, my
skin so tender—free of hair to hide it. I hoped it was not light
enough for her to see it too. I looked into her eyes, bent upon
mine.

'You are my sweet, good friend, and I am sorry to have burdened you with this my confession. I beg you to forget....' And
then, most odd, she said, 'You have the most beautiful eyes in
the world. Like the blue flowers that grow between the rocks,
high upon Snowdon ... the bluest things they are at all, at all
...' It was a little thing only, and a sentence spoke suddenly
and without thought. But remember it I did, and always, and
to my death-day. Oh, Margaret, my love ... that burned in me
like a flame and would not go out!

SEVEN

Owen returned, bringing back the young Morgan, now grown to full maidenhood; she must have been near fourteen. 'Trouble is brewing there in Richard's realm, one can smell it,' Owen said. 'I could not leave her there. Richard is off to Ireland, another mistake. He thinks to placate his war-hungry peers and subjects, too, but it will not happen. The road is clear now...'

'My God, what do you mean?' asked Margaret, her face paling.

'In Brittany and in Burgundy and other parts, too, Henry of Bolingbroke is rallying sympathy to his cause...'

'But what cause has he? He was banished for a time—as punishment—that is all...'

'No—Richard has made more mistakes than one can count,' said Owen, and sighed heavily. 'He has extended the banishment to life-exile...'

Margaret gasped, putting her hand to her mouth, not to cry out.

'He has confiscated the estates of Lancaster, pulled down the arms from Kenilworth, taken the Lancaster heir as hostage. John of Gaunt is dead. To his uncle, that John, Richard promised that nothing would be taken from the great Lancaster inheritance. It seems that after Gaunt's death, Richard dishonored those vows. Now has Henry of Lancaster cause aplenty. And he is a fighter. He will not take it lying down.'

Margaret cried, 'What of his son, his heir ... in hostage to Richard? He can do nothing ... there Richard has him ...'

'That will not stop Henry of Bolingbroke,' said Owen. 'He has three other sons, close on the heir in age. He will count him expendable.'

'Then is he the monster that as a boy he showed promise of,' said Margaret, and angry as I had never seen her. 'He is no father ... not human is he....'

Owen made a sound, deep in his throat. 'Not by your standards, no. But ambition is a thing that drives and with its

driving mows down whatever stands in its path. Shame it is, for
I saw the Lancaster boy there, at Richard's court. Pouring the
wine at table he was, as page. Comely he is and of a lively
intelligence. Nothing of his father shows in him. But,' he said,
and putting his arm around her shoulders, 'I do not fear overmuch for his life, in truth, unless Dickon flies into a rage. For
to me has he said, Dickon, that he would make the boy *his*
heir....'

Margaret spoke slowly, her brow puckering with thought.
'Then, Richard will make another mistake—in policy. He will
let him live, and his father Bolingbroke will have all....'

'It may not come to that,' said Owen. 'It may be I am over-
fearful. We must wait and see which way the cat will jump. I
have my own spies there—in Ireland, with Richard's expedition ... and at the court in England, too. Meantime, I shall
muster what Welsh forces I can—to Richard's succor, if the
need arises. Our Welsh love Richard. Under his rule they are
respected and left alone.... I must ride out tonight, my love.
There is not all that much time. I must make sure of my support....'

'If you think it ... yes, go! Go to Rob, your brother-in-law.
And to my brothers—they will be with Richard all the way, if
the need arises. I would you might stay ... but go! Go now!'

The girl Morgan had been listening, but none had noticed
her or sent her out. She said then, 'I beg pardon for my inter-
fering ... but I have seen myself the old stripes of beatings on
Harry's back ... done long ago they were by his Lancaster
father ... and he is not yet fourteen! That father does not love
him overmuch either, besides his cruelty. I have spoke much
with Harry, he is my friend ...' and she smiled. 'We spoke a
little Welsh together ... rusty it was, for both, for I had been
long away from here, and he was born among the Welsh, at
Monmouth, and spoke it with his nurse as a babe, but much
has he forgot.... I know, though, that he lacks his father's love
and that he feels that lack sore....' She cried out then, 'Oh,
Owen, can you not save him, save Harry? Bring him back here
to Wales, make him safe! Richard loves him well, but Richard
is not quite sane anymore ... you do not know! Wild he can
be, and unreasonable, and all his sweet merriness gone on a

sudden.... I fear for Harry, and he hostage ... I fear....'

Margaret took the maid by the shoulders, looking almost level into her eyes, for Morgan too was tall. She spoke low, for the girl's ears only, but mine are sharp for any thought of my lady's. 'Then, you love this Lancaster boy ... you love him....'

Morgan colored deep. 'Oh, Lady, no! It is not that at all. We are children only ... but he is a goodly youth. I would not see him destroyed ... you do not know his qualities! He is—he is, of all the boys there, at court ... he is—himself. There is none other like him....' She turned to Owen, her hands clasped together. 'Oh, sire, remember Harry, too! When that you come to Richard, remember Harry. He may be England's hope—and the hope of Wales too—after Richard!'

'I know, Morgan. I will remember.... But Richard's cause is now all our concern ... and maybe I am a frightened old dotard, smelling disaster where it does not live....'

'I pray it so,' said Margaret. 'I pray to Jesus it be so.'

'And I, too,' said Morgan, fingering the little enameled cross she wore at her neck. I saw that Margaret looked sharply at her and made as if to speak, but held her peace and bade Owen good-bye.

After, Margaret said to the girl, 'I would wish you would not wear that gaud in this house.'

It was plain that Morgan did not understand; she looked her question. Margaret spoke again, kind but a little stern, as she is sometimes now. 'That gaud about your neck. That cross.'

'Oh, Lady,' said Morgan quickly, 'it was given to me by Isabelle, a remembrance gift; I thought it a pretty thing and meant no disrespect to your faith....'

'Ah, child, probably you did not know.... I am of the New Learning, as are most of us in this house—except for Owen and some of the bards and minstrels....'

'I *did* know that, Lady, but it is such a small thing, smaller than the brooch you yourself wear.' She did not lack courage, that damsel, but spoke up to the Lady, and still with respect.

'It is not that.' Margaret shook her head. 'It is true some of the more zealous of our order frown on ornament of any kind ... but I am not one of them. But—the Cross ... it is a symbol of Christ's agony. We do not like to see it embellished and jeweled, as though there were rejoicing in His pain.'

'I see, Lady—I take the point....' Morgan's brows drew together, a small line between; so like to Owen she was then that I nearly smiled. 'But some of those that love Jesus believe that it was upon the Cross that He saved the souls of all men. And so, in a sort, they rejoice in the splendor of His sacrifice. Is it not so—with some?'

'It is so ... with the Papists. And I believe one or two of them, perhaps, believe it and understand it. But the rich and jeweled cross is a symbol of the Church's greed.'

'I see, Lady ... but she who gave it me was young only, younger than I—and in that French court she has had little thoughtful teaching. Indeed, Lady, you would wonder, if you knew, how she had escaped corruption ... but for sure it has not touched her. She is sweet of heart and pure of soul, a grave, good, merry damsel. She thought to give me a gift of her very own, not something Richard gave her. What she brought with her was not much.... I took it as a token of her love. The only other thing she has is a little ring, too small, with a green stone, given to her by her father, the French king, when she was a little child.'

Margaret colored a little. 'I am sorry, child. You have a good heart. You may wear it.'

Morgan said quickly, 'Lady, I will wear it so....' And she dropped the chain below her dress so that the cross was hid. 'I would not offend any.'

Margaret, much moved, took the maiden's face between her hands and kissed her gravely on the lips. 'Much fine discussion will we have—you and I, Morgan. For you are a thinking lass. And I enjoy good honest talk, even when it is not in agreement with me....' And musingly she said, still looking at Morgan, 'How like him you are ...' And shook her head a little in wonderment.

'So I have been told, Lady ... and I am glad of it.'

And so she was, truly, the damsel Morgan. The image of Owen, tall and tawny-fair, with the amber eyes and the mouth with a curl to it that mocked and beckoned. And only I knew that her eyes were set on a slant, like to her mother's, and that the grace that moved her long limbs was not of Owen.

Owen rode hard and mustered many adherents among our Welsh for Richard, but Bolingbroke was too fast for them. He landed at Ravenspur while Richard was still in Ireland; within the day he had ten thousand followers. He gave out that he only came for his own—that is, to win back his rightful estates —but the army at his back grew and grew. All the nobles with grievances against the king flocked to his standards, the powerful Percys chief among them. Richard fled to Flint Castle, and it was there that he was taken, stripped of his powers, even of his kingly robes, and, finally, of the crown itself.

When Owen returned, much later, looking on a sudden old and grim, we heard the whole dread tale. Richard, in Ireland, heard the news of Lancaster's return to English shores. He flew into a rage and threatened to kill his hostage, Harry of Monmouth, Lancaster's son, and the other boy, hostage, too, Humphrey of Gloucester. But he did not; instead he sent them out of his presence, to the castle of Ath Trium, sometimes called Trim Castle. Perhaps he did not trust his own temper and wanted them out of his sight. The powerful Burghs of Ulster owned this castle of Trim. The earl himself was away, but his lady received the two boys with kind care and made them feel safe and welcome. Humphrey died there; some laid it to Richard, poisoning, but others said it was plague. Owen said it was neither, but that the boy had been sickly always. The heir of Lancaster, though, was safe, until his father sent for him after his victory.

It is hard to explain how Richard lost all; perhaps it was true, as Owen said, that the poor king made mistake after mistake. But, in my opinion, fate was against him, that unhappy monarch, all the way. Storms over the Irish Sea prevented him from hearing soon enough of Lancaster's landing. Those same storms delayed Richard's crossing. Owen said that those close to the king advised him to cross to North Wales and land his royal troops at Conway Castle. This would have brought him under the protection of his loyal Welshmen and the royal stronghold of Chester. Instead, Richard sent the Earl of Salisbury to Conway and ordered his army and fleet to cross with him, Richard, to Milford Haven; he thought it would take six days, but instead it took sixteen, for Richard's forces were scattered all over Ireland. It was not till early August that Richard finally came ashore at Milford Haven; by that time disaster had struck in two ways. Salisbury's troops at Conway had dispersed, foul traitorous English that they were, and Lancaster's army had taken the city of Bristol.

Owen rode to the king at Milford Haven; disguised as friars, they made their way to Conway; reaching there, it was seen that not many defenders remained. Owen rode forth again, through the mountains, to recruit more Welsh. Meanwhile, Richard, playing for time, sent his half brothers, the Hollands, to negotiate terms with Lancaster. This was a mistake, said the Lady Margaret, for they could not be trusted, those men; she remembered that long ago, during the Peasants' Revolt, they had fled from danger. At any rate, they went to the wrong place, either from error or purpose; they went to Chester and found Lancaster gone, consolidating his forces in London and the western shires. The garrison at Chester was under the command of Earl Percy of Northumberland. He put the Hollands into close confinement, taking matters into his own hands, and proceeded to occupy the Conway territories. Then, feeling he had hemmed Richard in, he came, Percy, to Conway Castle and demanded audience with him.

Owen, returning to Conway with what small forces he could rally, seeing Percy's troops disposed about the castle in great array, bade his own men hide in the hills and went inside to stand with the king. Percy never left them alone for a moment; Owen had not the means to tell Richard how few men were at hand. He stood helplessly by while Richard stormed and raged, boasting that he would scatter Lancaster's army and put his rebellious cousin to death; let Parliament be the judge! Percy suggested that he meet with Lancaster at Flint Castle and discuss terms there. Owen did not trust the man and said so, even in his hearing, but Richard believed him and agreed.

It was a trap, of course. Lancaster had moved fast, faster than could be believed. 'Like a mole!' cried Owen. 'Like a mole that burrows under the ground!' For even before the turrets of Flint came in sight, they were surrounded by the swelling ranks of Lancaster; the country round about was covered, valley and hill, with the blue-and-silver-clad men, the enemies of the king.

'I am betrayed!' cried Richard. And Owen said then that Percy smiled and could not hide it. 'Evil it was to see, that smile, with the blackened teeth that the elder Percy was famous for always.... Turncoats they are, the Percys....'

Percy called orders to draw close about Richard and those few faithful who were with him. They were put into separate rooms and so spent the night. Henry of Bolingbroke, a mole indeed, arrived next morning before sunup. He sent word that he would not enter the castle till after dinner. But the meal was not served in peace, for he sent his officials in—'jailers' Owen called them—to watch and scorn. 'Eat well,' they said over and over. 'Eat well, for soon your heads will be off and no mouths to eat with.'

'None ate,' said Owen. 'We picked at our food only—ill served, the dishes, and almost raw the meat, and no doubt tainted. Though it did not poison Dickon's dog ... he had it all.'

When the sorry repast was finished, the king rose—Owen, and Salisbury, and those other faithful few with him—and made his way to the court below. There stood Henry of Lancaster, in full armorplate; he had removed his helm, and an angry red welt stood upon his forehead where it had cut into his tender redhead's skin. His hair, the color of scraped carrots, stood tousled and on end, and his face, ruddy, was marked with what appeared to be insect bites, though summer was long gone.

'I am come before my time,' said he. The wretched king said nothing, though he stood straight in all his golden slenderness.

'I will tell you why,' that Henry went on. 'Your people complain that you have ruled them harshly. However, with the held of God'—and here he made the sign of the cross—'I am come to help you to rule them better.'

Owen could not read Richard's face, so outwardly calm, his thoughts. But it was some time before he answered; Owen said he knew that Richard then made count of all his foolish errors, the first and worst, that he had let this man, his near kinsman, live.

Finally he spoke, Richard, his voice flat. 'Fair cousin,' he said, with the faintest of smiles, 'if it pleases you to do so ... it pleases me well.'

This reply seemed to infuriate Henry. The veins swelled in his neck, and his face grew redder still. 'Here is no son of the Black Prince,' he shouted. 'Here is a broken-spirited coward, and always was! And your people know it, sire! Your people know it! They know that your mother *had* to present her husband with an heir! And so it is well known too—many handsome churchmen lived there—in the household at Bordeaux ... Richard of Bordeaux!'

Richard stood white and shaken, too shocked to move, a frozen look. Salisbury started forward, his hand going of itself to the place where his sword should have been; of course, they all had been disarmed. Owen put out his hand to stay Salisbury. Then did he himself walk forward slowly, to where Henry stood, legs in their armor planted far apart, face a mask of fury. Owen came within a yard of that lord, perhaps, and stopped, looking down, for Owen is much the taller. Quietly he spoke, but all heard; Owen has learned how to throw his voice, in a whisper even. 'My Lord Henry,' he said, 'you have demeaned and insulted the highest lady of your land, who is not present to defend herself.' He stepped back a little, leaning as if idle upon one leg, his arms crossed as in reposeful contemplation, and looking at Henry in his own pure Owen way (I can see it in my mind), one eyebrow shooting up and the mouth showing a little curl. 'Red Bolingbroke,' he said, still quite, but each word barbed, 'I wondered when first I encountered you—and shaved your red head and saved your babyish life—who had had the rearing of you....' And he shook his head, making a little clucking noise. 'Poor lady—whoever it was! The shame she suffers now and forever must burn upon her soul always ... I pity her.... We wait all, sir, upon your apology.' And so he waited in that same idle pose and downlooking. He said later that he thought the blood vessels in Henry's throat would burst, and so end it all. But of course they did not; life does not grant such large mercies. There was a long silence. Not a mouse squeaked. Then Owen uncrossed his arms and with his hand took the embroidered glove that had been thrust through his belt as was his custom, weighing it in his hand. 'I am unarmed, sir, but I have this—though shame it is to so waste it. A pretty thing, embroidered by my own fair lady's fingers....' And he raised it slowly above his head and, with a sudden flick of his wrist, flung it hard onto the ground at Henry's feet. The color left Henry's face, as though he had been struck a hard blow, and he reeled where he stood.

'You will not pick up my gage?' asked Owen.

After a moment, Henry said heavily, 'I do not fight unarmed men.'

'A brave saying.' Owen smiled. 'It is easier, sure, to have me seized. Give the order.'

After a moment Henry said, 'I am no tyrant, Sir Welshman.'

'Glad I am to hear it,' said Owen, smiling again. 'And now I will take back my glove, for Marred would never forgive me that I should throw it away in such wise....' And he smoothed the fine leather and tucked it back into his belt.

'You have my leave to go now ... back to Wales,' said Henry. 'Fetch his sword'—he flung over his shoulder—'and saddle his mount in the courtyard.' He turned back to Owen. 'Go now, sirrah—before I change my mind.'

'You will not,' said Owen, deadly quiet. 'It is not a Lancaster trait.'

Henry turned on his heel and strode away, clanking in his plate, to seat himself in the small throne on the raised dais. At this point Richard's dog, a nervous, quivering hound, his favorite that was with him ever, broke from Richard's hand that was on his collar and ran bounding to Henry where he sat, jumping up to him and licking his face, his cropped tail wagging.

Henry half-rose from his seat; perhaps he thought the dog meant to sink his teeth into him. 'What is the meaning of this?' he cried. The great dog climbed into his lap like a puppy, snuggling his pointed nose into Lancaster's armpit.

'Cousin,' said Richard now, and very sad, 'it means that even my dog knows the right side to choose.'

'Dickon,' said Owen, loud, 'he has got a taste for raw meat from our dinner here, that is all. He smells it again.... Do not give him a man's heart. He is a beast only....'

'One brings your sword, Welshman!' roared Henry. 'And now begone!'

Owen took the sword and bowed his head, perhaps an inch, to Lancaster. Then he turned and knelt before Richard, placing his hands between his, in the sign of homage. 'I shall be faithful,' he said. And under his breath, for Richard only, he whispered low, 'We shall be at the heels of the Lancaster army, we Welsh. At Litchfield, let yourself down from the window— it is unbarred. We shall be there, waiting....' And he rose, raising his arm in a kind of salute. 'Au revoir, my Dickon....'

'Farewell, good friend,' said the king. I guess in his heart he knew that never again would they meet.

For though Owen and his Welsh forces stayed close on the army of Lancaster, their ranks swelling each day as more loyal Welsh joined them, still was there never enough strength of numbers to challenge the thirty thousand that followed Henry. And on the road from Chester to London, when they rested with the imprisoned king at Litchfield, Richard failed in his bid for freedom.

Owen told us, sighing heavy, 'He managed to get hold of a stout rope, or maybe some faithful soul among his guards helped, and he let himself down without hurt from his high window. I saw it all; I was there, as promised. There was a high wall around the castle, and soldiers posted at every gate and at every corner of the wall. I climbed the wall and throttled one, taking his place and waving our dragon flag on a white ground to show Richard where I stood. It was a moonless night and he did not see, his eyes not yet accustomed to the darkness, after his lighted chamber. I gave a low whistle, hoping; we had had no chance to agree on signals. He heard and started toward me. But the guard nearest had sharp ears, too, and gave the alarm. They seized him, and I melted away—down the wall and back to where my men waited.... It was our last chance. I never saw him again.... Nor ever will.' And he lowered his head into his hands and wept. It was a thing I had never seen him do before, even as a boy; he was not a man for weeping, Owen.

The remainder of the sad tale came to us in pieces, second-hand; I will put it together as best I can. It is said that at Chester, where they rested three days, young Harry of Monmouth, Lancaster's heir, was brought to his father. Stunned he was to see Richard prisoner and protested loud. 'But he has made me knight!' cried Harry. 'And he is the king!'

His father stared from a cold eye, unmoving. 'Parliament will decide that,' he said.

We heard, too, though it may not be true, that young Harry drew the sword that Richard had given him at his knighting, and ran at his father with it, and had to be subdued. Morgan, who knew the boy, nodded and said she believed it. 'For Richard was good to Harry—and a better father than that odious mole Bolingbroke!' The young are ever quick to hate. My own Sibli named him Molewarp, for moles warp the earth they burrow; it stuck, and we heard it often in Wales in the years that followed.

It was said, too, that Richard was made to ride all the way to London on a small and wretched steed, a sorry hack not worth two pounds, and that he was dressed in rough wadmal. Owen says this cannot be, for Bolingbroke was too canny; never would he so set the people of London against him, to demean their rightful king in such wise. Not so would he accomplish his purpose. But that is what the chroniclers say, and for what it is worth, I have told it.

When they came to London, the Lord Mayor and some guild leaders rode out to meet them. 'Fair sirs,' said Bolingbroke, 'here is your king. Think what you will do with him.' Owen said that by this speech Henry hoped to be offered the crown, but he was not; Richard was taken to the Tower and lodged in the royal apartments, Henry putting him under heavy guard by his own orders.

The next day Richard was told that his cousin Henry was below and wished him to come down. 'Let my cousin,' cried Richard, with a flash of his former spirit, 'come to me!'

After a long delay and Richard pacing the floor, Henry came to Richard's chambers and greeted him, bending the knee.

'Why am I under lock and key?' cried Richard. 'Am I not King of England?'

'You are my king, sire,' answered Henry, 'but the council thinks fit to put a guard upon you until Parliament has reached a decision.'

Richard burst out in fury, crying out that he would meet in combat any of his foes. 'It is forbidden,' answered Henry.

Richard demanded to see his queen. 'Bring her to me. Bring Isabelle!'

'It is forbidden.' Henry rose from his knees then, his armor creaking—I guess it needed oiling.

'Why are you in armor?' demanded Richard.

'I am used to it—it is my normal wear,' said Henry.

'It cannot be comfortable, even for a seasoned warrior like yourself,' said Richard, with a secret smile. 'What does it cover ... the French sickness? Your face shows signs ... like my father's. ...'

Henry's hands went to the marks on his face, some old and healing, some new and raw. 'I have a breaking out—some food does not agree with me. ...'

'You are too old for pimples, Henry. ...' And Richard turned away.

It was his last defiance. Next day Henry came, bringing with him the archbishop, Arundel, deposed by Richard and Henry's great friend. With them too was a deputation of bishops and peers; their faces were hostile, for each had his own grievance against that poor king. Richard, in a quiet voice and with great composure, read a statement agreeing to abdicate the throne, if Parliament so decreed. He then placed his signet ring on Henry's finger and expressed his wish that that man should be his successor.

On September the thirtieth, in the year thirteen hundred and ninety-nine, at Westminster Hall, he formally abdicated the throne, reading that same statement, by wish of Parliament. He wore his royal robes and crown and held the scepter of his rule in his hand.

But the members of the House were not content. They read a paper of thirty-three counts of accusation; Richard was compelled to hear it, a long humiliation. He made no interruption or denial but remained quiet, standing beside his throne. After, he was bidden to withdraw. He said nothing, but handed his scepter to Henry, and took the crown from his head, and gave it also. Then he bowed to the members there and left the chamber, his dignity alive in him like a white flame. All who heard it, our whole household at Glendower House—servants, bards, minstrels, and family—wept.

The story went on. Bolingbroke stood up and addressed his peers; these were his words, recorded by the scribe: 'In the name of the Father, Son, and Holy Ghost, I, Henry of Lancaster, challenge the realm of England and the Crown, with all the members and appurtenances; as that I am descended by the right line of blood, coming from the good lord Henry III, and through that right God of His grace hath sent me with the help of my kin and of my friends to recover it; the which realm was in point to be undone for default of governance and undoing of good laws.'

The Lords and Commons were challenged for their opinions and responded that they assented. The ex-archbishop Arundel (soon, of course, to be reinstated by Henry) then took Henry by the hand and conducted him to the throne of England.

The great hall where we sat, hearing this news, was crowded with all our folk; the doorways, too, were full, and the corridors outside, the stream of people going right out through the courtyard and into the road itself. How the word had spread none knows, but I think not one tenant or shireperson was missing from that throng. Rising slowly, like an old man whose joints ache in him, Owen made his way to the door, and on into the courtyard, the folk falling away to let him pass. Raising his voice so that all heard, like thunder it was, or doom, he said, 'Sweet Richard is deposed and his crown stolen from him. Henry of Bolingbroke, Duke of Hereford and Lancaster, Earl of Derby—that Henry now is the king of the realm of England.'

A loud sobbing wail went up from the women, and cries of 'Sweet Richard! Sweet Richard!' were heard from all sides. Suddenly above them all came a high piercing sound like a battle cry. 'Vengeance!' it cried, and in one great throbbing roar from a thousand Welsh throats it came then, 'Vengeance —vengeance for sweet Richard! Death to the traitor mole!' I shall never forget that sound, so wild, so barbarous. From a people of pastoral simplicity. From our own Cymry.

After, my own young Sibli sat late at her harp, playing soft and trying over notes, sweet and wild. From that long night came the long-sung 'Sweet Richard,' the lament that was heard for years all over Wales. After, it was said that Owen wrote it. But he could not, Owen, though there was much he could do, and did. No, it was my Sibli, that liked to be called Sybil in the antique way. It was the song of the Small Bird. It was a lament, as I have said, and a prophecy. For within the year was Richard dead and gone.

EIGHT

'The king is dead ... long live the king!' has always been a cry that chilled my heart. Though, truly, it is no more than the father dying and the son succeeding, in the usual way of all men's lives, even in low places. In England, though, it could not be cried, that cry, for Richard lived still—for a while. Even after his abdication and he still prisoner in the Tower, the people loved him, the poor of London stood packed close in the thousands, looking upward to the Tower room that held their rightful king. Three days they stood, even in the driving rain, for word had gone round that one loyal and powerful friend to Richard, Bishop Merks of Carlisle, was protesting the Bolingbroke seizure of the crown. Though he spoke valiantly, that good bishop, and with eloquence, stony silence met him, and he was even put under guard and taken away to prison himself. This announcement was made to the waiting people; they wailed, mourning, and some, armed with picks and axes, even tried to storm the Tower, but they were driven away finally by the soldiers of Bolingbroke.

One came to Richard in the Tower, head of a deputation of the House; he shook his finger at the king, as one reprimands a bad schoolboy, and read from a paper in his hand. 'None of all these states or people,' read he, 'from this time forward either bear you faith or do you obeisance as to their king.'

It is hard to know what passed through Richard's mind; he did not storm or rage as formerly, nor did he faint like the coward Bolingbroke had named him, but stood still and calm throughout. Finally he said, 'I look not hereafter ... but I hope my cousin will be good lord to me . . .'

It is said that, on hearing the news in France, the Duke of
Burgundy said, 'Since the English peers have imprisoned their
king, they will surely put him to death. They always hated him
because he preferred peace to war.' And the poor French king,
Charles of Valois, father of Isabelle, Richard's queen, fell into
one of his worst fits of mad melancholy, fearing his daughter's
fate.

All her ladies-in-waiting were sent from her without ceremony, back to France (we at home thanked God that Owen
had brought Morgan away in time!), and she herself, Isabelle,
was taken from Windsor, under guard, and put in the charge
of the Bishop of Salisbury at his manor house on the Thames.
As for Richard, the demand had been made in the House that
he be confined in 'some sure and secret place.' He was sent first
to Leeds Castle, then to Yorkshire, where he was kept succes-
sively in three of Henry's own castles: Pickering, Knares-
borough, and, finally, Pontefract.

The next Bolingbroke step was to punish those who had
been loyal to Richard. To do him credit, that red man with the
black heart, he contented himself with stripping these nobles
of their estates, greedy for money he was always, Henry. In our
Wales the evil Statutes of Rhuddallt, long ignored by Richard
and by his grandfather before him, were enforced again. No
Welshman might intermarry with English, own land in England, seek employment in England, or set up trade in England.
Those who already owned property in English lands were
stripped of it and beggared. Even the lowest serving-folk, be
they Welsh, were flung out onto the streets, penniless, by their
English masters. And so it went, in all manner of ways. And
there came flocking back to Wales all these unfortunates, bearing in their hearts a painful burden of hate and a buried hope
of revenge. Our Welsh manorhouses were filled with impover-
ished guests, bitter and plotting; the villages overflowed with
the many dispossessed; even the cottage-folk took into their
tiny hovels their kin among these poor. Unrest there was
among them and talk of rebellion, and some went mad, poor
souls. Many a sad creature wandered, ragged and filthy, homeless, through the lanes of our towns, crying, 'Sweet Richard is

coming to help us.... Richard will avenge us!' By that time, of course, their Richard, that sweet monarch, was dead.

Plots there were in plenty, before his death and after even, to get back his throne, but all failed. Chief among them was led by that faithful Salisbury who had stood by him always; in this was the little queen implicated, too. And she a lass of not yet fourteen! She tore down the arms of Lancaster from the walls of the castle where she was kept, putting up Richard's white hart badge in all those places. Gladly did she plot with those who managed to have her ear; they had, among them, the conspirators, one Richard Maudelyne, a priest, said to be Richard's very double for looks—though Owen said only from a distance did he resemble the deposed king. He was dressed in Richard's clothes and paraded through the streets, crying out to the people that here was their king, alive and well. I do not know the rights of it or ever will, but all were caught and suffered cruel deaths, except for the young queen, who had been got away, back to her native shores. There were poison plots, too, and the new usurping monarch near died, and his sons with him; shame that they did not. And I say it who have never had the bloodthirst! But all the havoc that was wrought in this our green and lovesome Wales I lay to his door, Bolingbroke. For here did it start, with the deposing of a lawful king that was gentle and good.

On the night of February fourteenth of the new century, Richard, sweet Richard, died at Pontefract. A tale went about, smelling, as Owen said, of much rehearsing, that the unhappy king had starved himself to death. The other, from French sources, had it that he was murdered by one Piers Exton, tool of Lancaster, struck down by a poleax. The right will never be known. But for sure he was dead; his body was shown to all in the London streets. Weeping women and cursing men filed by the coffin and looked upon his face. Our Griffith, son of this house, went up to London from his Oxford lodgings and saw it. No marks were upon the face, and beautiful it looked in death as in life. No signs of starvation either, no sunken cheeks or shrunken eyelids. But the head only was on view; the body was completely sealed in lead! What was the sight the lead hid? A wasted frame, severed limbs, marks of the ax? We shall never know.

All Wales mourned. And still did the displaced people pour in across our borders from the cruel new England. Poor friars that Richard had befriended came, their monasteries snatched from them by the new churchmen. And all those of the New Learning came in throngs, fleeing from the horror that was to come.

Archbishop Arundel, deposed from office by Richard for treachery, had returned at Ravenspur with Henry of Bolingbroke, and went with his army, offering churchly pardons to all who would join them against the king. Many were thus recruited, and he had his reward. He was reinstated, Arundel; again was he Archbishop of Canterbury, the highest church office in the realm. An evil man he was ever, and grasping; he seized lands and wealth upon the slightest pretext. And Henry was in his debt and did not stay him, for his was a shaky throne and needed all the support coming to it. That bishop was a fierce heretic hunter, too. He issued the infamous *De haeretico comburendo*—the blackest document in English history. The Latin words meant, in effect, that any confessed heretic would be burned at the stake. Alive. All those of the New Learning, called Lollards by some, spoke what the established church called heresy. The Lollards had many new thoughts and beliefs. They did not believe in war. They did not believe in punishment by death. These were not heresies, but other of their ideas were. For they did not believe that a corrupt priest was fit to save souls. They did not believe that the bread and wine became the body and blood of Jesus because they were blessed. They believed that Jesus spoke in metaphor, something as we poets do, and not literally. Many things they held true, the Lollards; chief of them all was that the Bible should be known to all, not told through a priest only for whatever gain he hoped from the telling. The whole movement had started with Master Wycliffe, a generation ago, who had translated the Bible into English. There were now quite a few of these precious copies about, the Testament in English, and Morris Stove, my lady's tutor, had been working for years on the Welshing of it. In the Bohemian lands, too, had this Lollard heresy spread, and many martyrs made. And now it was to happen here, in this island of ours! Folk would die in flames and in agony ... and all for using their minds, which are all poor humans have to call their own. So it is easy to see how they, too, those Lollards, in fear of their lives, fled here to us in Wales, as to a sanctuary. So many, indeed, came to our own doors that the Lady Margaret gave them a house of their own, with a little room, plain, where they might meet and read the Scriptures. But mostly they were homeless, for there was not room for all; at every hedge corner were preachers of the New Learning and folk gathering to hear them. And in every tavern was insurrection spoke and whispered, men weeping drunkenly for the lost golden days of Richard.

Our greedy neighbor, Reginald Grey, the Lord of Ruthin, pulled his same trick again, that had been put right by law in Richard's reign. Again he seized Owen's hereditary lands, the Common of Croisau, and expelled all Owen's tenants, a thing he had not dared to do the first time. These poor dispossessed fled to Sycharth for succor and shelter; in the hundreds they came, poor souls, with young crying children, fretful and weary, beasts of burden piled high with all they could salvage from Ruthin's soldiers, and terror whitening the eyes of all. Tudor was living there, at Sycharth, ruling it well and getting good harvests, though he had no lady-wife and only a few country concubines. He took in those people, making room in the many buildings that had been empty since our household moved here to Glendower House; there were so many, though, that tents and lean-tos had to be built to house them all, and many fatted beasts slaughtered to feed them. Tudor came riding furiously up to our manor, crying war and vengeance and bearing our dragon standard. He was, like his horse, wet with sweat; his face, too, was flushed, with anger and with mead; he had stopped at every tavern on the way. 'Calm yourself, brother,' said Owen, as Tudor reeled against him. 'You are like to drop from exhaustion, and you are flown with wine, too. Best duck your head in a pail of cold water and then sleep it off. We will talk in the morning.'

It was plain that Tudor could do no other than take his advice; he could not stand and his words slurred; he stank, too, of the wine cask so that we held our noses. Still was he as drunk on anger as on strong waters; could he hold weapon, he would have slain any Grey's man or king's man that appeared in his sight. Owen was his opposite, as brothers often are, and slow to kindle into fire; still was his face grim and set as he pondered his course.

'I shall go to London again,' he said next morning. 'This must be settled by law, once and for all. Those are our lands, by hereditary right and ancient custom, and the people that live upon them are our tenants and our care. I shall have the law ... and I shall have payment in full for the damages I have suffered. You will stay here, Tudor, for you inflame too easily. Come with me, Griffith, friend, and Brother John.'

For Margaret's brother, John Hanmer, was visiting. He was much like his father, the judge, loving the law, and his neat-featured clerk's face lit; then the light faded and he said mournfully, 'I cannot go. My wife will have my head. I cannot go.'

Owen laughed. 'I will send to her. And she will listen. I will send word that all our Welsh lands stand in jeopardy ... this is the beginning only. That will do it, for she will not want to lose all ... land-greedy your lady is, John.'

'But wait till we have gone, fair Owen ... else will she ride with us—and all the joy be gone....'

What joy there was in the mission I cannot tell; perhaps the journey held its pleasures for him, for at least he had his freedom, briefly, from his shrew. For sure, though, it was no joy to remember.

We came before the King's Court; three days did we wait, through interminable hearings, such slight matters as poaching or the stealing of two bags of wool being fully considered, while we chafed. Then was our case dismissed without a hearing, by king's order, it was said. Among those present at the court was Bishop Trevor of St. Asaph; this man knew Owen and Owen's ancestry, and he stood up and said, 'Honorable gentlemen, you are making a mistake, a grave mistake. This man has much power. Provoke him and he will cause trouble. He can cause more serious trouble than anyone today in all these British isles.'

They seemed, in part, to consider this, for they adjourned for the day, promising a final answer on the morrow. We were the next day denied entrance even. The bishop came to us privately, saying he had gone to the king himself.

'Henry of Bolingbroke, you mean,' said Owen. 'I do not count him king. What was his word?'

Bishop Trevor hesitated, a little color flooding his pale churchman's cheeks. 'He said, my Lord Owen, rough words that I put down to his illness—or his choler. This king was always rash, even from a boy.'

'This do I know well,' said Owen, 'and from long ago.... Say on, good friend. I will not hold it against you.'

'They are *his* words only,' said the bishop, with a hangdog look. 'He said, Henry—he said, "What care I for the barefoot rascal Welsh? Send him about his business—the Welsh magician!"'

'I thank you most kindly, good Father,' said Owen. 'Tell him from me—your king—that I *shall* be about my business . . . and soon!'

But still Owen did not act. He waited and watched, while Tudor stormed in impotence, and all the bards and minstrels composed their songs of war and vengeance. 'This is no war,' said Owen, 'but an unfair seizure and an unwise verdict. I know Henry of Bolingbroke. He is not so foolish as he seems. A bad day it was for him that day of our hearing . . . he is given to temper-fits. One more chance I will give him to settle all lawfully.' And he wrote letters, Owen, more than one. No answer came to any. And still he would not move, Owen, and waited still.

Grey moved his own people in, onto those lands belonging to Owen, taking over the cotter's huts with his own settlers, English churls and his unfree serfs wearing his rings of iron around their necks and tilling Owen's soil with lash and goad where our free tenants had lived for time out of mind. Soldiers he brought in too, hired mercenaries, hardened to their brutal life. And still did Owen wait, that man of peace.

Glendower House had not been built as a fort; there were no walls, no towers, no arrow slits. From all the shires round came bowmen, trained warriors that had fought in the battles past, offering their services to Owen for the defense of the proudest manor in the land. Upwards of a thousand we had in the space of a month. Rhys Dhu of Cardigan came down from his hills with another thousand, hill-fighters, toughened by their stony life. No need now for fortifications; ringed by an army we were. Barracks were built and tents erected, and the clash of arms and the thwang of arrow-practice was heard all the day long.

Many of the soldiers brought their familes with them; Glendower House had become a city, crowded with folk and spreading out far into the hills. Still were there many single fellows among them, with a roving eye and a careless heart. The Lady Margaret made Owen build a latticed barrier between our small cluster of houses and that bustling new-risen soldier-town. The damsels she bade to stay within it, though they could look through the latticework and watch the men at their drilling. She was grown very stately, my lady, pious, too, and a little stern; the maidens called her the Argylwyddes, giggling, behind her back. The young are cruel in their careless, golden way. Not one of those damels is as willow-slender as was Margaret in days gone; yet do they whisper among themselves that there are no more links left to put into the Lady's gold dragon belt. My sweet love, that is still the fairest lady in the land and no fuller than she should be, like a petaled yellow rose, at the prime of her beauty now. Morgan and my Sibli do not join in; they are thoughtful maidens and too tender of soul, each in her own way. It is the nun's foundling, Efa, that starts them off. She is giddy and gay and has a harlot way about her, young and innocent as she is; prettiest of them all she is, Efa, sweetly curving, white of skin, and with hair red-gold as the sun at its setting—but I do not like her. She is a bad girl, Efa, peeping at the men in their bath and rubbing against them as they pass, whoever they may be, even myself! But I am getting old, and I am not moved. My heart was given long ago and the flesh is quiet now.

NINE

All over North Wales that year there were lands seized by English border lords, and rebellions flared, even as far away as Mona, in Anglesey, where William and Rhys, sons of Tudor ap Gronw and cousins to Owen, raised the dragon standard and slew many of the would-be English masters. The English retaliated by burning down a Cistercian monastery and killing all the Welsh monks. And in our own near parts the Ruthin mercenaries roamed far and wide, looting, raping, and killing. Our own defenders, bowmen and lance-bearers, sought the Ruthin men out and punished where they could; still, scarce a day went by that one of our men did not come back, and each night there was mourning in the little city that had been our own Glendower House. Lady Margaret sent the damsels to the bereaved women in their makeshift homes, bearing death-gifts, and services were held for the soul-peace of the slain. And in the spring came Owen's answer from the usurper, Bolingbroke.

'You have been bid,' it read, 'to attend me, as your liege lord, into Scotland, to do battle there. Thrice now have I commanded you, through my good and trusted friend, and your own near neighbor, Reginald Grey, Lord of Ruthin, and thrice you have not replied. Henceforth all your lands shall be confiscate to the Crown of England, excepting those called the Common of Croisau, which I, Henry IV of England, have granted to that same Lord Grey; and you and your heirs are outlawed from this day, and a price upon your head.' Owen looked up, chuckling. 'He does not name the price. Wary he was always, Henry.'

'But, Owen,' cried Margaret. 'You were never informed! No command was sent to you!'

'Either he sent too late, that wily red one ... or Grey has played me false to en-anger his king. He wants my lands, Grey, by law. And so he has them now....'

'What will you do?' cried Margaret.

Owen tore the paper across and tossed it into the fire. 'I will wait,' said Owen, 'and I will send....'

And Owen sent his messengers out all over Wales, to his kinsmen, both close and distant. Even before they had had time to reach them, some came, as though Merlin had called them. For the prophecy had been, always, that at Welsh need another Arthur would rise, of the Pendragon line. Owen's lineage is from all the ruling houses of Wales, including this, and all Welshmen know it. Perhaps Owen himself knew it, in a way. As I have said, he had been dressing the part. As I saw him now, with my eyes new-peeled, there stood Arthur in all his glory, as the bards have sung him. Tall, with a lion look, and eyes that flashed command in yellow fire. Only the mouth, curling a little below the proud arched nose, held a hint of the old urbanity of the courtier Owen that the world had known.

Fresh news came from Sycharth, news of horror and outrage. Grey's men and the men of Lord Talbot, close follower of the Lancaster, had fallen upon our Sycharth manor; numbering in the thousands, they had stormed the place, torn down the drawbridge, and slain all the poor people who had refuged there. Tudor and two others had got away into the hills. After, when the marauders had left, they stole back; Sycharth, that lovely manor, was a smoking ruin, though it stood, still. Everything of value had been taken away, the walls even stripped of their hangings, and the pictures slashed, the furniture hacked to pieces. The folk, too, lay about in crumpled heaps, even women and little children. The walls were blackened with smoke and the smell of burning still hung in the air, and another smell, too, of rotting flesh.

Black vultures circled above the once-fair manor, too stupid to find the chimney holes. So, at least, when we rode over in force, there was enough left to bury decently.

'We will wait,' said Owen, impassively. 'We will wait till we have assembled our full strength.' For even Margaret, who preached the peace of Jesus, was aflame to avenge this dreadful deed. But 'We will wait,' said Owen.

The word had gone out throughout the countryside, and even into England. All the Oxford students, Welsh, left their hospices and inns and came home. Welsh laborers that had lived all their lives on English soil threw down their plows or melted them into weapons and came. The churchmen came, most militant of all. And all came to us at Glendower House, or so it seemed. We were besieged by them and by the cries of vengeance, and the blood-songs of the bards and minstrels. The dragon banner blew above every tent and hovel, home-sewn by outraged women. Even the children carried them, playing at war. The young men had their hair cropped about their ears in the new fashion called the helm-cut. It was in-vented by Harry Percy, the hero of the Scottish wars, that was nicknamed Hotspur, for his speed in battle. Even the young men of our house wore this new fashion, even Griffith, that all had thought of as clerk and scholar. For he had come home from Oxford too, with the younger Meredith and the four bastard sons of Owen. Hot were they all for war, to hear them speak, and their studies forgot.

With them came a young cousin of Owen, Rhisiart; half-Norman he was, but wild with love of Wales and steeped in its traditions. Born and reared in Hereford he was, and an Eng-lish subject, but he fell upon his knees before Owen, begging to go along to battle. 'For I am a scribe and secretary already,' he said, and holding out samples of his work.

I could not see them, but I saw Owen's face as he scanned them, and the old Owen showed then, amusement warming his eyes. 'Get up, get up, cousin,' he said. 'There are no battles to go to ... but I need a secretary ... and you shall have the post.'

And indeed he did need a secretary, Owen; forever writing letters he was, in the months and years that followed, and each one with its copy to preserve it for the records, or for posterity. A strange thought that; when time has passed me by, and Owen, too, and my dear love all unaware—the pretty damsels gone, and the rough soldiers, and Red Bolingbroke and all the kings to follow—will they survive still, those fragile flutterings of paper and the thin scratchings from the pen of the long-dead scribe? Perhaps. For Ovid is more alive today than I my-self, and a tiny scrap of Sappho has power still to tear the heart. An idle thought. But I am given to them. It is my pro-fession, after all, I can do no other.

With all the young men about, cropped heads, and merry, bold eyes, the Lady Margaret made barriers stricter than any nunnery. The damsels she kept by her mostly, at useless tasks, or sent Nurse, old now but still a watchdog, to accompany them as they moved about the house. And never was a lad welcomed in the ladies' solar after twilight fell. Still did they snatch their trysting-moments, for youth will have its day, and pair off two by two they did, no matter. Young Rhisiart mooned after Catherine; most like her mother she was, this youngest of the daughters, a silver-pale moon-maiden. And she liked him, too, or his attentions; more than once did I see notes passed between them, a tender look, or a soft touch of fingers in the shadows. Tudor's rosy-dark twins, Gwynneth and Gwenllian, old now for maidens but still unwed, found a pair of twins for themselves, like drawn to like. Big bright freckled lads they were, Irish, and looking for a cause to fight for; classmates of Meredith they were, but bored with Oxford, and come to Owen they did to offer their arms, spoiling for a fight. Chieftain's sons they were, they said, and told their lineage; there are more chieftains in the bogs of Ireland than in our Welsh hills even. And shy glances, full of meaning, passed between our Meredith and Rhys Dhu's Elliw, an almond-pale lass as insubstantial as a thread of song. And so it went, under my eyes, gold sparks amid the dark days, and I, grown old now and ugly, but the poor heart leaping still.

Letters he sent, and messengers, and a bidding to all to rise for Wales and her right, against the usurper-oppressor. And they came, all, his kindred and the great lords of our land, and held counsel. It was on the day of the sixteenth of September in the year 1400. I remember it well, for it is also my birthday and I was a half-century old and sad of it.

It was a true council, sage and wise and everything planned; I know, for I was present. But such meetings, with papers and maps and much talk, do not make a good story. The events of the summer before, when told, are like shows put on by minstrels and mountebanks; one like me might almost suspect they are.

As I have said, we were much crowded at Glendower House; every night the great dining-hall was filled to overflowing, particularly since the young men of our house had come home from school, bringing many others with them, all flaming with war-passion. Except one. I am getting old and forgetful, or I would have mentioned him before. Or perhaps that is not true, and I left him out from envy. For my Lady Margaret was much beside him, talking low, and I sat beside my harp, gnawed within. He was a famous Lollard, named Master Walter Brut, and came from Hereford, like young Rhisiart. Even here in Wales we had heard of this man, for he was a confessed heretic, yet had been set free by his judges. He was the only one in all England to escape the burning fate; already there had been many cases of this infamous punishment. But he, this Walter, had a great fund of knowledge, much wit, and a persuasive tongue, and his answers, while still remaining true to his faith, were couched in such terms that his accusers could not convict him. That is not to say that he was sly, far from it; I have never seen a more open countenance or less guile in an eye. And I say it, who harbored much resentment toward him for my lady's sake! I have told myself again and again that of a certainty she would find much interest in this man, Margaret, for he is a hero and a saint, in her faith. And so he has proved himself over and over; the only man I ever met who followed the teachings, truly, of his Christ. So I have got over it, my jealousy, in the end. Besides, he is near young enough to be her son; and so I told myself that I maligned her, Margaret. Still did they sit in corners talking, and eagerness lighting up both faces like the flickering from a fire. Well, let it pass; I am making a poor history.

That same night, when arrived all at once the young Oxford men, and Hall was noisy with their din, and sweat coming out on all from the folk packed like herring, there appeared suddenly that Rhys of the Hills, Rhys Gethin; it had been years since he had come to our door even. He had grown to manhood now, of course, though he looked more beast than man, clad as he was in black goatskin, and the black hair of him growing down his back and chest and up his legs to meet it. Wild he looked and savage, with the whites of his eyes rolling, and savage was his deed, too. For he dragged by a heel another man, stunned to senselessness, or nearly, and bloody in places. A cry rose from all round the hall, soldiers, mostly, that were squatting against the walls at their meal. 'A spy! A Ruthin spy! A man of Lancaster!'

It must have been so, for he wore Grey's livery, with the Lancaster blue and silver badge at his breast. And the cry roused him, and he raised himself up and cried, 'Long live King Harry.... Long live Lancaster!' And that Rhys drew knife, and, as one would slaughter a sheep, pulled back the man's head by the hair, and slit his throat!

Then Rhys Gethin looked toward Owen from under his low-jutting brow, and began to walk toward him where he sat on the dais. We were frozen, all, and the thought crossed my mind that he might be crazed, and use that dripping knife on Owen. But he threw it down with a ring upon the flags of the floor, and knelt before Owen, bowing his head and putting out a dark hand to bring up the hem of Owen's robe and kiss it. 'I have done wrong, master, in your eyes.... I have done wrong as always.... Do with me what you will. Only save Wales! Save Wales!'

And the soldiers rose up and echoed him from all the walls around. 'Owen for Wales! Wales and Prince Owen! The Red Dragon for Wales! ... Owen and the Red Dragon! Owen and Saint David!'

And Rhys Gethin cried out then where he knelt, 'Owen and Saint Derfel!'

Near him at the high table sat Margaret, horror on her face, and down the board our two churchmen guests, sly, satyr-faced Father Domitius and the fat dumpling, Father Simon, crossed themselves and fingered their beads.

Owen sat, staring before him, like stone, in the brief strange way that comes upon him now and then, and I saw from my place that tears glittered like gems in his eye-corners. I turned my own eyes, shy on a sudden, and saw that none was near the fallen dead man, save for that Lollard, Walter Brut, who was tearing his own shirt and using it to bind up the gaping second mouth in the throat. Then he drew out his plain wooden cross and kissing it, placed it between the hands that he crossed on the dead man's chest.

There was silence now in Hall, for all eyes were on Owen, staring still. Then he gave a great sigh, Owen, and reaching out, pulled Rhys the Savage to his feet and, standing, kissed the brutish forehead. 'My son,' he said. 'My poor, poor beast....' And he signed for a guard to come. 'I must put you away, my boy ... till I can think what must be done with you....' And he held out his hand for the knife. Rhys picked it up and gave it to him, meek as a lamb now.

'Kinsman,' said Rhys, 'and my heart's father ... do with me what you will. I could not stay my hand....' Not all understood, though he spoke clear, for the hill-Welsh is odd-sounding and full of little clicks and grunts. 'But it was for Wales I did it ... and in my hills are five hundred more like me. They will bring their bows and lay down their lives ... five hundred fierce warriors, maybe more....' So he had remembered how to count so far!

'I know you good ... under ...' said Owen. 'I will think....' And he laid his hand briefly on the shoulder of the beast-man. 'Go now with these....' And Rhys Gethin walked out peaceably between the two soldiers. I thought dimly: Where will they take him? We have no dungeon here ...

After, soon after, came a great din from the courtyard, women's voices squealing in rage, the sound of blows and heels on the stones, and then a long-drawn-out cry of grief and terror, unearthly clear and high and cut off short as if chopped. Men ran out into the yard, the Lollard with them, and came back bearing a woman, young, and big-bellied with child. The Lady Margaret started up and made her way to where she lay; by then the girl had roused and was screaming again, this time harsh, animal sounds. 'Sweet Jesus, she is about to bear!' cried Margaret softly, and sinking to her knees. 'Bring serving maids, quickly—and towels and water....'

But it was all over before they arrived; the babe came forth, a frog-thing, tiny and covered with blood and slime, dead. The young woman sank into unconsciousness again and lay quite still while the maids fussed around her, mopping the floor and wrapping the little scrap of humanity in a piece of silk, the lady's own head-veil that she snatched from her head. Weeping she was, Margaret, and no wonder; it was a fearful sight.

She gave orders for the girl to be brought to the upstairs chambers where the maidens slept. 'Can she have been the wife of the slain Lancaster man?' she asked.

Walter Brut nodded. 'It must be ... poor girl ... no husband —and now no child....' But busy all the while he was, placing the babe within the arms of the boy from Ruthin, and cleaning the corpse-face and smoothing the hair. Then he walked to Owen, who sat like a sleepwalker still. 'Sir,' he said, and sharply, to rouse him, unfearing he was, that Lollard. 'Sir Owen, I ask permission to place these bodies in the chapel. I have laid them out and they are decent now.... Could someone direct me, for I do not know where, in this Constantinople of yours, that it lies....' And he smiled, frank and easy, as one equal to another.

Owen's eyes came back from wherever they had been, and he smiled also. 'It has become a very city, indeed, this house of ours...' And he beckoned a page. 'Gwalchmai will lead you....

Father Domitius rose, his dark face growing darker from the blood which flooded it, and his eyes hot. 'I forbid it,' he cried. 'The Church forbids it! An enemy and an unbaptized infant ... they cannot lie in a holy place!'

'It is *my* holy place, Father,' said Owen, very quiet. 'This is my domain.' And he turned to the page and to Master Walter, who had been stayed by the priest's cry. 'Find bearers and take the bodies there. And light candles ... wax ones.'

The angry priest stood defiant, and the sparks, silent, flew between those two men, Owen and Father Domitius. Then did that priest grab the cassock of the other one, still seated at table, gnawing at a capon leg. He yanked him to his feet, his hands still holding the greasy drumstick, and bewilderment sitting upon his moon face. 'We cannot stay in this house of sin!' cried the angry one. 'Holy Church has been flouted! You will rue this, Baron Owen!'

Owen bowed slightly. 'That may be, Father. But I think not.... Must you go? ... It has been most pleasant having you at my board this last fortnight.' Owen could be adder-tongued; you could see the priest took his meaning. For sure they had been dining off Owen's bounty twice that time! And to the other one, little and greedy, Owen bowed also, holding out a cloth. 'Here is a napkin ... you may take the drumstick.'

And so did Owen place his cause in jeopardy, for the sake of his Lollard lady, or for his own whim, who can tell? The two priests left the hall, to spread sly word against its master. For he held no preferences, Owen—save perhaps for us bards—and gave all, high or low, the same respect, be they good folk and true. And always was he enemy to evil, except where it lurked, small, in his own heart. But no man is proof against that.

After, the girl from Ruthin that had birthed the little dead babe recovered, under Nathan's ministrations and my lady's care. She was pure Saxon, named, in the Saxon way, Alice Oxerd, for the tasks she labored at; she was born a byre-maid, on the Ruthin estates, and unfree. Her mother, she said, the Lord of Ruthin had burned for a witch, before the girl's eyes, and she a little maid then. She grew up under their yoke, working hard; but she grew comely, and they took her, the Greys, both father and son, on her wedding night. A Norman custom and filthy, like all those foreign ways. The *lord's right*, they call it, in their fancy tongue. After, they threw her back to her husband, like a worn-out rag; she wept all night. But they were happy then for a little, she and the poor unfortunate that had been killed by Rhys Gethin's knife. He *was* a Ruthin spy, but what would you? He had no choice, being unfree. Theirs was a sad story.

When she cried out in the courtyard, having followed her man there, the furious Welsh women knew that Alice for English, and beat her and cut her with knives; thirst for blood have they, women, after too much wine. It was a miracle that she was saved. Another miracle was her swift conversion to the New Learning; she had called herself witch before, like her mother. And that must be laid to Master Walter's door. For he was forever beside her, talking at her, after she healed of her bruises, and it was seen she was passable-fair. She hung on his every word, her eyes all hungry. He took her to wife later, Walter, and gave her his name. So from the serf Alice Oxerd she became Mistress Brut, with estates in Hereford. Another miracle. But it is not part of my story, that, so I will let it pass.

On Midsummer Night, when the fires were lit in all the shires round about and could be seen for miles, a fair wild sight, old Iolo died. He had been abed for many months, complaining of a weight on his chest that crushed him and took his breath. His words wheezed and whistled and were hard to hear; by that Midsummer Night the death rattle had begun in his throat too. He gave sign he wished to be carried into Hall; a litter was made and he was brought there, while all the folk wept. Word had spread somehow, as it does, mysteriously, that the great bard was at the gate of death, and hundreds crowded along the lanes and byways and thronged the courtyard, up to the very doors.

Sad it was to see, so wasted was he; I had thought him a big man, even a year ago, but now was he shrunk to child's size. His age was great; he boasted that he was over a hundred years. It was not so; I that am his younger kinsman know, for I have traced it out, and think he was not much above eighty. Still had he lived hard; much travel, and little sleep, and the bardic *awen* (that is our word for inspiration) eating at him always. Sad it was to hear also, in that hall, all silent now; he labored to speak, the cords of his old neck standing out and his eyes glaring, wild with frustration. Nothing but wheezes and rattles came from his throat; his voice was gone forever, ahead of him.

Owen bent over him, tears glittering, but could not make out any words. Many tried, and I among them, and I say there *were* no words. But little Elliw Dhu, who was his godchild, ran forward, and bending very close, said that she heard and understood. She repeated his words to all, and then fainted, conveniently, so that none could question her.

She said that his last words, for he died just after, were 'Burn Ruthin—on St. Matthew's Day, burn Ruthin!' ... and then 'Owen, Prince of Wales!'

I have lived among bards, minstrels, and mountebanks all my life, and I can smell a made-up scene. Whether the young people did it, all hot for war, or the patriotic bards, or Owen himself, to get the common folk behind him, I do not know. I do know it was his plan all along to burn the town of Ruthin on a fair-day, when the folk would be out of their houses, and suffer less hurt, and loss only; I was privy to that plan, and so were others; waiting for greater forces was he, Owen, only.

But it was a scene of antique horror and noble grief, and it served the purpose well. For all men present there came forward and swore fealty to Owen, and proclaimed him the rightful Prince of Wales. The hall rang with battle-cries and with swords clashed in promise, and women wept and wailed in token of the grief to come.

Owen spoke then, and in some measure was quiet restored. For his words were calm and full of reason. He said that he was true prince of our land, by right of his descent from the three princely lines, but that he wanted not to rule, but to govern, with the help of an elected Parliament. 'We are a land of petty princedoms,' he said, 'and little cities and baronies. We must weld out of them one Wales—and cast off the Saxon yoke!'

And 'One Wales!' became the cry. 'One Wales! Owen for Wales! Wales and Owen!' And one cry came: 'Down with Lancaster! Owen for Wales and England!'

He held up his hand for silence. 'I seek no power in England,' he said, and though he spoke soft, he was heard. 'I seek no power in England and no crown to wear.... But Wales has suffered long ... and it has not yet begun.... For Lancaster will make slaves of our people. We must unite and stand against him and his house.... One Wales, I say! There must be a Welsh Council, a Welsh Parliament, Welsh laws ... and the Welsh tongue spoken free. A university, too, we shall have ... These are my dreams ...' And a clamor rose, and he held up his hand again. 'First must we regain the rights that have been taken from us ... and the lands that have been grabbed. But it must be done with purpose—and with plan. I ask you in the name of all Wales ... trust me. Trust your prince that does not seek a crown. Trust me!'

And the cries came back, as from one throat, ringing above the dead bard where he lay at Owen's feet, crumpled and small. 'Owen, our prince! Owen, savior of Wales! The dragon banner! Wales forever!' I have forgot them now, all the words shouted, but they were behind him, all, and even from the countryside above the cries echoed through the hills.

The body was taken away, borne to the chapel by Owen himself and his sons, and the tears streaming down every cheek. And there was feasting and wine and mead in Hall until midnight. Margaret came to me and whispered that I play. I took harp and played, songs of Iolo and older bards still, songs of Wales in her great days that are gone, and songs of triumph. And one of my own I played; rough it was and not perfect, but felt at the moment, and some merit in it, a lament for Iolo at the end of his days. I have polished it up since, but still is it sung as I sang it that night, for folk have long memories.

Some of the younger people had gone out into the night to watch our Midsummer fire that had been kindled on an old barrow-mound. And in the skies there flamed many others, and with them, another, that was no bonfire, but a long wall of flame. Valle Crucis was burning!

When Owen's men got there, the monastery was a ruin, the old stones charred and black, and many of the monks slain. There was no sign of any of the nuns; they had been captured by the Ruthin enemy. Years after we heard; they had been made into army whores, to serve the Lancaster soldiers. It was a deed of indecency and outrage, and it got back for us the churchmen that Owen had offended. So does all tragedy have its meaning and its purpose, though if I were God I would not rule it so.

TEN

Owen's first council met, as I have said, on the sixteenth of September; it was only a crude and hasty copy of a lawful proceeding, but it served. By then all that were with us had arrived, nobles mostly that had lost their lands, but some others, too. Rhys Gethin was admitted there, a strange sight in his goatskins, but welcomed by virtue of his promise of five hundred fierce hill-warriors. Hiding with him in the hills and caves was one Edmund Outlaw, and he came too. Owen had known this man in London long ago, when he led some of the peasants in the revolt. He had escaped the horrible fate of John Ball and the others and made his way to Wales. Commons in the thousands he would bring to our banner, he said, for he had been going forth among the border peasantry all those years, rousing them against their English masters. They would come out, he promised, for they wanted the old days of Wales back, where each man tilled his own piece of land and was paid in gold coin, and none was unfree. 'Some have been drilling, even, in secret, awaiting this day. Rough weapons they have only, but hearts of steel!' He had been so long in our Wales that he had picked up our speech and even its rhythms.

I will not name all that formed the council, for so many names confuse; Owen there was, of course, and all his sons, even to Meredith, just fourteen, Robert Pulestan, and all the Hanmer in-laws, Rhys Dhu, brother Tudor, and the dean of St. Asaph. One came, too, that was strange and piteous to look upon, though he was a wealthy landowner. They called him *Crach Ffinnant, the Scab*, a nickname given by his English border neighbors. He was of goodly height and person and dressed in rich raiment, but one side of his face was covered wholly by a blue-red birthmark, hideous. Though when he turned and it was hid, his features showed straight and neat. The young folk were afraid of him, and the servants also, poor man. And it had twisted his mind, this deformity; it was whispered that he practiced dark rites, rites of Derfel, though there was no proof. He himself said that he was a prophet, smiling thinly. I never heard him prophesy; only sense came from his mouth at the council, and that wise and shrewd. Later, Nathan the Jew made a thick paste, flesh-colored, and he wore it always; one had to get very close to detect it. The name *Scab* stuck, though, as such things do. I heard many false tales from folk who had never laid eyes upon this Crach Ffinnant; they said he was a leper, his nose rotted away, or that he was covered from head to toe with sores, running and raw. It was not so; he was a man like any other, though his mouth wore a bitter look. Owen, I know, heeded his wise counsel more than once; nor did he flinch by so much as a flick of the eye but looked upon him straight.

This council proclaimed Owen, and recorded it on paper, with Rhisiart for scribe; they proclaimed him rightful Prince of Wales, through the lineage that stretched back beyond

Arthur to the mythical Brutus of Troy that some believe founded Britain. And then they planned, as their first step, the burning of Ruthin. 'It shall be at first darkness, and we will divide into three groups. One group will carry the resin torches and ride behind; another will infiltrate the city at sword's point, but harming none. Surround those celebrants in the market and confine them there. They will be most of the population. Fire no houses until it is sure none are inside, sick or babes. Get them out first and bring them to the market. Then fire every house, shop, and church in Ruthin city. The last group will storm the castle; it will fall, for surely Grey will send to the aid of his tenants in the city.'

Such was the plan, and on St. Matthew's Eve it was accomplished, the firing of Ruthin town. The first blow struck for Welsh freedom, and no blood shed, except for one of our men, who snagged his hand on a nail from a loose plank. The nail must have been rusty, for it festered, the wound, and the arm swelled up like a bladder, red streaks running up, and he lost the hand later, for Nathan had to cut it away to save the man's life. It was a great price, of course, for him, but a little one for a whole raid.

The Castle of Ruthin did not fall, though, for Grey kept all his defenders by him and let his town burn, no matter. What cared he for humanity that was not his own kin? So the defense was too strong, and we did not gain the castle, though our marksmen hit a few, and they toppled off the walls. Owen rode among them, the arrow-bolts whanging past him, to look for the Greys among them; of course they were not, though, and were hid deep within the walls. They would have to be smoked out later.

We rode away, all of us still alive, and a great host we were, and the taste of triumph boiling up within us. At the crest of a hill we turned our mounts and watched the fires we had set. Like hell it was, and fearful to see, with the flames leaping high to reach out for the stars. 'Look,' said Owen, pointing with his spear. 'Look—to the west ... The flames take the shape of——'

'Yes,' I said, beside him. 'It is the dragon shape, as near as near ... the Red Dragon of Wales....'

BOOK V

THE COMET OF FIRE

Told by Nathan ben Arran,

physician to Owen

ONE

I was born old; it is my heritage. I cannot remember playing
with other children, though I must have done. Books, books,
books are all I remember of my early days, and they are still
my greatest joy; or perhaps by now they are a habit with me. I
come of a proud and old Hebrew family; like Owen ap
Griffith, my master, I can trace my lineage back to the earliest
heroes of my people, David the Singer and Solomon the Wise.
Though it has not availed me much in this world, for my
people are despised, except here, in this country of Wales. And
that may be because of Owen, who has much power here, like a
king, although he wears no crown.

The country of my birth I cannot recall much of; somewhere
in the Turkish lands, among the hostile folk, for we Hebrews
all are dispersed and have no country of our own now. I have
vague memories of stonings in the streets, and my mother
moaning and lying in a pool of blood; it was not her own, I
think, for we escaped whatever anger was being vented upon
us and fled to other shores; I remember still how sick I was on
the boat. I had a baby sister then who died on that sea voyage
and was dumped over the side tied up in a sack. Those were
the first Kaddish—prayers for the dead—that I myself said; I
was just old enough to have learned them. I cannot count the
times since then; for wherever we have gone, Jews die, and
lucky are those who find burial places.

I was reared to be a rabbi; that is to say, a priest. I was the
only child that lived, and the eldest son also. My mother had
many miscarried babes, and three stillborn, after the small
sister who had lived a little while. Thinking upon it now, I
know she must have been hurt inside, that time long ago when
she was stoned, for she never bore healthy babe again, my
mother.

We were not bad off, in Spain, where we lived most of my
childhood, for my father had some wealth; his had been a

merchant family, and, for a time, he was allowed to deal in rich cloths and jewels from the Orient, which stuffs were much prized. His money did not buy as much as other coin, though; our people are always cheated, though it is said to be the other way around. But we lived in some comfort, while it lasted, and I had all the holy books, the Torah, the Talmud and all the books of The Law that we live by.

My rabbinical studies played me false, though, for I conceived a taste for all reading matter, even in the pagan tongues. Greek I knew already, for my father had used a form of it in his trade, and taught me, and I picking it up fast. Debased it was, though, as he and the others used it, with Arabic words thrown in, and the writings of the ancients difficult to draw the meaning from. The Spanish that was spoken and writ in the outer city was near to the Latin, so that was easy. I say outer city because we Jews lived behind thick, high walls and must not venture out of them, except on licensed business. But many a noon hour I spent, stolen from my father's errands, in the marketplaces and bookstalls near the great university, poring over books and dusty scrolls, and even sometimes making a purchase. I never had the price that Jews were charged, for my father was a careful man with his money; but if I turned my striped cloak, badge of our people, inside out, I could pass for any ordinary Spaniard, and my accent was good. So the shopkeepers took me for a student and gave me a fair price.

It was my undoing, that. For never did I become a rabbi; my mind was exposed to too many thoughts of men other than my own kind, and I began to doubt and to question, even our Law itself.

My journeys to the outer city also saved my dear ones, in the end, for I overheard a persecution plot. In other parts, and the word had filtered down to us somehow, there had been mass slaughtering of Jews, senseless and horrible in the telling; here, in the city of Toledo, there had for years been nothing but the casual look of contempt in the street, and perhaps an order to move on, or a curfew warning.

We were a thriving community, we Jews, behind our thick walls, we had a temple and a rabbi, butchers, bakers, and the like. I loved the rabbi's younger daughter and, like Jacob, had waited, labouring at my studies, for my Rachel. That was not her name, of course, but it was like the Bible story, for her father put me off, saying he would give her only to another rabbi. Though he offered me her older sister with no such scruples, for she was fat and hard to get rid of. Again like the Bible story, though I have forgot that daughter's name. My beloved was called Deborah, and she loved me in turn. We had our stolen night moments, kisses, no more, and waited for her father to relent. For my mind was restless now and wandering many places; I knew I would make no fit religious leader.

One morning, in the thin sunlight of a waning winter, I browsed among the bookstalls outside the university; it was almost Passover time, and I lingered longer than usual, knowing that during the high holy days I would be forbidden to leave our inner city. Some students lounged among the stalls, eating their midday meal, hot rolls filled with a spicy sausage meat; it smelled wonderful, and my mouth watered, though I knew it was ground from swine flesh. They spoke a kind of careless Latin; it distinguished them from lowlier folk, but I understood, from my reading. I heard, through the munching, the words 'Good Friday,' 'crucify,' and 'City of the Jew-devils.' I looked up sharply at the nearest; I could not help it. He stared back. 'I have not seen you before.... What master do you hear? Whose lectures?' He spoke in an insolent fashion; these students are all arrogant beyond bearing.

I could not think for a moment, at a loss for words. Then I felt, rather than saw, that they were all, some eight or ten, creeping closer, surrounding me, faces hostile, I said, 'I am a-visiting only, from ... Milan.' It was the first place that popped into my head.

'Where?' asked one, the biggest, swallowing the last of his sausage. 'Where do you visit?'

I jerked my thumb over my left shoulder. 'There,' I said. 'Just there—in the Street of the Silversmiths.... My father has business with—with Master Leone.' He did, from time to time, so I knew the name. I hoped they did not. 'The third house from the corner,' I said. It is the largest and most ornate, and I knew them impressed. I felt them look me up and down; I

wore the striped cloak inside out, as always, and a fur mantle
over, against the chill; also I had combed my Jewish side-locks
behind my ears and did not look so very different from any of
them, except more richly dressed.

'Do you study at the university there—in Milan?' asked one.

'Of course,' I lied, hoping there *was* one.

'What do you read for?'

I knew their vernacular, having listened to student-talk before.

'Oh,' I said lightly, 'Greek . . . and medicine . . . anatomy. . . .'

'Anatomy? Do they offer anatomy there? It is so new. . . .'

'They have a teacher from the Eastern lands,' I said, lying
easily now and almost enjoying it.

'A Saracen dog!' said the biggest, and spat.

'Well,' I said, shrugging, 'they have much knowledge in the
East that we have not. . . .'

We chatted, mostly questions from their side, and I not only
lying, but inventing. When they asked about the science of
anatomy, I said, 'Why . . . we dig up cadavers from the pauper-
graves or buy them from the almshouse. And we carve them up
to study how they are made—and what is under the skin.'

One of them grinned, sly, and nudged me in the ribs. 'I can
tell you where to find a few . . . come Good Friday. Look in the
City of the Jews. . . .'

Another shushed him fiercely. 'Hold your tongue, fool! Do
you want the soldiers after us?'

'We have upwards of a hundred *with* us, did you not know?'

'Soldiers? What great news! It will be the best pig-slaughter
in all Spain!' It was the big fellow. He turned to me, lowering
his voice. 'Want a bit of fun? They say some of the Jew-women
are pretty, too. We could run them through after. . . .'

'When did you say it would be?' I asked, hoping my voice
did not tremble.

'Good Friday . . . when they killed our Saviour. They have a
feast time then too and none will be missing. They call it the
Feast of the Passover. . . .'

I counted it up in my head; we had barely a week to plan
our escape.

Then I answered them, shaking my head sadly. 'Afraid I

can't make it ... have to get home for Easter, you know, and the Mass of Christ Risen....' I thanked my ancestors, wily David and sly Solomon, for the slippery tongue they had bequeathed me, and gave thanks silently, too, for my reading knowledge that had let me understand the Latin prayer books.

'Oh, too bad,' said one, and put out his hand to clasp mine. 'If I ever get to Milan, I'll look you up. What is your name?'

I paused a fraction only. 'Visconti,' I said. It was the only Italian name I knew; I cannot think where I had heard it. 'Raphael Visconti.'

Their eyes popped then, all, a comical sight. I felt that, given another moment, they would fall upon their knees to a man and kiss the hem of my robe. I gave them no time for it, though, but raised my hand in farewell, smiling my most lordly smile.

I knew nothing of the modern world outside, the Gentile world. Only some bits of the ancient world, pagan, had I heard of through my books. Old names I knew, Ovid and Julius Caesar, and, older still, Socrates. Antique cities I dimly remembered, Athens, Cairo, Thebes. Were they named so still? And of the science of anatomy I knew nothing, save for some half-rubbed-out charts in a scroll I could not afford.

But, sure, I was a prophet that day; or as the Welsh say, I had the Sight, for once. For three words had I said, unthinking, out of nowhere, and they were to be later, in varying degrees, tied up with my life. A city, a man's name, and a profession.

But I did not think of that then. I hurried home, to my own walled city, to spread the word of terror.

TWO

'But the unleavened bread is baked already,' wailed my mother. 'Sheets and sheets of it, thin as paper, if I do say it myself ... and is crisping even now on the top of the oven ... and the fish ordered, and the Passover wine.... We cannot go!'

And she threw her apron over her head and wept aloud.

My news was received everywhere with suspicion, even open disbelief. As if I would invent such a tale! 'A chance word heard in the market, spoken by goyim ... what is that?' said the butcher, spreading his hands.

'Students—pah! Street-boys!' cried the rabbi, in a voice of thunder, such as he used sometimes when speaking of hell in the temple. 'What can they do, a few fired-up youths? Our gates are barred and heavily. . . .'

'But from the *outside*!' I protested, trying to speak with reason.

'Just so,' said the rabbi. 'The duke will protect us ... we are his subjects. His soldiers will guard the gates!'

I looked to where my Deborah stood, white-faced, in the corner. 'But—my honored father-in-God,' I said, and very low and calm, 'I have heard them say it. They have a hundred soldiers with them ... on their side. . . .'

My own father sat silent, brooding. After a moment he said, heavily, 'It has happened in other places ... we have had word. Dreadful things have happened. . . .'

'They cannot happen here!' thundered the rabbi again. 'Even the Christians respect the Passover ... their own Jesus was one of us!'

'But,' I said, 'their Jesus was killed at the Passover time, when He came into Jerusalem. And their priests tell them that the Jews of the temple did it ... that they of the temple, in those days and in that place, turned him over to the Romans and let one of their own be crucified. . . .'

'And,' offered Deborah, timidly, twisting her hands in her skirt, 'and, Father, they blame us for it. They say we killed their Christ, their Saviour ... I myself have heard them. They fling it at us in the streets. . . .'

He turned on her a face of wrath. 'And when have you been in the street? When have you been outside the walls, girl?'

'Now and then,' she said, growing pink. 'Sometimes to buy a little fruit ... it is hard to come by here. . . .'

'I forbid it!' he cried. 'I forbid you to go outside these walls! If any such fruit is needed, let Shana go!' (I have remembered her name after all, the older sister, and the name lovely on the lips.) And the rabbi threw a look of scorn at his other maiden, wretched and ugly in her doughy flesh. 'She can go, for even the goyim will pass her by....' I knew him then for a cruel man and knew I would never be one of his sort, no matter how much my mother wept that her only son would not own the highest office among us.

And the rabbi went on, saying, 'And I forbid any to leave these walls from fear! I forbid it. Jews cannot run about on these, our holiest days!'

And the word of the rabbi spread about our little commune, and folk shuttered their windows against us, my father and me, as we went about the narrow lanes. 'We will leave at first light,' said my father to the closed doors. 'At first light tomorrow, as soon as the gates are unbarred and the guards gone. We will go disguised, and we will get away ... I have the means.' But none would heed us, or answer even, in all that sad walled town.

And at home my mother pleaded to stay, for she feared the rabbi as she feared God; she was not a thinking woman. 'We will go,' said my father, 'as I have decided.' He opened a chest, filled with beautiful lengths of silks and velvets, his trading-ware. 'Make yourself a gown,' he commanded, 'such as the Gentiles wear, that drags upon the ground ... cut like a long sack it is and will not be difficult. Sew!' And he rummaged again in another chest, bringing out wide, hanging sleeves, furred surcoats, and a headdress, called a wimple, that covered the hair. 'Take off your sheitel and wear this,' he said, holding it out. Her hands flew to her head, her soft mouth in an 'o' of horror. I felt pity stirring for her, Mother. The young wives hate the sheitel, that ugly black goat-hair wig, and some refuse to wear it. But it is, among my people, an old, old custom (begun, I privately believe, to make the married woman an unattractive object to other men), and women like my mother feel naked without it, after long years of wearing. She took the wimple, head bowed in submission, and took up her scissors to cut into the gleaming cloth.

Out came hose and tunic, robes, bonnets of velvet, hanging purses, belts, shoes with pointed toes; we were to be fashionable goyim. Father cut my hair straight below my ears and bade me shave clean. 'It is the new style for youths,' he said.

His own full patriarch's beard he trimmed to a small, close point; he looked ten years younger. He brought out saddle-bags; I had not even known he owned them, as there were no horses inside the walls, only goats for pulling carts. He stuffed the bags with gold and silver coin, wrapped in silk pieces, and rough-cut gems in a little casket. He divided all the other monies we possessed into the purses that would hang at our belts. Finally, he brought out two daggers, beautiful things, all silver-chased, the blades very sharp. 'One must carry them everywhere,' he said, 'in the world outside.'

Mother, at her sewing, had been making little whimpering sounds; we had almost grown used to it as a background. Then came a little tap at the window, barely heard. We looked at each other, Father and I, something abashed to be found in such dress and guise. 'Open the shutter,' he said finally.

I went to the window. A small voice whispered, 'Quick—let me in!' It was Deborah! She was breathless, in her shift, and shivering. She carried a large bundle, unidentifiable. 'Take me with you,' she said, once I had drawn her inside. 'I want to go with you ... wherever you go ...'

The bundle was the sheets from her bed; she had tied them together and let herself down from her window while all slept. And I had thought her a very doe for shyness!

She looked at me then, hard, and laughed, shakily. 'Oh, Nathan, you look like one of ... *them*!'

I did not know whether to laugh or frown, but Mother wept louder still, crying out that we could not travel with an unwed couple.

'Cease, woman!' My father spoke sharply for once; it went well with his new grandee look. 'She is the only one in all this congregation with sense. Shall we leave her to be slaughtered?'

'Besides,' I said, 'we will marry as soon as we can find one to bind us legally. There are other rabbis. ...'

I glanced at Deborah; there were unshed tears in her eyes, but she blinked them back and said, 'What must I do to help?'

Father found gauds for her too, saying that her shift would have to do as an underdress, with a long surcoat. 'No wimple for you,' he said. 'But unbraid your hair and let it flow. You will be our daughter and, for now, Nathan's sister.'

'You are beautiful,' I said, on a breath let out, when she was ready. I had thought her the loveliest maid in our little company, but I saw now she would have few rivals in the outer world either. I had not known how lustrous was her black, black hair, curling sweetly at her temples and falling in deep waves down her back. Her surcoat was violet-colored, of some heavy weave, and trimmed with pale-gray fur; above it her skin was white as milk, and her eyes deep and dark. They widened with horror when she saw the little jeweled cross my father gave her to hang about her neck, but she did as he bade.

'Think of it as an ornament only,' he said, 'for so do all the Christians wear these things—except for the most devout among them, and they are mostly hid away in convents and monasteries.'

In the end we all wore them, these symbols; our daggers had the cross embossed on the hilts, and Mother wore a string of beads, cross-hung, at her girdle. 'Finger them when you cannot find words,' said Father. For my mother had not picked up much Spanish.

We looked our parts, for, in the end, we got away, through the unbolted gates, and picking our way in the first rays of dawn through the back streets to a place where my father bought horses. Two only, and the women riding pillion behind, and a fierce Basque guard for protection. He spoke no Spanish, and his own language was well-nigh unpronounceable, though Father knew a few of the words. I saw then that Father had had a secret life all along, in his trading; this Basque man had accompanied him on all his travels, and there were places, too, where we were almost welcomed, though we paid handsomely. And so we made our way out of the cruel Spanish lands.

It was a long, long journey; we skirted all the larger cities, and crossed the wild Pyrénées, and made our way along the French coast, and finally into Italy. The rough peasant folk were kind and not suspicious; they had rarely seen silver, much less gold, and one piece of it bought provision for a week. We told them all, by sign mostly and a few words picked up along the way, that we were on a pilgrimage to Rome. Magic words these were, for sure the Christians are forever on the move, to visit their holy places! I suppose we Jews would do it also, save that we are not allowed to travel, except in trade.

It is too long a story, mine, to tell here; it would fill a book. We came finally to Milan, that city that had popped into my head; Father had named it as a place where Jews could flourish, in part, and where there was a thriving community of us. He laughed long, Father, when I told him the name I had picked for myself, Visconti. 'No wonder they stared, those youths. It is one of the ruling houses of Lombardy. And Milan is ruled by one of them, the Duke Bernabò; very modern he is, and the city all newly laid out. He welcomes our people, for they bring wealth, if they are allowed to thrive. That duke is shrewd enough to be Jew himself!'

And so we settled there, in the Place of the Jews; it was pleasant and nearly as clean as the rest of that city, without walls, and all of us allowed to come and go as we pleased, so be it we had the price of our living. There was a temple and a rabbi, and Deborah and I were married in our Law and were happy for a time.

None wore the sheitel there, not even Mother; no striped cloaks either, and you could hardly tell us from the natives. The plague, when it came, made no distinctions either; nearly half the population died, in all the districts both high and low. They say all Europe suffered that year. We all took it, and I alone survived. The black boils came out on me and burst, and I lived. Where they turned inward, the poison consumed the vitals. I was too sick to know what happened; the plague carts took all the dead, dumping them in common graves, unmarked, outside the city. So there was no place to mourn beside; only in the heart.

I knew where Father's monies were hid and used them to pay my way to study the science of medicine, that I had named so lightly, long before. I was clever and learned quickly, and I found solace, of a sort, in the knowledge that I gained. Perhaps I would save some few lives, and make some easier. I prospered, and even the Gentiles called me to their bedsides. I was lucky, for I lost no patients; luckier still, I saved the life of the duke's son. So I was scorned by none, though I was known for a Jew. I say not scorned, and that is true. Folk mostly just looked through me, as if I were not there. I grew cynical, telling myself I had some magic that rendered me invisible.

Until, sometime later, I met the young man, Owen of Wales. He, like me, spent much time in the bookstalls; they were the finest in Europe, there in Milan. I was looking at an old book, writ in Hebrew, but very smudged and difficult to decipher. I was deep in it and did not hear him when he addressed me the first time. The second time I heard, for he spoke my name. 'Master Nathan,' he said, and I turned, wondering, for the voice had a lilt to it, not of Lombardy. I saw a tall young man, golden in color, even to the eyes, and dressed in a dazzling courtier way, everything the latest. At first glance he had the beauty of an angel out of our Bible tales, for so are they described, taller than men and of a golden brightness; I blinked, and saw he was a young men like any other, but with a face all his own, long and strong, high-nosed as my own, and his eyes keen with intelligence.

'I surprise you that I know your name? I did not mean to presume, but Nathan the physician is famous in this city. I had one point you out.... Will you take me for pupil?'

'But I am not a master,' I said. 'You must enroll at the university...'

He shook his head, smiling. 'I have not time for that.... I am here for a little only, on leave from Westminster, where I study law ... and the humanities.'

'That is—in England?' I said. I was not sure of my northern geography. 'You have no medical studies there?'

'Well——' he said. 'We do ... though they are mainly blood-letting and prayers ...' and he smiled. It was a look of extra-ordinary charm, lighting his stern-made features like a lamp. 'No,' he said, tapping the book I held. 'It is this language that you have there ... I would know something of it. A little Greek I have learned to read ... but this, I think, is more ancient. I have a passion for antique studies—almost a vice it is with me....' And he smiled again, and so won me. For such passions, too, have I had always, and more now that my beloved is gone from me.

'Hebrew, it is,' I said, 'and very ancient. I cannot read it well, for some words have changed a little in the many years....'

'Like our Old Welsh,' he said. 'Few but the bards use it nowadays....'

And so it began, our friendship that has lasted so very long and deepened and grown stronger. He is a man to follow, a very lodestar, and I was one of the first to follow. I went back to England with him, and finally to Wales, his home. His children have I brought into the world, and I love his people, the Welsh, that call themselves the Cymry. They are much like my own, or at least I feel it so. For once did they own all this island kingdom and have been pushed back into the mountain parts, first by the Romans, as were my own people, then by the Saxon barbarians, and, more recently, the Norman conquerors. They have lived in the fastnesses of the hills and have been content to have it so, making a culture of their own there, and keeping alive their old traditions. But now has come another king to the throne of England, a usurper, who will not let them have even this, but has demeaned them and shown much injustice. And so they have risen, and are still rising, all over Wales. And they have proclaimed Owen their prince to lead them, for he is descended from all their old princely lines, back as far as one can count. Besides, as I have said, he is a lodestar, a man to follow.

Owen is a man of peace, and I even more so. And now he is above forty years of age, old to learn war. Long did he put this from him, hoping to avert it. But the revolt has begun now and cannot be stopped, and they will follow no other.

I am a man of peace, as I have said, and older still than my master, and lame now. But though I cannot fight, I can mend the fighters' wounds. And I can train up others to serve me at my business.

I took off a man's hand the other day, after the first event, the burning of Ruthin. His was the only wound, but it festered, and he lost the hand. But he lives still. No lives were taken, in this first act of Welsh aggression, on either side. May the God of my fathers, Yahweh, whose name is not said, grant it be always so!

THREE

It never happened again, one casualty on a foray; I was a fool to dream it might be! War is a bloody business, and worse, almost, from my view of it. The cries of the wounded ring always in my ears, and the moaning is the background to it. The flung dead, grotesquely twisted, the smashed bodies, spilled guts trailing, and limbs that hung by a thread of sinew—these haunt my dreams. For we raiders had bows and arrows, and lances, and fiery torches. But the English defenders had great hurling-stones, the new Greek fire, and boiling oil poured from the tops of their thick stone walls.

For three days, after Ruthin, Owen and his captains used the same tactics, rounding up the citizens in the square, unharmed, and burning the settlements at Denbigh, Rhuddlan, Flint, Hawarden, and Holt. The towns were destroyed, but the castles could not be taken, not by men armed as we were. Soldiers toppled from the walls, picked off by our arrows, and Owen's men stripped these dead and took their armor and their weaponry; we had enough to armor a hundred. The next castle we took, Oswestry; it was our first real victory. The price that we paid was high, though; we lost more than a dozen men, and upwards of fifty suffered grave wounds. I worked all day and all night, for few were trained to help me. Gwalchmai, a page, offered his services and begged to learn from me; he had the name, by accident, of Arthur's army doctor, and he took it seriously. He was not cut out for soldier, anyway; small he was and of a shy speech, like a maid. But his hand was steady and his stomach strong; he learned quickly. I valued him from the first, and more still in the years to come. There were other pages, too, good boys and handy, but they were not doctors, nor would ever be. The Lady Margaret was a tower of strength; she herself could dress small wounds without blanching, and a word of comfort and cheer always on her lips. All her damsels tore linen for bandages, and prepared salves and pounded herbs, and one, the bard's daughter, little dark Sibli with a voice of silver, might have made a doctor herself, so clever she was and so quick. And the Lollard, Walter Brut, though he fought beside Owen, stayed awake all the nights, holding down the sore-wounded during their agonizing ordeals, the amputations and the painful probing for arrow-heads; he had the strength of twenty, that man, and a face and a voice that calmed the sorest souls. And so I had some aid, and we made do with it and served as best we could.

All of this attack and counter-attack happened fast, within a few days only; it was Owen's strategy that brought success, for blow after blow was struck at the English garrisons before the first surprise had worn off. 'It will not last,' he said. 'The word will spread and a check in our fortunes will come, as it must. Meantime, we must strike over and over, and quickly.'

He was right, Owen, for at Welshpool, on the twenty-fourth of September, came our first setback, barely a week after the beginning of the rising. We had fired the town, and it blazed as we rode away from it, none caring to look back. We rode for the castle; over the first hill we saw plumed helmets, lance tips, and banners flying. It was a huge force, levied from Shropshire, Staffordshire, and Warwickshire, trained warriors under the command of Hugh Burnell, a war veteran and sheriff of the region. There was nothing for it but to join battle, though Owen's people were vastly outnumbered. Fighting began on the banks of the Severn, and the waters ran red with the blood of friend and foe alike. It was hand-to-hand combat, and we slew as many as our own fallen, but still they came at us, full-armored men against our bowmen in their leather jerkins and chain-mail shirts. There was nothing for it but to retreat, back into the hills and forests. We were safe there, for the enemy did not know the terrain; to their minds we must have melted into the atmosphere. We heard, after, that this was the beginning of the legend that Owen had magic powers and could appear and disappear at will, with all his followers!

We had to leave our dead, though, and our worst wounded, for the battle site was patrolled for days by that Burnell; a canny and shrewd commander he was, enemy or not. 'These are the men we must watch,' said Owen, 'and fear.' We sat around a small fire, in the deep of the woods, the tall trees hiding all trace of us. Other fires burned too, many, but low-dug in trenches, so that one could stumble upon them almost, before they were seen. This was a trick learned from the hill-tribes and served us well always, for our 'magic.' 'Men like Burnell,' he said, 'are tenacious as wolfhounds and know the arts of war. Many such will come against us; our only weapons are our knowledge of our land. We must disappear, or seem to, until they leave. For our army'—and he spread his hands, smiling—'it is no army as the English know armies. We are scholars and peasants, monks and bards, and a few savages from the hills.... But,' he went on, 'take heart—for that is our advantage. We must think how to make it work against them. There are ways....' And he sat staring into the little fire, deep in thought. 'Send Rhys to me—Rhys of the Hills....' None moved, for all feared this hill-man, so strange he was and fierce.

Walter Brut, the Lollard, looked up from where he tended a moaning Oxford lad whose ear had been sliced off by a sword. 'A moment only, till I make this one comfortable,' he said, tipping a potion into the boy's mouth. When he had finished, he said, 'Sire Owen, where does Rhys camp this night?'

Owen gave him a keen look. 'You will have to search ... take this.' And he pulled from his finger a ring that all knew for his, with a dragon raised upon it in gold. 'He will be farther up the hill ... in a cave maybe—he is used to them ... as we will all be, perhaps, before this thing is resolved.' And he smiled thinly. 'Unsheath your sword, Walter—just to be on the safe side.'

Walter smiled. 'I do not fear the hill-men,' he said. 'They are like children. Many of them have I converted already to Jesus. ...' And so saying, he slipped away, swallowed by the darkness, for there was no moon.

It was not long; he came, Walter, with that Rhys and two others, as savage as himself. One man, I noticed, had a green slime plastered all over his forearm.

They conferred, Owen and these hill-people, but I understood little, for their speech is hard for a foreigner to understand; only a few words I caught. After, I stopped the man with the strange salve on his arm. 'What is that?' I asked. But of course it had to be translated, everyone talking at once and laughing. I understood finally that it was a moss that grew under certain trees and had a marvelous healing property. He scraped off a bit of it, and I saw the wound under, healing and the skin already growing back. 'Fetch me all you can find of this moss,' I said. 'It may well be another magic—to work for us.' And indeed, though I never knew why, this moss, which was not fresh but more of a kind of mold, had power to heal quickly and prevent infection. It would not keep, though, and had to be gathered often. The man had mixed it with his own urine to make a paste. I tried this, though it smacked of witchcraft and I could not believe was healthy. It worked, but so did pure spring water. Later, much later, I found a way to mix it with Eastern oil; that was scarce, though, and we settled, after, for lard, and I wrinkling my nose, for my Hebrew upbringing still made swine obnoxious to me. Thus, though, we could carry it with us; it was a fine ointment, and I believe, truly, saved many lives.

But I digress; healing interests me more than the making of wounds. But this Rhys, though the most uncivilized of men, had a keen mind. It was he, that night, who thought out many of our tactics of raiding and attack. At his suggestion, our men smeared themselves, face and hands, with earth, to blend into the surroundings, and in spring and summer wore leaves and branches fastened on, so that they moved against the hill slopes like blowing trees or bushes; from a distance they could not be seen at all. And so, often and often, in the years that followed, they crept down upon the enemy, unaware, and devastated and wrought havoc. Another witchcraft, and it worked. For not only was it effective in itself, but these island people are so riddled with superstition that their minds and souls suffered, the English soldiers thinking they were pitted against warlocks or worse. Many deserted Lancaster for this reason, or had to be beaten into service; an army without heart is almost as bad as an unfed one. And often, for he was stingy, Bolingbroke had both.

We Welsh—and I counted myself one, before the end—had these things only in our favor: high hearts, new tactics, and full stomachs. I never knew a Welsh cotter, howsoever poor, that would not give the last of his bread and onions to one of his defenders. And we had the hills, of course, the rough forbidding wild hills of Wales, where no Englishman dare follow.

It was no war of chivalry, this rising that spread over all Wales. It was, indeed, to the English, no war at all. It was a nuisance only, at first like something that gnawed at the edges of the English life; but the gnawing spread, and great pieces of that England were eaten away, before it was done. Among us were no fancy rules, no sparing of nobles. All were equal, even to the lowest. I have seen the great Owen get down from his horse and lift a wounded man upon it and lead it himself. Or horseless, I have seen Owen, for he was a big man and strong, though growing older, gather up the poor unfortunate and carry him, so that he should not be left behind.

As I have said, it was no war at all; it was a rage in the heart of a people. And I understood it well, for I am a Jew.

FOUR

The news of the revolt in Wales got to Henry of Bolingbroke early, and he moved fast, warning that Hugh Burnell that routed us and sending word to many distant shires to levy forces against Owen. He was not called by our people the Molewarp for nothing; in October he made a complete circuit of North Wales, from Bangor, through Caernarvon, and thence through the mountain passes of Mawddwy to Shrewsbury. And, like the mole, the ground beneath him was left humped, hollow, and devastated. He did not burn property only, as Owen did, but all the folk within their houses perished, roasted alive. They were not heretics even, going to their deaths with courage for the faith they held, as had been happening all over England; these had no chance to recant and be spared. They were burned along with their towns and abbeys, as casually as a boy will destroy an anthill; most were innocent, even of rebelling. Some, in the remoter villages, had not even heard of Owen. Still did they perish and their countrymen counted them martyrs, chalking up another deed of horror to the Molewarp.

All over Wales, rebellion had broken out, but they were scattered, and, on the whole, the Molewarp put them down successfully, and viciously. On Henry of Bolingbroke's return to England, he took drastic action against the chief rebels, though none of them had been captured, and it was all on paper. The estates of the Hanmers and of Robert Pulestan were declared forfeit to the Crown, and on November eighth, a grant was made to John Beaufort, Earl of Somerset, Henry's half brother (on the wrong side of the blanket, as is said, but no matter; Richard, sweet Richard had legitimized all the Beauforts, and they were now a great force in Henry's realm, an ironic thought). This grant included all the manors and lands of 'Owinus de Glyndordy' in North and South Wales, with all 'royalties, knights' fees, advowsons, franchises, liberties, customs, wards, marriages, reliefs, escheats, forfeitures, chaces, parks, warrens, wreck of sea....' At this Owen grinned and said, 'He takes me for a scavenger, it seems—one who scours the beaches to pick over old derelict vessels and rip the jewels from the poor bloated drowned bodies....' And he tore the document across; something of a feat, for it was parchment, and not many could have made a rip in it. 'Worthless,' he said, 'for he has not the power to enforce it. Let him try.... Meanwhile, let us send to our kinsmen in the South.' And he summoned his secretary, the young Rhisiart with the hawk face, to him, and composed letter after letter, to rouse up the barons of the South.

Little fighting was done that last part of the year, for it was cold and snow lay upon the mountain passes, blocking the trails. Owen waited at Glendower House, making plans. New recruits came every day, and drilled and practiced with the bow, no matter what the weather; the wounded healed and joined in the drill; armorers were at work, fashioning plate and chain mail on the pattern of the captured armor. The Molewarp did not move either, but in January, 1401, the English Parliament met to consider the 'Welsh rascals.' The Crown agreed to seize the lands and property of any Welshman living on English soil and to execute immediately any Welsh person suspected of any crime, without trial. This was an act of infamy; masses were said in chapel for the souls of these unjustly murdered dead, and the prayers of the Lollards, too, went up for them.

Henry of Bolingbroke had given control of North Wales to the council of his eldest son, young Harry, styled by the English custom Prince of Wales. Chief of this council was Henry Percy, he that was called Hotspur. In effect, this man, adored by all of England, was the young prince's war tutor. And well did he tutor him, as was seen in afteryears; too well, for in time he became a very Alexander, mad for power and conquest. But now was he only fourteen years of age, a tender stripling to throw into the red maw of the war dragon. I have made a kind of pun there, not intended, as I will explain; the device and the banner of Wales is, from ancient times, a red dragon. Owen has adapted it a bit; his banner shows a gold dragon on a white ground, said to be the device of Uther Pendragon, father of the great Arthur. But among the common folk the red dragon means Wales still, and there is not a house, even the humblest, that does not fly one.

Hotspur, that hero, suffered a rude defeat almost at the beginning of his wardship. He had come to terms with some of the Welsh, in Denbigh and in Flint, for there are always some prudent men who will not commit themselves to rebellion. On Good Friday (which I remember with horror in my own life, though I escaped)—it was then April first, and all the garrison of Conway Castle were at mass in the chapel. A band of less than forty Welsh, led by William and Rhys ap Tudor of Anglesey, already with an English price on their heads for earlier revolt, forced the gates of that strong and supposedly impregnable castle and occupied it, locking the worshipers within the chapel and securely establishing themselves as the new castle-keepers. It was a bold stroke, and it worked. The garrison stores were plentiful, and they could not be starved out, and the walls were very strong. Also, the Welsh country folk round about made attacks and forays upon the town and its defenses, melting away into the hills at the first sign of reprisal. Hotspur was forced to negotiate a peace, though it took till June. Those lords of Wales, those Tudors, were given full pardon, with all their followers, in return for giving back the castle. They were beginning to run out of supplies by then anyway, so it was just as well. It was not glorious—but, in a sense, it was a Welsh victory, and we heard of it with no little comfort.

But Hotspur, with the young prince by his side, learning his trade, went up and down the Welsh borders and into the interior, too, their forces occupying abandoned manors, old forts, or burned-out monasteries. I guess it was more comfortable than the bare ground.

There was one such force at Dinas Brân, not too far from Glendower House; we were not aware of it, our spies had not done their work well. One warm day, when all the green was beginning to show and the mountain snows to melt and run down in little smiling streams, some of the young people of our house rode out in a body, to enjoy the day; they had been cooped up all the winter, and there had been no sign of the enemy. The girls wore hose and their hair braided tightly under little caps so that the whole looked like a train of pages; the Lady Margaret thought it safer so, among so many of our woman-hungry soldiery.

But four there were who lagged behind a little; great scholars and talkers they were, three of them, at least—the damsel Morgan, intelligent as any Oxford student, young Rhisiart, would-be lawyer, and Walter Brut, that learned Lollard. The fourth was that Alice from Ruthin; she forever hung about Walter, though she said little in that company, I am sure. They must have dallied, letting their mounts eat the new grasses, and arguing about some Latin phrase or such; at any rate, they were captured and taken to the ruins at Dinas Brân, now occupied by English mercenaries. Word came to us at Glendower House; they were to be held as hostages till Owen should come to terms, and harsh terms they were.

Shame to say, there were some Welsh who sided with Lancaster. Among them was a cousin of Owen's, his father's brother's son. This man, called Howell Sele, was of old childhood days an enemy of Owen. None knew the tale for sure, though it was whispered that it was over a woman that the quarrel started. Privately, Owen told me that they had been unfriends from boyhood; their temperaments would not mix. And, he said, great injustice was done by this Howell, too, to one beloved of Owen. So I surmised that the rumor was, in some part, true. Never had I seen Owen's face black with anger; when he spoke this man's name, the look upon it was dreadful to see. This man was said to be there, at Dinas Brân, with more than a hundred of his followers, in the train of the young Prince Harry. I have wondered often if that did not enter into Owen's decision to go into that enemy camp in person and bring back his hostages. Although he loved the damsel Morgan, his daughter, well, for sure, and could not let her come to harm. I think both factors forced him to choose.

I, being lame, could not go on this particular raid, for all went in a disguise, and I would have called attention to them all with my infirmity. Dressed as mendicant friars and beggars they were, who are everywhere accepted in these Christian countries as innocents of God, and suffered to sit beside the fire and warm their bones, and perhaps snap up a crust that is thrown them.

He rode out, Owen, in long white beard and flowing robes, and some others dressed so also, but with a force of soldiery along and weapons hid beneath their monks' gowns. Griffith Lloyd the bard was with them, and I have heard the tale from him, so it is only secondhand.

Leaving the greater part of his army below the conical mountain where stood old Dinas Brân, and in darkness, some twenty, in their disguise, Owen among them, walked up to the gate of the ruined castle. They were given their grudging welcome and their scraps from the tables; the Lancaster forces were mostly wine-flown, and many were in a drunken stupor and lay snoring among the rushes on the floor of the great hall.

The man Howell, though, spied Owen, just a second after Morgan recognized him and made signal. Owen moved, and the arrow from Howell's bow missed his brain and lodged in his upper arm, near the shoulder. Owen drew bow, quicker than quick, with all sitting numb with horror, and shot his old enemy through the throat, a deadly and fatal mark. Then, in a voice of thunder, Owen claimed his hostages. With the arrow still sticking out from his flesh, for it had gone right through and come out the other side, and unflinching, he cried. 'The next man to make a move will get my next arrow—and my hand is steady.' And he fitted arrow to bow and stood waiting. None moved, and he brought the hostages, all four, away to safety, down the hill to the waiting soldiers and horses, and thence home to Glendower House. It is an unlikely tale, but so did it happen, as I heard it from eyewitnesses.

After, Owen said that again it was the element of surprise that succeeded here. 'For we were armed, all, under our robes, and most of that so-called army lay drunk upon the floor; we had seen how to do it, the killing of Howell was an accident only and done to defend myself. Though, for once, and I am sorry to say it, I was glad. For he is gone, my enemy, and the enemy of Wales.... I think those others at table there, Harry Percy, the constable, and the rest, were stunned, simply. Besides, my men had thrown off their disguises and shown themselves ready to shoot us out. Hotspur was unarmed; so were the others. None spoke—only that Lancaster sprig, the boy Harry, answered me and boldly, daring me to shoot him and saying he would take his farewell of my daughter, his old friend from Richard's court long ago. Then came he forward, like a very courtier, with my arrow pointed at him, and gave each hostage into my keeping.... I have six fine sons, and mayhap seven'—and here he bent his look on the brutish Rhys of the Hills—'still would I welcome another such. I do not wonder now that Richard spared his life and would have made him his heir. Marred, my dear, if you had had the training of that one, then should we see a man of greatness, indeed. As it is, he will make his mark, that Harry.... Some things he must grow out of—he has a name for whoring in all the taverns—and a name, too, for father-hate....'

'What of Hotspur?' asked Margaret, his lady.

Owen sat silent a moment. 'He is a man of goodly parts and not resembling his turncoat father.... Yet do I think that in time he will come over to us ... for the Percy monies are being used up by Henry of Bolingbroke, and they resent it. They are not men to trifle with—the Percys. His men, Hotspur's, are all paid for from his own pocket ... such will not last forever. The Percy loyalty must be bought. King Harry goes in error there and in arrogance.... Well, we shall see....'

Owen had made contact with the barons of the South, and

in the opening days of summer, we marched there in great force, leaving only enough men behind to defend Glendower House. Word had been brought Owen that there was a large army of Lancaster soldiery in Montgomeryshire, on the river Hyddgen. We encamped in a remote and hidden glen of a wild mountain there. They could not see us, the Lancaster army, for we were smeared with earth and covered with new foliage, all; we watched them, their every move. They were camped where two great stone blocks stood, in the river valley; dolmen graves, Owen said they were, from old, old times, raised up by the ancients.

Before sunrise, we came down upon them where they lay sleeping on the ground; few escaped, but we lost none. There was no work for me and my assistants.

The word of this great victory spread, and great numbers rallied to Owen in the marches of Carmarthen. Our forces had swelled by the thousands. Most of Wales was now behind Owen. I wondered what the English king thought and what his dreams were or if he closed his eyes at all. His throne was shaky enough, having been seized by force, and here was near a whole nation at his throat!

FIVE

During the summer, more and more rallied to the red dragon flag. All over Central Wales, men laid down their plows and followed Owen's heralds. Each village had its small army, and more mustered from the hills beyond. Wealthy landowners took arms, knowing that all was at stake—that Wales now must fight or die, crushed by this new and cruel England.

Henry of Lancaster, in the fall of that year, marched into South Wales, spreading ruin as he went. He carried off little children as captives, giving them to his toadies for slaves; a barbarism that none could believe in this modern day. He executed all who were in any way loyal to Owen, even powerful nobles, creating a hatred that would never die. Lands and estates were confiscated, noble Welshwomen raped or carried off to live in English concubinage. We heard with horror how it was—that many a Welshman, tortured in the Norman way, died in agony without betraying the counsels and plans of Owen.

Owen called me to him privately, speaking in calm wise. 'Old friend,' he said, 'shall I submit? I cannot bear this slaughter in my name....'

I pondered long, for I hate war and see no glory in it. Finally I answered. 'I am not one of your people, Owen, but I think that now you cannot submit.... We are in it now—for good or evil.... Even a peaceful people will defend what is theirs—they can do no other. And you are the leader, by lineage and by strength ... they will follow only you....'

'I shall make a try for peace,' he said, heavily, gazing before him. 'But first we will strengthen our position—take what castles we can, rout as many of the enemy as possible.... If Henry is hard-pressed, he may listen. We may yet stop this war before it destroys both countries. I want no power in England. Only my lands returned, and my rights as a Welshman, and all the other Welsh rights restored ... and a Welsh recognition as a nation. Let us work for that....'

And so Owen directed attacks all over Wales, with much success. He took Welshpool; he put an army at the town and castle of Caernarvon, placing it under siege.

At this point, Henry Percy, ill-advised, or perhaps sick of being unpaid, went north to his own lands that bordered Scotland, for there was insurrection there always; the Scots do not love their English masters either. In his absence, the young Prince Harry was vulnerable, being still a fledgling warrior. Our Welsh attacked his train as he traveled through the mountain passes; few were slain, but much spoil was carried off, plate and armor, horses and gold. It was a treasure to us, for we were still weapon-poor, not being bred to war. Now most of our soldiers had some sort of weapon and some sort of protective armor, and many were mounted; the 'barefoot rascals' were no more. Shields glittered in the sun, and swords gleamed bright, plumes tossing from helmed heads. And all stolen, beggaring none but the enemy!

From our spies we learned that indeed Henry of Bolingbroke was entertaining the thought of a negotiated peace. The Percys, both father and son, urged this upon him; Hotspur, in council, spoke up for the wrongs done to Owen and of the power that Owen wielded in all Wales. 'He is not a man to affront!' he cried. 'But you have done so.... Beg his pardon, reinstate him—and you will avert disaster!'

'And poverty,' added the sly father of Hotspur, knowing well the stinginess of the Lancaster.

Others of the king's council felt differently, mainly the border lords, Grey of Ruthin among them. They had their own rows to hoe, as they say in these parts. None knows why, but these border views prevailed, and Henry determined to pursue the struggle until the traitor Owen was utterly crushed. 'For I hate that tall man with all my soul—and always have!' he was heard to cry, Bolingbroke.

His life had been saved as a boy by that same 'tall man,' but I have noticed often that humans do not respond as one would think they should. The nature of man is perverse; I think King Henry could not bear to be in Owen's debt. There was little reason to continue the fight; Henry was a sick man already; his realm was poor and in debt to many; the commons were against this Welsh war, and many of the nobles, too.

Of course, as the Lady Margaret said, if Owen had not smuggled out that Henry during the revolt of the peasants, he would have been killed, and none of this would be happening. For Richard would be king still, and peace would reign all over the isles of his realm. So does fortune hang upon a thread!

Said Owen, wryly, 'Then did I shave his head only.... To-day it would be somewhat further down the razor would cut!' And he drew his hand across his throat in a slicing gesture and grinned; one could almost see the old Owen, looking out, merry. For he had changed, Owen; I saw it on a sudden. Now was his face like stone, and bleak about the eyes, though he was godlike still. But now was Apollo vanished, and thundering Zeus in his place. But I am a fanciful old man; he was a man only, Owen, like any other. The difference was within, and who knows what accident put it there? Man is a mystery—and all life—and the world, and the stars, and whatever lies beyond.

I cannot but remember how, once, as I walked, after some battle or other, among the pitiful dead and soft noisy wounded, the big bald Griffith the poet beside me, helping to carry off those who could not walk alone, I looked by chance into his eyes, beautiful and blue but bleak as Owen's then. He turned and pointed to an outjutting crag, bare rock, with a tiny fissure in it. And from the fissure grew a tender small blossom on a thread of stalk. 'Man is frail,' he said, 'so frail ... can you doubt? Look where the flower grows. So small and delicate, a thumbnail could tear it loose ... yet is it rooted in rock, and man has no roots at all, at all....' A poet's thought. Yet did I understand, and tremble within.

There came to us at Glendower House two new recruits, more suited to clerical work and to doctoring, but valuable and welcome. With tears in his eyes Owen clasped his old tutor, Iorweth Sulien, vicar of the little church near Dolgelly where Owen spent his boyhood, and another friend with him, the miller, Iestyn, a cripple like myself, but born so. This man was used to walking miles, for all his life had he lived with his deformity; in after times he marched with the army and never lagged behind, though I truly believe he was nearing eighty. A powerful man he was; I asked to examine his foot, for it was strange and twisted. Thick it was, like the hoof of an animal; the ancients had exposed babes born with such feet, believing them nastily and inhumanly conceived. We know this cannot happen; still did his parents, whom he never knew, put him out upon a hillside to die, but by luck was he found and adopted. A fine, keen mind he had and a great heart, this man; shame would it have been to lose such to the world. I know that in the East such deformities have been corrected; early enough, it can be done with clever binding by tight cloths, while the bone is malleable, and even by the knife, if the child is older. So much is there to learn of this art of healing, and I with so few years left.

But Iestyn warned Owen that he must find a place deep in the hills and take his household there, for, as he said, Glendower House is wood and can burn, and all fall to Lancaster while the armies are elsewhere. And so did he send out scouts, Owen, through all the slopes of Snowdon; Rhys Gethin, that lived most of his life in the hills, found it, finally, an old stone fort, hid deep in the fastnesses of that great Mount Snowdon, thick-walled and impregnable. Built by earlier folk than the Romas even, it seemed to be, though the Romans had used it and added on later. Below were deep baths and conduits to run off water and waste, in the Roman way, and pipes where was once a heating system. Owen and Iestyn spent much study upon this and set up the old stove-place, too, and connected it to the pipes so that it worked, though imperfectly. The stone of the lower floors was warmed by it, though abovestairs all was cold as the tomb. Owen said that once it must have run clear through all the walls, for we could see broken bits of piping where a door had come off its hinges. If we had not been at war, we might have resurrected this and made a whole new miracle of warmth. Before the winter snows we all removed there, the Lady Margaret weeping. 'For never shall I see it again, our home—so beautiful....' Owen comforted her, saying we would move back later, but over her head I saw his eyes, sad and with a new hardness in them.

Before we left Glendower House, the four of us, Owen, Iestyn, Iorweth, and I spent many nights gazing at the stars through our glass roof, for that autumn were the skies very clear. Through our long tubes we saw, each, a new star, far to the north, and each night getting larger. 'Send out word,' said Owen, 'to the people to watch the skies over Anglesey for a sign.... I think it will soon be visible to all. Say it is a sign of Welsh victory....' And he shrugged. 'We have nothing to lose if I am wrong ... and much to gain if such a star appears, all new to the sight.'

And so we sent, by messenger and by letter, to spread the word. Even to Scotland, to King Robert, calling upon him for help in our need, and to the Irish chieftains, too. I think they never reached their destination, those letters, for no help came, though both peoples, Celts also, were sore oppressed by Bolingbroke and his adherents and would have joined us, for sure, comet or no.

For it did appear, as we predicted, but later, much later,

after we had removed to the stone fort in the wilds of Snowdon. One icy night in the month of February, came Walter Brut and his Alice, from where they walked upon the ramparts to be alone, as lovers should. They clutched, each, their plain wood crosses, for she was a very Lollard too, by now, for love of him, and both faces filled with a white awe. They were wordless, but beckoned us all outside. The breath froze in our nostrils, clogging them, and steam blew from our open mouths, but we could not feel the cold. For there, in the north, over the isle of Anglesey, as we had predicted, flamed a huge body of fire; the ancients named such comets. It was round as a sun and near as bright, and from it trailed a fiery shower of sparks, like a myriad diamonds, filling the whole northern sky; it was near as light as day. All our household crowded out to watch it, fear upon their faces. Owen turned. 'It is not a sight to fear,' he said. 'It is a comet, and it is far, far away, and moving so slowly to our eyes that we cannot notice its progress ... for I have studied these things, and Nathan, too, in the old lore of the East.... It is, in fact, hurling through the night, but so far, far away it is ... it seems to us motionless....'

And Walter Brut said, ' "Fear not, for I bring you tidings of great joy"... so said the angel to the shepherds.... Such was the star that flamed over Bethlehem, I have no doubt....'

Owen rubbed his chin, and nodded. 'So it must have been...'

And Griffith Lloyd spoke too, then, he that spoke mostly in these latter days in his music only. 'I have heard, too, and so have all us true Britons, how such a star flamed in the heavens when Arthur was born.... So will we take it for a sign....'

And a voice cried, loud upon the clear cold air, 'Victory ... victory for Wales! Read it—written in the sky!' And other voices took it up and all the dark hills rang with those cries and flamed in the light of the blazing comet.

And in England was it seen, and the enemy trembled. And in France even, so huge it was.

And we in Wales rejoiced, for to every heart it was a sign of victory and a new Wales.

SIX

All through the months of February and March the fiery comet flamed in the sky; by day, even, one could see it, pale and trailing its tail like a faint snail's track. By April it had gone, it seemed on a sudden; but, as Owen said, it had been moving all along. Whether it fell to earth somewhere and buried itself deep in a waste place, or destroyed some far city, or whether it traveled still its lonely path, we never knew. We had seen it, we, and taken it for our own, our comet of Wales.

And in April it fulfilled its promise. For Owen captured Lord Reginald Grey of Ruthin, his archenemy. This is how it happened. Reginald was at Ruthin; his own desire was to capture Owen, whether to kill him or force him to sign away his lands, I cannot say. But so strong was his desire that he lost all caution and allowed himself to be drawn into a trap set by Owen, not far from his castle, having been informed that Owen was there, hiding. And so he was, Owen, but with a huge force of hill-fighters. It happened that from the Ruthin side came some of Grey's own men, those that were of Welsh birth and waiting for this chance, and betrayed him to us. We took him as easily as one traps a rabbit in a snare; he was securely fettered and carried back to our mountain fort. His only son, too, was taken with him. As they were dragged between guards up the hills and into the fortress gates, the women spit upon them and threw rotten fruit, eggs, and manure from the stables. They were covered from head to foot with filth by the time they were brought inside the walls. That Alice, who had been so misused by these men and whose mother they had burned years ago, had horrid vengeance working in her eyes and approached them with a knife, meaning to work heaven knows what horror upon them. Her Walter, wed to her by now, restrained her, saying good Christians leave such things to God and to the human conscience. 'They have none!' Alice cried. 'They have no consciences! They deserve to die!'

But Owen said, 'So it may be, poor girl, but I have other

plans, and I am master here. Get you gone now, or you yourself will be tied up too!'

It was Owen's idea to hold this man hostage, demanding a crippling ransom from the stingy Bolingbroke. Grey knew his master well; one could see upon his face that he saw no hope coming from there.

It was thought to throw them belowstairs, into the dungeon there, but Owen said, no, that was the warmest place, now that the piping worked, and they should be held in a wooden outhouse that had once served as a latrine and smelled still, after so many centuries. 'It is a fine joke,' he said. 'I grow cruel with my old age. . . .' And so they were kept there, and in chains, and fed on low fare, but plenty, for Owen wanted them alive to use against the king's greed.

The women—maidservants, that is, for the maidens and wives of Owen's house were nobly reared and would not stoop to such—the women of the people came every hour of the day to jeer and sing derisive songs and poke through the slats of that wood structure with sharp sticks, hoping to wound them. It was a sort of hell, for sure, though truly they were not harmed. Yet did I feel pity for them; it is my nature. And the Lollard, Walter Brut, went every day, chiding those women, who crept away shamefaced; each day would Walter sit outside their small prison and read to them his New Learning Scriptures. It was a punishment perhaps for them, as Owen said, laughing, for they were Norman-bred to orthodoxy, and each of Walter's words to them dripped heresy and blasphemy to their church. 'Another fine joke,' he said. 'Let their God save them from his preaching. I love our Walter well, yet would I grow weary, even sitting on a soft cushion. . . .'

The Lady Margaret looked at him with censure, for she is much given to Scripture-reading herself. He looked back and smiled. 'From you, Marred, it is like the dripping of honey. . . . I *forbid* you to preach to the Greys!'

She smiled too, it was almost like old times, and the faces unharried. 'I would not go near them at all, at all,' she said. 'For I have learned to hate . . . though it is a sin.' And her face set again in its sorrowful lines. She had been the fairest, sweetest maid ... I remembered her well. She must have seen me staring, for her hands went quickly to her head, and she bit her lip. 'Nathan, come,' she said. 'I would speak privately with you....'

As we went aside, I saw a strange look on Owen, a look half wary, half of worry. Well, we are all changed nowadays.

She would not come right away to the point, Margaret, but pointed out where some daffodils still bloomed late on the shaded side of the hill. 'It is a wild spot he has chosen for us, Owen. I could believe myself Guinevere, here in this place ... so old it is, so savage.' And her eyes cast down at her own words. 'Except, of course, that none would look on me with longing or with love ... for I have changed ... so changed.'

'Lady, you have not,' I lied. 'You are beautiful still.' And that was no lie, for so, in a way, she was, and different only. 'And, besides your loving husband—and myself'—and here I bowed a little, deprecatory—'there is one whose eyes follow you always, and always have...'

Her own eyes widened, for she truly did not know; I had always thought she flirted, mildly, as women will, when they know they are admired. 'Who ... ?' she asked softly. 'Is there someone, truly?' Her face fell. 'Oh, a soldier, maybe, yes ... they are so long kept from women...'

'Oh, Lady ...' I said, and could not hold it back, for I felt the man's passion burning in him silently, enough to scorch me as I walked near him. And it was safe enough now, for he was away with a raiding force, and it might be long before she saw him again.

'Lady, it is the poet Griffith. He burns with love for you ... did you not know? ... I have seen the look in his eye, ever and ever, hungry and naked. All can see it plain ... only you have not....'

She was aghast. 'And do they jest of it?'

'Oh, Lady, no never.... He is the greatest poet of your country. And all respect him ... They call you Helen, the folk....'

Her brow wrinkled. 'That was Owen's mother's name...'

'Helen of Troy, they mean, Lady.... She who was more beautiful than all other women, so that Homer sang of her....'

'His songs of love, then, Griffith's—they are to me....'

'But surely, Lady.'

'And Owen?'

'I think he is proud. For that he would wish to have written them himself. . . .'

'Shall I tell you something, friend Nathan?' And she wore an odd look; like a girl it was and artless. 'I would that he *were* jealous, Owen.'

'You have not given him cause, Lady. . . .'

'I would that I had, Nathan, for now I am growing old. . . .' She walked a little ways off and turned; I saw her lip trembled a little. 'Friend, I asked you here to feed my vanity . . . you have done it, but in an unexpected way. I thought to ask you for a—dye . . . my hair, it is losing all its color. . . .'

'It does not show, Lady. It was always such pale gold, almost silver. . . .'

'But now is it silver truly. Look close. White almost, it is, and Owen still has all the yellow in his hair and beard. Have you not something among your herbs? A long while back, in peacetime, I had a paste that I got from a peddler that came each six-month. But I have not seen him of late, and there is none left. . . . I would not have Owen turn from me, for that I am old and ugly. . . .'

'He will not, Lady, for you will never be. But I will mix something, yes. Tonight I will mix it. You shall have it to-morrow.'

'And it will be our secret?'

'None will know, Lady. I will make it a very subtle color, the gold faint only.'

'I thank you,' she said simply. 'And I am glad that you told me about—Griffith. . . . I am a woman only . . . and vain like all my kind. I am glad.' And she left me, wearing a little sweet secret smile that made a damsel of her again, just for a fleeting moment.

SEVEN

When Owen captured Grey at Ruthin, he avoided Denbigh, knowing that Hotspur was constable there; he had a plan, Owen, for he knew the man Hotspur had some sympathy for his cause, and cause, too, to be estranged from the king. For it was rumored that never had he received any pay and had given his soldiers their wages from his own pocket.

This Hotspur was royal lieutenant in North Wales now and had many duties. Among others, he organized a naval expedition, which left Chester on May 26, to relieve the castles on the Welsh coast, which were being constantly harried by raiders among our Welsh followers. On June 4 he summoned all the English lords of those parts to Denbigh, to discuss what should be done and how to deal with these rebels of ours.

Owen, true to his reputation for magic powers, appeared in a new quarter, along about the middle of June. This was the district of northeast Radnorshire, a mountainous land well suited to our kind of fighting. Now this whole district had been for years, even centuries, under the hereditary rule of the ancient house of Mortimer. These Mortimers were, far back, partly Welsh, having married among the Cymry. I must explain a very touchy situation, known well, of course, to Owen.

The Mortimer heir, at present, was a lad of ten, Edmund Mortimer, the Earl of March. He was kept in close confinement in the Tower of London by King Henry, for he was, by the proper rules of descent, the closest linear heir to the crown of England. That he was not murdered is one of the few mercies that can be granted to the soul of Red Bolingbroke. But here, in Radnorshire, there was another Edmund Mortimer, not heir but close cousin to him. He was a man full grown, twenty-five, perhaps, and it was he who gathered together the forces of the county of Hereford and led them against Owen. This was the great battle which took place on St. Alban's Day, June 22, on a hill to the west of the village of Pilleth. This hill was called, in the Welsh tongue, Bryn Glas, and I was there.

I lurked in the background, for sure, as did all the doctors and pages. We had one woman with us, a maid, rather. This was the bard's daughter Sibli, who was more like page than damsel, with her small, unformed, slim body, her cropped hair, and a certain strange sharpness of feature. She was a fine, unflinching nurse when needed, and at night she could sing songs to her harp that would melt the heart. Of her own making they were, sadder than her father's, and smaller, somehow. She sang of small things, the eaglet in its nest, the sapling, tender and green, the child with its milky mouth, the gentle, tingling touch of hand on hand. Her songs spoke to the hardened soldiers, even the wild hill-folk, so that they wept like babes. And so when she ran away to follow us, Owen did not send her back, but let her stay, surrounding her with other pages and some soldiers to protect her, and keeping her well away from the fighting. I grew to love her well, this Sibli, over the years, and she was a favorite of all the common people; they called her the Small Bird after one of her own songs, and for her small size also, maybe. I privately think she won the battle for us, this battle of Bryn Glas.

The fighting was fierce, for, true to our custom, we leaped upon the armored riders unaware, throwing them from their horses and finishing them off with lances as they lay helpless in their heavy gear. He must have thought, many a poor English warrior, that a tree had smote him, like the hand of an old Druidic god. For we wore always all about us that foliage, tucked into and wrapped around our own light armor, and smeared our faces and hands, our plate, too, to keep it from shining, with earth and mold.

Still was there that day a great force of them, the Englishmen, and more sprang up for each one slain, as in the old Greek tales.

I saw whatever I saw from the crest of the hill only, the hill above; still could I see us, friend and foe, sliding and slipping in the soft earth made soggy with blood; sometimes a fallen arm, an enemy arm, raised upward, bearing a sword, and it going through one of ours. So did they fall, both sides, like mayflies at their end of days. I despaired, for there were more of the enemy beyond; it looked to be in the thousands. Many of our own were fallen and lay under the feet of those fighting above.

Suddenly, from behind me, higher still upon the hill, came one loud note from a harp-string; strange it sounded, as from another world, and echoing among the hills. And then a voice, clear and sweet as a bell and heard, for a miracle, above the clash of sword and shield. There came the beautiful strains of 'Sweet Richard,' the lament, and she who wrote it was singing, to her little Welsh harp; it was a lament for that unhappy king, but as she sang it, pure and very high, it was no lament, but a war-cry. The fighting stopped, and the men's heads lifted, till she reached the refrain; one by one voices joined in, till the mountain rang with it.

And I saw, among the English ranks, not one by one, but two by two, and clusterings of soldiers, step forward from their ranks and come to us, singing and crying the Welsh word for 'brother.' In the hundreds and thousands they came, and turned upon their English masters, for they were Welshmen, mustered up by force, and fought beside us. And the voice went on behind, the harp not sounding, but the sword and shield accompanying it, and the high whanging of our Welsh arrows from the English ranks.

It was the great bard-sung victory of Bryn Glas; when it was over, more than eight thousand of the English lay dead upon the hill-slopes. Among them were slain many of the finest Norman-English knights; the 'flower of chivalry,' as they were called in their world. And two famous men were captured, Thomas Clanvowe, an English poet and high lord, and that same Edmund Mortimer, who led the army.

There were in the English rear guard a host of Franciscan monks, who had been used to tend their wounded; these left the field of slaughter and marched back to our camp with us, singing the strains of 'Sweet Richard,' and some even spreading the rumor that Richard lived still and was hidden here, in Wales.

We ourselves had, on this day, many gravely wounded men, great victory though it had been. We had all we could do to get them off that field and into shelter where they could be cared for. The dead we could do nothing about; they would have to lie there one more night until we could bring back the bodies for burial.

We worked through the night, binding up wounds and administering poppy juice to those in dreadful pain. The maiden Sibli worked as hard as any two of us; quick and deft she was and always with a word of cheer. A dark face she had, like a Moorish damsel, and the features too sharp and strong for a woman, but her eyes were huge and filled with a sort of glow, warm and moist. The soldiers grew to love her that night, and in the years that followed. One fellow, his arm shredded and a smash of blood, watched her, grinning, as she washed his blood off her hands. 'The red-hand maid, you are, for sure,' he said. 'Someday the blood will not come off, and you'll be stained with it forever....'

'And it is proud I'd be,' she said, with a smile, and drying her arms. 'Get you some sleep now, silly boy,' for he was no more than a lad. And she dipped up some water, mixed with my poppy-brew, and held it to his lips. 'Drink,' she said, her dark face grave now.

He lay back in her arms and, looking up at her, said, in a voice growing blurry from the drug, 'A good thing it is that 'tis my left arm that is hurt. I'll make a banner, sweet singer-lady, just for you....' And a look of pride flitted over his pain-filled face. 'An artist I am at it—ask anyone ...'

And true to his word he was, for he recovered, though not all did. He fashioned, while his bad arm healed, and only with his right, a beautiful great banner on silk; none knew where he had got the stuff. Thereon was painted, in beauty and perfection, a pair of young rounded arms, in a position half suppliant, half blessing, the palms open, and the hands reddened with bright blood clear up the forearms. Chased round the edges were small gold dragons; it struck horror and beauty to all who saw it, for it was a true work of art, the kind to move the heart. The common bowmen, those that had been once wounded and knew the damsel Sibli, carried it always as their own banner; for years did they bear it into battle until, one dread day, it was trodden into the dirt and mud and taken by the foe as trophy. But that was much later, and I am ahead of myself.

We made camp that whole night upon another hill and in the forest beyond, for there were too many unable to ride for home. We had settled down, most of us, except for us few who nursed and gave succor to the wounded, and many slept. Owen walked among us, his face sad in pity for those fallen who had followed him. To each still awake he spoke a word, intimate and for him alone; their poor faces shone with it, for to them all he was a god, an Arthur come again.

And before the maiden Sibli he sank to his knees, Owen, and she not reaching much above his head even so. He took her small dark face, made oddly beautiful in the moonlight, between his two hands and looked into her eyes. 'You are our savior, sweet damsel, this day. Your song won the battle for us.' And he leaned to her and kissed, full upon the lips, her down-turned face. I saw the look upon it after, that face, a shining look, a struck look, the look of a maiden in her first love. Poor damsel, caught in war, and wasting her own strange beauty upon an old man. For he was old already, Owen, though not much above forty. Golden still he was, Owen, as he was as a youth when first I knew him; but some men age in another way and subtler, and he was one. A man of stone he was now, and his grave responsibilities writ upon his face for always. For he knew the height and the depths, too, of the task that lay before him, Owen. It is the price of intellect, such knowledge. Lesser men do not feel it.

During the night, the long night, and close to the dawn hour, we heard noises upon the battlefield below us. Could it be another enemy force come upon us? Softly we crept, we few, down the mountain, keeping to the forest edge and out of sight below. We saw, among the dead English, the thousands that were strewn there, filling the plain and the foothills, figures dimly made out, walking among them and stooping down; now and again we saw the flashing silver of an upheld knife.

'They are women!' whispered Sibli, in a kind of horror. We crept near; she was right. We could see, in the moonlight, the flowing hair and robes, the white arms. There were some twenty perhaps, going among those fallen dead creatures. One looked up; in the moon's glow and the faint rose of early dawning her face was Medusa's, the hair about it wild and writhing like snakes; or at least in my sick fancy it was so. She looked round at the others quickly, making a sign, and they fled, into the woods beyond the plain.

We crept on down the hill, leaving the shelter of the trees; there was none left to see us as we came. Only the silent dead.

It was a sight of horror; I heard Sibli's breath catch in her throat. The Welsh, our own fallen, lay in their green jerkins, Owen's livery; the others, the English, in their thousands, had been stripped naked; their bodies gleamed white, and blood lay in pools about them. Rough crosses were carved into their foreheads, running blood still, but discernible; upon some was carved another sign, like a pair of horns. Owen's breath hissed. 'It is the Derfel-sign! They were Derfel-women from the hills. . . .'

Some corpses, too, were slashed across the chest and belly; fresh wounds, for the blood was red still. There were some with ears missing and noses, and eyes gouged out, leaving black blood pits. And in all the dead throng, there was none, naked, that still wore its genitals.

The scene was dread; it was a war scene in all its glory. And no victory was worth the sight, to my mind, or ever can be. 'Turn away your eyes, my Sibli,' said Owen, soft. He put his arm about her shaking shoulders. 'Come away. Come back up the hill.'

And after, he said to me, his eyes like yellow-pebbles washed up on a beach. 'Thus will the English see my people always . . . butchers, and worse. For the work of a handful of crazed women are we undone . . . and history will name us savage. We proud Cymry . . . we poor remnant . . .'

EIGHT

The two captives, Mortimer and Clanvowe, were received into our temporary manor, the old stone fortress on Snowdon, with much cordiality; Owen had no quarrel with them, and they had committed no atrocities. They were enemies only in that they owed loyalty to their liege lord, Henry of Bolingbroke, and, when called upon, had gone forth to do battle in his name. Mortimer, who had heard of the capture of Grey, asked where he was kept; when he heard, he laughed loud and long. 'It serves him right, the whoreson!' he exclaimed. 'A latrine is too good for him!' His pleasant face darkened, and he added, 'Upon my own people, too, my cotters and those who live upon my lands—upon them, too, has he worked much oppression and injustice. Do not ask me to meet him face-to-face, for one of us will have a broken nose!'

Owen smiled, clasping the man's shoulder in friendly wise. 'And do you think, friend—I plan to cast you into the latrine with him?'

Indeed, it was impossible not to like this young Edmund Mortimer. He was a personable fellow, slim and of a good height, with curling brown hair and candid eyes. All the damsels looked upon him with favor, for he was comely and had much charm. The Lady Margaret, too, seemed happy in his presence, for it had been long since she had had converse with a courtly gentleman, and she listened with eagerness to his descriptions of life at court. His tales of the new king, though, were something upsetting; the man was so unlike Richard. He had a new queen, too, Joanna of Navarre; Margaret was curious about her, as women will be, asking all manner of questions about her person, her dress, and her disposition.

Edmund answered that she was not beautiful, being swarthy of complexion, older than Henry, and inclined to plumpness. 'She consumes pounds of sweetmeats a day,' he said gaily. 'An expense to the exchequer, you can be sure, though perhaps they come out of her dowry—who knows? It was a large one.... She brought with her upwards of a hundred fine gowns, each with several pairs of sleeves, and many surcoats—and changes them sometimes a dozen times a day.'

Margaret began counting on her fingers, merry as I had not seen her in many months. 'Then would she need them all, the gowns!' she exclaimed brightly. 'For before the year is out she must start all over again!'

Owen pointed at me. 'Master Nathan has an abacus from the

Far East,' he said. 'It will do your counting for you, if you needs must know for sure....'

'Oh, Owen, I jested only,' she said, her face falling.

'I know,' he said. And putting his arms about her, he said, 'How sad these times ... when we do not recognize each other's little japes. Oh, my Marred....' And he buried his head in her neck, holding her tight. When he brought his head up, one could see tears glittering in his eyes. And Edmund, that courtly gentleman, turned away his eyes, embarrassed. 'It is this sickly war,' he said. 'I would it were resolved....'

'God grant it will be!' cried Margaret, her hands clasped together.

'I am asking from Henry ransoms of ten thousand marks for you, Edmund, and for Grey—and five thousand for the poet....' Clanvowe was not present; he might have been offended at the small sum asked for his person.

Edmund shook his head. 'I think you had best forget it ... where I am concerned, at least. Lancaster will pay nothing—except it be for my head. I am too close to the throne for his comfort.' And he smiled, a wry, twisted line to his mouth. 'And so, friend Owen, I am at your mercy....' His open countenance shut in upon itself a little, as he sat thinking. Then he said slowly, 'I can raise that much myself, perhaps, but I wonder if I am prepared to do it in his cause....' A look passed between them, he and Owen, and a little silence hung in the air. Then Edmund laughed shortly. 'As for Clanvowe'—and he spread his hands, like a very Jew—'what think you a poem is worth to Bolingbroke? He has left Chaucer unpaid for a year ... and he is the greatest flower of England's verse! The young prince, Harry, paid him last out of his own pocket, or so it is said....'

The damsel Morgan clapped her hands together from the corner where she stood. 'Oh, he would do so, Father ... he would! Harry loves all manner of song and verse——' And then she stopped, her words hanging in the air. None had marked where the damsels stood, listening with eager ears to all the news.

Margaret turned to bend her look upon them, frowning a little. 'I think you girls are needed abovestairs,' she said. 'Nurse has little help now, with all the serving-maids fled to the hills with their men. Make your farewells and go now....'

And so each stepped forward, to curtsey before the Mortimer; all shy they were at this fine gentleman, except the last, Efa. She went very close and, rising from her curtsey, managed to brush her breast against his arm; he reddened. And I saw, before they left, a look of pure hatred on the sweet maiden face of Catherine. Efa is a wanton, I fear. Even I, who never notice such things and live with eyes in the heavens or some book, have seen it; she has dallied with all the young men of the house, even her own half brothers, even the roughest soldiers, those she can manage to encounter. I think there is a kind of madness in her; she is not made quite right and cannot help it. But of course the other maids resent it; it gives her an advantage the others cannot take. And it is wartime, and marriages far from thinking on. Poor damsels!

The Lady Margaret thought with me, it seemed, for she bit her lip after and said, 'Owen ... we must send her away—Efa —to her father. She will infect the others with her—unseemly ways....'

Owen said, 'Yet was it Morgan's speech that caused you to dismiss them ... and is so always ...' he added, low.

'Oh, no, Owen! Believe me ... I love Morgan well——' And she took his hand. 'It is all over, long ago—my bad feelings ... truly. But Morgan—she is sick with love for this Lancaster boy. There is a ring from him, his mother's arms upon it, a rich thing, a state thing. She wears it upon a string about her neck under her gown. And a shirt she has, too, that he lent her when she was captive there where he was, at Dinas Brân. I have seen her kiss it and hug it to her...'

'It is a childish passion only,' said Owen. 'She knew the boy at Richard's court when they were children....'

'Well,' said Margaret. 'She is fifteen and old for her age, in body and mind, too.' And she cast down her eyes. 'So I was— her age—when first I loved you, my lord....'

'Well,' he said heavily, 'we must find a husband for her. There are likely lads about...'

'It should not be difficult,' said Edmund in his courtly way. 'She is a bewitching beauty, your daughter Morgan. She would not need a dowry even.'

A look passed between Owen and Margaret; Mortimer reddened again. He had guessed the truth, I think, that there was
nothing of Margaret in the girl and that she was not true-born.
It was a touchy moment for all. But he carried it off, Edmund.
For he said, bowing to both host and hostess, and his hands
over his heart, 'But all the maidens of your house are lovely,
for sure. A man would be hard put to choose....' He was a man
of much tact and some sensitivity; I liked him from the first,
enemy though he was.

The other, the poet, was another cut of cloth. He was, to my
mind, an arrogant bore, forever quoting from the Latin, as
though he alone had knowledge, and expounding on such
idiotic matters as the elixir of life, the Philosophers' Stone, and
all manner of foolishness, which no man of sense can credit. He
was fascinated beyond belief by astrology and by magic; one
could see he really thought that the tales of Owen's witchcraft
were true! 'Where is it?' he asked, rubbing his soft plump
hands together. 'Where is the Tower of Magic, with the Merlin
signs writ upon the walls and the crystal ball that tells the
future, and the stone—oh, that I wish to see very much indeed! The stone ... that renders you invisible, Lord Owen....'

'Is that what they say?' asked Owen, laughing. 'That I have
such a stone? But then would I disappear before your eyes—at
will! Or journey all through the isles, unmarked, to cleave the
skull of my Lancaster enemy! Be sure, friend poet, it is all
foolishness....'

The poet's face fell. 'But many have seen you call the wind.
At Richard's court you did it often....'

Then Owen laughed loud and long, and Margaret with
him; I had heard the story only, so I merely smiled. 'Friend,'
said Owen, 'once only did I perform magic.... As you know,
when I met Richard first he was but a lad of ten—at his coronation. I was not yet twenty myself. I fancy myself as a mummer, having lived among such folk, minstrels and bards, all my
life. I played in a masque for him at his coronation feast, foam
from my mouth and all manner of fooling ... so he loved this
foolery. There was much solemnity about that poor little boy,
his dark-minded, scheming uncles.... I was forever on the
lookout for some new amusement for him and I was much in

his favor ... a kind of unpaid jester, one might say. And later, much later, when we two, Richard and I, were wed, and he keeping court at Sheen Palace, that is gone now, he was minded I should play another trick on the more gullible high-noses, for he loved to mock them, Richard. I saw, as any who looked to the north might, that a storm was a-brewing. So, dressed up like Merlin, in robes all covered with Druidic signs—though made-up they were, for sure, none of us knowing the right ones—and wearing a long beard to my waist and a tall Merlin cone-hat, I climbed upon the ramparts of the castle, and all the glittering throng below, watching, in the courtyard. I made strange passes with my hands in the air, and strange guttural sounds in my throat and high keening noises, too, giving it out that I was calling the wind.... Well, it took a while, and I growing hoarse, and feeling somewhat silly, too, but a great wind blew up then, bringing thunder and lightning with it and a drenching rain. Any fool could have seen it coming or felt it, for it was that kind of sultry day, still before the storm will break. I had to run for shelter, like all the rest ... And that is my magic.'

Edmund Mortimer laughed till the tears streamed, but the poor poet Thomas Clanvowe wore a face that fell into deep jowls of disappointment.

'Oh, dear,' he said. 'I did so want to see some magic ... have my fortune told.... Can you not do just a little something, sire?' he wheedled.

'Why, man,' said Owen, 'any hill-woman will tell your fortune in your palm for a coin....' But then he snapped his fingers. 'Marred,' he cried. 'We might call Hopkin!'

She hid her face that could not stop smiling; I saw it was an old joke between them.

'Hopkin ap Thomas—yes, that is the very thing!' said Owen, keeping a straight face.

So, for our entertainment, one night while the two prisoners waited to hear from their ransomers, Hopkin ap Thomas put on a great show. All the household was there, the man being summoned from his lair, wherever it was, and taking it seriously, too, one could see, dressed exactly as Owen had described himself, as the folk say Merlin dressed, but richly, and no minstrel-costume; in fact, it was his daily wear. He had no teeth in his head, and the words came out strange and lisping and in Welsh, too; the young maids and youths giggled and hid their smiles at the gibberish, but the English poet hung on every word. He could not understand the Welsh, so the bard Griffith Lloyd translated, making each sentence into a song, so that in afteryears we all remembered it differently, forgetting the man himself. He said that England would be at war a hundred years or more, that a Tudor of Mona would sit upon the throne and spawn the greatest of monarchs, a virgin queen; all nonsense, and more besides, that predicted a victory for Wales, at which all cheered. Then he said that a maid in armour would lead a king to his anointing and create a nation. This was an odd thing indeed, but Sibli said, softly, into my ear, for she was ever shy in company, 'He means me, Nathan ... I have asked for mail. And I am ever with the army. Perhaps I shall lead Owen to his crown....' And her face wore a dreaming look; I shushed her, so that none should hear.

'Owen does not want a crown,' I said. 'I had thought you a maid of much sense. Hold your tongue, for it is all silliness....'

But it was an entertainment, and some of the lesser folk were impressed, and worked and fought the harder for Owen and Wales, so all was not wasted. I noticed, too, how Edmund sat between the damsels Morgan and Catherine, and laughed and joked with both, but that his hand rested in Catherine's lap and their fingers were intertwined.

The bard sang after, and his daughter, dark Sibli, and the minstrels put on a show, tumbling and dancing, and their own lute-playing, different from the harp. It was a merry night, and the last I remember in Wales.

NINE

In the early fall, September, Owen's magic powers looked to be in evidence, for the weather was as if called by him to work evil against the 'Saxon Horde.' There were weeks of rain, pouring in torrents from the sky, and hailstones as big as your fist every other day; in some parts, where in normal times it was summer still, snow lay upon the hills and frost in the valleys. Owen himself said it must have something to do with the movement of the comet, now vanished from our sight. 'For,' he said, 'we know nothing of the firmament, less than nothing. . . . Surely it is all tied together, somehow. . . .'

But our enemies were confounded, for the whole border had been put into a state of defense by King Henry, one army at Shrewsbury, under the king himself, another at Chester, commanded by the young Prince Harry, and yet another at Hereford, led by Lord Stafford, a veteran commander. But by now, along with the weather, Owen had the whole of Glamorgan with him; he attacked successfully Gwent, Abergavenny, Usk, Caerleon, Newport and Cardiff. It was told that on September 7 Henry encamped for the night in a very pleasant, lovely meadow, under a balmy, star-filled sky; in an hour a storm broke, rain drenched his tent, a strong wind blew it down, and a hail of arrows fell upon him from the hills, where some of the 'barefoot savages' had been waiting the chance. His habit of wearing full armor always, even in sleep, saved him, however, for arrows cannot pierce iron. He had to have an entire new suit forged, though, and in a hurry, for it was so dented and smashed shapeless that it was painful to wear. Owen, hearing this, chuckled and said, 'Good! He will hate that more than a wound, Red Henry . . . for he cannot bear to part with a farthing, and armor is costly.'

A new ordinance was passed by the next Parliament; no 'waster, rhymer, minstrel, or vagabond' was to be allowed to maintain himself in Wales by 'making commorthas or gatherings upon the common people.' I have reported it as it was writ, and an effort was made to enforce it, but the bards and minstrels of Wales are beloved by all, and never was one taken, though a reward was posted also. These wandering bard-folk went everywhere, stirring up the cause of Owen and of Wales by their songs. This same Parliament urged the king to ransom Lord Grey, believing that it would ease matters.

The king did not; instead he granted that Lord of Ruthin permission to ransom himself! Grey could not gather such a sum as ten thousand marks, that Owen asked; he paid six thousand and left his son as hostage till the rest was paid, months after.

Mortimer was another story; King Henry would give no permission to Mortimer even; he could rot in Owen's hands for all he cared. 'Indeed,' exclaimed Edmund, 'it would be simpler for him if I did!'

One night in Hall, and all the household present, Edmund Mortimer swore allegiance to the Welsh cause, his hand upon an old sword, said to belong to an ancient hero, Eliseg; Owen had dug it up somewhere, and said to me, privately, that it would serve, for who could tell, it might have been Eliseg's, if indeed there had been an Eliseg!

After, Owen led forth Catherine and announced her betrothal to Edmund; it was no surprise, really. Even I, who notice little of such things, could see it was a love match from the first. Only the young hawk-face, Rhisiart, looked glum, for he had mooned after Catherine and written bad poems to her; I had heard the maidens giggling over them, cruel children! After the marriage, in November, this Rhisiart was much in the company of Morgan, though I never saw that they held hands or exchanged love-looks.

Now, this Edmund Mortimer, son-in-law to Owen, was also brother to the wife of Harry Percy, that Hotspur. It must have rankled deep in Hotspur that the king, whom the Percys had backed with arms, men, and money, would not even so much as countenance the ransom of Mortimer. Indeed, he had much cause for discontent; he was owed money in the thousands, he had paid his army from his own pocket, and his lady-wife had, in a sense, been insulted, through her close kin. Mortimer sent a letter to Hotspur, informing him of his marriage, 'and well content am I, for my bride is a delight.' He informed him also of his intention henceforward to throw in his whole allegiance to the cause of Owen and Wales, against the usurper Bolingbroke, with the express purpose, as he stated, of restoring the crown to its rightful heir, the young Mortimer, captive of the usurper, and of restoring to his friend and ally, Prince Owen, his rights in Wales, and all other Welsh claims.

There was no answer till the spring.

Night had all but fallen; every tree and bush in small new leaf was in clear-cut lead color against a darkling pearl sky; the gates had not yet been closed for the night. There was no road really, up to our mountain fastness, just a sort of winding path worn by random feet, and a dirt track in the rear where oxcarts could carry proviser. Came that evening loud ringing hoofbeats on the rocky path and a clear 'Hallo!' and after 'Peace! We come in peace!' And the first we saw, in the fast-gathering dark, and all poking our noses out at windows at once, or at door, was a white banner that shone like marsh-fire. Carrying it was a rider on horseback, full-armed, and another rode behind, and two squires.

They two in front, knights, for sure, at least, by their bearing, sprang off their mounts and stode into Hall, all falling away to make a path and stare. For, none such had been seen in our manor-houses, ever. These were like beings from another world, one in shining silver, one in black with a high polish, and no faces, but pointed face-masks, like birds of prey; clanking too they were. The first, who bore the white flag, snatched off his helm, showing cropped dark hair, a high-colored face bright with charm, white teeth, crooked in a crooked smile. A step behind, the other, too, removed his helm. They were much alike, with the Celtic dark I have come to know, but the second had a thin high nose and a long-chinned face, bearded, and much hair falling to the shoulders. 'It is Hotspur!' cried young Rhisiart, behind me, in a voice awestruck, and came forward to kneel before the first warrior; I saw he wore that same helm-cut all the young men were affecting. Of course, I remembered, it was he who had started it; it had been freshly done, probably that morning by his squire, for his neck and the place above his ears was bluish-white against the sunburnt skin below.

He looked down, puzzled, then snapped his fingers, laughing. 'Why, it is our flown captive of Dinas Brân!' he cried. 'Rhys ... Rees....' He hunted for the name in his head.

'Rhisiart ab Owen, sire' came the answer.

'Well,' said Hotspur, turning to his companion and gesturing, 'this is another captive—not flown yet ... and the most famous in the world!' And he smiled a broad smile that made one's own face twitch to imitate it; even the thin-faced one smiled his own wintry one, grudging. 'This,' Hotspur went on, 'is the famous Earl of Douglas. Even you must have heard of him—the Black Douglas ... and my friend-prisoner!'

We had all known of his famous victory over the Scots, the fabled hand-to-hand combat that lasted twenty-eight hours and ended in a draw, and now, it seemed, had resulted in a kind of partnership. For the two were as easy with each other as brothers. I guess, though it is odd to contemplate, to some men war is the whole world and can bring each to each as can love. Such were these, certainly, though I never got to know either of them, yet was it plain to see, each would die for the other, if need be. And they had been from childhood the strongest enemies!

And so an alliance was formed, between Owen and these men, one honored captive of the other. Hotspur brought his father's seal, the great ring of the Northumberland lords, in earnest of their break with Lancaster and their sponsoring of the Welsh cause.

After, Owen said, and meditating deep, 'Well ... the elder Percy was turncoat to Richard, and now has he turned his coat from the house of Lancaster and to me, with his son, too.... But I like the man well, Hotspur ... and we need them and badly. Let us trust them—for the time, at least.'

In the early weeks of May, the prince, young Harry of Monmouth, as was his title (in Wales he was never called Prince of Wales, of course), led a raid of considerable proportions. An attack was made on all the Glendower properties and lands; Sycharth manor and all the other houses in the vicinity were burned to the ground, and all those left there put to death. There were none of Owen's household there or at Glendower House, either, which was the next object; all of it was utterly destroyed, that lovely place, and the poor Lady Margaret wept bitter tears. 'Do not care, sweet,' said Owen. 'We will build other, better houses ... we have all Wales almost, even now ... and we *will* have all. There are many castles in Wales. You can live in any you choose...'

Our spies found a letter from the prince to his father; it begged for money to pay the troops within ten days—'or, your respected Highness, they will leave us in the lurch, and we must strike while the iron is hot.' And it went on to say that the Welsh had besieged for months the castles of Harlech and Aberystwyth, which must be relieved or they would fall. We rejoiced to read it, for we knew him afraid, the prince.

Owen said, 'There is a canny man—boy that he is. His father should thank God for him. Let us hope that he does not realize his worth....'

Owen was right, in a way, for the king did nothing, saying he would attend to it when he returned from the Scottish border. In the meantime, he sent a thousand pounds to the prince for payment to his soldiers, but not before many had deserted. And, though it seemed a large sum, it was a paltry one against what was needed; this, again, we got from our spies.

Meanwhile, Owen took the field in person, with more than eight thousand men, and deposed other armies, under Rhys the Savage, Rhys Dhu of Cardigan, Henry Don, and other loyal followers. Owen himself concentrated his forces on the Towy valley, and I was with him there. Everywhere he was hailed by his title that was hereditary, Prince of Wales, and everywhere the noble Welshmen swore fealty to him. He looked like Arthur come again, as I have said; Owen always played his parts well. Like a very Jupiter he was, in his great height and goldenness, all stern and stony, upon a huge white steed caparisoned in gold, with the gold dragon banner blowing proud above him.

He was expected by the enemy to march either to the north, south, or east; instead he made for the comparatively open west. All along the way we were joined by loyal Welsh. On the road to Carmarthen, all the great castles and strongholds surrendered to him, including the great castle-fort of Newcastle Emlyn, which left his road open to the north. All day we besieged the castle and town of Carmarthen, and the next day they surrendered; we lost no lives.

Leaving a force there to hold it, Owen advanced upon Pembrokeshire. On July tenth, word was brought to us that Henry Percy, Hotspur, had raised the standard of revolt at Chester. Deposing small bands to police the neighborhoods where he had a foothold, Owen decided to attempt to join forces with the Percys, and so make an end.

Communications were slow, and we never got our rightful news in time; I will try to tell it as I learned it after.

Henry Percy was joined by his uncle, the Earl of Worcester, and by great numbers of the Cheshire folk and the Welshmen of the March, who up to now had been almost converted English and hardly spoke the Welsh tongue. It was said that Hotspur got them to his side by telling them that Richard was still alive, but of this I am not sure.

Up to the last moment, the king suspected nothing; he thought he was joining with the Percys against the Scots, and it was not till he got to Nottingham that he learned of their defection to Owen. They say he swore a great oath, too terrible to write, and turned sharp west, following the River Trent, and thus to Burton, where he summoned twelve counties to come to his aid. Hotspur was meanwhile marching south, hoping to reach Shrewsbury and capture the young prince, who was holding the town.

But the Molewarp, as Sibli called the king, moved too fast. He reached Shrewsbury on the twentieth day of July with all his army and closed the gates, just before Hotspur got there. Hotspur camped some three miles from the closed town, in open country, and on the next day, the twenty-first, battle was joined.

Owen anticipated this move; we struggled to reach Shrewsbury, but in this one case, at least, the elements were not with us. There was no rain, but all the rivers were in flood, as they had never been, and fording-places could not be found. We were miles and miles away from the scene still, when that dreadful battle was fought. If we could have got there, it would have won the struggle for us. But that is hindsight, as Owen himself would say.

Neither was the elder Percy there; he was still in the far north with his army; Hotspur and his men fought alone. And there was he slain, the great Hotspur, and his head stuck up after on London Bridge, and pieces of him displayed in other towns all over England, as a warning; it is a filthy Norman barbarism and makes me sick to my stomach to think on it.

The king was victorious there, at Shrewsbury, and the Percys named as traitors. Yet was the young Prince Harry wounded and badly. We heard some of the story in this wise.

The remains of Hotspur's army made its way to us at Snowdon, where Owen had come, too, leaving his armies to hold the castles he had won. They came limping up the mountain, one man bearing another, in all condition of pain and rotting flesh; the mountain moaned with the poor sounds of those beaten men, and they lay in the shelter of the great trees, for there was not room in the courtyards or keeps for such a horde. All night we worked, I and my helpers, binding up the long-festering wounds; Owen walked among them, and his lady, too, and all the sons and maidens of the house, for much help was needed.

One man we came to, a doughty fellow, though an arrow-bolt was lodged in his eye. He called himself Tom Franklin, and explained proudly that he was free. Owen said that there was a law in England that a serf who could run away from his home county and reside by some means, hook or crook, in another for a period of three years—or perhaps it was five, I have forgot—became therefore free, and serf no longer. One can imagine how difficult this would be, for who would succor such a one or give him employment? Anyway, those who managed it usually took the name of Franklin, which is Old Norman for 'freedman.'

This man told us much of the battle; he was strong and sinewy and never flinched when I took out the arrow, though the pain must have been near unbearable. His other eye wept great tears when he told of the death of Hotspur. '... for he was a man to love well,' he said, 'and a man to follow.... And so, Lord,' he said, looking up at Owen, 'he was bound to you and your cause, and I will be too. Besides, I like well that there are no unfree here in this place....'

'Except on the border lands,' said Owen. 'But we will change that. All men must be free, as far as can be.... There are enough bonds upon us set by nature and our own failings....'

Tom Franklin watched him still, not moving while I laid ointment on the raw pit of his lost eye. 'A rare king you are, for sure,' he said. 'More like a wise man or a holy hermit....'

'I am no king, Master Franklin,' said Owen, 'nor wish to be. Nor am I holy at all, at all.' And he laughed, shortly, his face grim after. He bent over the man then. 'I am sorry for your pain and your loss. I salute your spirit. Look well with the eye that is left ... look long and hard.'

And he left us, Owen, moving to speak to another poor maimed creature. 'Now what did he mean by that?' said Tom Franklin. 'Never mind. I will think it out. . . .' He went on then, to tell us tales of the battle.

'Just let loose an arrow,' he said, 'and fitting another to my bow I was, when I saw the prince upon the ramparts, and close to me he was too, close enough to see his pretty looks. I see him clap his hand to his eye, and an arrow sticking out between his fingers. . . .' Behind me I heard the maiden Morgan gasp, catching her breath on a sob. He went on. 'I looked too long upward ... that's when I got mine'—and he pointed to his own wound. 'Never look up in battle ... I heard it all my days. I was a fool, and so was he, the young one. . . .' He stopped a moment while I tied on a bandage, then went on. 'I got it in the eye—like he did—and it hurt, it hurt bad ... and the blood running down into my nose and mouth, and the other eye tearing up in sympathy, like ... and I think: Well, Tom, this be the end ... just lay down here, boy, you're a goner, free or no.' He paused for a moment. 'Then, through all the muck, tears and blood and all, I see that brawly boy, that prince, and a white rag tied round his head, out again on the ramparts, with his sword, and directing the battle like a cockerel. And so I goes on, taking heart, like. . . .' He was running down, I could see, for I had given him poppy to drink and it was beginning to work.

The damsel Morgan bent down to him, saying soft in his ear, 'Was it his eye—the prince? Was it his eye?' But he had fallen asleep and did not answer.

TEN

We learned later that the arrow had just missed the eye of the English prince and lodged beside it, near his temple. When I heard, I was puzzled, for that place, the temple, most often means sure death or, at the very least, a living death of insanity. The reports must have had it something wrong; near the eye it was and near the temple, most like, but missing both. But it was not properly tended, the prince's wound, and it festered and sent him into a raving fever; for weeks he lay close to death, but in the end, as we heard, he escaped it. And the damsel Morgan, who had gone about red-eyed, took heart again. Poor little maiden, I thought, you love that boy-king, and when will you ever lay eyes on him again? Poor child, that will not find another object for her love!

Catherine bore a boy to Mortimer at the end of August; they had wasted no time! He was called Edmund, too, as is the English custom often. Owen said that in Wales he would be Edmund Vaughan, as Owen's own father was called Griffith Vaughan, being named for his father. So I surmised that it meant, somehow, 'son of the same name.' My Welsh was improving, but not up to the finer points. 'It is an old word,' said Owen. 'I think, in truth, it means, "the small," he said, laughing. 'And so he is—very small—my first grandson. Takes after the Mortimers.' And he nudged his son-in-law in the ribs; there was always much fond accord and japing between these two. And so he was, the babe, quite small, but perfect in every way, and healthy; the midwives say, in these parts, that small children come from too young a mother. I myself have not found it so; it lies in the heredity somewhere.

In the meantime, castle after castle fell to Owen, and we removed, all to Harlech, the nearest, under heavy escort and moving slowly through the wild mountain passes.

It is a noble and awesome sight, Harlech Castle, set high upon a jagged hill and with its back to the sea. It is one of the larger in this country, built sometime near the tenth century; though it is old, it is strong-built and secure, with walls more than a foot thick and all of native stone, gray and melting to silver in the twilight, as I first saw it. It looked like a place where Arthur went still, and Merlin, but Owen shook his head, laughing. 'It is nowhere near so ancient,' he said. 'But I agree, it has a look of fable and of heroic times. Remember, Arthur was Roman, or as good as so, and Merlin, too ... all those old heroes had some Roman blood mixed in.... This is no Roman

place. . . .' And so we fell to argument as we rode; most pleasant
it was, for it was long since we had found the time. It was like
the old days for a little, and the others like us, Iestyn and
Iorweth, and Griffith Lloyd the bard joining in, and faces lit
with love of learning and disputation. But of course it did not
last long. Nothing is normal in wartime.

We settled in at Harlech; though it was not the lovely modern place we had been used to, still it was better than that cold
mountain lair where we had been so long. The part that faced
inland was cheerless and dank, dark, too; but on the seaward
side there were no defenses, none being needed, and the windows were cut larger and light flooded in, white from the sea.
The Lady Margaret made her solar there, and mostly everyone
gathered in that part, whoever was at home and not on the
battle trail or at a siege.

It was from this storied castle of Harlech that Owen sent out
his formal ambassadors to the French king, suing for an alliance. There were French boats already off the coast, so we
knew that the French were sympathetic to the cause of Wales.
For months there had been six and sometimes more ships,
harrying the English towns along the coastlands and firing
upon them with cannon. Though none hit a mark, for they
could not get in close enough. Still, it was enough to frighten
those English folk who lived there; many beseeching letters
were sent to the king, asking for help against them, but no help
came. The French ships hovered still, keeping the fishing boats
inshore and frighting the people. Once we saw a sea battle
joined; four English ships against four French, and another
French vessel coming in at last to turn the battle. All the English boats were sunk, and there was cheering from us all,
though after, the Lady Margaret wept, thinking of the poor
sailors in their watery graves.

Owen had, earlier in the year, held a Parliament at Machyn-
lleth modeled somewhat on the English form, for he was familiar with all the statutes, laws and procedures from his studies
at the Inns of Court. The great difference was that Owen had
gone back to the old Welsh Assembly called at Whitland by
Howell the Good in the tenth century, and summoned four
men from each commote under his sway, as that Howell had

done long ago. I was with a segment of the army, and I did not see these men assembled or hear the judgments or decisions which were made there; I think, in fact, it was a preparation only for the formal coronation of Owen as prince and the formal declaration of Wales as a principate. All his sons were there and his kinsmen; also there were envoys from Scotland, France, and Spain, at that time a close ally of France. I am not one that loves ceremony, but I should have liked to have been there, just to see Owen's face. We had been four years at struggle for this thing, and now it had come to pass! His son Griffith told me later that Owen refused to wear royal robes, and simply gave that old crown he wore always into the hands of the bishop and bade him use that. 'It is hardly fit to be called a crown,' said Griffith. 'Old iron it is, and has lain in the ground for centuries, worn thin by time ... more does it resemble the rim of a cooking-pot!'

This was not true of course; to my eyes it was beautiful for its antique look and the delicacy of the tracings upon it, worn, as he said, by time. But of course, not all folk see with the eyes of an antiquarian. In my heart I was glad he had forgone pomp, though I said nothing and only shrugged my shoulders, in that way that Owen jests only *my* people can do.

In the spring of 1404, Owen summoned his envoys that were to go to France, as had been decided by the Parliament earlier. They were Griffith Young (there are so many Griffiths here!), who was his chancellor, a doctor-in-law degrees; and his brother-in-law, John Hanmer. They were to be accompanied by some others, a Tudor of Mona in Anglesey, and representatives of North, South, and West Wales as well. But the negotiations were to be put into the hands of Chancellor Young and of Hanmer. It was a very timely expedition; Owen had a master statesman's mind. Charles VI of France had never been favorable to the usurper Bolingbroke, who now sat on the throne, and he had been outraged, as had all his court, at the pulling down of Richard and his ultimate death; Richard had been the French king's friend, in the years before his madness took him badly, and his daughter had been Richard's last queen. Though the two countries were not actually at war, the French never left off harassing and injuring the regime of

Henry of Lancaster. One perfect channel for this ill will was, of course, our Welsh revolt; the ears of the French king were willing to listen to our suit, for certain, and it was now or never.

Owen wrote to the French king, giving this document to his chancellor. It was in Latin, and he styled himself 'Owynus dei gratia princeps Wallie,' writing on the tenth of May in the fourth year of his principate. He stated that 'his envoys have the fullest powers to treat with the French king, in the hope of establishing an alliance of friendship and affection between Charles the king and Owen the prince, a league between independent powers on the basis of mutual goodwill.' He asked for an ample supply of weapons, including the modern cannon, just coming into use, to be shipped to Wales from the mouth of the Seine, and, later, an expedition under the Count of La Marche, one of France's most renowned commanders and brilliant warriors. He authenticated this *procuratio* with the impress of his privy seal, bearing his title, Prince of Wales, the princely coronet, and the four lions rampant of Gwynned; he had decided at the Parliament that, as successor to the great Llewellyn, he should take these arms for his own. The arms of Powys, his father's house, had been for many years a single lion.

When the envoys returned, Chancellor Young told us all, and we had been successful in all. 'Thank God,' said Owen, 'Charles was in good health!' This was a delicate way of putting it; as all knew, the poor king had frequent fits of madness. Chancellor Young stared out of his shortsighted clerk's eyes, so apparently he had known little of international gossip.

Charles had received them graciously, seated upon his throne; John Hanmer said the throne's gilt needed polishing and that the king's hose had many holes and were not over clean, but Owen said, laughing, that it had always been so, Isabeau being busy with other things. At this, Chancellor Young stared again; truly the man must be of a monkish turn! John Hanmer, though, laughed and made a rude gesture, at which Lady Margaret clucked her tongue.

'What a woman!' said John. 'Even fat, one would pray hard for long arms to embrace her and a long——'

'Hush!' said Owen. 'Your sister is present, to say nothing of the damsels. . . .' But his sternness had a lightness under.

This Isabeau is a man's joke, for true! Privately, after, John told us how her eyes roved, and her hands, too, and other parts, also, at the presence of a goodly male. 'She had a supper for us, and she was the only woman present,' he said. 'Wine flowed . . . but never fear, I was continent. It was not such business I was sent on . . . much to my regret. . . .'

At any rate, King Charles asked what kind of gift would most please Prince Owen; the chancellor replied that in nothing did Owen take more pleasure than the trappings of war, for he was above all things a soldier.

Owen laughed long at this, but said, 'A politic answer . . . the perfect thing to say . . . and I congratulate you, Master Young.' The poor chancellor, pulled to and fro by Owen's moods and not understanding him, looked like a terrier confronted by a playful lion and wondering when the great beast would pounce. He brought out the gifts, proud; a gilt casque, with a cuirass and a sword. Owen took them, turning them over in his hands and examining them with great curiosity. 'These are things for show,' he said finally. 'The sword will not cut through butter, and the cuirass is as thin as hammered gold. I will hang them upon the wall. It needs some ornament.'

Besides this fooling, we found that business was not neglected. On June fourteenth at Paris, James of Bourbon, Count of La Marche, and John, Bishop of Chartres, were formally authorized by the king to conclude an agreement with the envoys of the 'magnificent and mighty Owen, Prince of Wales,' and negotiations were begun. A document was drawn up, witnessed by the French chancellor Arnaud de Corbie, the bishops of Noyon, Meaux, and Arras, and the Count of Vendôme. This document bound the French king and the Welsh prince in a close league against 'Henry of Lancaster,' their common foe, and all his adherents. They promised that neither would make a separate peace or truce with Henry and that each would welcome in friendly wise the ships and merchants of the other. They agreed that any local trouble which might arise should be amicably composed by the proper local authority. There was nothing explicit in the document about a French expedition into Wales, but such was implied; Owen had provided his envoys with full information as to the ports of Wales, the routes to be traversed, and the facilities for getting provisions. This information was duly given to the French. And so Owen, rubbing his hands together, said, 'It is accomplished then.... French help will come, and I am confident. Thank you, gentlemen....'

A few small castles still held out against us, but all the open country was Owen's. So great was his power, and so feared, that at Shropshire the citizens forced the authorities to make a three month truce with 'the land of Wales'; even the royal council had to concede this truce, a great thing for Welsh morale.

There were a number of forays at this time; our forces were deployed to harry every English border settlement. In fact, at one point, the English were pursued to the very gates of the town of Monmouth, which only got them shut in time. And this was not Welsh land, but the very earth of Saxon England!

Cardiff, a great town, fell to us; only one street was spared, the street where the house of the Poor Friars stood, the Poor Friars that had been ever loyal to Richard. All else was burned to the ground and the citizens dispersed.

There came over to Owen also one who had been up to now an active supporter of the Crown. This was John Trevor, Bishop of St. Asaph; he was a man ever against insurrection and had held out long. Now did he espouse the cause of Welsh independence and wrote so, saying that in all things was Owen in his rights and that Wales should be free of the foreign oppressor. Owen rejoiced to hear this, for, though he was a man without formal religion, yet did he need the support of the Church and its sanction.

About this time, the French alliance bore fruit; sixty ships, under the command of the Count of La Marche, sailed out of Breton and Norman harbors and gathered in the English Channel, like a storm threatening the House of Lancaster. But that storm never broke; none knows why. Through the summer and autumn, the count with his fleet sailed up and down the English Channel, putting fear into every English heart. He did not bring it to Wales and, in November, sailed back to France. Owen swore at this news. 'What in God's name can the man have been doing? Does he think he was on a pleasure cruise? Or can it be he is as insane as his master?'

Indeed, it was a grave disappointment; the news that came from the English side, though, showed that Parliament took a very gloomy view. They felt that this cruising was a fine examination of English shores and harbors and that at any moment, the French, with their new knowledge, might land anywhere.

It was now that we had our months of waiting ... waiting for the French.

ELEVEN

In February, 1405, the famous Tripartite Indenture was drawn up. This was a formal alliance between Owen, Mortimer, and the crafty Earl of Northumberland, who had survived his great son, Hotspur. The occasion was moved by a new conspiracy against the House of Lancaster in which many leading English barons had a part. The chief among them was Thomas, Lord Bardolf, who had been a trusted councillor of King Henry; it was plain to see that this king had made himself most unpopular! I will not go into details of this plot; it was put down, finally, but serves to show that much dissatisfaction existed still in the realm of England. A usurper's throne is never solid.

The treaty between the three powers, the Tripartite Indenture, was drawn up at the house of the Bishop of Bangor, with that man and the Bishop Trevor witnessing and concurring. By the terms of this indenture, the three magnates promised to warn each other of any danger and swore to defend the realm of England (which was to be theirs) against all men, saving the oath of alliance which Owen had sworn to the King of France.

The plan was, when the defeat of Lancaster was accomplished, to set the boy-heir of Mortimer, our Edmund's kinsman, upon the throne, and the kingdom would be divided thusly: Mortimer, his house, would have the Thames valley and the region to the south, while Northumberland would receive a share which projects far north and also into the midlands; Owen's new Welsh principality would encroach no less boldly. The new Wales would be bounded by the Severn to the north gate of the city of Worcester, thence to a group of ash trees known as Onennau Meigon and which is in the depth of England, thence by the old road north to the source of the Trent, and thence to the source of the Mersey and along that river to the sea. Since the days of Cadwallon of Gwynned, so Griffith Lloyd, the bard-historian told me, no Welsh prince has presumed to claim so large an area of these British islands. And that was many years ago, in the days of Welsh power and pride!

In this same year did Owen call another Parliament, this time here at Harlech, again with the four men from each commote. So that, in one way, it was a year of hope and the realization, coming nearer, of Welsh independence.

In another way, though, it was a year of deep tragedy. And being a Jew, it hit me deep, for I recognize it well. I saw doom coming, though I am no seer.

I will leave the broad ribbon of history for a moment and tell of the little webs of our own private fortunes, all woven together as they were and more poignant than any records can show.

Owen and his lady, between them, having worried much about the unwed damsels of their house, made plans to marry off those maidens before it was too late and they were left without protectors.

Owen's second son, Meredith, was wed to Elliw, daughter of Rhys Dhu of Cardigan, whom Welshmen call the Black, for his coloring and his temper in war. These two young people had long doted on each other; it was no hardship.

The bard Griffith's daughter, Megolin, a sweet lass, was wed to a Tudor of Mona, one Meredith, too, and went away with him to his home on the isle of Anglesey. The other daughter, Sibli, refused, with wild weeping, to be wed at all, saying she was needed at my side; I must confess I argued for her, for she was an excellent nurse. Besides, she had the genius of her father, which, in its way, is above the laws of man. So Owen gave in, but exacted vows from all his house to protect this maid as though she were their own.

I cannot remember all the damsels or all the youths, but most were joined somehow and happy, too, in a sort, and for a little.

The wild and wanton Efa ran away with Rhys of the Hills, a strange match, one would think, she so delicately made and softly seductive, and he as rough and brutish as a creature from old tales. But Owen said, no, let them be—the two wildnesses in them would merge and meld. Though he said, too, rubbing his forehead and his eyes looking far, 'Let us hope it will not be as Arthur, who lay first with his half sister, unknowing, and spawned his own downfall, Mordred ... for she is said to be Tudor's daughter—and God knows'—and here he cast a shamed look at Margaret——'God knows which of our house made that Rhys! Privately I think none of us did; he much resembles that hill chief Gethin, for whom he was named....' Of course, I had heard the story, that Rhys Gethin's mother had bedded with all three, Griffith the father, and the two sons, Owen and Tudor, long ago. One cannot blame her for wishing to claim that her son came from the loins of the greatest house of Wales!

Tudor's twins had over a year ago married in double ceremony those Irish twins and had each, already a son.

And those are all I can remember. Except for Griffith, Owen's eldest, who said he had yet found none to please him; indeed, it was rumored that, unlike his family on either side, he was as celibate as any priest. The Lady, I think, privately, was glad, for she much adored this, her firstborn, and was as jealous of his affections as any wife! She tried and tried not to show it, but it stuck out all over her, no matter; her other son, Meredith, was a youth with great charm and handsome looks, far surpassing, to my mind, his brother. But what will you, women are strange creatures; perhaps it was Griffith's lesser qualities that endeared him to her. He was no longer sickly, except for sudden bouts of the choking asthma, that she herself had also. Perhaps the kinship lay there, beyond the mother love. At any rate, we are what we are, we humans. We are not gods.

I have forgot to tell of the marriage of Morgan, poor love-lorn lass. She was nearing twenty and, of all the damsels, one of the most glorious to look upon. Like Owen she was, a lioness, with a proud and noble face and a beckoning smile. Her love for the English prince was a faraway thing, a dream. But for this war she would have forgot it long ago. But still did she tend his horse, called Mercury, that he had given her, letting none other ride it, or even curry it or feed it. And still did she sit gazing far out into the seascape, caught in her private dream; the look upon her face was like that look of ice and fire that came upon Owen at times, of being some other where. When Owen came to her, saying that Rhisiart, the young eaglet, his secretary, had asked for her hand, she stared, and said, simply, 'Father, I do not love him.'

He looked at her hard, Owen, and said, 'I know ... you love a dream—as I did once, long ago.... But can you not *like* Rhisiart? I can see you agree well, and I would not have you live without a protector, in these hard times that I have brought upon us....' And a look of great sadness came over his face; she caught his arm.

'Oh, Father, you could do no other! It was for Wales ... and for us all. I know....' And she sat silent awhile. 'Yes, Father, I will wed with him. We have much fine converse, and he is a good youth ... and he asked for me, did he not? You spoke truly? You are not forcing him to wed with me?'

'Oh, my Morgan,' said Owen. 'Any man would want you ... no matter that you are not true born. If there were no war, you would have your pick of all the goodly knights of all the shires. But they die like flies, and the times are not normal. In normal times——' And he stopped. 'But, my dearest daughter, even in normal times, the one you long for—*that* one you could not have....'

'I know, Father,' she said, and smiling small and sad, as no beauteous damsel should. 'I know. And I will take Rhisiart, and gladly.'

And they two, Morgan and Rhisiart, were married on the eve of the battle of Usk. Not even was it evening, and they had no wedding night.

For the portion of the army that was to go to Usk left that

very day, under the command of Griffith, son of the house. He had begged to command a force, and finally Owen had given in, considering that this town and castle might be taken with comparative ease. He himself would lead that force that was deployed into the town, and Griffith would lead the besiegers of the castle. Most of the men of Harlech were going, leaving only a handful of defenders; I was left behind this time, Owen being confident that not much doctoring would be needed. Besides, Catherine was due to be brought to bed of her second child any day now. (I have said that these two, the Mortimer and his lady, wasted no time!)

It was the worst defeat, in a way, in our history, for it came as a total surprise. The town, under Owen's army, was put to the torch and its citizens driven out, but the army of Griffith encountered a huge force at the site of the castle, some miles away, and was put to rout. The battle was at a hill, close to the castle, called the Yellow Pool, and the Welsh were pursued across the River Usk and into the great forest of Monkswood, many dying on the way. Even so, some reached us at Harlech, to tell the tale.

The page Gwalchmai, my most trusted assistant, and the miller Iestyn between them bore on a litter the huge frame of Griffith Lloyd the bard. His daughter Sibli walked beside him, her face set like a man's, hard, to keep back the weeping; it was plain he had not long to last, for a cannonball had crushed his legs and the whole lower part of his body. When I lifted the sheet they had spread over him, I saw that the whole was nothing but pulp.

He must have been suffering agonies, for great beads of sweat stood out upon his face and head, but he spoke clear. They carried him into the hall, placing the litter before the fire, which always burned, even though it was late in the month of May. The Lady Margaret hurried to him, dropping to her knees, her eyes searching his face. 'Oh, my friend——' she said softly on a sob. And then, 'Owen...?'

'Lady,' he said. 'I know not, for he was with the others.... Tudor is dead.'

She lowered her head into her hands for a moment, and her lips moved. I knew she was saying her own prayers.

'Let me tell it, Lady,' said Griffith. 'I can tell it ... before I go. There is time....'

Though he had said it, still he did not speak. Wordlessly, Sibli brought a goblet of wine and held it to his lips. He sipped a little, and his head fell back; he was growing ever weaker. The Lady brought a cushion to set beneath his shoulders, and he spoke.

'They were four times our number, Lady, at least ... and he was brave, my namesake....' His lips curved ever so slightly in a smile.

'My Griffith ... is he——'

'No, Lady, he is not dead, but captive only.... They captured him and took his sword. Rhisiart, too, they have taken, and Master Brut....' At this came a high, loud shrieking; Alice Brut, with all the other maidens, had heard, too.

Sibli turned on her, fierce. 'Hush!' she cried. 'Hear him out!' I saw the damsel Morgan white as whey and the little Elliw beside her, their hands clasped.

'But they are prisoners only ... I saw it with my own eyes,' said the bard. 'Marched off they were, with their hands tied. Some were killed on the spot—put to the sword like common felons before the castle....' His head fell to one side; I thought he was gone. But he lifted it, with a great effort, gazing with his deep beautiful eyes into the Lady's. 'Lady ...' he whispered low, 'will you take me in your arms ... this once ... so will I die ... and happy....'

Tears stood in her eyes, Margaret, and she gathered him to her as if he were her beloved, holding his heavy head close to her bosom. And so was it for a long moment, she staring, unblinking, above his head, and all the damsels still as still where they stood.

He lifted his head a little. 'Long have I loved you, Lady ... and you did not know?'

'No,' she said gravely, but her eyes catching mine for a moment, 'no, my dearest friend ... I never knew.'

'One kiss from you I beg ...' and his lips curved again. 'Like a knight in a tale ... like Lawnslot....'

'But Lawnslot had his love,' she said.

'It is too late for that,' he said, gesturing to his smashed body. 'Only a kiss from your sweet lips, my silver lady ... my own love....'

And she bent and kissed him long upon the lips, and on that kiss he died. A scene from an old tale of heroes, and I watching, and all the others.

And the Lady wept, after, and all the damsels, and the serving folk crowded in to look upon his makeshift bier and lament loud, throwing their aprons above their heads.

And only his daughter Sibli stared, dry-eyed, her odd little face made perfect by its carven grief; like a face in marble was it that day, done by a master hand. I saw she was beautiful, and none had known.

TWELVE

In that great rout of Usk, many were killed; all Owen's bastard sons were put to the sword before the castle, and the two Irish twins that were married to Tudor's daughters, and many others. Meredith came back, sore wounded, borne in his father's arms. His left arm, Meredith's, had been broken in two places; he had swooned from the pain, but when I examined him I saw that, with care, he would recover. I set the bones, a painful business, and drugged him so that he could sleep away the horror. His wife Elliw sat by his side, staring before her. A strange little creature she was always, this Elliw. She looked up at me suddenly and whispered fiercely, that little brown wren, 'Master Nathan, I will not bear child ... I will not bear child! To hurt and die ... to kill others. I will not....'

I was full harried with the work that was before me and could not talk to her, poor child; besides, she was half-crazed with worry, I could see.

We heard that they had struck off Tudor's head, rejoicing, for they took him for his great brother and felt that now the rebellion was put down. Efa, that was Tudor's daughter, swore vengeance, and her man, Rhys Gethin, had it before the year was out. With some of his savage hill-raiders, he crept up by night to the gate of Usk castle and, taking the sentries by surprise, brought back Tudor's head, which had been displayed upon the wall there, along with six others, the enemy. The Lady Margaret insisted on honorable burial for all those poor relics, and prayers given to Jesus for the souls of those men.

Gwalchmai, my assistant, showed me a crushed hand; he had hidden it, waiting till the more sorely wounded were cared for. As I wrapped it about with linen and the green salve under, he told me, with not a little pride, how he had got it. 'The banner of The Maiden,' he said, 'the Red-handed Maiden, Sibli's banner ... I saw it trampled in the mud, the standard-bearer fallen, slain. I darted into the thick of the battle and made to snatch it up. A rearing horse brought its hoof down on my hand.... I cannot remember much—only clashings above me where I lay, and horses snorting, their reins flying loose, riderless. For a miracle, I was not trampled again. But the banner was picked up by the enemy.... I saw one look at it curiously, standing still in the thick of the fray, and then stuff it into his doublet and, with his bloody sword, run a man through.... Someone dragged me off the field, finally. I do not know who it was, for I had lost my senses.... How I escaped more hurt is God's divine mercy, indeed....'

'The more fool you, though,' I said, 'to run into a battle unarmed for a rag of cloth! And now you have lost the use of your right hand, that could have helped heal your countrymen....'

His young face fell at my reproof. 'I will learn to use my left hand. And, master, the banner meant much....'

'I know——' I said, relenting. 'Perhaps that craftsman who made it can fashion another.'

'No,' he said sadly, 'for he is dead....'

Truly, there was much work for me that whole week; I did not see until it had festered that Owen's old neck wound had opened up, for he hid it from me, deeming it a small thing in the face of all the other serious woundings. And so he lay abed with a fever; a blessing, in a way, for he did not hear his lady weep aloud, in the whole household's hearing, that he, Owen, had taken the safer course and let his son go into danger and be captured, and perhaps killed after.

'Lady,' I said, 'they will not kill him. They will hold him hostage ... it is their custom. They will use him to wring concessions from Owen. And,' I said, censuring her, though I have no right, 'Owen chose the easier task for Griffith, and long had he begged, your son, for the chance to lead. None knew those great armies lay in wait ... there at the castle. It is the fortunes of war. Calm yourself, and be true lady to your lord....'

She wept then and begged the pardon of all. 'For he is the darling of my heart, Griffith, my firstborn ... and I lost my wits for a moment.' And she looked at me with an anguished face. 'Master Nathan, truly, do you believe they will not kill him?'

'Lady, I am sure of it.' I was not, of course, far from it, but it was what she needed, and it worked. She left off weeping and said, 'How is my lord? How is Owen?'

'He is resting better now,' I said. 'The fever will break to-night.' And I put my arm around her; war permits such familiarities. 'And now you must rest—or your *nerves* will break, and then where should we be? For we depend upon you, Lady—all of us in this house.' And I looked at her, seeing for the first time how she had lost flesh; her arms that were round as a very Ceres' once were now like sticks, and her lovely face was marked by deep blue marks beneath the eyes, and two long lines replaced the dimples of her cheeks. She never had worn the wimple, that kindly fashion that hides much on women; the flesh beneath her chin showed a little sag beginning. I counted up; she was approaching forty.

We were all aging, truly, in this struggle; close to, I saw that Owen's tawny looks were gone. Only a few lights gleamed, like ghost things, in his hair and beard. He was all iron now, nearly matching the iron circlet that crowned his brow.

I myself was white, hair and beard, too; my sooty eyebrows looked strange to me against them. Owen, recovering, jested. 'Friend Nathan, once, long ago, at little Richard's crowning, I mummed that prophet of your people, Nathan, another Nathan. Full overacted was it, I see now, for my white beard reached to my waist and foam came from my mouth.... Soap it was, my secret, and I would not divulge it to the boy-king....' And he made a wry face. 'What a taste! For sure I was taken with myself and my doubtful arts, to endure such for a paltry show....'

'Sire,' I said, 'that show is famous yet, I have no doubt. Folk talked of it still, when I was there, in the court.'

'No,' he said, shaking his head. 'I knew none of your people then, Nathan ... and I made him different from other men.... Such is not so—not of any ... prophet or no.'

'Well, it was a pastime only,' I said. 'You do not make your living as a mummer....'

'Perhaps I should have, Nathan. Perhaps all this havoc could have been avoided....'

'Oh, no,' I said quickly, 'you cannot take the whole thing upon your shoulders. It is the heart of Wales that shouted out, and they could follow only you ... as once my people needed their Moses to lead them out of captivity....'

'But God talked to him, did He not?' There was a phantom twinkle in his eye. 'He does not talk to me....'

I was silent for a while. Then I said, 'Sometimes I think He has no voice, Owen ... as my people believe He has no face and forbid images of Him to be fashioned.'

'Ah, yes,' said he. 'Those were the first glimmerings of thought, truly ... in your people. Faceless, bodiless, voiceless, is He.... Some order, some force, which holds all together—that must exist, if we can find it....' Then he stopped, his eyes far away as happened now so often with this man. But he was still for a moment only. 'Nathan, go to your work. I am well and have kept you too long. We must not indulge in our sport longer ... for it is our sport, truly ... philosophy.' And he caught my arm, strong. 'What days we used to have, you and I.... What talk! ... No longer, friend....' And he turned his head, weary, on the pillow and closed his eyes; after a moment I left him.

THIRTEEN

After our long waiting, the French actually set sail. A force of 800 men-at-arms, 600 crossbowmen, and 1,200 light-armed troops set sail from the harbor of Brest on July 22. Some great warriors led them. Jean de Hangest, lord of Hugueville, led the bowmen; this man was a diplomat as well and had much knowledge of the English court. With him were Jean de Rieux, marshal of France, Renaut de Trie, admiral, Patrouillart de Trie, his kinsman and one of the most renowned knights of the world of chivalry (what would he think of our skin-clad hillmen?), and Robert de la Heuze, known as the One-Eyed. Tom Franklin, whose remaining eye could still flash wit, said, 'Ah, a Frenchy brother!'

The French fleet finally reached Milford Haven on the first day of August; we met them there. We Welsh, under Owen, numbered upwards of ten thousand.

Our first battle was at Haverford West, where we captured the town, but not the castle. The great warrior, that Patrouillart de Trie, fell there, assaulted by more than a dozen English and fighting them off successfully for more than a half hour. In the end, a stray sword thrust went through the gap between his neck armor and his helm and severed the great vein; the man who had done it grinned and took his head for trophy. All the others lay dead around him; we counted eleven Englishmen he had slain by his own hand, Patrouillart. A great warrior, truly, and songs were written of him, but only in Welsh; for one who worshiped war and lived by it, it was not much glory, poor fellow.

In a few days we had taken the town and castle of Carmarthen and of Cardigan; Owen had control now of the valley of the Teivy and the whole of southwest Wales. From there we marched eastward; we passed Caerleon, where there is an ancient Roman amphitheater. From there the French would not budge, but must spend the night, camping there. It was popularly thought to be the site of Arthur's Round Table; this, Owen said, was a French invention, a romance only. The true Arthur, Owen said, will never be known; they have so surrounded him with their own chivalric legends. 'Surely,' said Owen, 'there can have been no such figure.... Arthur was half Roman, half hill chieftain, trying in vain to preserve the Roman way in Britain, with no help from Rome ... for Rome had fallen to its own barbarians.' But nothing he said meant anything to the French; they would have their own Arthur, all done up in the trappings of knightly deeds and Christian valor. Owen says Arthur was sure to have been a follower of Mithras, for it was the accepted religion of the Roman legions, and he followed legionary tactics always. But again, I am doing my favorite thing, disputation with myself, and am not following my story.

We came victoriously through the county of Hereford and camped at Woodbury Hill, eight miles from the city of Worcester; there we settled to await the coming of Henry of Lancaster.

He had a long wait, almost a week. It was a miserable time, for our men did not get along with 'the Frenchies,' as they called them; many fights broke out among them, especially the bowmen. The Welsh used the longbow, and were contemptuous of the complicated crossbow of the French, aping the winding up of it and the slowness that ensued. 'Five men would I kill, Frenchy, while you were a-winding!' I heard one Welsh bowman say. Whereupon the Frenchman, understanding by his motions only and facial expression, cracked his tormentor over the head with the same heavy crossbow. And so it went, always, among the common soldiery; they could not communicate and would not try. We lost a considerable number in small battling among those warring allies.

Nor did their leaders approve of our leaders' operations. They scorned the hill-men and would take no advice, though they did not know the terrain. Full armor always they wore, even to their horses. Once they were unhorsed, that was the end of them, for they could not get up and were butchered by the English, who by now had learned a little from us. Also, the French, accustomed to their own rules of war, usually, when confronted by difficulties, would hand over their glove, as a sign of surrender and ransom; we lost many that way.

We had many small forays with the English; Henry himself was very ill and did not take the field, though he was present in his tent. Each week swelled the English ranks, though we slew many. For from all the shires of England came more mustered men. And each week diminished our supplies; we were far into enemy ground and could get nothing through. By the end of the month we had nothing left but a few onions, moldy, and some hard crusts of bread, with no relief in sight. There was nothing for Owen to do but retreat, outnumbered and half-starved as we were.

We marched back into the heart of Wales, where supplies were easy to obtain from every village. That September the weather was all for us again, and the word spread again that Owen was working his old magic. Henry was unable to make any headway at all in our own territory, for the rivers of Glamorgan were in raging torrents, and streams poured down the hills to swell them. Fighting was at a standstill, and many of the French deserted us, not enjoying the prospect of a Welsh winter.

As for us, we came back for a bit to Harlech, leaving commanders in all our castles to hold them against enemy action. Owen still owned control of much of Wales, though he had not been able to gain a foothold in England itself.

A letter was brought to him that winter from the French king. He read it, wrinkling his brow. 'I must switch Popes, it seems,' he said, looking at his lady-wife.

'I do not understand,' said Margaret. 'You are not under the Pope!'

'The church of Wales is,' he said.

I must explain a thing known to all, but not much thought on in this country of my adoption. There existed at this time a sort of schism in the Church rule. The Pope at Rome, hitherto unquestioned, had now a rival at Avignon. The rights and wrongs of it I have not studied; I know only that it was more political than theological. England, and Wales, too, in the churchly hierarchies, gave allegiance to Boniface IX at Rome, whereas France, Spain, and Scotland swore obedience to Benedict XIII at Avignon. So France being an ally, and Scotland a potential one, Owen must play statesman, in his own words.

What he had, in short, to do that year was to persuade the powers of the Welsh church to switch with him; in order to gain this, he had to make strong Welsh demands.

Owen summoned to him in March a large conclave of church magnates and his own Parliament to discuss this matter. After much talk, a document was dispatched to the French king, conveying the decision of this assembly to adopt the French proposal and transfer the ecclesiastical allegiance of Wales to the Pope at Avignon.

There were, however, many conditions: Owen spent much thought upon them. Pope Benedict of Avignon was to withdraw all censures which had been launched against Wales in the past; he was to grant relief from all oaths of obedience which had been sworn to the Roman pontiffs; he was to confirm all orders, titles, and dispensations granted by Rome since the outbreak of the schism. These conditions were but to be expected. Owen went further.

He declared for an independent Welsh church, as the counterpart of the independent principality. St. David's was to be restored to its ancient position as a metropolitan church, long disregarded by English interference and influence. Benedict must appoint churchmen in Wales who were Welsh-speaking; there must be no English bishopries. He was to revoke all grants of Welsh parishes to English monasteries and colleges and to restore such monies to their true Welsh counterparts. Welsh chapels would be free of Episcopal control. He was to grant plenary remission from all sin to those who fought on the Welsh side and to bless the Welsh struggle as a holy war. (At this, Owen privately held his nose but remarked that it must be in there, for the churchmen's sake. 'There is no such thing as a holy war,' he said. 'The terms are contradictory.' He shrugged his shoulders, though; he had learned by now to imitate me!)

Then Owen came to the part that he himself had fought for. Wales was to have two universities, or *studia generalia*, one in the north and one in the south of Wales, completely independent of England.

Though all these conditions were granted, still matters had come to a standstill. This is hindsight vision, but I believe that it was at this point that Owen's fortunes and the fortunes of Wales began to decline. One may imagine that, being a Jew, I put it down to Papal interference. This is not true. Many outside matters were brought to bear; it was fortune alone which turned the tide. Bad fortune. Which takes a myriad forms and, at the last, merges into one.

In the season of Passover, which is the Christian Easter and the pagan spring solstice, those few French troops which had wintered in Wales quit the country. There are small gains to be had by foreigners in a land ravaged from end to end by war. 'No pickings,' as Tom Franklin put it, spitting in disgust. 'That for the Frenchies!'

More French ships were dispatched, but most of them were captured by the English, and only one came ashore in Wales. This was the one, unfortunately, which had no arms or armor aboard, and few soldiers; it was the small private vessel, richly painted and adorned, which bore gifts from the famous collector, the Duc de Berry. There were some beautiful paintings and statues, missals, and fine jewels; there was also a menagerie of all manner of strange animals, specimens from all over the world, collected with care. Among them, for the Lady Margaret, was a cage of singing birds no bigger than her finger, and the cage of gold, a pure white bratchet-hound wearing a collar of diamonds, and a bright bird that spoke Latin. For Owen, there was a creature, manlike, called a gorilla, from the distant African lands. It could walk upright, though its long arms swung almost to the ground. Owen laughed and snapped his fingers. 'He is the very image of Davy Gam!' he said. This was cruel, though funny, and I could not help but smile. This Davy Gam had been an adherent of that Howell, cousin-enemy of Owen's and slain by him at the beginning of the war. This Davy, too, was a staunch Lancaster. Though he was of a good and noble Welsh family, the lords of Brecon, yet did he resemble the wildest and most primitive of the hill-men. At least in looks; they say his wits were razor-sharp, though I never came to know him. He had been captured, in a way, by Sibli, strange as it may seem.

She was walking at night in the woods' edge at Harlech; it was a thing forbidden to the damsels, for there was always menace to their virtue from the stray soldiery camped nearby. But often and often I had heard her say that inspiration came to her in the dark of the moon and when none was about, and so she risked the Lady's displeasure and censure. She caught a glimpse of Owen's white robe as it gleamed among the bushes and lagged a little, hoping not to be discovered. Suddenly, beside her, she saw a flash of something bright and stood still as a wood animal, listening. A twig cracked softly, and she heard an indrawn breath; someone was near, very near. Out of the corner of her eye she half-saw it, a crouching figure armed with a knife; the moon was just rising. Without a thought, she chopped downward with the sharp edge of the back of her hand, and the knife dropped; at the same time she cried out to Owen ahead. After he said she shrieked loud enough to wake the dead, though she herself felt it was no more than a hoarse whisper. Owen turned and, running quickly, caught the fellow and pinioned his arms. 'Run! Fetch someone, quick——' he shouted. 'This fish is squirming!' She swiftly roused two guards; when they arrived on the scene, Owen was sitting on the man's head, pressing the face down into the dirt and bracken, and had bent the legs back under his own; he was like a trussed pig. And this was Davy Gam, bent on assassination. He was kept in a dungeon, chained, and behind bars; Owen was growing harder with the hard years. It seemed, though, that this Gam was a great favorite of Lancaster, for he sent word that ransom would be forthcoming from his own pocket! The Brecon people were connected, in some dim fashion, with Henry's first wife, long dead, Mary de Bohun; the castle there had been one of her inheritance holdings, so perhaps that was it. I had not dreamed there had been anything of sentiment or feeling in the Molewarp!

That year saw much sadness; Iorweth Sulien, Owen's first boyhood tutor, died. It was not in war or of a sickness, either, though he was growing old. It happened this way. He, being curious as a cat and avid for all knowledge, had got it into his head that this manlike parody, that great ape, the gorilla sent from the Duc de Berry, might have been, or its ancestors, a forerunner of man himself, and that the two species developed differently because of conditions under which each lived. He spent much time with this animal, declaring that its intelligence was superior to all other animals, and trying vainly to teach it speech. One could see it trying, hard, its short jutting brow wrinkled in the effort, but the sounds which came out were clicks and whistles. 'Something is missing here,' said Iorweth, puzzled, and pointing to its throat. 'Come, Nathan, take a look'—and he pried open the great beast's jaws. 'Something is amiss there ... mayhap you can cut it away.... It may be just a tendon holding the tongue, or a cord closed in the throat....' I looked, for I was interested, but I could not think to operate on the creature, for I feared it. I could see nothing anyway, for the gorilla thought the whole thing a game and would not keep its mouth open long enough.

It became a familiar sight, the small, shrunken old man and the manlike beast covered with hair walking hand in hand like brothers. The gorilla would kiss him, too, Iorweth, smacking his lips; hug him it would, too, hard to break his ribs. And in the end that is what happened. Iorweth was found dead, his chest crushed, on the path that led down to the sea, where they had been used to walk. Beside him sat the gorilla, stroking him and slapping at his face to wake him. I never saw a more mournful sight than the beast's face, for the features of it were all exaggeration; it resembled those old masks that the pagans made for tragic dancing; the Druids used them and Owen had dug many up from the old earth hereabouts.

When the priests came to take the body, with the women, to lay it out decently for burial, the gorilla would not loose it and defied all who came near, clutching it in a kind of angry terror. None could approach. But Sibli remembered that the poor creature loved marchpane and fetched a bit from our almost vanished store of sweets, holding it out to him at arm's length and moving slowly backward, so that it loosed the body, its mouth watering, and came where she stood, snatching it from her hand and cramming it into its great jaws. I shall never forget the sight. The beast, sad-eyed, pushing the last of the marchpane down with both hairy hands, and the jaws working. Then it stood very still, staring at all as though we had done the deed, a kind of rage mingled with reproach showing on it, or so I fancied; swiftly it turned and ran down the seaward path to fling its squat body into the sea. Owen went in after it and some others, too, who could swim, but they found no trace. It had come to us from the sea, and there it had returned. Poor beast. I think my heart broke for it, and Owen's, too, for we saw at last what Iorweth, wiser, had seen at once. Poor Man!

Owen's hopes were still high for a final victory, but the heart was out of most of the rest of us. The Lady Margaret languished for her eldest son, dead or captive, and none knew for certain, and her other son, Meredith, maimed and broken, and his young wife, almost witless. All four of Owen's bastard sons were gone too; she had had much fondness for them. Her older daughters were far away and no word came from them; Margaret in the south was thought to be dead and her husband with her, and Janet had fled Dolgelly, and the manor there was left deserted. Catherine was busy with her children, one each years, so fast that even I, who attended the births, could not keep track of them. Only Morgan and Sibli were left to the Lady for comfort, and Morgan dreamed still of her English princeling, while Sibli's harp was all her world. Tragedy surrounded us all; the death of Rhys Gethin the Savage tore at our hearts, wild man that he was.

He had been out on foray; never could he sleep within walls, and this was a small raid, such that he did without thinking, a part of his life. Efa, his wife, was at the castle, for she was with child, and his cave-lairs were not healthy for her. One dark night came a hammering at the gates, and some of his hill-men brought his body in on a shield. He was red with blood all over; the Lady wiped it away to see his face. None could tell what had killed him, so covered with wounds he was. His sword was still clutched in his right hand and dragged upon the floor; it, too, was covered in blood, right up to the hilt, so we knew he had given as good as he had got. Efa, on a high wail, tore at the stiffened fingers and loosed the sword; before any could stop her, she had held it before her and fallen upon it; it went through her chest and out the other side, and she never uttered another cry. It must have killed her instantly. The child within her was not more than five months, too young to save; three deaths there were that night, and the running blood like a flooding stream upon the flags of the castle floor.

The French had now all left us; a letter came from the king, an apology, in a sort, for the small assistance that had been given. The words were careful; the expedition would have been larger, so it ran, had there been reason to look for a cordial welcome in England from the late King Richard's friends! 'He means,' said Owen bitterly, 'that he has cooled off. He has seen I could not throw open the door to England itself.... I had hoped for more valor in a just cause! But chivalry is a word only.... I knew it, but I had forgot....'

Another serious blow to the Welsh struggle was the thing that happened in Scotland. The heir, young James, had been sent by his father, King Robert of Scotland, to be educated in France; on his way, he was captured by the English. His father the king died within the month; the English had the good fortune of holding the new King James as hostage for Scottish good behavior. The regency which governed the realm of Scotland during James' long capitivity could, of course, do nothing to endanger his person. Which meant, in effect, that no help, or even sympathy, could be expected from that quarter.

Many of the Welsh turned traitor, too, with the changes of fortune. Dozens of nobles submitted to the English and were pardoned for their part in the revolt. One cannot blame the peasantry, who deserted in the hundreds; they were not soldiers, but poor farmers, and could not forever let their fields go untended. In the end, Owen was left with the two great castles of Aberystwyth and our own Harlech, and not much more.

The English king, Henry, was very sick; some say he had leprosy and wore full armor always to cover its ravages. I do not privately believe this; the disease does not fit with the descriptions of his person that I have heard. On his face were running sores and half-healed scabs, none of the white marks or eaten-away flesh of the leper. Besides, he is reported to suffer from dread pains within; this speaks more to me of the disease that the ancients called the crab, that pinches and gnaws at the vital organs. His symptoms were fascinating; I should have liked to have had the opportunity to examine the man and make my own diagnosis. Even in the midst of war and tragedy, we are what we are.

The full burden of the Wales campaign was now given to his son, Prince Henry. Owen swore a great oath when he heard. 'For the boy is a soldier-born, and hag-ridden with ambition. Much of the arts of war, too, has he learned, this sprig of Lancaster. He will fight us to the death and beyond ... for the sport of it—and to rule after. For his father is sick and dying, and the throne is there.... He will want to make it strong by victory after victory. Seeing that it was not come by honestly, he has no choice. A canny lad. But a war lover ... it will kill him young—in the end.' He paused, smiling a little. 'I grow old and am getting the Welsh failing ... I fancy I have the Sight. ... Forget my words, my Nathan. We must fight on, no matter. There is no choice left now.'

The prince appeared in person with a strong force to besiege the castle of Aberystwyth; siege engines, very new, were directed against the fortress and its fall looked to be imminent. But in the Lancaster camp, too, there were traitors, and many deserted the prince. He decided he must make an 'honorable retreat,' as he called it, and began negotiations with Rhys Dhu, Elliw's father, who held the castle. A truce was reached between them; for six weeks there would be a halt in battle on both sides; after, Owen was to be given one week to raise the siege. If he did not succeed, the castle would be turned over to the prince, and in return, Rhys Dhu and all his followers would receive a full pardon. Again Owen swore.

Assembling a large host (there were still some loyal Welsh to be mustered), Owen appeared before the walls of Aberystwyth and threatened death to all traitors. 'And that means you, Rhys the Black!' I was there and I heard it. No lives were lost; we were admitted straightaway, and the prince forced to abandon all hope of capturing the castle.

It was not for long, though; he returned with a huge force, mustered from all the shires of England, and with many engines of war and cannon. Aberystwyth fell, though most of us escaped to the woods and the hills. Owen carried me, for we had no mounts, and I slowed us all by my lameness. This was the second time the House of Owen had brought me safe through danger. Long ago, when my knee was first shattered, in the English Peasants' Revolt, Owen's lady, then the maiden Margaret, refused to abandon me and, with her maid, Branwen, dragged me to safety. And here I was again, slung over the great Owen's shoulder like a sack of meal, and that man of iron striding through the forest and climbing up mountains like a lion of the hills, that is aging, but has power still. And the song of Sibli coming to us faint from far ahead.

BOOK VI

THE DARK BLUE HILLS

Told by Sibli, the bard's daughter, called by

the people the Small Bird

ONE

I knew from the first, I think, that I was different from other maidens; not because of my talent for music and the singing words that go with it, but in all ways. All the damsels of Owen's house, where I was reared, were pretty as flowers, fair and fresh and softly curving, even when they were no more than babies; I was thin as a weed and dark as a Moor, and of no stature to speak of. I did not mind not being beautiful, for there was enough beauty within me to say upon the harp; but they were forever laughing, laughing at nothing, and their bright eyes dancing, even Elliw, the shyest of them all. I thought them silly.

The boys were better; I could climb higher than any of them, to the top of the tallest tree, and shoot an arrow straighter, and catch a ball when it was thrown; they respected me for this and let me share their play; they too despised the giggling girls.

Until the time I broke a finger of my right hand. We had been throwing a hard ball made of cured leather, like a stone it was, and I not looking for once, and it caught my hand and bent the finger backward; I heard the bone snap, and the pain made everything swim around me. After that, my father forbade me any rough play, though Master Nathan set the bone with skill and it grew back as good as ever. My father is the greatest bard of Wales, perhaps of the world; he would not suffer me to injure my harp-hands, for I had inherited the feel of music from him, and he had no sons.

I did not love my father; to me he was teacher only. I think he did not love me either; my sister Megolin he sometimes used to fondle and place upon his lap, for she was sweet-faced and golden-fair, like the Lady Margaret, to whom his heart was given forever. It was hard for me to like that Lady, kind and good as she was always; I blamed her for stealing my father's love, and she all unknowing and uncaring.

But this was when I was very young; I know now that no blame attaches to any for such things. For, as he loved, my father—so I did also. I loved Owen, and no other. And my life was sad and beautiful and blazing with it, till the end.

All of us, the maidens of that house, were petted and spoiled and given much. Taught we were, too, by masters, as girls are not, they tell me, in other places. Even I, the ugliest, had fair new gowns and ribbons for my hair and slippers of leather that were made to fit my very feet. We grew up learned in Latin and logic, and accomplished at the arts of sewing and embroidery, and our manners were good, modeled on courtly ways, for Owen and his lady had spent years at the English court. Music we learned, too, and all the bardic songs, and how to play upon the lute and the small harp of the Cymry.

Once, when I was nearly grown, I remember a morning, sunny and warm. We damsels were all with the Lady in her solar, sewing at a great wall-hanging; I was assigned to the bottom border, for that I was so small and did not have to bend low. It was before any wars had started, and through the great window, if we looked up, we could see green grass and trees and, in the distance, the far peak of Snowdon, shrouded in blue mist. There were no sounds of drilling or of arrow-practice; only humming of bees, close, at the flowers, and, faint and far, the shouts of the boys as they swam in the moat, and soft splashings. I longed to be with them, but we were too old for swimming and water-play, and must play at ladies instead.

Owen came in, carrying the leather gloves he wore for riding, and kissed his lady so hard that she blushed, and he laughing with it. They sat together on a settle by the window, talking low, in whispers, his arm around her. We were quiet as field mice at our work, trying to hear their words; I think that all of us, not just me, were in love, each in her own way, with Owen, even his daughters. For he was golden and godlike, and gay, too, in those years.

He rose and, looking round at us and smiling small, said, 'Lady sweet, you have a casket of jewels here, your damsels. So fair they are and gleaming. . . .' And he looked at each in turn, and she flushing. 'Here are the twins—like dark glowing rubies . . . and Catherine and Efa are yellow diamonds . . . Morgan a topaz, and Elliw is an amethyst....' I have forgot the rest, but he left none out, even me, stooping beside me so that I hung my head in confusion. He put his finger under my chin and lifted it. 'You are the rarest, child,' he said. 'Have you ever seen an opal?' I shook my head.

Morgan cried, 'I have, Father!' Morgan was ever bold and fearless, like to Owen himself. 'Yes, I see ...' she said, her tawny head to one side, examining me. 'Darkly pearl on the outside, and when you turn it, fire flashes from somewhere at its heart....'

'Yes,' he said, looking deep at me and smoothing back a strand of hair. 'Yes ... fire under....'

I lived on that for long, remembering it again in the dark, in my bed.

In the years that led up to the war, I found another to worship from even farther; from death and beyond even. For the tales of Richard, that gentle and art-loving king, fascinated me. And Owen, with his gift of mimicry and the telling arts, made the man stand alive before me. I saw him as Galahad, in the old tales, as Owen was Arthur come again. The men and boys I saw close to meant nothing; they were just rough creatures, and, mostly, to my mind, without heart, and worshiping war and battles. Besides, I knew they did not find me fair; in my heart I knew that Richard would have. When he was murdered, most foully, as I do believe, by Red Bolingbroke, my heart near broke, for never would I meet him face-to-face. I made a song for him, a lament it was, and the best I ever have writ. Folk sang it for many years in these parts, the 'Song for Sweet Richard.'

I grew to love Morgan well, for she too languished, in a sort, for one she could not have. She loved—and told me of it and no other—that Red Bolingbroke's son, called Harry, that she had known at Richard's court. She is base-born, like me, though she is Owen's daughter, and so they could never come together, for now was his father king—the Molewarp I called him, and it stuck!

In the first years of the war, many were wounded; all our household were needed to help in whatever way they could. Because my fingers were trained to the harp-strings they were deft and quick, and my stomach was strong; the sight of blood did not sicken me. Master Nathan said I was his best nurse, near as good as Gwalchmai; I truly think I might have made a doctor, if a woman could be such a thing. There are no women who are bards either; yet am I a bard and thought so by all. I lost much of my shyness, and did not spend hours brooding over my differences, for those differences now were needed.

We all had hose and page's gear, we girls, for riding out; the Lady Margaret thought it more seemly so. Gwalchmai gave me an old helm and a leather cuirass that he had outgrown. My long hair would not fit comfortably under; I stole scissors and cut it to my nape. I could not care how I looked; indeed, with my shape that is no shape truly I looked like a boy. On one of the first forays, I managed to go along, none seeing till we were well away. And I carried my harp, hidden in a bag that hung from my saddle. I was much needed, as it turned out, for I could tend the wounded, and after, when they were resting comfortably, sing and play to them softly in the long forest night. Master Nathan and my father, too, pretended to be very angry, but when Owen found out, he said merely, looking hard at me, that I might stay. 'But mind you ride well in the rear,' he said, 'with the baggage and supplies, and put yourself in no danger—or Marred will have my head....' He always called her that, his lady; it was the Welshing of her name and prettier to the ear.

After, I rode always to battle, minding what he had said. In the great victory of Bryn Glas, my song, in the midst of the battle, brought many of the English-mustered Welsh over to our side. Owen said I turned the tide for Wales, and kissed me on the lips. It was the first time I had felt a man's mouth on mine; I thought that I would melt.

When we came back to the castle at Harlech, the word of my part in the battle had spread, and I was a kind of hero, as much as a girl can be. One made a banner for me, and I was called the Red-Hand Maid. Though most of the folk called me still the Small Bird. I was as near happy as I had ever been, though it were shame to say it, since it all had been brought about by war!

Peak after peak of victory was reached, and I with my part in it always; at home the other girls crowded round me and asked me for my own tales; I think there was not one that did not envy me. For they were cooped up dreadfully within doors, with little to do but tear strips of cloth for bandages, and pray, if they felt it. Most of them were Lollards true, for love of Lady Margaret, and swayed, too, by Master Walter Brut, whose goodness shone in his countenance, like the Jesus that he preached. I could not feel to worship any god, for I had seen too much ugliness and pain. Surely no god would allow it! Or, if he did, he was a bad god. Or so I thought, to put it simply. Morgan agreed, but she had many learned arguments to support her ideas, for she read much. I was too busy for reading.

And then, though I do not know the rights of it or the reason why, setback after setback occurred, and often we lost battles or had to retreat. Owen spent much time in council with his Parliament, trying by policy to win right for Wales. When we were at the castle, I trembled inside whenever he entered the solar or the great Hall, though in the field I was easy with him.

In the great final retreat from Aberystwyth, all was backward; being in the rear, I led; I had no banner anymore, for it had been lost long before, captured by the foe. But my harp I had and played it, to give us a little heart.

We had to sleep wherever we could find shelter; more and more left us; soon we were a remnant. Many had been captured or killed; all Owen's sons except for Meredith, who was badly wounded, and many of our captains, including Rhys Gethin the Savage, who had been our greatest warrior. I had always hated Efa, his wife; jealousy, perhaps, of her beauty, or because she had cruelly teased me when we were very young. Besides, I thought her always not quite right in the head, talking of witches and Derfel and hanging without shame about all the men, even the commonest soldiers. But when he died, she killed herself, and pity and terror ran through me and shame. What had we come to, to work such horror upon a young woman, and she with a child in her belly?

Often and often I thought about this; I knew that others did too. Especially Owen, for he felt the blame of it all, being the leader of the rebellion.

My father, the great Griffith Lloyd, died also; happy at the end he was for a little, for he breathed his last in Lady Margaret's arms; it was the place he had ever wanted to be.

The years of our outcast were long, so long, but now they seem to have passed in a moment, as I look back. We never lacked for food, for all the folk brought us offerings, we who still held out in the hills. Not so the house-people left at Harlech; they were under siege by Prince Harry. For eight months he stood before the thick stone walls with his vast army, fed and comfortable, while within our dear ones starved, a slow death and dreadful. We had spies still, in the army of Lancaster, and we heard all. The first to go was Edmund Mortimer, who had the command. It was the plague-death he died of, and many caught it; the others were too weak to bury the bodies, and the infection spread. For Master Nathan said that that is the way it happens; the rotting flesh lets off an infection into the very air. In the end, the few who were left surrendered; Meredith, maimed, was the only man among them, and they could not hold out. They were brought to England half-dead, Morgan, Catherine and her little son, the last left, and Elliw, Meredith, Alice Brut, and the twins, Gwynneth and Gwenllian and their small sons. The story of Lady Margaret was the saddest of all; none dared tell Owen, only that she had perished. But she must have lost her wits, for, starving, she killed some rats and made a sort of stew, railing at the others that they would not eat it; she died horribly, as poisoned people do.

All the deaths were a great grief, I know, and to me also. But somehow, in a sort, I felt worse about a lesser thing. Morgan had had a horse that Prince Harry had given her; long had she cherished this beast, a noble creature, Arab-bred, called Mercury for his swiftness and beauty. When the folk within the walls were starving, she gave him up to be killed and eaten. Mayhap he saved a few lives, he that was born to ride free, his mane flying, or to carry a great warrior, or lead a parade.

Our spies told us later that most of the prisoners taken were kept in the Tower; there was no word of Morgan, though, for she had been imprisoned in some other place. I prayed, though I had no one to pray to, that she lived still.

Years went by, and our small band dwindled with those years. Some left us to go back to their untended homes or to find if their families still awaited them; some were picked off by a stray arrow in our little futile raids.

We had for a while moved about the valleys, staying each night in a different place: a cotter's hut, a stable, a ruined monastery. Once a noble lady took us in, a lady without menfolk, and only one attendant; I have forgot her name and her rank. She was another one like Efa, but older and not beautiful anymore; when Owen did not come to her bed, she flew at me next morning and drove me out, thinking I was her supplanter! The others did not stay either of course; by now we few were very close, and none could part us. Though there was food of the finest and horses, and all manner of things in the lady's castle, not one of our band abandoned me for the comforts that she offered.

After a while—I cannot now remember how long—the searching parties of English were so numerous that we feared to come to any house or town, and slept in caves, cold and dank, and smelling of old mold.

Owen sat thinking, one night, in one of these caves, before the tiny fire that barely warmed our bones. 'Nathan,' he said, 'remember the place I told you of—long ago ... the House of the Snake? There is a great cave there, dry and comfortable, used long ago by the ancient peoples....'

So we came, by slow stages and at night, to the foot of the conical hill upon which stood the ruined fortress of Dinas Brân; there was now reported a very high price on Owen's head. He thought that truly none of his countrymen would give him up for gold, but Master Nathan said remember Jesus and that there was always a Judas. 'Old friend,' said Owen, laughing in almost his old way, 'I am not a Jesus, nor does any think it ... but mayhap you are right.... Who knows what unhappiness made Judas? .... And my people are unhappy ... much of it brought on by me. I have brought all to ruin....'

It was a mood that came upon him often in his latter years; it seemed he took all the burdens and woes of poor Wales upon his shoulders, and none could say him nay.

He had described to us this House of the Snake, an old temple that had stood at the foot of Dinas Brân, with a cave behind. When we came to the place, we could find no trace of it, no foundations even. It was first light, Dinas Brân was touched with gold atop its hill, looking like a place within a dream. Later we saw it grim and forbidding, with its jagged rooftops and fallen walls.

Owen said, musing, 'It was just here....' And he walked about the trampled earth, looking for a sign. I saw it first; a small stone image, toppled onto its side, its pedestal smashed, and half-hidden in the long grass. 'This is it ... this is the site!' exclaimed Owen. 'The image of Epona ... they could not carry it away, or smash it either, seemingly....'

And Gwalchmai nodded, looking grim. 'They have utterly destroyed the temple ... the Lancaster men....'

'Do you remember it then?' asked Owen.

'My mother ... she used to come here ... in secret.' And his face held shame. I knew why, for I had heard tales of the place from my father. It was a nasty cult of woman-worship, a throwback from long-ago pagan times, and those who came here dabbled in blood and worse.

'But where is the cave opening?' said Owen, searching.

'Perhaps,' said Nathan, 'they have filled it in with earth....'

Owen paced off distances from the fallen image. 'It must be here ... just here, as I remember.' And he looked close at the hillside. 'Yes!' he cried, excited. 'See—where the fine new grass grows ... all along this part.'

And true it was that it was almost discernible, almost a doorshape, once one knew what to look for. Owen plunged his lance into the hill face. When he brought it out, a few clods of earth fell. 'It is there!' he cried. 'I can feel the emptiness beyond. Let us dig!'

We could make no headway with what we had at hand, sword, dagger, or lance, though we dislodged more bits of earth, exposing raw yellow soil.

'I will go up to the castle,' said Gwalchmai. 'Somewhere there must be something lying about—a broken shovel, or a fallen beam to batter with....'

'I, too,' said Iestyn, the aged miller that walked crookedly.

They, with Nathan, Owen and myself, were all of us that were left.

They found some old picks with broken handles and a great curving shield that would scoop away the earth as it was dislodged; with all of us working at it, it still took most of two hours before we uncovered the cave-opening. Inside looked to be vast, we could see from the light that now poured full from the sun. 'Come in,' said Owen. 'Follow me, for I remember it well, and the floor is level.'

We went in a few paces; I saw that all the walls that were discernible were covered with crude paintings, though I could not make them out in the half-light.

'We must light rushes,' said Owen, 'and get a fire going, too. Though the air is sweet here, and not moldy or damp ... strange....'

After we had done this, I almost fainted in horror, for there were great barbarous pictures of old fierce gods, or goddesses, rather, in colors most garish still. 'When was it done, do you think?' I whispered, for I went in awe.

'Oh, it is older than time remembered,' said Owen airily. 'Who can tell? The colors look fresh because they have never been exposed ... but it is a very ancient culture....'

Master Nathan, who loves all manner of curious old things, was peering close, though Gwalchmai sat cowering in a corner; perhaps he felt guilt that his mother had worshiped these horrid images. I roused him from his fear or lethargy or whatever it was, and the two of us set about making a meal over the fire we had built.

In the end, we explored the passages of that cave, finding that it went clear through the mountain and led to another opening, well hidden by a ledge of rock. 'That is why the air is fresh,' said Owen. 'If we cover over the one by which we entered, that the enemy knows of, we will be safe here—safe forever, maybe....' He was smiling like a boy, his iron-gray locks no longer aging him, and the little roundness that had lain on his shoulders this long while gone; he was much excited by this place.

We settled in there, the cave becoming our home. It was not so bad, dry and warm and safe; during the day we hunted game, and cooked it over the fire at nightfall. All summer we stayed there.

We found a great painted chest there, too, with odd things all mixed together in it; robes made of some scarlet stuff, red dyes, and gold beads and rings. An ivory comb, too, we found; Owen passed it through my hair, and smiling. 'There is a mirror, too, little Sibli. We shall make you beautiful.'

'There do you ask the impossible,' I said, smiling too.

'Not so,' said Owen, with a strange look. 'It is not so. Look into it.' And he held out the mirror. In it I saw a face I did not know, all eyes and with a pointed chin, catlike. The sun had made me darker still, but with a reddish color that was not unsightly. My hair had grown too and reached well below my shoulders. 'Come, look at her well, Nathan. Is she not a lady out of old Egypt?'

Nathan nodded and smiled. 'And a woman, too, now, Sibli....'

Owen rummaged in the chest, pulling out a skirt, all flounced and sewn with beads of glass, and a little jacket that looked to be made for a child. 'Put them on,' said Owen. 'And the bangles, too ... I would see a woman before me again....'

I went aside into a dark corner and took off my boy's gear, changing it for the strange pagan clothes and tying a long cloth, striped silk in yellow and red, about my head to hide, partly, my rough untended hair. When I came forward again into the firelight, I heard Gwalchmai gasp. 'Why, you are beautiful ... and none ever knew!'

'I knew,' said Owen softly, taking my hand and drawing me down to sit beside him. He held the mirror again; what I saw delighted me, and I smiled; I saw that my teeth were white and small.

The little top did not quite meet in the middle, for I had grown larger; I held it together with my hand.

Owen laughed. 'It was not meant to close,' he said, 'a wanton fashion, but pleasant. Here is a brooch.' And he took his own from the shoulder of his cloak and fastened it; his fingers trembled against my bare skin, and within me all turned to water.

TWO

Little bands of the hill-men came to us there, in the great painted cave; how they knew of it I could not guess, but they came by the secret entrance in the rock; the place became Owen's headquarters, in a sort. For they fought on still, those men from the hills, harrying the English border settlements, and picking off a few now and then. Horrid it was for sure, for always they brought some grisly trophy for show, a severed hand, or finger, or worse; Owen had forbade them to take heads. They were savage and barbarous, but they were all that was left of battling Wales. I think that Owen hoped still for some reverse of fortune, a word from the French, or that James of Scotland might make his escape and bring his country's might with us. But, as Master Nathan explained to me privately, that would be in the nature of a miracle, and who believes in them nowadays?

I was not unhappy; I still had my harp and made many songs, more than I had had time for before. I knew, too, that Gwalchmai admired me, in my new self that the odd clothes had brought to light. He that I had thought of as just another girl! He had been gentle as a maiden in many ways before; now was he hardened by privation, and sinewy as a mountain animal, and grown to a man, too. We were both of us above twenty by now and showing our natures, male and female; it was about time! So it happened that, when he was ready for it, I was the only woman about. Alas for him. For he was not the only man. Where Owen was, there was no other ... for me. Never mind that he was near as old as my father would have been. Or that he was gray and lined deep. The lines were beautiful, deep god-strokes in his cheeks. In the end, of course, he knew my love, if he had not always. He knew that I shook within me when he came near. And that all my little songs were made for him.

I had all manner of fineries now; we had sneaked up to the old castle and brought down all sorts of necessaries that had been forgot by the conquerors. Pots and pans, goblets, even a dish or two. And in the Ladies' Tower, roofless now, gowns of a century or more ago, still beautiful and shimmering; they were made in the old fashion, that clung to the body and trailed upon the floor behind; I could not have worn them all in a six-month.

Soaps we found too, lavender-scented, so that we all laughed like children at our new sweet-smelling selves; pomades for the hair and paints for the lips and cheeks. Owen showed me how to use them; he had many skills that other men would scorn. But he was a master, and I a great lady of marvelous beauty when he was done. 'How did you think then that these fair creatures did it?' he asked me, smiling broad. 'There are many secrets and they are not witchcraft either....'

'But the Lady Margaret——' I began, and could have bit my tongue out after.

He was silent for a little, and his face in sad brooding. Then he said slowly, 'No ... she did not need them, very fair she was ... Marred. Yet did she redden her lips a little and her cheeks, too, as did all the others. It is a fashion only.... Once, in bar-barous times, it was the men who painted—as it is the male bird that has the finest plumage. Did you know that the early Saxons painted themselves blue?' And so it passed, a touchy moment.

There came a day when Gwalchmai, who followed me al-ways with his eyes, asked Owen for my hand—as though he stood in place of father to me! When Owen asked me if I would have him and if I wished it so, I cried out, without thinking, 'Oh, no!' And then I put my hand before my mouth, fearing that Gwalchmai had heard. 'I mean'—and I was all confusion—'how could it be, for there is none to marry us at all, at all....'

'Well,' said Owen, 'that is true, but laws of church and state do not pertain in the wilderness ... and man will call to maid, as ever since time began....' And he looked at me, hard.

I hung my head. 'I do not love him,' I whispered, very low. 'I do not love him....'

He tipped my chin up, as he had done once long ago, when I was a young, half-grown maid. He remembered, too, for he said, 'I likened you once to an opal.... Is there then no fire under ... is the fire for your harp only?'

'There is,' I whispered. 'I—I would come to you, Owen. I would come to your bed ... and happy....'

'And I would have you, little Sibli—and for these many months have I waited for a sign.'

My heart was pounding in me, so hard I thought the others could not help but hear, and that my whole body must be shaking with it. 'I have not slept at night,' I said, 'waiting....'

'Nor I....' We had slept, the five of us, far apart, my pallet nearest to the fire, Gwalchmai guarding the one entrance, and Iestyn the other, and Nathan and Owen in the farther corners.

'The night is still mild,' said Owen, 'and we have fur cloaks. Will you come outside with me?'

And so did I give up my maidenhood, my *maidenhead*, as it was writ in the old songs, under the stars that flamed above and the moon that blazed, naked upon a covering of warm animal fur that smelled of it, and us, and the heavy scent of grasses in their last yellow dying, for the autumn was coming on.

Our bodies were hard, both, against each other, hard from our hard life, but yielding too, and sweet, so sweet—and wild, unlike anything I had heard or imagined. Women and girls pretend it is not pleasant and a duty only; they are liars. There is nothing to match it except the harp song, and that only sometimes, when it truly speaks to the soul. This thing, this marriage, is for all; I had thought, in my ignorance, that the muse spoke only to those like me.

'You are a little pagan,' he whispered to me when I would not let him go from me but held him close within, fierce. 'The idea is to rest ... and do it all again.' In the moonlight I saw the flash of his teeth above my face. 'Even though I am old ... yet can I manage....'

He was not old, or only as a god is old, and knowing much. After, near to dawning, he said, 'Only once have I bedded beneath the moon ... and that long years ago—my first girl....'

'I want to be your last,' I whispered.

'You shall be—never doubt it, little one,' he said and laughing. 'I promise you....'

'Have there been many?' I asked, jealous on a sudden.

'Not as many as the tales would have it,' he said. 'But

enough that I have forgot some of their names....' It was all that he would say, but pulled my hair, playful, and bit my shoulder, sharp and sweet. I did not press him; I knew myself the most fortunate of women.

When we came back into the painted cave, our home, Iestyn was building up the fire and Nathan stirring porridge in a pot. Their movements were elaborately casual, and they were careful not to look at us. Behind them, Owen lifted me in his arms, as one might a child, for I am little; he held me close and said, 'We are handfast, from this day ... this lady and I. I would have you know it....'

Later, after we had breakfasted, Iestyn left us, coming back in the afternoon. 'Gwalchmai is gone from his place. His bow and his lance are there, where he sleeps. I searched the woods, but found no trace....'

He never came back, Gwalchmai. Pride had driven him away, or love, perhaps. I could not blame myself, for I could do no other. Sad it was to break a young man's heart, in its first giving. Yet was I glad and always, of my love.

THREE

The winter was long and hard, but we weathered it, like bears that hibernate. Iestyn and Nathan studied the painted walls and disputed what the images meant, telling each his own lore, race-memories, and much the same, in the end, as Owen said. 'For all men have their beginnings in some like way,' he said. 'All men have looked at the sky, seen storms, watched the moon move and the tides run ... and all have wondered, and worshiped, and questioned ... much as we do still. Not much have we learned in the millions upon millions of years that have gone by. And they are still there, outside these painted walls we cower in, the same stars, the same blue hills. And will be, too, when we have gone, all....'

Though we lay together each night, Owen and I, yet I bore no child, nor showed any sign of it. Perhaps my soldiering life had broken something within me ... or perhaps he was past it, Owen. Though he was not very old, really, in his middle fifties only. They say old Iolo Goch, the dead bard, had fathered many, and in his eighties. But perhaps that is just a tale, like so many others.

One can become accustomed to most anything; the low fire-light flickerings on the ceiling above made the bloody war-goddess seem to move and writhe, and at first I hid my head. But after, I watched it, wakeful beside my lord, picking out patterns of leaves and flowers in the dim-seen painted figures. So does the mind, in its mysterious workings, protect itself from its own dreads.

In the first spring thaw, we left the cave, glorying in the outside air, though it was still damp, and the hills ran rivulets from the melting snow of the peaks. It grew warmer, and the stream from the mountain made a little pool, protected from the wind by rock falls, centuries old. We swam there, Owen and I, happy to feel the water on our bodies, that had gone unwashed all winter, except for the bits that we could manage from the snow that we had melted, scarce enough to go around and precious, for we had to use it for drinking also.

Owen was like a young man still, white beneath his neck and above his weathered hands. He had been spare always, though very tall; if one did not look at his face, one might have thought him Apollo, with the head of a Jove. I saw myself too in the water's mirror when I stood very still; no longer was I like a boy, but curving in all the right places. Love had worked this magic, and happiness, for we ate little.

I caught a heaviness in my chest, though, after, and a raging fever, and lay long abed; gravely ill I was, though I recovered. I gave that infection to all, to my sorrow; the cave rang, hollow, with our separate coughing. Nathan made little of his own ailment, saying that doctors were immune; he was wrong, for one day he did not rise from his pallet.

I went to him; he was very weak and could barely give directions for the brew that I should concoct for him. Three days he lay, in a kind of coma, while we walked tiptoe and grieving, not knowing how to help. On the last day he roused and, in a kind of croaking whisper, called Owen to him. 'I am going, dear friend,' he said. 'Hold my hand ... for much comfort and joy have I had of you ... and say the Kaddish for me....' A little ghost-smile came over his sunken features. 'Do you remember? Long ago it was—in the days of our youth that I taught you ... you promised....' And so he died, on a smile. Owen bent and kissed his forehead and, very grave, began the prayers for the dead in the Hebrew tongue; strange to my ears the language, but full of music, and touching my heart.

We buried him in the foothills and placed a stone at his head to mark the place; full hard it was for us, for we were all very weak.

Iestyn recovered first, that old, old man; like a granite-stone he was and no mistake. My cough, too, disappeared, finally, for I had my own young strength. But Owen had fits of choking and spitting, bringing up a yellow mucus. 'I am come down with Marred's disease,' he said. 'And so long after....' But it was not so. I remembered the lady when she was seized this way; she gasped for breath and her chest heaved, but it was soon over. Owen's trouble was constant and grew worse; I remembered the herbs the lady used, brewing them over a fire and making him breathe the steam that was given off. But it did not help; he complained at night, too, of heavy pains in his chest and back. I held him in my arms to comfort him; wild I was that I could not help him. I saw him growing weaker, sitting all day by the fire, even when the warm weeks of spring were greening the trees outside.

Iestyn and I hunted every day, and there was game aplenty and game birds to tempt him, but he could not swallow more than a bite before the choking took him. Mostly he drank broth, and so he kept alive. But he had grown very thin, with shadowed eyes and a hollow look to his great chest.

One day in summer, almost at dawning, we heard a tapping on the rock-face of the entrance. It was done in our own rhythm, a signal from a friend. Iestyn crept up to the cave opening, holding his ax. But it was two hill-men that we recognized, or he did; to me they all looked alike. They brought with them two strangers, gray-cloaked. When they came forward into the firelight, something clicked in my head, some feeling that I had seen these men before. They were like wraiths, so thin they were and insubstantial, and walking with a peculiar shuffling gait.

Owen looked up from his place; his face lit, but before he could speak a racking cough caught him, and we waited till it was over, one of the strange men coming forward to place a hand upon Owen's shoulder, and the other kneeling before him. Owen put his hand up to cover the other upon his shoulder. Hoarsely he cried, 'It is Walter—Master Walter ... and young Rhisiart, Cousin Rhisiart! Given you up I had by now....'

'They have released us,' said Rhisiart, the kneeling one, for now did I, too, recognize him, though he was much changed. 'Four years did they keep us there, in filth, and naught but bread and water....' His hawk's eyes glittered, angry.

'We were captured, sire ... at Usk.' And Walter bent a look of reproach upon the other. 'Give thanks we should to Jesus that we live still—and prayers for the souls of those that do not....' He had lost much flesh, and his smooth round face was no longer smooth and round, though the same constant sweetness played upon it.

'Yes,' said Rhisiart bitterly. 'They let one in three go—a kind of game they played, killing two and releasing the third ... and laughing all the while. We were the lucky ones....'

'And—Griffith?' whispered Owen.

'He was taken some other place, some said the Tower ...' said Rhisiart. 'But we know not overmuch ... prisoners so long we have been and chained always, so that we cannot move freely any longer, and must grow into walking again....'

'But we will—never fear,' said Walter. 'With the help of Jesus.' The name of Jesus was always on his lips, even long ago; he was a devout New Christian, as Owen's lady had been.

'How did you find us here?' said Owen, in some alarm.

'There is a kind of grapevine that goes from mouth to mouth, secret, here in Wales,' said Walter. 'But never fear that any will give you up, sire. You are their lodestar ... the hope of Wales....'

Owen laughed, a dry sound. 'Not much am I now ... no man to lead any, except if it be to ruin and beyond....'

'Oh, sire, never say it!' And Rhisiart caught his hand and

kissed it; he had the power still, Owen, to stir all hearts. 'Sire, when you are well——'

Owen shook his head, but Rhisiart went on. 'You must get away from here ... Sire, listen! We passed through Dolgelly on our way. Most of the outbuildings still stand. Rhug Hall, too, did not burn ... only the manor house is gone. We must go there. There we can make a home for you ... and you will be well again—and lead us again....'

Owen asked of Janet, his oldest daughter, that had lived there, but they had found no trace of her or of her family. Some of the folk that had fled those parts and come back after the invaders had left, thought that the manor people had fled, all, before the place was sacked. 'So she is safe, your daughter, somewhere ... and we will find her....'

We made our way, by slow stages, to that place, Rhug Hall, hearing Owen on a litter and taking turns to carry it. It was the home of his boyhood; his eyes flashed with their old eagerness when we came to the familiar places. I walked beside him, and he pointing them out; already he seemed to draw strength from these parts, and I rejoiced. 'There is the Vale of Eden,' he said, and truly did it seem so, in the summer's glory, so lush and green it was. 'And there is the abbey, where the friars had trod the grapes in the fall. Sour wine it was, and the honey not fine either, but I remember it all with joy....' The place looked deserted; I wondered what had happened to those poor monks.

'There,' he said, pointing upward to a small hill that rose in a smooth mound. 'There is Moel Offrwym....' I looked at his face; it was sadder than I had ever seen it. Moel Offrwym, I thought, the Hill of Offering.... And I wondered what had made the sadness; something in the name itself that implied a sacrifice? I was never to know.

FOUR

Morgan came to us there, at Rhug Hall, with Alice, Walter Brut's wife. They had made their way at night, riding hard, and hiding by day, all the way from London.

They brought news, all of it sad. Catherine had died in the Tower of the plague, and her remaining child with her; there was now none that we knew of the male line of Owen, no child. Some others had died too, the twins, Tudor's daughters, and their offspring. Griffith, too, was dead; they thought he had been held in some other castle, near the border. Meredith lived but was still a prisoner in the Tower, held in a way as hostage, I suppose, for Owen, though I said nothing.

They two, Morgan and Alice, had been kept in the prince's own house; I looked keen at Morgan, but saw nothing in her face. She was still as beautiful as a great golden flower, and so like to Owen in his prime that my breath caught in love.

Alice flew, sobbing with happiness, into her husband Walter's arms. Morgan, too, came forward, shy, to embrace her lord; they had been wed, she and Rhisiart, just hours before the battle where he was taken. Alice's face shone like the visage of an angel, though she was plain of feature, but over Rhisiart's shoulder I saw the face of Morgan, set in an old sadness; I put two and two together and understood. Poor lovely lady, I thought, and your heart was always given ... and now you have given up your heart's happiness. For I knew, on a sudden, that she had been lover to Prince Harry.

She bore a child, Morgan, a seven-month child, brought on, all said, by her hard journey. He looked like Owen, too, except for his dark coloring, that he got from his father. I knew it was not Rhisiart, but I never said.

None knew me but as nurse to Owen, either, though I was sure that Morgan guessed, as I had guessed *her* secret. Owen was too weak to leave his bed, except for odd moments, when we would carry him to a chair beside the window; he liked to look at his hills, the hills of Wales and his youth.

Others came to us there, loyal folk and good, to help us till the land and make a new start out of the havoc that had been wrought. Meredith came, bringing Elliw, his wife. She was released, but he had given word to the prince that he would return. He bore the news that King Henry had died at last; the prince was king now, King Henry V his title. He bore also a full pardon for Owen.

Owen looked long at the paper with its royal seals; then smiling like the proud Owen he had been in his full strength, he made to tear it. His fingers were too weak; he gave it to me. 'Put it in the fire, my Sibli.... I want no pardon from the Lancasters. I have done no crime against them.... I did all for Wales....'

Meredith returned to his bondage, for he had given his word as one man to another. 'And I cannot stay,' he said, holding his wife close. 'For I am too proud. Farewell, my little sweet Elliw....'

He did return, though, Meredith, within a fortnight; the new young king had given him the pardon that was meant for Owen, and now he was forever free.

As I sat sewing beside the sleeping Owen in his bed, I heard Meredith speak to Morgan, low, and words not meant for me to hear '... and he begs you for the love you bore him....'

She shook her head. 'My place is here, beside my husband and my father ... and my son is in Wales—where he belongs....' She held her head high and color came and went in her cheeks and she breathing hard; I knew she held back tears. After a little she said, 'How is he—Harry? How does he look?'

'He languishes,' said Meredith, simply. And then, 'He drinks too much wine also ... and composes sad love songs that all the minstrels sing....'

I knew her heart was broke, Morgan. But she was proud, like to her father. Good wife she was to Rhisiart always, though, and none else knew.

In the next spring, Owen died. He had had a dreadful fit of coughing in the night, and great heavy pains across his chest, so that he cried out between the coughing. In the morning he was quiet; I thought he had gone.

I ran to summon the nearest, Morgan; she was in the buttery below. When we came up the stone stairs, though, and into the chamber, his eyes were open and clear. He spoke very low, so that we had to bend close to hear. He was not coughing now. 'I would see the hills once again,' he said. 'The dark blue hills of my Wales....'

Between us we bore him, we two women, to the window. He was light as a very sapling, that big man; the skin above his cheekbones was transparent, and the yellow eyes of him were sunk deep. He looked; the dawn tipped the peaks with rose, but below all was dark, the forested slopes.

'They are still there, my hills ...' he said. And on those words he died. We lowered him to the floor, for he was heavy now in death. Morgan, in a gesture of ineffable grace, brought down her hand, gentling her palm over his eyes, and closing them.

I have never been a weeping woman.

But I lifted my eyes to the dark blue hills and wept.